D0113715

MAR - - 2016

THE
NEWSMAKERS

Center Point
Large Print

Also by Lis Wiehl and available from
Center Point Large Print:

The Mia Quinn Mysteries (with April Henry)
A Matter of Trust
A Deadly Business
Lethal Beauty

**This Large Print Book carries the
Seal of Approval of N.A.V.H.**

THE NEWSMAKERS

Lis Wiehl
with
Sebastian Stuart

CENTER POINT LARGE PRINT
THORNDIKE, MAINE

This Center Point Large Print edition is published in the year 2016 by arrangement with Thomas Nelson.

The text of this Large Print edition is unabridged. In other aspects, this book may vary from the original edition. Printed in the United States of America on permanent paper. Set in 16-point Times New Roman type.

ISBN: 978-1-62899-899-3

Library of Congress Cataloging-in-Publication Data

Names: Wiehl, Lis W., author. | Stuart, Sebastian, author.
Title: The newsmakers / Lis Wiehl with Sebastian Stuart.
Description: Center Point Large Print edition. | Thorndike, Maine : Center Point Large Print, 2016. | ©2016
Identifiers: LCCN 2015046868 | ISBN 9781628998993 (hardcover : alk. paper)
Subjects: LCSH: Women journalists—Fiction. | Reporters and reporting—Fiction. | Conspiracy theories—Fiction. | Large type books. | GSAFD: Mystery fiction. | Suspense fiction.
Classification: LCC PS3623.I382 N49 2016b | DDC 813/.6—dc23
LC record available at http://lccn.loc.gov/2015046868

For Jacob and Dani.
I love you to the moon and back.
—Mom

THE
NEWSMAKERS

Prologue

It's a clear, hard winter day, and blinding sunlight pours into the conference room, glinting off metal surfaces, triggering migraines, and making the room uncomfortably hot, stifling. But in these tall midtown towers, you can't turn down the heat. You're trapped.

Nylan Hastings is not happy. But he won't let them know it—the dozen executives and producers who are sitting around the large table. He doesn't do sweat. But they're failing him. Failure is another thing he doesn't do. He does success, excessive historic success.

But Global News Network is floundering, bleeding well over a million dollars a week, searching for a voice and an identity in a hyper-competitive market where every smartphone spews out the latest headlines in what has become a never-ending, unrelenting, assaultive news cycle.

Nylan scans the assembled faces. They're smart, competent men and women—an eager bunch of pathetic fools, toiling away on the middle rung of life's ladder. He pays these people well and it's time for them to deliver.

A week ago he called them all together and said, "I need a star. Someone I can mold and nurture and transform into the face of GNN."

Today he says simply, "Let's see what you've found."

The mood is tense as they open laptops and pull up videos. An associate producer he hired away from CNN goes first—she presses a key, and her candidate's greatest-hits reel plays on the room's large screen. He's a man in his late twenties, as handsome as a movie star but a cipher; he reads the news well and knows the power of his dark-eyed smile, but beyond that he has all the presence of negative space. Besides, Nylan doesn't really want a man.

Then another reel plays, and now Nylan watches a serious young woman who's attractive and seems to know her stuff and is quick on her feet, but she has no real appeal; there's something schoolmarmish, almost condescending, in her tone. People don't want to be lectured when they watch the news.

The pretty young woman in the third reel is so sunny Nylan wishes he had his dark glasses handy.

Then there's another reel and another and another, and the brittle baking sun sets the stage for the parade of mediocrity—do these people really think looks and diversity and intensity are a substitute for raw talent, for that intangible quality that makes someone leap off the screen and into the mind and heart? And maybe even the soul? Speaking of mediocrities, Nylan makes a note to thin this pack; he asked for a star and these mongrels drop half-dead ducks at his feet. He feels himself getting angry, that hard, bitter rage that festers deep inside him, dormant but ever ready to flare to monstrous life. He loves his rage. It's his best friend and has been since he was a little boy. A little boy in a big house. But he reins it in, modulates it as he's so diligently trained himself to do.

"You're disappointing me here," he says. "All I see is adequacy. I don't like being disappointed and I don't like adequate. In anyone."

He stands up abruptly, paces back and forth. He looks at the people around the table—fear shadows their faces. How Nylan loves their fear. It's a tonic, a balm, a power surge. They're all expendable. Everyone is, really. Except the man at the very top.

"You're disappointing me," he says again, his voice growing louder. "And you're boring me. You're giving me beauty queens and prom kings. No soul, no guts, nothing that anyone with a B+ in communications from a third-rate safety school and the money for a nose job couldn't have."

He looks around the table and sees it in their eyes, that their fear has a new companion—shame. It excites him to see them bow their heads and avoid eye contact.

"I don't want to see another tape unless you're

11

so sure of it you're willing to put your own job on the line. Otherwise you're wasting my time." Naturally, there's silence from the lambs. He waits another beat, lets them squirm.

"I didn't think so. This meeting is over." As he's walking toward the door, a male voice speaks up.

"Actually, Nylan, I have someone I think you'll be interested in."

He turns. The speaker is Greg Underwood. Greg is one of the smart ones, has some fresh ideas and a vibrancy that seems to pulse off of him in waves. Everyone else at the table tries to disguise their relief that Greg's head is on the chopping block and not theirs.

"I hope you're right. For both our sakes."

"She's working at a small New Hampshire station right now, but I don't think she'll be there for long. She's got real talent."

"Let's see her," Nylan says.

The tension around the table ratchets up as Greg presses a key and a young woman who looks a little north of thirty comes on-screen. As they watch her report from the news desk and then from the site of a deadly house fire and then interview the parents of a missing child at their modest home, the room goes quiet. She's blonde, very attractive, polished but not too polished, and she gives the news urgency and import; she draws the viewer in, makes that intangible connection that transcends thought and reason.

Nylan stands very still and watches, rapt. There's something intriguing in her gaze, an intelligent, exquisite vulnerability. She's hiding something and almost getting away with it. A pained darkness lurking behind that bright blonde beauty.

"I've seen enough," he announces.

Greg looks at him with a firm expression—he's no cowering fool. He stops the presentation and closes his computer. Nylan goes to the window and looks down at the line of traffic snaking slowly up Sixth Avenue—the sun bouncing off the cars momentarily dazes him and he turns away. It's so nice to be above it all. And now, for the first time in weeks, he feels he's starting to ascend even higher. He turns back to the table, to the eager, anxious, tragic faces.

Greg speaks before he has a chance to. "What do you think, Nylan?"

Nylan makes eye contact with Greg, letting the rest of the nonentities blur in his peripheral vision.

"I want her," he says, and walks out of the room.

Chapter 1

Erica Sparks strides down Ninth Avenue on her way to the Global News Network headquarters on Sixth Avenue. It's her first day on her new job as a field reporter, her first job in New York City. And, if things go well, the first step toward scaling the heights of television news. She feels a little shiver of pinch-me excitement race up her spine. *Stay cool, one step at a time, one foot in front of the other.* Getting here was hard, but she's made it. Now she just has to stay on the beam. It's five thirty a.m., her call time is six, and she's just three blocks from the studio. Erica believes just being "on time" means you're already five minutes late.

She reaches West Fifty-First Street and heads east, and catches a glimpse of herself in a storefront window. The tailored coral suit looks just right. Her hair is hidden under a cap and her face is plain. She's going to leave hair and makeup to the pros. She got up at four, showered, had a cup of Irish breakfast tea and a banana, did her half hour of Tae Kwon Do exercises, and then scoured the Web looking for potential stories. She's not going to sit back and wait for the world to come to her; it doesn't work that way. The inquisitive bird gets the worm. The corporate rental she leased for six months is convenient if soulless, but that's all right for now. She doesn't want anything fancy, no chicken counting, budget-budget, focus-focus.

It's mid-April, a mild morning. Around her the city is kicking to life, trucks rumbling down the pavement, early commuters rushing past, empty taxis cruising for fares, maintenance men hosing down sidewalks, food vendors pushing carts from their garages to take up their stations on the mid-town streets. The neighborhood is a mix of shiny, new condo buildings, all glass and amenity-filled, and tenements, home to long-term New Yorkers and immigrant families of all stripes and colors. Erica loves the city's gorgeous mosaic, the crazy cacophony, the sense of endless possibility and promise.

Suddenly she hears yelling, a woman's voice, slurred and hysterical. Up ahead there's some kind of commotion. A police car pulls up, the doors fly open, and two cops leap out. Erica's reporter instincts kick in and she picks up her pace, remembering her maxim: always rush *toward* the sound of gunfire. When she gets close, she sees the wailing woman sprawled on the sidewalk, skinny and strung out, pale-skinned with skanky hair. A Hispanic man stands nearby, clean and bright-eyed, holding a little girl.

"The bastard won't let me in my own apartment," the woman screams at the cops.

"She's been out all night doing drugs and I don't know what else. I don't want her around my daughter," the man explains, soft-spoken and sure.

"She's my daughter too, you filthy creep!" the woman wails. She jumps up and races to the man, grabbing for the girl. The little girl starts crying, "Mommy, Mommy."

One of the cops pulls the wasted woman off the man. She turns and slaps the cop, hard. Out come the cuffs.

Erica watches. The little girl is crying, crying so hard. Domestic disturbance. Unfit mother. Unfit mother.

Suddenly Erica feels that terrible, raw hurt come crashing down and hears another little girl crying. *Mommy, Mommy, wake up, wake up! It's twelve o'clock, Mommy, please wake up! I'll miss kindergarten, Mommy.* And Erica, curled on her side on the living room floor, does wake up. Her head feels like concrete being chipped at by a jackhammer, her mouth tastes like sand and dirt and shame.

Erica blinks and she's back on the sidewalk. She knows what she needs to do. She ducks into the nearest doorway and takes five deep breaths. Then she says, in a strong, low voice: "God, grant me the serenity to accept the things I can't change . . . and the courage to change the things I can."

She steps out of the doorway. The woman is being loaded into the police car. The little girl is clinging to her daddy's neck. As Erica approaches, the father gives her a rueful smile. He's a good man. The little girl looks at her with wide eyes, and Erica has an urge to gather her up in her arms and shower her with kisses. She smiles at the girl and continues on her way.

And now here she is in front of GNN's headquarters in the Time and Life Building on Sixth Avenue—right in the heart of America's media capital, just blocks from NBC, FOX, and CBS. Nylan Hastings, the network's founder, is sending an unmistakable message: watch out, big boys, there's a new kid in town. And Erica is about to start a fresh chapter in her life. The incident on the street has only strengthened her resolve. She's come this far—and now she wants to go all the way to the top.

Erica Sparks walks into the soaring lobby, passes through security, walks over to the elevator, and presses the button that reads UP.

Chapter 2

As the elevator shoots skyward, Erica feels her excitement rising with equal velocity. There's a poster of Nylan Hastings—charismatic, idiosyncratic, enigmatic—on one wall of the elevator. Below his picture is his one-sentence mission statement for the network: *To connect and unite humanity—and write a bold new history for our planet.* Erica, like the rest of the world, is fascinated by Hastings. She studies his boyishly handsome, artfully airbrushed face, half smile, and inscrutable blue eyes for a moment, thinking: *You and me, buddy.*

The elevator doors open on the tenth floor. Erica gets off and heads down to her office. Greg Underwood, her executive producer and designated mentor, gave her an orientation tour last week, so she knows the lay of the land. She smiles modestly and says a warm hello to the colleagues she passes. Her greetings are returned with quick nods and an occasional tight smile. The vibe is serious, heads-down, we're-all-here-to-work. But do things feel just a little *too* reserved—almost coiled, protective, suspicious? As if everyone is looking out for numero uno. It's such a contrast with the casual, freewheeling

New England news stations she's used to. *Welcome to the big time, kiddo.* Erica feels ready. She's going to show them all what she's made of.

Her office is small with a large desk, a wall of shelving, and a spectacular view of the vents and pipes on the roof of the building next door. Fine for now—she remembers the Hollywood axiom: small office, big movie. Erica puts down her carryall, sits at her desk, and turns on the computer.

She reaches into her bag and takes out a well-worn deck of playing cards and tucks them into the top drawer, in easy reach. Nothing relaxes her like a few hands of old-fashioned, played-with-real-cards solitaire. No matter how stressed she is, if she can find the time and space for a few rounds, her blood pressure drops. There's something about the tactile feel of the cards and the finite parameters of the game that make her feel in control. And she never ever cheats.

Next Erica unloads her glittery armada of clip-on earrings. Back when every girl was getting her ears pierced, Erica declined. She suffered enough pain at home not to voluntarily inflict more. She spreads the costume jewelry— which she buys at flea markets and on eBay—on a side table. A neatnik she isn't. Then out come two framed pictures of Jenny, her smart, brave, funny eight-year-old. Jenny. Who paid such a terrible price for Erica's mistakes.

• • •

"We're going to make you a star," Greg Underwood told Erica at her first interview.

We'll see, she answered to herself. Global News Network is only a year and a half old, still finding its footing in the cable news network galaxy. But it's well capitalized and aggressive, with an uncanny knack for breaking stories before its rivals. Ratings are going up. Erica could be in on the ground floor of something big. She could become a star. She really could. And then . . . and then she could build a new life for herself and Jenny, and give her daughter all the advantages she never had. Which is what she wants more than anything in the world.

Erica turns to her computer screen and starts to scour the Web for possible stories. As a field reporter, she's near the bottom of the food chain, and she expects Greg to appear at any minute with her first assignment. But she's not about to sit around waiting. She knows from experience that there are stories out there just waiting to be told. She races through the major news sites, then skips over to the celebrity gossip sites. Something catches her eye: Kate Middleton, the Duchess of Cambridge, is arriving in New York for a short visit timed to coincide with the opening of a Turner exhibition at the Frick Museum. Erica feels her blood race—the fastest route to fame is through the famous. If she can snare an inter-

20

view with the duchess, it will be a major coup. Fluff? Maybe. A smart move? Definitely.

Erica picks up her phone and calls the Smart Room, the network's research nerve center, staffed 24/7 by lawyers, accountants, scientists, and researchers. Between them they can answer just about any question within minutes.

"This is Judith Wexler."

"Judith, hi. It's Erica Sparks, newly hired field reporter."

"You're not wasting any time. What can we do for you?"

"I need any information you can find on the Duchess of Cambridge's visit to the city."

"We're on it."

Erica hangs up just as Greg Underwood appears in the doorway. He's in his early forties—a decade older than Erica—tall and off-kilter handsome, with green eyes, skin tawny from years of sun, and a shock of black hair that looks like it rarely connects with a comb. There's something haunted in his eyes, as if he's battle scarred, but at the same time an ironic smile plays at the corners of his mouth. There's a raw physicality about him, and he looks lean and fit in jeans and a gray work shirt with the sleeves rolled up to his elbows. He smiles at Erica, and when he does, a little spark comes into his eyes.

"Good morning, Erica. And welcome."

"I'm happy to be here."

"I've got a story for you. E. coli was discovered in one of the city's reservoirs up in Putnam County, about an hour north of town. The city is expected to order a boil alert for parts of Upper Manhattan and the Bronx. I want you to go up there and cover it. Frame it as a story with national implications—how do we protect our water supplies?"

Erica does the math: E. coli or the duchess? No-brainer. "That sounds like an interesting and important story. But may I suggest something else?"

"I love suggestions."

"The Duchess of Cambridge is coming to town and I've been granted a short interview."

"You've been on the job for half an hour and you've landed an interview with the future Queen of England?"

"A plucky reporter gathers no moss."

"Where is this happening?"

"I'm just waiting for confirmation of that." Her phone rings.

"Erica, it's Judith. The duchess is arriving this morning. Lunch today under a tent at Battery Park, hosted by the Anglo-American Alliance. She's touring the Turner exhibition in the afternoon, and then there's a formal dinner dance at the Frick. Press contact is Reginald Beckwith."

Erica jots down Beckwith's number. Then she

hangs up and tells Greg, "Battery Park, this afternoon. What do you think?"

Greg rubs his jaw and whistles in appreciation. "Run with it. I'll find somebody else to send up to the reservoir."

"Thank you. I want to do a little bit of research on Turner and on Battery Park, think about the strongest visuals, and figure out the best way to frame the story. I think I'll go with how the duchess has revived the royal brand. Of course I won't call her a brand to her face."

"She's right up there with Coke and Disney," Greg says with that ironic smile. "When you've nailed things down, come see me. I'll get your pod together."

When he's gone, Erica googles Kate Middleton as she dials Beckwith. She explains to him that, coincidentally, she's been working on a piece about the duchess and how she's become the shining star of the Royal Family. Erica lays it on thick—but not too thick—throwing in a few facts about the duchess's background and interests (as she reads them off the screen). Could she please get five minutes of face time this afternoon at Battery Park?

Beckwith demurs, in a crisp British accent: the duchess is already doing CNN and NBC, and she doesn't like to spread herself thin. "Can't you use some pool footage?"

Erica adds a note of urgency to her voice. "Mr.

Beckwith, Global News Network is the most exciting thing to happen to news in thirty years. Our founder, Nylan Hastings, has an exciting vision of a synergistic network that seamlessly spans broadcast and social media. The duchess will receive a depth of positive coverage that the other networks simply can't deliver." There's a pause on the line. Erica softens her voice, warm and sincere. "I would deeply appreciate anything you can do for me."

There's another pause before Beckwith sighs with a mixture of exasperation and appreciation. "I can never resist the charms of American reporters. The duchess will give you five minutes. Be at the luncheon tent at noon."

"Many thanks, sir. Cool Britannia."

Beckwith laughs. "Oh, you are good."

Erica hangs up, stands up, crosses her office, and closes the door. Then she does a little jig.

Chapter 3

Carrying her notes, Erica heads down the hall to hair and makeup. She already feels supported by Greg. What a pro he is. And what a fascinating man—where does that war-weary, knowing edge come from? And he's strikingly attractive. She quickly pushes that thought away. Romance is simply not on her radar. This first year (at least) is all about work. And the vodka-soaked wounds of her failed marriage are still healing.

Not that she's counting, but she's been sober for one year, eleven months, and eleven days. She was working as the nighttime coanchor on a Boston station and probably drinking a little too much when she discovered Dirk's affair. He said he wanted a divorce—and everything just spun out of control. She went from two glasses of wine a night to three cocktails to four cocktails to an all-vodka diet. Dirk moved out and took Jenny with him. Erica spent a month crashing around her empty house, drinking, cursing the world, and crying for her daughter. Then the station fired her for on-air intoxication. That pushed her right to the bottom and she did the unimaginable—and ended up in the hospital, under arrest. The judge gave her a choice of rehab or six months in jail. She took rehab, and something clicked at that first meeting. The surrender . . . the acceptance . . . the *grace*.

Erica took off six months to get clean, then pleaded her way into a job as a reporter for a small New Hampshire station. She scoured the hills and towns for interesting stories—and she delivered. Soon she was anchoring, and the station's ratings soared. Boston wanted her back.

And then she got the call from Greg Underwood.

There is a hair and makeup station on each of GNN's six floors; most have three chairs and two experts at the ready. When Erica arrives, all three chairs are empty and two women are standing by. One is middle-aged and Hispanic, carrying a few extra pounds, with a pleasant, open face, brown skin, and lovely, expertly made-up gray-green eyes; the other is young, pierced, tattooed, and bleached blonde.

"Good morning. I'm Erica Sparks."

The older of the two women says, "I'm Rosario, and this is Andi."

"What a pleasure to meet you both. And thank you in advance for helping me look my best."

Rosario and Andi exchange a glance: nice lady. The vibe here is decidedly more relaxed than at the rest of the network.

Erica sits in the chair in front of the wall of mirrors. Rosario studies her face for a moment as Andi picks up a brush and gets to work on her hair.

"You're beautiful," Rosario says.

Erica smiles. She knows that her looks are a marketable commodity in the news business, but she also understands the limits of beauty. Looks may get you in the door but they won't earn you your own show. And they can engender resentment and even subterfuge among colleagues who don't have the same advantage.

"If possible, go easy. I hate that caked-on look," Erica says.

Rosario picks up a small metal sprayer and proceeds to coat Erica's face with a thin, translucent layer of makeup. Some genius invented the spray applicator after traditional makeup proved inadequate to the merciless clarity of high definition. Flaws that were once invisible on camera were suddenly there for the whole world to see. The sprayer erases them like magic. Then Rosario applies lipstick, a little eye shadow, and mascara. Meanwhile Andi magically doubles the volume of Erica's hair and sweeps it back to frame her face.

As they work, Erica asks them about their families and how they ended up at GNN. They even manage to get in a little industry gossip. Erica realizes that Rosario and Andi must hear confessions, rumors, and plans all day long. They have their ears to the ground—and while Erica finds them warm and lively, they could also be valuable allies.

"I like you, Erica," Rosario says as she brushes on a light powder. Then she leans in and lowers her voice. "Be careful around here."

Erica is taken aback and looks at her quizzically. Rosario reaches over and turns on a hair dryer, adding under cover of its whirr, "Nylan Hastings is a strange man. He plays games. Be careful. Please." She turns off the hair dryer and finishes the powdering as Andi gives Erica's hair a final pass.

When they're done, Erica looks in the mirror. The transformation is both subtle and striking. Her eyes have never looked bluer, her cheekbones more sculpted, or her hair fuller or glossier.

"Very pretty," comes a honeyed voice from over Erica's shoulder as a tall brunette strides into view. "I'm Claire Wilcox. Welcome to GNN."

Erica catches the look that Rosario and Andi exchange. She gets out of the chair and extends her hand. "Erica Sparks. What a pleasure. I'm a fan."

It's true—she is a fan of Wilcox's prime-time show, a fast-paced mix of hard news and human-interest stories. Claire has been with the network since its launch and is its biggest star, although her ratings are erratic. Tall and thin with a killer body, shrewd brown eyes, hair so thick it must be extension-enhanced, and a face that looks more angular in person than on-screen—she radiates drive, intensity, and a buttery charm. Chilled butter.

Claire steps past Erica and sits in the makeup chair with a proprietary air. The two women make eye contact in the mirror. "I hear you've scored three hundred seconds with Kate Middleton."

How did Claire learn that so quickly? What

pulse does she have her finger on? Erica takes note: there are no secrets at GNN and word travels like wildfire.

Just be careful. Please.

"I have, yes," Erica answers.

"Good luck getting five interesting words out of her. She's the plastic princess, a yawn in a tailored suit. The Royal Family was determined not to have a second Diana. I think they over-corrected." Claire examines herself in the mirror, turning her head from side to side. "I have Chelsea Clinton on tonight. *She* has some substance. And Diane Von Furstenberg is giving us a sneak peek at her fall collection." Claire drops eye contact and turns to Rosario and Andi. "Girls, work your magic."

Erica stands there, slightly stunned by Claire's energy and nerve. The woman is a force of nature. Good. Having a colleague that sharp will only force her to up her own game. Still, there's something feral and predatory about Claire that unsettles Erica.

Focus on yourself.

She heads back down the hall, determined to get more than five interesting words out of the duchess.

Chapter 4

Erica is fascinated by Battery Park, that stretch of green that lies at the very southern tip of Manhattan. The view it affords of New York Harbor—deep and protected, the reason the city originally grew and prospered five centuries ago—is breathtaking. The nautical bustle of barges, tugs, yachts, cruise ships, and kayaks reflects the enlivening mix of commerce, pleasure, and grit that defines the city today. The Statue of Liberty stands guard over the scene, and Ellis Island—first stop on the American dream for so many millions—is visible close to the New Jersey waterfront. Turn around and the towers of Wall Street loom, potent symbols of Manhattan's economic might. Anchoring the east side of the park is the Staten Island Ferry terminal, where the workhouse ferries chug in and out twenty-four hours a day.

On this early spring day—blue-skied and sparkly—the park is groomed and lovely, filled with daffodils and tulips, a respite for city workers on their lunch hour, tourists, and dreamers. As Erica takes it all in, she can hardly believe this is *her* city now. But there will be a time for swooning. Right now she's working. And

Battery Park is a prop in her piece on the duchess, setting the scene and providing context.

She goes over her notes as Manny, her cameraman, and Derek, her soundman, get set up. They and associate producer Lesli Gaston make up her pod, the crew that will travel with her to cover local stories. They all got to know one another a little on the drive downtown. Manny is Puerto Rican, Derek grew up on an Iowa farm, and Lesli is gay. Erica loves that her crew reflects the diversity and unity that make New York great. In this town it's about *the work*—not what language you speak, the color of your skin, or who you love.

Erica stands on the promenade with the harbor behind her, establishing the visual she wants. Behind her, a Staten Island ferry approaches the terminal. A little ways away is Castle Clinton, a circular stone fort that is the remaining vestige of the ramparts that originally lined the battery and protected the city. Beside the castle is an enormous tent, site of the luncheon in honor of the duchess. There's a lot of buzzing about the tent. Waiters, florists, and chefs finish their prep; Secret Service agents and their British counterparts in dark suits and dark glasses hover and observe; and socialites in spring dresses anxiously triple-check their clipboards and smartphones (nobody worships royalty with the fervor of the American upper class).

This isn't a live report—it will be edited and aired later in the day—which takes some of the pressure off. But it's Erica's first assignment with GNN, and she's determined to make it perfect.

"Whenever you're ready, Erica," Lesli says.

Erica takes a deep breath and puts on her game face. "Let's roll." She smiles into the camera and begins, "This is Erica Sparks reporting from Battery Park at the southern tip of Manhattan, where a luncheon is being held in honor of the Duchess of Cambridge, better known to most Americans as Kate Middleton." Erica walks a few steps down the promenade and gestures to the park. "This piece of land has hosted a great deal of history. Today it welcomes the British, but on November 25, 1783, great crowds gathered here to watch the last British troops leave after their defeat in the Revolutionary War. The patriots jeered King George's vanquished army as it sailed away, and in response one of the British warships fired a cannonball at the crowd. It was the last shot fired in the war—and it fell far short of land. Later that day George Washington marched triumphantly down the island of Manhattan and claimed the battery as American soil. Today the future Queen of England returns to reclaim the land—over a lunch of poached salmon and baby vegetables—"

Suddenly screams, screams of terror, fill the

soft spring air. Like a great crashing wave, they grow louder, stronger, more panicked. Erica looks around wildly and sees the Staten Island ferryboat heading full speed ahead, not toward its berth in the terminal, but directly toward the seawall that encircles the park. The passengers on deck are screaming, and now the pedestrians in the park are screaming too, running, running away from the hulking tons of steel heading right at them.

Erica lowers her mic and cries, "Get the shot, Manny! Go live, Lesli!" Then she raises the mic. "We're witnessing a tragedy unfolding as a Staten Island ferryboat seems to be off course, out of control, and unable to stop."

The boat makes a desperate last-second attempt to veer back toward open water, but it's too late. It slams into the seawall, tossing scores of passengers like rag dolls into the choppy harbor waters. Erica watches as a man is crushed between the boat's steel and the seawall's stone. The boat grinds along the seawall for what seems like an eternity before finally slowing and stopping with a fierce rumbling shudder. Inside the upper-deck cabin Erica can see crumpled and flailing bodies. Other passengers were thrown onto land by the impact. Screams of agony fill the air.

Erica continues to broadcast. "A Staten Island ferry has just crashed into the Battery Park seawall, killing and injuring many of the passengers."

As she speaks, scores of New Yorkers and tourists rush toward the carnage. They staunch wounds with anything available, often articles of their own clothing, offering comfort and calling for help on their cell phones. Erica sees several people jump into the water to rescue the drowning.

A young Asian girl—*she's Jenny's age*—is lying on the ground, blood pouring from a head wound, her right leg twisted backward at an ominous angle. Erica shouts to Manny, "Don't follow me—stay on the boat," drops her mic, and runs to the child. She kneels beside her. "You're going to be okay, sweet baby. You're going to be okay." Erica's dress is useless as a tourniquet, so she tears off the girl's blouse, rolls it up, and wraps it around the child's head, pressing on the wound. She cradles the girl to her chest. "You're going to be okay, sweet thing, you're going to be okay."

Now the girl starts to cry, to wail, "Mommy? Daddy!"

"We're going to find them, sweet girl, don't you worry. We're going to find your mommy and daddy. You're going to be okay, baby girl. I promise, you're going to be okay."

Now the air is pierced with a hundred sirens as ambulances, fire trucks, and police cars pour onto the scene. Two EMTs run to Erica and the girl; they load the child onto a stretcher with something close to tenderness. As they carry her away, the girl reaches out to Erica, who grabs her hand and kisses it again and again. "You're going to be okay, I promise, sweet baby, I promise."

Similar rescues are happening all around Erica. Now she's just in the way. Derek and Lesli have also been offering help to the injured. Manny stays true to his training, filming the scene. "Let's get back to work," Erica says.

She picks up the mic. Her dress is crumpled and bloodstained, her hair flattened, her makeup smeared. "This is Erica Sparks reporting live from Battery Park in New York City, where a Staten Island ferry slammed into the seawall just minutes ago. You can see from the terrible scene around me that there have been numerous injuries and fatalities. We have no idea why the pilot of the boat lost control. The New York City Police Department has arrived in force. I see several Coast Guard boats speeding toward the scene, where passengers who were thrown into the water are being assisted by brave civilians who leapt in to save them. Other passengers have managed to swim to shore on their own. Medical crews have arrived and are transporting the injured to hospitals."

Erica looks over at the party tent—all concerned are standing in shock watching the scene.

Clearly, there will be no luncheon for the Duchess of Cambridge. News trucks from the other networks are arriving and reporters begin to broadcast.

Erica spots a dazed but uninjured man, a ferry passenger, sitting on a bench in shock. She knows a good interview subject when she sees one.

"Come on, crew, follow me," she says.

Chapter 5

Six hours later Erica arrives back at her office. She's in some realm beyond exhaustion, running on fumes. She's covered fires, car crashes, and propane explosions, but never a disaster on this scale. By some miracle only five people died, but over eighty are hospitalized, two dozen of them in critical condition. As for the cause of the crash, the ferry's pilot says the controls "just froze, like someone flicked a switch." The National Transportation Safety Board arrived on the scene and has started its investigation. A computer malfunction is the suspected culprit.

Erica sits down behind her desk, closes her eyes, and takes a deep breath. Suddenly a terrible loneliness descends on her. How do you come down from a day like today?

By making dinner for your daughter and then helping her with her homework.

Of course that's out of the question. Still, the yearning feels like an open wound. She picks up her phone and dials.

"Hello."

"Dirk, it's Erica. May I speak to Jenny?"

"I'm not sure that's a good idea. I didn't let her watch you today. It would have been traumatic for her."

Erica takes a deep breath and struggles to control the anger rising inside her. "I won't mention it. Can I please just say a quick hello?"

Dirk sighs in that disapproving way of his. "All right. A quick hello."

She hears him calling Jenny to the phone.

"Mommy?"

"Hi, baby. How was school today?"

"Good. We drew a huge map of America. Where are you?"

"I'm in New York City."

"Can I come see you?"

"Yes, sweetheart, of course you can. We'll go see *The Lion King*."

"I'd rather see *Aladdin*."

"How about both?"

There's a pause, and then Jenny asks, "Are you okay, Mom?" There's such concern in her voice, and a peculiar maturity. A maturity that comes from having seen her mother descending

37

to the depths—something no child should have to witness. Something that forced Jenny to become the parent, at least for those last terrible months.

Erica feels her throat tighten. "Yes, I'm fine. I had a hard workday, but that's a good thing."

"I'm happy about your new job."

"I miss you, Jenny, I miss you so much. Be good. I love you."

Erica hangs up and feels nurtured by her daughter—she only hopes that Jenny feels nurtured by her. Sometimes amends take a long time.

"How are you holding up?"

Erica looks up. Greg is standing in the doorway, looking concerned.

"I'm good."

"You are good. You're *very* good." He steps into the office. Evening stubble makes his jawline look even stronger. "Have you eaten?"

"Actually, I don't think I have."

"How about I take you out?"

"What a nice offer. But I just want to decompress a little and head home. I've got some leftovers in the fridge. Early call tomorrow."

"You're a pro, Erica," Greg says.

"Listen, Greg, I'd like to do an in-depth follow-up on today's crash. Find out what happened, why, and what can be done to prevent it happening again."

"Great idea."

"I'll get my first report in this week, while the story is still fresh."

"There she is," Nylan Hastings says as he appears in the doorway.

Erica has never met Hastings before and— remembering Rosario's words—she feels a little wary. This emotion is followed by a sudden surge of insecurity and inadequacy. She's the kid with the dirty cheeks and the dirty clothes, the kid who never invited other kids over to her house, ashamed of what they would find. She's the student at Yale on a scholarship, all the privileged kids with their prep school pedigrees and condescension masked as curiosity. She suddenly remembers Suki Waterson, who carried a Hermès purse and wore Chanel flats to class, saying, "Oh, you grew up in rural Maine? What was *that* like?"

Using all her psychic might, Erica pushes the dreaded feelings aside. She's *proud* of what she's accomplished. She's *earned* that pride. And her experiences at Yale made her determined to treat everyone she meets with respect and dignity —it's one of her core credos.

Hastings steps into the room and extends his hand. "Nylan Hastings."

"I think I figured that out." Erica stands, shakes his hand, and smiles. "After all, I am an investigative reporter."

"What a charmer." Hastings laughs, but it's a hollow laugh, almost like a learned behavior.

Hastings, who is in his midthirties, is lanky. He's wearing jeans, some very hip Nikes, and a T-shirt that reads ROCK THE COSMOS. The cool-kid effect is undercut by an emergent potbelly and dark circles under his eyes—they hint at something unsavory going on behind the façade. A shock of sandy hair hangs over his forehead, and his skin is unnaturally smooth— has he started Botox already? He radiates casual confidence, even entitlement.

And no wonder. Hastings invented Universe, a video game in which users explore the galaxy and interact with intelligent life on other planets. It quickly became a global phenomenon, with over two hundred million monthly users. He sold Universe—which he solely owned—to Facebook for $5.7 billion. And then he founded Global News Network.

"We made history today," Hastings says. "Our ratings spiked, and for three hours we beat every other cable network. That's never happened before."

"I was just doing my job."

"Greg told me you were a world-class talent"— his eyes roam up and down Erica's body—"and so very attractive."

It's inappropriate and unnerving. And why doesn't he look her in the eye? She suddenly feels like an object, something to be admired and owned. It's disquieting, but so be it. You don't become a billionaire and then found a network without being a little bit—as Rosario put it—strange.

"Good work, both of you. Keep it up," Hastings says, suddenly perfunctory, as if he has better things to do. He turns and leaves.

Erica looks at Greg and raises her eyebrows. He closes her office door and lowers his voice. "That's our Nylan. Listen, Erica, you've made a big splash right out of the gate. But take it slow and play things close to the chest. Sometimes caution is the better part of valor."

"I'm not sure I understand."

"Nylan is sole owner of GNN. He doesn't have to answer to a board or to shareholders. That gives him a lot of freedom and a lot of power. As long as we keep our heads down and deliver, he pretty much leaves us alone." Greg looks over his shoulder, claps his hands together, and raises his voice. "We'll continue this discussion. Meanwhile, congratulations!" He goes to the door, opens it, and then turns back to Erica. "See you tomorrow," he says. Their eyes meet, and a frisson of attraction crackles between them.

As she walks home, Erica both marvels at and rues her good fortune. It came at the expense of people's lives, and she knows that the horrific scene she witnessed—the screams, the blood, the little girl she held, the man getting crushed—will haunt her for a long time.

But the undeniable fact is that the tragedy benefited her career. Erica has always felt that success is 90 percent work and 10 percent luck. Well, today she got lucky. What were the odds that the boat would careen out of control just as she was standing there? But it *did*. And she seized the moment.

As Erica navigates the midtown crowds, she feels a surge of elation and hardly registers the odd looks she's getting from passersby. She's completely forgotten that her dress is covered in blood.

Chapter 6

It's five a.m. and Erica is running north through Central Park. She loves this time of day, just before sunrise, as the light grows stronger and the powerful beast awakens around her. She also loves the sense of momentum that she feels in the city—of fearlessly racing toward the future. To her, this intangible energy, verve, and promise define the city more than any of its touristy landmarks. Then there's the sheer beauty of the park—rolling lawns, lakes, flower beds filled with bursts of color, swaying grasses, towering trees, promenades, and vistas.

She reaches Seventy-Second Street and Fifth and turns west, running past stately Bethesda Fountain with the lake beyond, crossed by a graceful arched footbridge, the boathouse anchoring its northern shore. Erica can hardly believe this is her home—it's a million miles from bleak St. Albans, Maine, and a prefab house that sat on a concrete slab and welcomed the bitter winter winds with loose windows and hollow doors, and tall plastic glasses filled with generic soda and off-brand booze paid for by selling the family's food stamps for fifty cents on the dollar.

Erica picks up her pace, even though she knows she can't outrun her past. The best she can do is turn it into a source of strength and drive and compassion. The footage of the Staten Island ferry crash two days ago has been getting a lot of play, and her follow-up investigation into the cause is proceeding. She has interviewed an inspector from the NTSB and the pilot of the boat and is starting to pull the story together. The inspector wasn't willing to go on record with a reason for the crash, but he did hint at a computer malfunction.

The words *computer malfunction* caught her attention. Erica closely followed the Sony hacking case, which the United States pinned on North Korea, and the cybertheft of customer

43

information at Target. There can be no doubt: the world faces a growing threat from cyberterrorism—computer systems from Zappos to the Pentagon are at risk. When Erica asked the NTSB inspector if the crash could possibly have been an act of cyberterrorism, he grew very tight-lipped. Which only stoked her curiosity.

She loves having a story like this, one with real consequences, one that takes some searching, some groundwork, some *reporting*. It's easy to forget, in the glamorous, supercharged world of cable news—where Megyn Kelly and Anderson Cooper and Rachel Maddow have become celebrities in their own right—that in the end journalism is about finding out *the truth*.

Erica reaches the west side of the park and runs past Strawberry Fields and its *Imagine* mosaic, donated by Yoko Ono in memory of John Lennon and his fallen idealism. She thinks of another idealist: Archie Hallowell, her professor and mentor at Yale. Rail-thin and patrician, wild-haired and vital, perpetually covered with a thin layer of chalk dust, bits of his breakfast stuck to his Harris tweeds—Hallowell looked like some relic of a long-gone age, as if he should be stuffed and displayed in a glass cabinet at the Smithsonian: *Professorus americanus*—extinct. But oh, what a passion for the truth burned in Archie's heart! And he took Erica—the fish out of water, flopping around in the thin Ivy League air—under his wing. At least once a week he would invite her into his cluttered office where—in a voice urgent and impassioned—he impressed on her that journalism is a noble profession, an important profession, one that lies at the very beating heart of a functioning democracy. And Erica learned that if she kept her eye on that prize, all the pain in her life fell away. At least while she was working on assignment for the *Yale Daily News*.

In social situations with her prep-schooled peers, her anxiety remained. But then she found a magic elixir that assuaged it, smoothed out the edges, made her eyes sparkle and her wit sharpen: booze. And so began her bifurcated life: kick-ass journalist on the one hand, insecure girl with a secret blighted past and a growing dependence on alcohol on the other.

As Erica runs past the Tavern on the Green—where delivery trucks are unloading meat and produce—her cell phone rings: it's Moira Connelly, a fellow newscaster, her best friend from the early years of her career in Boston. Moira stayed loyal through Erica's troubles and drove her to rehab when the day of reckoning arrived. She lives in LA now, where she anchors the local evening news on NBC affiliate WPIX.

"Hey, Moy. You're up early."

"Haven't been to bed yet. Your Battery Park

report is at a hundred twenty thousand hits on YouTube."

"And I've got eleven thousand new Twitter followers."

"It's a wonder you're still talking to me."

"What was your name again?"

"I'm so proud of you."

"It's a start."

Moira's tone grows serious. "Are you feeling solid?"

"Trying my best. And how are you?"

"I'm great. I covered an important story last night: a water main break in Tarzana."

"How did you handle the pressure?"

"The water pressure? There was none." The friends laugh.

"Actually, Moy, the vibe at GNN is a little weird. Uptight. Secretive. Two different people have basically warned me that Nylan Hastings is a little . . . weird."

"Seriously?"

"They told me to be careful."

"I'd heed those words. You're in the big leagues now—the rules are different. I'm here for you 24/7."

Erica feels a swell of emotion. "Thanks, Moira. The time may come . . ."

". . . and when it does."

Another call comes in. "Gotta go, Moy, this is my producer . . . Good morning, Greg."

"Are you sitting down?"

"I'm running."

"I just got a call from a producer at *The View.* They want you on the show tomorrow to talk about the ferry crash."

"You're kidding me."

"I'm serious as stone. This is a *big* break."

Erica's first thought is: *I deserve a glass of champagne to celebrate.* What she says is: "I'll see you in about an hour."

Chapter 7

Erica arrives at GNN hoping for words of congratulations from her colleagues. The few she receives are cursory, belied by the envy in the speakers' eyes. There's no doubt—an edge of suspicion, even fear, permeates the network. She'll take Rosario and Greg's advice to be cautious, but she's not going to put a wall up around herself. In the kitchen, as she brews a cup of Irish breakfast tea, she allows herself a cheese Danish. It's not Dom Pérignon, but Moira taught her that it was important to celebrate success, even if only with a flaky pastry.

No sooner does Erica sit down in her office than a woman wheeling a rack of dresses appears in her doorway. Black, tall, slender, about forty, she's the picture of workday chic in perfectly tailored black slacks and a bluish-gray three-quarter-sleeve blouse that has a little bit of shimmer. Her hair is a tight Afro, a little thicker on top. She has high cheekbones and full lips, and she's wearing a large geometric silver bracelet and black sandal heels. In spite of her elegance, she radiates a friendly professionalism.

"Hi, Erica, I'm Nancy Huffman, wardrobe supervisor. I've brought some outfits for you to consider for your *View* appearance."

This is a perk she didn't have yesterday. "Can you make me look like you?"

Nancy glances down at her arms and says with a sly smile, "That might be a stretch." The two women laugh. "Ready for my unsolicited and probably unwanted advice?"

"I need all the help I can get."

Nancy gestures for her to stand up, and Erica complies. "First of all, I hate you for all eternity. Please tell me you *live* at the gym."

"Tae Kwon Do."

"Tae Kwon *did*—you're stunning."

"I may be pretty, Nancy, but *you're* stunning."

"It's an occupational hazard." Nancy turns to the rack and pulls a simple but beautifully cut sleeveless, above-the-knee blue satin dress.

"Gorgeous, but is it a little bit too cocktail-y for daytime?"

"If it were any shorter or tighter, it would be.

Remember, this is *The View,* not a hard news report. The ladies are going to be asking you Oprah-y questions about how witnessing the crash made you *feel,* what it was like seeing injured children, touchy-squishy stuff. I want you to look feminine—and your very best. Try it on."

Erica slips out of her cream suit (which seems so dull in comparison) and into the dress. She looks in the full-length mirror on the back of her office door. The dress is lovely and flattering.

"Move a little. See how it feels."

Erica walks around the office, sits, crosses her legs, stands up.

Nancy clocks how the dress moves on her body. "Does it feel comfortable, relaxed?"

"It feels . . . *fabulous!*" Erica says, breaking into a huge grin.

"There's nothing I like better than a happy customer. Hold still." Nancy takes a piece of tailor's chalk out of a bag hanging on the rack and makes quick marks on the waist and hem of the dress. "A couple of small alterations and you'll be good to go."

Erica changes back into her suit and hands Nancy the dress.

"I'll get this back to you ASAP," Nancy says.

"I can't thank you enough."

"Rosario told me you were one of the nice ones."

"Hey, we're all in this together."

Nancy's face darkens, she lowers her chin and raises her eyebrows—the message is unmistakable: not everyone at GNN shares *that* sentiment.

As soon as she's alone, Erica turns back to the ferry story. She wants to understand the mechanics of how the boat's controls could have frozen like they did. She needs to talk to an IT expert. She picks up the phone and calls the Smart Room. "Judith, it's Erica."

"Congratulations on *The View.* I'm sure Nancy Huffman found you a nice dress."

Boy, there's no privacy around this place. Two men Erica has never seen before, wearing sunglasses and dark suits, walk past her office. She gets up and closes the door.

"Listen, I want to find an IT expert who can explain how the Staten Island ferry's computer systems work."

"We've got one of the best in-house, Mark Benton. He's in charge of keeping our work computers up-to-date and running smoothly. He's on the third floor. Extension 4437."

Erica decides to go down to the third floor and meet Benton in person. Just as she gets up, there's a rap on her door and—before Erica has a chance to answer—Claire Wilcox's head pops in. "Peek-a-boo!" she chirps in a failed attempt at girlish charm. She strides into the room, slaps on a serious expression, and says, "*Good* work."

"Thank you."

"We're a team here at GNN, and when one of us does well, it reflects well on all of us."

Erica's bullcrap alarm starts to sound.

"You probably know that my show is our highest rated. Which lifts us all up." She gives Erica a meaningful glance. "I mean without a flagship show, the network would be floundering. Nylan might decide he can't continue to bleed money and shut the whole thing down."

Erica doesn't remind Claire that her ratings are far from stellar, and that Erica broke the network's viewership records with her ferry coverage. "Your point is taken."

"Good. Then I'm sure you'll understand why I'm taking over the Staten Island ferry story."

"You're *what!*"

"I'm just much better equipped to handle it. I've got a staff of five, including a full-time researcher. I'm running a special segment on the tragedy on my show today. I've already got the footage of your interviews with the NTSB and the pilot. We're editing you out. Scott Lansing, the nation's top expert on boat safety, is going to be my live guest."

Erica thinks, *This isn't a story about boat safety. It's about what caused the ferry's computer system to freeze up.* But she doesn't say a peep.

"Are you going to use my live footage of the crash?"

51

"It's not *your* footage, Erica. It belongs to the network. Of course I'm going to use *pieces* of it. The visuals in particular are very strong."

"And *The View*?"

"I've spoken to Nan Sterling, the lead producer over there, and she insists that I do the show. Nan and I were at Stanford together," Claire says, letting a little country club seep into her inflections. "But the decision was *purely* a professional one."

"No doubt."

"Well. There we have it." There's an awkward moment. Claire looks around the office, spies Erica's array of earrings. She reaches up and casually fingers the fat diamond stud in her right ear. "Those earrings are *so* darling. Target?"

And then she's gone, leaving behind a whiff of some perfume Erica can't afford.

Erica gets up, crosses the office, and shuts the door. The blood is pulsing in her temples so fast and hard she thinks she might faint. Or throw up. *That witch!*

"I'm just much better equipped."

"It's not your *footage, Erica."*

"The decision was purely *a professional one."*

Suddenly Erica is back in that dark-paneled freshman dining hall at Yale, afraid to open her mouth, ashamed of her broad Maine accent, slumping further and further down in her chair, hoping her classmates will forget she's there.

They even hold their knives and forks differently. Did their parents *buy* their social ease, their casual confidence, all the talk of horses and Vail and the school their family is funding in "Bolivia—or is it Namibia? Ha-ha!"

Erica leans against her desk and sucks air. She closes her eyes and recites the Serenity Prayer, repeating the second phrase three times.

Courage!

She strides into the hall, turns left, and heads toward Greg's office.

Chapter 8

"What's up?" Greg asks in alarm, looking up from his computer.

"Claire Wilcox stole my ferry story!"

There's a pause, and then Greg nods in resignation and looks down at his desk. Why isn't he more upset? Why isn't he outraged?

"Did you know?" Erica demands.

"No, I did *not* know. But to be honest, Erica, I'm not surprised." He looks her in the eye. "Why don't you sit down a minute."

Erica fights the urge to rant. She knows from experience that impulse comes before error. She sits and crosses her legs, tries to compose herself, but her top leg is bouncing.

Greg sits back at his desk, gives her a rueful look, and runs his fingers through his thick black mop. "I'm very sorry this has happened." His soulful green eyes are so sympathetic that for a moment Erica is afraid she'll burst into tears. Like tears ever got her anywhere.

Greg leans across the desk toward her. She smells his piney soap. "You have a lot of talent, Erica. I *believe* in you. I think you can make it to the top in this business, and I want to do everything in my power to help make that happen." He leans back and crosses his arms. "But Claire Wilcox has some clout at GNN. A chunk of the network's revenues come from advertising sold on her show. Yes, your ferry coverage did well, and that's been noted by Nylan—you're firmly on his radar."

"Can we take this up with him?"

Greg gets up, closes his office door, sits back down at his desk, and lowers his voice. "Claire wouldn't have pulled this without his okay. Nylan is a shrewd bird, Erica. He likes to pit people against each other. And even play mind games. He's a little perverse."

"Do you think he put Claire up to it?"

"That's not something I want to get into here and now." He gives Erica a meaningful look and switches gears. "I think we have to be very smart and very strategic. We're in the news *business*."

Erica tries to push Greg's words about Nylan out of her mind. "Greg, Claire is going at the story the wrong way. I believe we have to look into the possibility of cyberterrorism."

"Say more."

"What if someone hacked into the ferry's computer system and shut down the controls?"

Greg drums the desktop with his fingertips, wheels turning. "Cyberterrorism *is* the twenty-first century's battlefield. And there's so much hacking going on these days. But terrorists are usually eager to take credit, and no one has."

"Yet."

Greg is silent for a moment. "I think you should write Claire a memo and copy it to me and Nylan, laying out your theory."

"She just stole my story and you want me to hand her a promising lead?"

"Absolutely. If it does turn out to be cyber-terrorism, you'll look like the brilliant reporter you are. And there will be a record of it. Plus you'll earn points for being a team player."

Erica knows he's right, but it's a hard pill to swallow.

"The best thing we can do is accept what's happened, keep our heads down, work like dogs, and find a story Claire Wilcox *can't* steal."

Greg's voice is so calm, so reasonable, and there's no sugarcoating. He's speaking the simple truth. And presenting a way forward. Erica lets out a deep exhale and feels herself relax. She has an ally. Someone she can trust.

Greg smiles at her. She looks at his hands, the dusting of hair, the prominent veins, the long, supple fingers—and has a sudden urge to be held by those hands, cared for, caressed.

Alarmed by her desire, Erica stands up, paces a moment, and then stops. "You're right, of course. Thanks for talking me down. Any promising stories on the horizon?"

"Kay Barrish's plans are *the* hot topic these days." The former movie star and California governor is considering a run for the presidency, a race she would enter as the clear favorite.

"She's said she'll announce her decision on a White House run in the next couple of weeks. Landing an interview with her would be a big coup."

Erica nods. "I'll work on that."

"It won't be easy. Everyone in the business is trying to snag her." Greg smiles at her. "Of course you're not everyone."

"I appreciate your support and sound advice." Erica heads toward the door.

"Erica?"

She turns.

"Any chance we could continue our discussion over dinner?"

Greg looks so hopeful, both strong and vulnerable. Erica swore to herself that romance was off the table for her first year. But this isn't romance. It's just two colleagues having a casual dinner. Right?

He holds up his palms in surrender. "We'll go Dutch," he says with a smile.

"Out of the question," Erica says. And then she returns his smile. "*I'm* paying."

Chapter 9

Erica steps into the elevator and presses 3. Sure, she'll write Claire a memo raising the possibility that the ferry crash was an act of cyber-terrorism. When she's good and ready.

The doors open on the third floor, and Erica walks down the hall toward GNN's IT department. It's a large, open space split into cubicles. There's a single private office at the far end of the room with its door open. It must be Mark Benton's. Erica walks past the cubicles—some of the employees look like they were bused in from a Star Wars convention: geeky, goofy, gender-indeterminate, sporting a rainbow of hair colors. Others are wearing bland clothes and don't have a hair out of place. Both camps are focused on their computer screens with the maniacal intensity of obsessive-compulsives. The room is eerily silent except for the click of fingers on keyboards, a disembodied, malevolent sound.

Erica reaches the office. Inside, a man of about thirty is sitting in front of a huge computer screen with several other large screens nearby. The main screen is filled with a diagram of mathematical symbols—at least Erica thinks that's what they are. Each time he hits the keyboard, the configuration of the diagram changes.

"Mark Benton?"

"Not now!" he barks, not taking his eyes off the screen.

"When?"

"Later."

"That's not very specific."

"Can't you see I'm working?"

"Well, I'm not exactly on the beach in Cabo."

He turns and looks at her, his mouth twisted in annoyance.

"Erica Sparks. Sorry to interrupt your work. Can you give me a good time to come back?"

Mark looks from the screen to Erica and back. He sighs. "Fine. Go ahead. What's up?"

"I have a few questions."

"About?"

"The computer systems on the Staten Island ferry."

"I'm not paid to help reporters conduct research." He has a roundish face that still seems to hold traces of baby fat, pale skin, and curly brown hair. He's wearing black-rimmed glasses that are too big for his face and give him a buglike look, a wrinkled work shirt, and baggy black cords. In spite of his best efforts, he's attractive in a nerdy sort of way.

"Can you make an exception?"

"Doubtful."

"Could the Staten Island ferry crash have been an act of cyberterrorism?"

That grabs him—his expression goes from aggrieved to engaged. "That was *my* first thought."

"Seriously?"

"No, I just said it to prove what a genius I am." He blows air out through his mouth, his lips whinnying like a horse, then reaches up and scratches his scalp. "I'm sorry I'm being such a jerk. We had a software glitch yesterday and I pulled an all-nighter. It's almost resolved but not quite."

"Gotcha. This is a bad time. But you think cyberterrorism is a possibility?"

"Absolutely. It would be a tough system to hack into, but once you were in, you could control that ferry from the Kremlin."

"Can you back up a little? How would that work?"

Mark's eyes light up with techy enthusiasm. "Transportation systems—starting with airlines, of course—are high security risks. They're protected by a lot of firewalls—both software programs and hardware that identify and block hackers. So getting in would take time and skill. But it's certainly doable. Look at North Korea and Sony. ISIL shut down the French television network TV5 Monde and took over its website and social media. North Korea got into Sony by stealing the credentials and assuming the identity of a Sony IT systems manager. Once they were in, they could inflict damage at any time. It's really the equivalent of getting behind enemy lines. North Korea's initial salvos were phishing—e-mails that put malicious code into a computer system if the recipient unknowingly clicks on a link. The phishing started two months before they took total control of Sony's systems. With the ferry, I would guess that the hackers had been in the system for a while, waiting for the optimal time to freeze up the navigational controls."

"And the Kate Middleton lunch was the perfect moment to gain maximum media coverage."

"Exactly. You know GNN has a whole cyber-security department."

"I had no idea." How come no one has mentioned this to her?

"Oh yeah. It's located on the sixth floor. It's run by a guy named Dave Mullen. For obvious reasons, it's a locked ward."

"But you're in IT here."

"I take care of our internal functions. I'm basically a glorified repairman. Dave Mullen protects us from the big bad world. He used to work for the Pentagon and then for a big defense contractor. Won't give me the time of day."

"How do I contact Mullen?"

"Through your executive producer. But I doubt he'll talk to you. Like I said, they lie low. Nylan has a paranoid streak, but you know what they say: just because you're paranoid doesn't mean someone isn't after you. There's North Korea, ISIL, the Kremlin, rogue hackers. Imagine the panic a terrorist group could create if it simultaneously shut down all four cable news networks, the East Coast power grid, and the national air traffic control system."

"Terrifying thought."

"We're living in a brave new world, Erica. You know what I call anyone who claims to know where it will all lead?"

"What?"

"A fool."

Chapter 10

To wear or not to wear, that is the question. Erica is at home, standing in front of a full-length mirror, admiring the beautiful blue dress that she was going to wear on *The View*. Nancy Huffman returned it to her, perfectly altered. She's meeting

Greg in twenty minutes at a restaurant two blocks away. It's Italian, unpretentious and well lit. She didn't want some romantic place filled with candlelight and cozy corners. She's nervous enough as it is.

Yes, the dress is a dream, but does it send the wrong message? Would she be better off going simple—jeans and a white oxford, maybe, with the collar up? As soon as she got home, she washed the spray paint off her face, so maybe she can get away with the dress. It does make her feel . . . desirable. But is she comfortable with that?

She picks up her phone, takes a selfie, and texts it to Moira: Is this dress too much for a business dinner?

Within seconds she gets an answer: With a man?

Yes.

How attractive is he, on a scale of 1 to 10

I don't want to go on record.

Which means he's at least an eight.

More money.

Busted! Beauty is power. Wear it!

As she walks down Fifty-Seventh Street past Carnegie Hall, Erica is glad she took Moira's advice. The admiring looks she's getting lift her spirits and her confidence. It was a rough day but a good day, a learning day. Before she left the office, she wrote an e-mail to Claire Wilcox, copying Greg and Nylan:

Hi, Claire—I think it's worth exploring cyber-terrorism as the cause of the ferry crash. Internal IT head Mark Benton thinks it's a possibility. Let me know if there's anything else I can do to help with this story (or any other). Best—Erica

The big leagues are cutthroat. That's not her favorite way to roll, but if that's what it takes, she's in—as long as it's not at the expense of her integrity. Let Claire have the ferry crash story. It's a big, chaotic world out there and another important story will come along. And if it doesn't come along, she'll go out and find it.

She enters the restaurant and is greeted warmly by the maître d'. Greg is at the small bar and he crosses to her, drink in hand.

"Would it be unprofessional of me to tell you how great you look?"

"Probably—but why don't you say it again so I can be sure."

The maître d' leads them to a table and after they're seated asks, "May I get the lady something to drink?"

"I'm fine with water for now, thank you."

"I just read your e-mail to Claire," Greg says as they open their menus.

"And?"

"I thought it was pitch perfect: helpful and respectful but not obsequious. Have you heard back?"

"Not yet."

"Claire's no fool. I predict she'll take your advice."

"Mark Benton tells me GNN has a cyber-security department."

"So I've heard," Greg says with a sardonic half smile. "It's *very* secretive. Nylan is obsessed with all things secretive. And cyber. He believes in something he calls cyberpower, and he thinks it's going to define the twenty-first century. The man has ambitions that go way beyond GNN."

"Such as?"

"Well, I'm one of several dozen executive producers at the network, so I'm hardly in his inner circle, but offhand I'd say he's after world domination. Seriously, I think he craves power on a global scale. He's thirty-six, he's made his billions on Universe, he's gotten GNN up and running. What's next? I don't think he wants to get into politics per se, but I think he wants to be a major player behind the scenes."

"And you think he's perverse?"

"Under that boyish façade lies a very strange man. I don't pretend to understand him. But I do know I don't trust him. Nylan's main management tool is fear."

Erica gets a text and takes out her phone. "I

know this is rude, but reporters get a pass. . . . It's from Claire: Thank you for the valuable lead, teammate. Fair enough, although I could have done without the 'teammate.' What a cliché."

"With someone like Claire, you've got to beat them at their own game."

"Fool me twice . . ."

"Exactly."

The waiter comes over and takes their order. Erica goes for a simple angel hair Bolognese, Greg for mushroom ravioli. She also orders an Italian lemon soda.

"So . . . I've been thinking about your next move," Greg says.

"And . . . ?"

"In some ways the ferry incident is a mixed blessing. It launched you like a rocket, which is good. Nylan and everyone else at GNN—and all the other networks—know who you are, and that you're good at what you do. But it does raise the question of how do you top it."

"I don't want to get desperate and search for something sensational. I'm a workhorse, Greg, I'm in this for the long haul. I'd like to do some substantive stories even if they don't blaze across the screen."

"Good to hear. I've seen a lot of smart young reporters so anxious for a hot story that they made stupid mistakes."

"Like?"

"Not doing your homework is number one. You have to understand what you're covering. Showing up unprepared for an interview is a close—and closely related—second. Being so aggressive that it backfires is another—if you push too hard, people's natural instinct is to recoil. It's really Journalism 101."

"Still, it's good to be reminded."

The restaurant is filling up; everyone looks bright and attractive, leaning toward each other, saying fascinating things. Erica finds the chatter and hum enlivening, inspiring; who cares about food—this city nourishes her. And being here with Greg—savvy Greg—makes her feel a part of it all, a nascent New Yorker.

"If I quoted Shakespeare, would you think I was a pompous jerk?" Greg asks.

"Totally."

"I just had to make sure. Hamlet tells the actors that 'in the tempest and whirlwind of your passion, you must acquire and beget a temperament that will give it smoothness.' "

"Didn't you do a little editing?"

"I quit. You're too good."

They laugh. "I'm sorry, that was obnoxious of me," Erica says. "It's just that my mentor at Yale loved that quote too . . . *give it smoothness . . .*" The words hang in the air between them.

Their food arrives. Suddenly Erica is famished, and she digs in with gusto.

"How's the angel hair?" Greg asks.

"Heavenly. Listen, Greg, you know my history because you hired me. I'd like to know more of your story."

"I don't want to turn this into a dull dinner."

"How about I be the judge of that?"

"You have only yourself to blame. Grew up in a small town in western PA. Father mailman. Wants son to follow in footsteps. Son says no way and joins army day he graduates high school. Learns photography. Leaves army. Works as a free-lance photographer. In midthirties gets tired of hustling assignments and having roommates. Gets into news business. Works hard. Gets promoted. Makes good money. Is having dinner with recently hired, incredibly attractive reporter."

"Who thinks he uses irony as a defense."

"Which only makes her more attractive."

"Greg, I'm an investigative reporter. I know that you worked as a war photographer during the first Gulf War and then in other hot spots around the world. I'd like to hear about that."

Greg looks down at the table and something sets in his face, his mouth tightens. "You want to know what that was like? You want to know what it felt like to witness the fog of war, the wanton killing of civilians, the rapes, the piles of rubble where houses once stood and families once lived and where, from under the twisted wreckage, you hear the dying cry for help with their last breaths, where you see a six-year-old boy with his leg just blown off, where you see a mother nursing her infant until a piece of shrapnel decapitates the baby and you still hear her wail when you wake up in a sweat at three a.m.? Is that what you want to know?" Still not looking at Erica, Greg sits back in his chair and exhales. "I'm sorry. That was unfair and unkind."

Erica waits a moment and then says, "And honest."

He looks at her, and under the anger she sees loss and bewilderment. "I'll always be a prisoner of war."

Just as Erica will always be a prisoner of her childhood. She feels a connection to Greg, something that transcends physical attraction and professional rapport. While she doesn't equate her traumatic childhood with the horror of war, both she and Greg have seen humanity at its darkest, and have been left scarred.

For a long moment there is really nothing to say. They both eat in silence. And then Erica makes a decision to change the subject.

"So—I'm trying to figure out the best way to approach Kay Barrish. But please keep that under your hat—and don't let Claire Wilcox anywhere near your head!"

Greg taps his scalp. "Claire-free zone."

As they eat, they exchange safe banter about the city, politics, movies. They both decline dessert but do order decaf espressos. After the waiter brings the coffees, Greg says, "Now it's my turn to raise a tough issue."

"I'm here."

He puts down his cup and looks her in the eye. "You make no secret of your alcoholism."

"My firing from WBZ in Boston is public record."

"Did you feel it was justified?"

"I would have fired me."

"And you've come back."

"That's the great silver lining of addiction: if you can beat it—or even wrestle it to a draw—it makes you stronger, more empathetic and open-minded."

"There might be another silver lining. Like some terrific television."

"Say more."

"I'm thinking of an ongoing segment where you interview celebrities and politicians who are also recovering addicts. You could bond with them in a way no other reporter could. I want to make you a star, Erica. Your struggles make you sympathetic."

"And you think we should exploit them?"

He looks her right in the eye. "I'd use the word *leverage,* but yes, I do. We may call it the news business, but we all know it's just as much *show* business."

Erica ponders his suggestion for a moment. As

opposed to her alcoholism itself, she considers her sobriety sacred and private—it's a spiritual journey, one that connects her to millions of people fighting the same battle. The idea of parading it in front of the world gives her pause. But she's no Mary Poppins, and rose-colored glasses give her a migraine.

"If it's done the right way, I think it would be powerful," Erica says. "But I'm not interested in TMZ TV. I'm a serious journalist. Who went through a dark period."

"And you have a daughter."

"Jenny. Who is completely off-limits."

The conversation is moving into dangerous territory. Erica looks at her half-empty glass of lemon soda and wishes it had an inch of vodka in it. Instead she takes a sip of her espresso and signals for the check.

Chapter 11

Erica loves New York at night—the city relaxes a little, people's pace slows, the streets are filled with laughter and lovers, the neon casts a comforting glow. Greg lives on Riverside Drive and Erica's rental is on Fifty-Seventh between Ninth and Tenth. He walks her home in an easy silence. Several times their shoulders touch and she feels heat at the spot. And that scares her. She hasn't navigated the minefield of attraction since before her marriage a decade ago. It wasn't supposed to happen this way. Her life was going to be all work and nothing but. In a year maybe, but not now. And not with a colleague. She has to nip it in the bud. But the feeling of his closeness when she breathes, when she moves, is exquisite, and it makes her feel alive.

"Are you okay?" Greg asks softly. "Sometimes my curiosity gets the best of me."

"I guess we both have wounds that are still raw." Walking through the crowds creates, ironically, a feeling of intimacy between them. They're in their own private bubble surrounded by the soothing sea of humanity. It makes Erica feel safe, being with Greg like this. She decides to come clean. Well, clean-ish. She lowers her voice and leans into him.

"My drinking was escalating. My ex-husband began an affair with a family friend. He filed for divorce. There were ugly accusations on both sides. We got into a custody fight over Jenny. I got sober and he got into therapy. When you hired me, I didn't want to pull her out of her school, which she loves, and I knew my life would be so work-focused and my hours so erratic and I would probably be traveling a lot, so I gave Dirk sole custody for a year. I have visitation rights. So far it seems to be working, except that I miss her so much . . . Well, I'm not going to admit to you or anyone else that I sometimes cry myself to sleep."

"Was Jenny traumatized by the divorce?"

"Yes, she was. And is. And I have a lot of guilt about that. But we're moving forward. She's doing pretty well all in all. My lawyer got the court records sealed. I think we just need some time." Erica feels a sense of relief: her story is on the table. Even if it's not the whole story. Even if she left out the darkest details.

Greg walks with his head down, taking it all in. Then he says, "I'm sorry you had to go through that."

His words are so simple, his tone so sincere— Erica has an urge to take his hand in hers and kiss it, hold it to her cheek. She's saved by geography.

"This is my building."

They stand facing each other—his eyes are so soulful, he's a kind and intriguing man. She wants to know him, all of him.

"Thank you for dinner," he says.

"My pleasure."

"I had a nice time."

"So did I."

Some subterranean force, some wave, cosmic and undeniable, pulls their bodies toward each other. *No!* Erica turns a half step away. There will be another time for this. A look of disappointment flashes across Greg's face but is quickly gone. He understands.

Erica walks past the doorman, takes the elevator to the ninth floor, goes down the hall and into her apartment. Not even stopping to take off the beautiful dress, she sits in front of her computer and googles *hostas*.

Chapter 12

Erica is on her way to work. She's not sure what to make of the chemistry that sparked between her and Greg last night, but this morning she feels buoyant. In spite of her vow to avoid any emotional entanglements, she knows that the heart has a mind of its own.

As she approaches the Time and Life Building, she runs into Nancy Huffman.

"Good morning, starshine," Nancy says.

"I wore the blue dress last night. I think it brought me good luck."

"You strike me as the kind of woman who makes her own luck." As they near the building's entrance, Nancy lowers her voice. "I'm sorry about that stunt Claire Wilcox pulled, stealing the ferry story. She sees you as a real threat. I think she has her sights set on Nylan."

"Romantically?"

"Yes. She wants to create the ultimate power couple." They enter the building, and Nancy nods in the direction of Le Pain Quotidien at the far end of the lobby. "I'm going to grab a cup of coffee. Can I get you something?"

"I could use a cup of tea. I'll come with you."

Le Pain Quotidien is jammed with workers picking up morning sustenance. As they wait, Erica asks, "So where did you work before GNN?"

"On a couple of soaps. But they kept getting canceled. When this job opened, I pounced. The culture around here is . . . dark, but the pay is good and my mother has Alzheimer's and her nursing home ain't cheap."

"I'm sorry."

"Thanks. It is what it is. I do love the excitement at GNN—I'm a news junkie. And I just don't think you-know-who is a first-class journalist. She's a thimbleful of talent in an ocean of ambition. Of course, that ocean can trigger some mighty waves."

"I got swamped by one."

There's a tall handsome guy a little ways in front of them in the line. Dirty-blond shaggy hair, lean and toned, he has a cobalt stud in one ear, is wearing a linen Cuban shirt and cool sunglasses, and has a long string of beads around his neck. He looks like he should be wasting away in Margaritaville, not waiting in line with a thousand office drones. He orders a triple espresso in a low drawl and then favors the barista with a killer smile. As he walks away with his java, Nancy leans into Erica and says sotto voce, "That's Dave Mullen, the head of the cybersecurity division."

"You're kidding me. I thought it was Matthew McConaughey's younger brother."

"Good call. His favorite vacation spot is Colorado. And he's not a skier."

"You mean . . . ?"

Nancy brings her thumb and forefinger up to her mouth and mock inhales. "With some"—she makes a sharp inhalation through her nose—"as a capper."

"And *he's* protecting us from North Korea."

"Computer freaks are a breed apart. And apparently he's the best, a white-hot wizard. Plus—and you didn't hear this from me—he's been seen with Nylan after hours. In some pretty unsavory places."

"Like?"

"Clubs that cater to . . . listen, it's none of my business what two consenting adults do together."

"Oh come on, Nancy, you can't lead me on like that and not deliver the goods."

Nancy leans in to Erica. "We're both grown-ups; we know that some people get pleasure inflicting pain."

"I did read *Fifty Shades of Grey*. Or tried to."

"No, I mean real pain. I've heard rumors that one of Nylan's . . . *dates* . . . ended up in the emergency room."

"Oh no."

"I never bought that laid-back Zuckerberg act of his. That man is wound tight. And I don't want to be around when he snaps."

They reach the front of the line, and as Erica orders her tea, she thinks, *GNN is* very *tricky terrain.*

Chapter 13

Erica and her pod—Derek, Manny, and Lesli— are driving through the Hudson Valley on the Taconic Parkway. One of the many parkways built in the early twentieth century to showcase the pleasures of "motor touring," the road is simply gorgeous, winding through bucolic rolling hills and farmland. Erica imagines what it would be like to live in a landscape this soothing and pastoral. And she knows she'd be bored to tears.

It's been two weeks since the ferry crash, and the story has pretty much fallen off the news. Erica thought Claire's appearance on *The View* was embarrassing, borderline unprofessional. All she talked about were the victims, getting all sticky sincere and sentimental in a way that screamed *performance*. Yes, people died and that's a sad and legitimate part of the story, but uncovering the cause and hopefully preventing a recurrence are equally important. It feels to Erica as if Claire willfully ignored serious reporting. Yes, the NTSB released a preliminary finding that the crash was caused by a computer malfunction, but they didn't give a reason for the breakdown. In all of her coverage, Claire has only glancingly mentioned the possibility that it was cyber-terrorism. It's almost as if she was given orders to drop that line of inquiry.

Erica's extracurricular dinner with Greg felt like too much too soon, and she has reined in her growing feelings for him. She knows from experience that when she ventures into emotional terrain she has a tendency to lose her footing. She's more confident when she's working. Work is like solitaire—she understands the parameters. They're finite and defined. Emotions are amorphous and unpredictable. And sometimes dangerous.

Not that it's always easy to keep her emotions in check when she's around Greg. Yes, he's attractive and interesting, but it's his steady, unwavering support that affects her most deeply.

Support is something that was in short supply in Erica's childhood. Her mom was a sad, sloppy pot-and-pill-head. She did the laundry and cleaned the house every twelfth of never. At least she kept the refrigerator well stocked—with week-old KFC remnants and blocks of government cheese. Her dad was a mill worker who faked a disability claim and went into early retirement, leaving him all day to indulge his addictions to beer, Keno, and victimhood.

When Erica started bringing home report cards filled with As, they ridiculed her. "Oh, look at Little Miss La-di-da! Thinks she's better than we are." School was her sanctuary—if it hadn't been for the nurturing teachers and her guidance counselor, who recognized and encouraged her promise, she never would have made it to Yale, where Archie Hallowell took her under his wing.

And now, when she needs it most, when there is so much at stake, Greg has come into her life. As the van turns off the Taconic Parkway and heads down a quiet country road toward the subject of her interview, Erica says a silent prayer of gratitude.

They drive through more glorious landscapes, over rushing streams and past fields dotted with happy cows—Erica didn't realize the Hudson Valley was this beautiful. They turn onto an even quieter road and after a few minutes arrive at a charming house, rambling and old and wooden, with a wide, welcoming front porch. It sits on a small rise surrounded by ancient towering trees and . . . hostas. Literally thousands of hostas— small, medium, and gigantic, some with delicate little leaves and some with leaves the size of palm fronds, in colors from deep emerald to wispy pastel, or variegated—veined with white and cream and yellow. The hostas sweep across lawns, march alongside pathways, encircle trees, sprout atop stone walls, all of them so healthy they seem to be popping out of the earth to greet the world. It's a green dream, simply spectacular.

The four of them sit silently in the van, mesmerized. Then a small woman in her eighties comes around the side of the house, waving and smiling a radiant smile. She's wearing low rubber shoes and a gardening apron and gloves. Her shoulder-length gray hair is expertly cut and she's got on bright red lipstick.

Erica gets out to greet her. "You must be Anne Sweeney."

"Ya think?" Anne cracks.

"Thanks so much for having us. As I explained on the phone, I'm initiating a new segment called 80 Is the New 80. I want to counterbalance the denial of aging that's turning us into a culture of desperate youth seekers. I believe aging well isn't about *fighting* age, it's about working *with* it."

Anne nods. "Terrific idea, I'm happy to be a part of it."

What Erica doesn't need to mention is that 80 Is the New 80 is aimed at America's fifty-five million baby boomers—who just happen to watch cable news in disproportionate numbers.

The crew shoots some establishing footage and then follows Erica and Anne as they walk the grounds.

"Your garden is dazzling. How did it start?"

"My husband, Fred, was a lawyer, I was a housewife, we had one daughter. We had a very happy marriage. One morning Fred went into the office and sat at his desk. Five minutes later he was dead of a heart attack. He was thirty-four. My daughter was five. When the shock woreoff, I felt an urge, a *need* almost, to create beauty —I wanted to remember my husband, to honor him for our daughter. And I also wanted to do some-thing for myself, for my sanity, for my survival. When I was digging in the earth, my grief felt manageable. Sometimes, in the evenings, when I look around me, we're a young family again."

The woman is so honest and the story so sad that Erica unconsciously reaches out and touches Anne's arm.

"What did your daughter make of it?"

"At first she liked to help me plant. That wore off pretty quickly. Even as a five-year-old, she was fiercely independent."

"And why hostas?" Erica asks.

"The property has these old trees, which means lots of shade, which hostas enjoy. One hosta led to another. When I retired from teaching seven-teen years ago, I just went with it." She smiles in a self-deprecating, I-know-this-is-a-little-crazy way that makes Erica fall in love with her.

Erica looks around at the eccentric explosion of beauty and thinks, *There are worse ways to spend your retirement.*

Anne puts her hands on her hips and surveys her domain. "It's been great fun. I loan the place out for environmental fund-raisers—we *must* protect this glorious valley. A couple of friends have used it for family weddings. I call it God's Little 4.6 Acres. The deer call it a cafeteria."

After the tour, Erica continues the interview over iced coffee in Anne's modern kitchen. The table holds *New Yorker*s and a laptop open to Huff Post—clearly this is a woman who has learned how to balance the past and the present. Then the crew goes to pack up and Erica finds herself alone with Anne. Which is what she wants.

"I can't thank you enough for today. I think it will make a wonderful story."

"It's been my pleasure. If there's one thing I've learned in my eighty-four years, it's how to judge character. When you called to ask if you could come, I googled you. I read about your struggles, your firing in Boston. And now you're back on your feet." She reaches out and clasps Erica's hands. "*Bon courage,* young lady!"

"You know I have an ulterior motive?"

"Of course I know. Do you think you're the first

reporter who's developed a sudden, burning interest in hostas?"

Erica smiles sheepishly.

"However, you *are* the first to pass muster." Anne picks up her cell and dials, then speaks into the phone. "It's your mother, dear. You haven't called in six days, and please don't give me any of that time-difference nonsense. I'm sitting here with someone I want you to meet."

Anne hands the phone to Erica—who finds herself talking to Kay Barrish.

Chapter 14

Erica is in her office, a half-packed suitcase on her desk, preparing for her flight to LA for her preliminary meeting with Kay Barrish. She's one step away from landing the biggest interview of her career, one that everyone from Claire Wilcox to Katie Couric to Diane Sawyer covets. The Barrish camp has made it clear the assignment is NMNA—No Men Need Apply. A smart move, considering that women are her political base.

As focused as Erica is—she's put together a thirty-page file on Barrish—she can't stop thinking about the ferry crash. Computerized navigational systems don't just freeze up for no reason. She wants to find out the truth, and she frankly doesn't trust the NTSB. An act of cyberterrorism on American soil would be a real embarrassment for the Department of Homeland Security, the whole administration in fact. Could there be a cover-up?

And why has the network let Wilcox gloss over a story that is not only important but could drive viewership? The ratings went through the roof on the day of the crash. It just doesn't make sense—and it feels like a pebble in Erica's shoe. Only this is an irritant that she can't shake out.

She pulls a deck of cards out of her bag and shuffles them. Just that act—and the crisp sound it makes—relaxes her a little. As she deals, she thinks, *Yes, if I land the Kay Barrish interview, it will be the biggest break of my career, but I can't let the ferry story go without doing everything in my power to uncover the truth.* As she plays the hand, she formulates a plan. The cards are dismal and the game is soon over. But it's done the trick.

Erica heads down to Greg's office to say good-bye. "Ready to rumble?" he asks.

"A few butterflies, but maybe that's good."

"You sure you don't want me to fly out with you? I could clear my schedule for today and tomorrow—and I'll bring my butterfly net." His voice grows serious. "Nylan *really* wants this one."

"My instincts tell me Barrish will respond better to a simple one-on-one for our first meeting."

"Let's trust those instincts."

"Listen, Greg, very quickly: I think Claire has dropped the ball on the ferry crash."

Exasperation flashes across Greg's face. He's a tough pro who doesn't always welcome push-back. Which is probably how he got to where he is. Erica reminds herself that in the news business tough is good. Tough. Is. Good.

"I think we have to let this one go," he says.

"But I'm not convinced the NTSB is doing its job. People died in that crash."

"The public has lost interest. It was a terrible accident, but it's really a regional story. It's fallen off the radar screen. Let's move on."

She doesn't agree, but she nods.

"Call me as soon as you leave Barrish and let me know how it went. I doubt she'll sign on immediately. I'm sure you're not the only reporter she's auditioning."

"Will do."

"I'm with you, kid," Greg says. They look at each other—and in that moment Nylan and Barrish and the NTSB fall away—and Erica's breath catches.

She heads back to her office. She picks up her deck of cards to put it in her purse—and that's when she notices them. In front of her computer. A pair of black eyeglasses, open, facing the screen, carefully placed. Where did they come from? While she was down in Greg's office, someone came into her office and put them there. Were they searching her files, her history? She picks up the glasses—they're brand-new. She holds them up—no prescription.

You're being watched.

Erica looks over her shoulder as a spark of fear races up her spine. She tosses the glasses into the wastebasket just as Nancy and Rosario appear in her doorway. Nancy has two dresses draped over her arm, and Rosario is carrying a small cosmetics bag. Erica manages a wan smile.

"Are you all right?" Nancy asks.

"Yes, yes . . . I'm fine."

"A little emergency kit," Rosario says, opening the cosmetics bag and lifting out items. "An eye mask—works wonders after a long flight. Moisturizing lipstick—the air is very dry in LA. Argan oil if your hair needs a quick boost." She zips up the bag and hands it to Erica. Then she reaches out and grasps her hand. "We're all rooting for you out there."

"Tell Kay she has a lot of fans in the East," Nancy says. "I just *love* that woman."

"Me too," Rosario adds. "She's got a big heart. *And* big cojones."

The three women laugh. "It's time to see one of *us* in the White House," Nancy says.

Erica nods. No wonder President Garner—and every politician with presidential aspirations—is waiting to see what Barrish does. The woman

85

will be unbeatable if she runs—a billion dollars' worth of ads can't buy the kind of passionate support Nancy and Rosario have just expressed. Erica takes a deep breath—she *has* to be on her A game in Los Angeles and land this interview. It's historic.

"LA is so casual, I think these dresses will work," Nancy says. She holds them up quickly, almost as if she's embarrassed by them. They're short and low cut. Nancy quickly folds them and puts them in Erica's suitcase.

"I'm not sure about those dresses, Nancy. They're a little bit casual and . . . revealing. Maybe a pantsuit would be better."

Nancy doesn't look her in the eye, and her expression is rueful. Or is it fearful? Rosario just looks glum. There's a long pause, and then Nancy says, "Let me see what I can do."

The two women leave. Moments later her phone rings. "This is Erica."

"Hi, Erica, it's Nylan."

She sits up straight, instantly on red alert.

"I just wanted to wish you luck with Barrish." His tone is friendly, supportive.

"I'll do my best."

His tone does a one-eighty and he says condescendingly, "I sure as hell don't pay people to do anything *but* their best."

"Understood."

"I'm *counting* on you to land this, Erica."

"Nylan's main management tool is fear."

"I don't want to disappoint myself, either," Erica says.

"Good girl."

Did he call her *girl?* Just as she's leaving to interview Kay Barrish? The irony.

"Listen, Erica, Los Angeles is looks-obsessed. I think you should wear a flattering dress to meet Barrish."

Erica looks over at the suitcase with the two dresses, and Nancy's sheepishness suddenly makes sense.

"Don't hide your assets." Now his voice is calm and businesslike—too calm, too businesslike, and is there a slight leering edge? It doesn't feel like advice, or even a request—it feels like an order.

"I don't think a woman of Kay Barrish's stature is going to be judging me on what I'm wearing."

"You're representing my network, Erica."

"I better get moving or I'll miss my flight."

"*Don't* disappoint me, Erica."

Erica leaves the dresses in the suitcase and zips it up. Her car for the airport is arriving in twenty minutes. She picks up the phone to call Mark Benton and see if he has anything new on the ferry crash. Then, remembering the glasses on her desk and the tone in Nylan's voice, she hangs up. She grabs the suitcase and heads for the elevators.

Chapter 15

Erica looks at the elevator's control panel. She hears Greg's voice: *"Let it go. Let's move on."* Then she hears Archie Hallowell's, fierce with passion, quoting Shakespeare: *"Time's glory is to unmask falsehood and bring truth to light."*

Bring truth to light. Watched or not. Threatened or not.

Erica presses the button marked 3.

As the elevator descends, she says the Serenity Prayer. The doors open. Erica gets off and heads down the hall, suitcase in tow. Mark Benton is in his office, and she's surprised to see his face isn't inches from the computer screen, but buried in a windsurfing magazine.

"Mark, do you have a minute?"

He puts down the magazine. "Sure, it's a slow day."

She steps into the office and closes the door behind her. "I'm going to cut right to the chase." She lowers her voice, almost to a whisper. "Would it be possible for you, hypothetically, to get into the Staten Island ferry's computer system and figure out what happened that day?"

"Oh sure, no problem. I haven't committed any felonies lately. Seriously, it would be very difficult. Just speaking hypothetically."

"Of course."

They exchange a small smile as Mark's eyes light up and he swivels to his computer screen.

"Thanks for the information," Erica says.

"I have no idea what you're talking about," Mark says, already punching keys.

Erica starts to leave, then turns. "You wind-surf?"

Without taking his eyes off the screen, Mark smiles. "Yeah. I'm going out on the Hudson this weekend."

"Be careful. The currents are treacherous."

Chapter 16

As the plane descends toward LAX, Erica feels her pulse quicken. If she lands the interview, Greg and Lesli will follow to set up the shoot; they'll use local sound and camera people. She spent the flight reviewing her notes on Kay Barrish. What a dynamo. The day after she graduated high school in 1976 she moved to Los Angeles, determined to be an actress. To support herself she got a job selling cosmetics at Bullock's—within a month they asked her to take over the whole department. She had a brief first marriage to actor Kent Barrish—his connections helped her get cast in television movies.

Agents and producers noticed her strong screen presence—what she lacked in beauty she made up for in intelligence, vivacity, and charm. During those early years, she lived in Silver Lake, then a rundown part of town, and got involved in neighborhood cleanup efforts. Then she got her big break: a small but showy role in a Robert Altman film that earned her an Academy Award nomination for Best Supporting Actress. She moved up to leads, earning a reputation as one of the most versatile and gifted actors in the business. She won a Best Actress Oscar in 1996, the peak of her stardom.

Then she married Bert Winters, the butter king of the Southland (just about every pat in every restaurant comes from his company), had two children, and gradually gave up acting. She enrolled at UCLA and earned a degree in American history. Her philanthropic and community involvement grew and led her into politics. A moderate Republican, she was drafted by the party to run for governor and proved to be a natural on the stump, with seemingly endless stamina and a gift for inspiring audiences with her call for every Californian to look past self-interest and commit to the common good. She won the election in a landslide and became a star on the national political scene. She was considered a shoo-in for reelection—until a right-wing congressman mounted a primary challenge and beat her by a tiny margin. He went on to lose the general election by twenty points. Her grace after the defeat only increased her popularity.

Since that time, Barrish has kept a high profile as head of her family's foundation and the author of three books that detail her policy views. She cunningly leavens the books with down-to-earth personal anecdotes—and lessons learned—about being a woman, a mother, and a wife. Polls regularly name her one of the most admired women in America and the leading candidate for the presidency in the next election. It's all a long way from a lawn covered with hostas.

As the pilot announces their final descent, Erica looks out the window and marvels, as she always does, at the sheer size and sprawl of Los Angeles. She loves the energy and diversity of the city, its noir-tinged history, its exuberant architecture, its creative output. It's not New York, but it's a close second.

Erica gathers her things as she gets ready for the landing. Nylan's little power play with her outfits was a cheap trick, a head game designed to let her know who was calling the shots. And placing those glasses in front of her computer? That could have been Claire. GNN is definitely not a warm and fuzzy workplace. Erica reminds herself of her healthy paycheck and the opportunities—including gaining custody of Jenny—that lie in front of her. If she has to put up with some juvenile machinations, it's worth it. As she folds up her laptop, she can almost convince herself that the little ball of dread at the back of her neck is just a stress knot.

The plane lands and Erica finds her driver. She's going to meet Barrish, who lives in Brentwood, in the morning. Then she and her old pal Moira Connelly are going to have lunch. Erica is staying at the Miramar in Santa Monica. On the way to the hotel, she has the driver stop at a boutique on Montana Avenue, where she buys a pearl-gray pantsuit and a stylish above-the-knee dress. Maybe she should send Nylan a selfie of her wearing them.

After checking in, she goes up to her tenth-floor room and unpacks. Then she sits on the edge of the bed. It's late afternoon, the sun is softening, the room is silent. She looks out at the Pacific and the Santa Monica pier with its honky-tonk amusement rides. Suddenly a terrible wave of loneliness sweeps over her. She remembers a vacation she, Dirk, and Jenny took on the Maine coast when Jenny was three. One afternoon they played miniature golf, and she and Dirk let Jenny win. The winner got to pick the restaurant where they ate dinner. Who says a butterscotch sundae can't be called fine dining? And now here she is, alone in a hotel room, three thousand miles from home.

She picks up her phone and dials.

"Hello." Dirk's voice sounds oddly cheery.

"Hi, Dirk, it's Erica. May I speak to Jenny?"

There's a pause and then a perfunctory, "Hold on."

Out the window, she watches a hawk circling while she waits.

"Hi, Mommy."

"Hi, baby. How are you?"

"I'm okay."

"I miss you. I miss you so much. How was school?"

Jenny giggles. "I played hooky."

"You did?"

"Yes, we went to the aquarium in Boston. I fed the penguins!"

"You and Daddy went to the aquarium?"

"And Linda."

"Who's Linda?"

"Daddy's new friend."

"Oh. Okay."

"She's so nice. We had a lot of fun."

"I, uh, I don't think you should be skipping school, honey."

"It's only one day."

"You must be tired after all that excitement. Did you have a nice dinner?"

"Delicious."

"Your favorite mac 'n' cheese?"

"No, that's for babies. We had scallops with fennel, wild rice pilaf, and a kale soufflé."

"A kale soufflé?"

"Linda invented it. She's very creative. We're going to paint my bedroom."

Erica feels a welling up behind her eyes. Her baby—she's losing her baby, her little girl, her Jenny. And there's nothing she can do about it.

"I'm in Los Angeles, Jenny."

"Is it nice?"

"Yes, yes, it is. I wish you were here. Then it would be much nicer."

"I have to go to school tomorrow!"

"I know, I just meant . . . well, I just meant that I miss you terribly and I love you and I'm proud of you." Jenny doesn't say anything. "Bye-bye, baby girl."

Jenny sighs in exasperation. "I'm not a *baby!*"

"No, no, of course you're not." Erica sits up and exhales. "You're a girl, and soon you'll be a young woman. And you're going to do great things!"

"Bye, Mom."

Erica hangs up. She feels her throat tighten as her loneliness edges toward anxiety.

She looks over at the minibar. It looks friendly and welcoming. She walks over and opens it. The contents look so benign: the salted cashews, cheese and crackers, and, of course, those adorable little bottles. All the makings of a party. A party of one.

Think it through . . .

Erica reaches into the minibar and grabs a . . . Toblerone. Then she slips into shorts, a T-shirt, and sneakers, takes a huge bite of the candy bar, and heads out for a run.

Chapter 17

It's a sparkly Southern California day as Erica and her driver wend their way through Brentwood toward Kay Barrish's house. Erica is always dazzled by LA; the colors seem so much more vivid, varied, and saturated than back east, as if God was working with an extra box of paints when he created the landscape. Has it really only been three and a half weeks since the ferry crash? And now—wearing the pantsuit—she's meeting one of the most admired women in the country. To calm herself, and for good luck, Erica fingers her simple blue clip-on earrings. The car arrives at a large gate, and her driver pushes a button on an intercom stand.

"Yes?"

"Erica Sparks to see Ms. Barrish."

The gates swing open and they drive up a small rise and find themselves in a parking court in front of a rambling white house that looks as if it were airlifted in from Connecticut—except for the pop of neon color provided by the blooming vines that artfully climb the façade. It's a large house, yes, but not at all gaudy or intimidating.

Erica gets out of the car just as Kay Barrish comes out of the house. She's wearing Levi's, a white cotton shirt, a brown leather belt, and blue sneakers—the orange scarf tied around her neck gives her a splash of color. She looks lovely: fresh, fit, and vibrant. She grasps Erica's hands and gives her a radiant movie-star smile. "Erica, welcome. How terrific to meet you."

"It's a pleasure to meet you. Before we go any further, I have a message from Nancy Huffman, the head of wardrobe at GNN, and Rosario Acevado, one of our makeup artists: 'We *love* you.' I, on the other hand, reserve judgment."

Barrish roars with laughter. Her face looks unlifted, if pampered, she's wearing nothing more than lipstick, and her silver-blonde hair is swept back and picks up glints of sunlight. "Oh good, you'll keep me on my toes! And love back to those two ladies. Come in, come in."

Erica follows Kay into the house. The living room is large and comfortable, the furnishings a mix of traditional and modern, with bold abstract art on the walls. The far wall is all glass and looks out onto a large yard, a pool, and several outbuildings. Kay leads them down a wide hallway and into the kitchen/family room, which is huge and filled with sparkly appliances, but lived-in and homey at the same time.

"How about a cup of coffee?"

"Love one."

"And I made us some muffins."

"Did you really?"

"No." The women smile at each other. "I'm not much of a cook, although I do make delicious boiled water."

"You should taste my Cheerios."

Kay pours them both mugs of coffee. "So, Mom was very impressed with you."

"We had a nice time. She's really mastered aging, hasn't she?"

"I'm awfully proud of her." Kay leans forward, forearms on the counter, and lowers her voice, pulling Erica in. "It was so tough on her when Dad died. They just adored each other. If she hadn't had to take care of me, I think she would have drowned in her grief. But she got up every morning and did what she had to do. There wasn't any money. She went back to college and got her teaching degree. She cooked dinner every night and helped me with my homework. And, as you saw, she found a passion, a way to bring beauty into the world. When I look at her garden, I see grief transformed."

Listening to her, Erica completely forgets she's talking to one of the most famous and formidable women in the country, someone with a good chance of becoming president.

"How did it affect you?" she asks.

"It was a terrible shock, of course. I was Daddy's girl and then suddenly Daddy was gone. I'm not sure you ever fully recover from a shock that great." She takes a sip of coffee. "I think it gave me my drive. I was so little, but kids *feel* things that they may not understand intellectually. I could feel Mom's sadness, and to be honest, I wanted to get away from it. It was more than I could handle. And I wanted to *live,* fully and completely, to make my life *matter.* In honor of Dad, but also because I instinctively understood how fragile life is. We don't have forever." Kay looks out the window at the beautiful day.

Erica is moved by her words. Was there an element of performance? Of course there was. But all great performances contain truth—that's what makes them great.

Kay stands up tall, and when she speaks, her voice is full. "Well, we certainly got to the nitty-gritty in record time."

"I know your father would be very proud of you."

"I sure hope so." She makes an encompassing gesture. "None of this happened by accident. Come on, let me show you around."

For the next hour Erica gets a tour of Barrishland. She sees the pool, the children's playground, and the gardens with their crazy-quilt California colors and view of the Pacific, blue and crashing and infinite.

"Not a single hosta," Kay cracks.

The sprawling guesthouse has been turned into her office, nerve center, and de facto campaign headquarters. One room is home to half a dozen nicely dressed operatives and aides, several of them on their smartphones, the others hunched over computer screens, monitoring social media sites and keeping Kay's posts up to the minute. A second room is filled with younger, casually dressed interns who are working the phones, reaching out to voters across the country. There are a couple of private offices. In one Erica is introduced to Audra Ruiz, Kay's chief of staff, a woman whose fiercely intelligent eyes quickly size up Erica. The second is lined wall to wall with books and is home to a researcher and a speech writer. As Kay walks through the rooms, she answers questions, makes requests, asks about family members, and banters with an easy jocularity—she is clearly a much-loved boss. Doing her research, Erica discovered that many of Barrish's staff have been with her since she first entered politics. The whole place hums with a sense of unity, purpose, and momentum. People are working hard, very hard, but they are happy to be doing so.

Finally there's Kay's private office, the door guarded by a no-nonsense middle-aged male secretary.

"Bob Franklin, Erica Sparks," Kay says.

Franklin smiles but—like Audra Ruiz—there's a protective scrutiny in his eyes. Erica gets the sense these people would lay down their lives for Kay Barrish.

"Bob is an organizational genius. Without him I'd be nothing but Post-it notes and missed appointments."

"And gray roots," he adds.

"I've asked you not to reveal any state secrets."

Kay leads Erica into her office. One wall is book lined; there's an enormous desk, a comfortable seating area, and a view of the ocean out a picture window.

"Well, there you have it," Kay says. "Our foundation is headquartered downtown and is much more formal."

Unlike most successful people's offices, this one has no wall filled with plaques, awards, and certificates. "Where's the trophy wall?" Erica asks.

"I'm much more interested in where I'm going than where I've been."

"It's all very impressive. May I ask one question?"

"Shoot."

"When are you going to announce your decision on running for president?"

"Mom was right about you, Erica. You're direct and honest. I like that. Mom also told me about your struggles. I *admire* that."

Kay sits on one of two facing sofas and gestures to the other one. Erica sits.

"As to your question: Both my kids are off in college and doing well. My husband is supportive. People across the country and across the political spectrum are urging me to get into the race. I have concrete, well-thought-out ideas that I believe can unite the country and move us all forward." Barrish grows pensive; she looks around the room, gathers herself. "All that said, it's a *big* step and I have to be absolutely sure that I'm up for it and that it's the right move for my family. And I'm not quite there yet." There's a pause; she locks eyes with Erica. "Off the record, if you buy that denial, I have a nice bridge you might be interested in."

Erica sits there, stunned into momentary silence. Then Barrish lets out one of her warm, loud, down-to-earth laughs, calls Bob into the office, and sets up Erica's interview for the next day.

Chapter 18

Erica tries to contain her excitement as Kay walks her to the car and waves her off. As soon as she's past the gate, she takes out her phone and calls Greg.

"I got it."

"You got it?"

"Yup."

Greg lets out a holler, sounding like a Little Leaguer who just hit a game-winning home run. She smiles at his exuberance. "I am *so* proud of you, Erica."

"We're not home yet, Greg, I still have the interview to get through."

"Did she give you any hint of what her decision will be?"

"No comment."

"That speaks volumes. Nylan is going to be over the moon. Where and when?"

"Tomorrow at her house."

"That's fast. I've got to get to work putting together a promo. We'll broadcast it wall to wall on the network and all over social media. We'll drive the ratings through the roof: *Will she or won't she?* There's a lot to do on this end. I'll arrange for on-site hair and makeup, and I'll book the best lighting guy in LA. This interview is going to take you to the next level, and I want you to look sensational."

"We'll start with me outside the house. I'll establish the location, and the why and wherefore of the interview. Then Kay will show me around the grounds. We'll keep that segment light and family-centric. We can tape it in the afternoon. Then we'll shoot the actual interview live in her living room at eight eastern time," Erica says.

"Peak viewership," Greg says. "We're going to blow the other networks off the map."

"Let's not count any chickens. I'm nervous enough as is."

"You're going to be fantastic. I'll fly out tomorrow morning. Don't talk to anyone in the business until we've announced it. We don't want this leaked."

"Tight lips on your end too, please. Especially with Claire."

"No way she's stealing this story. Kay Barrish picked *you*."

"She's a pretty terrific woman."

Greg lowers his voice. "Look who's talking."

"I couldn't have done it without your support."

"I'll see you tomorrow, Erica."

There's a moment of silence between them. Erica feels something electric and anticipatory— a tingling in her short hairs—that has nothing to do with landing the Kay Barrish interview.

Chapter 19

When she gets back to her hotel, Erica calls Moira, tells her the news, and cancels their lunch. Of course Moira understands. Then Erica sits down at the desk and spends the afternoon writing and rewriting her introduction to the interview, her questions for the lightweight part of the segment as Kay shows her around the grounds, and then for the mother lode—the living-room exchange in which, Erica is fairly positive, Barrish will announce that she is running for president of the United States.

Erica is so absorbed in her work that she loses track of time. When she looks up, it's six o'clock and she realizes that she hasn't eaten since breakfast. Not that she's hungry, but she knows she needs to eat. She orders a tuna fish sandwich and a fruit salad from room service. While she's waiting for it to arrive, she does a half hour of Tae Kwon Do. The food is delivered, and she turns on GNN. Almost immediately a promo for her interview comes on. It features footage of Kay Barrish accepting her Oscar, addressing the California legislature as governor, and then visiting a clinic in rural Mexico funded by her foundation. The voice-over describes her many accomplishments and ends with a visual of the White House and: Will she or won't she? Find out tomorrow at eight p.m. in Erica Sparks's exclusive interview with Kay Barrish.

Erica clicks off the set, feeling a combination of excitement and almost overwhelming pressure. She retrieves her deck of cards, sits on the edge of the bed, and plays three hands of solitaire. Then she calls the front desk and asks for a printer to be sent up. When it arrives, she prints out the introduction and the questions she has written up. Then she starts to rehearse, walking around the room as if she were at Barrish's house. She goes over it again and again until she has it just about memorized. She wants to be prepared for any eventuality.

Before she knows it, it's almost ten o'clock. She takes a shower, slips into an oversize T-shirt, gets into bed, and turns out the lights. She lies there as her exhaustion battles her adrenaline. She *needs* to sleep. She closes her eyes and tries to clear her mind. Just as she's dozing off, her hotel phone rings.

"This is Erica."

"Erica, it's Mark Benton." His voice is charged and urgent. She sits up, throws off the covers, and swings her legs to the floor. "I've been working nonstop on our project. I was up all last night and called in sick to work today. I borrowed a page from the North Koreans and hacked into the computer of a midlevel manager at the NYC Department of Transportation. I took on his identity and then used it to maneuver through a maze of DOT systems. But I finally got into the ferry's system. Erica, the ferry's controls *were* hacked."

"Are you sure?"

"Yes. The log files on the DOT router I used to get into the ferry system show invasive activity minutes before the crash."

"Do you know by who?"

"No. Finding their identity is going to be a lot harder. I need an IP address or something else to go on, and these people are very good at covering their tracks. They use proxy servers to block or mask their IPs, and Tor, a freeware program that hides your identity online no matter what you're doing. It basically makes them invisible, or at least indistinguishable from millions of other people online. It could be anyone anywhere. The ferry could have been hacked from Beijing, or it could have been done from Fourteenth Street."

"But still, the crash was an act of cyber-terrorism."

"It certainly looks that way to me."

Erica stands up and starts pacing. "Where do we go from here?"

"I'm just going to keep digging, looking for anything that might tell us where the hacking originated. They may have been sloppy some-where along the line. But listen, forget about this until after the Barrish interview."

"That won't be easy. Five people *died* in that crash. A dozen more are still in the hospital."

"The closer we get to the hackers, the greater the danger that they'll find out about *us*. They're very sophisticated and are no doubt monitoring for intrusions, just like Dave Mullen is up on the sixth floor at GNN."

"Great work, Mark."

"It's exciting. And scary."

Erica suddenly feels cold. "We may have opened Pandora's box."

"Yeah, the demons are out."

They hang up. Erica grabs a throw and wraps it around her shoulders. She walks over to the window and looks out at the California night— the Pacific is glistening under a three-quarter moon, and the pier's amusement park is lit up like a pinwheel. But all she sees is darkness.

Chapter 20

Erica's introduction and the tour of the grounds with Kay Barrish have gone well. The crew is busy setting up for the live interview in the living room. Erica, Greg, and Kay are in the kitchen, alongside Kay's chief of staff, Audra Ruiz, and several other aides. Kay's husband, Bert Winters, is also there—he's older than she is, with a casual confidence, soft-spoken and self-effacing, known for standing by his woman and raising prodigious amounts of money for her campaigns.

Erica has been fighting all day to stay focused. She curses this break—the pause in the intensity of the work allows her mind to return to the news she got from Mark. She wants to tell Greg but she has to handle it very carefully, since

Mark's actions were both illegal and unsanctioned by GNN. And who are the perpetrators? Why haven't they claimed credit? Terrorists are usually quick to trumpet their carnage. Her wheels start turning, carrying her away from the moment. She wills herself back to here and now.

Lesli, Erica's associate producer, has hired Lisa Golden, LA's organic caterer to the stars—a woman of about forty, scrubbed and earnest—who has worked for Nylan several times when he was hosting parties in town. The kitchen island is filled with an array of salads and dishes so glistening and artfully presented they almost look fake. Golden describes every dish down to its last non-GMO grain of rice. When she's done, she introduces her assistant, a Hispanic teenager. "This is Arturo Yanez, who comes to me via Recipe for Success, a program that trains at-risk youth for jobs in the beautiful world of food. I'm a proud supporter."

"How wonderful!" Kay exclaims.

Arturo smiles with a modest pride that can't disguise his anxiety.

"Arturo has made you individual tamale pies for today's supper. Does he have any takers?"

"Me-me-me," Kay says.

Arturo opens the oven and carefully removes one of a dozen small baking dishes. He puts it on a plate with a fork and hands it to Kay, who takes a bite. "De-lish," she pronounces. Not for

108

the first time, Erica marvels at her warmth and charm, which flow as naturally as water.

There are other takers on the tamale pie, but not Erica. Food is the furthest thing from her mind. The most important fifteen minutes of her career are coming up. She steps into a quiet corner of the kitchen and reviews her notes. Since the earlier segments covered Kay's life and career up to this point, she's going to get right to the billion-dollar question. A little shiver runs up her spine—she's not sure where her excitement ends and her anxiety begins. Hair and makeup are set up at the kitchen table and she sits down for a quick touch-up. And then her mind—which seems to have a mind of its own—goes back to the unknown hackers, the *terrorists,* and then to the crash itself, and then she hears the man's scream as his body is crushed between the ferry and the seawall.

Lesli comes into the kitchen. "We're all set. It's five minutes till we go live."

Erica stands up. Kay comes over, locks arms, and leads her into the living room. "I'm so glad I'm doing this with *you,*" she says. Then she burps, a discreet burp but still. She smiles sheepishly. "Why aren't the cameras rolling when you need them?"

Erica and Barrish sit facing each other in straight-back chairs in front of the fireplace. A fire is roaring and the air-conditioning is on—

only in LA. Final adjustments are made in the sound and lighting. Greg, who has put on his headset and is communicating with the network back in New York, stands beside the cameraman and looks through the lens. "You both look terrific."

"Oh, we're women of substance, we don't care about *that,*" Kay says. Laughter ripples through the room, the tension is lightened, and Erica feels a sudden wave of confidence—and affection for this woman. Imagine her in the White House!

"Thirty seconds," Greg says. The room grows still. Kay sits up a little higher, puts on her game face. Erica takes a deep breath. "Ten seconds and . . . Go!"

"So, Kay," Erica begins, "we've seen your lovely house and grounds, and visited your office and met some of your staff. I know how busy you are with your foundation work and your books and speeches, but I sense that you're gearing up for something more."

"You know, Erica, I've been very fortunate, very blessed. My work so far has been deeply fulfilling on many levels."

Erica notices sweat break out on Barrish's hairline and upper lip.

"But when I look around me at the division and gridlock in this country, and the dangers we face in the world, I'm compelled to get involved." All

110

the color suddenly drains from Barrish's face and an odd look comes into her eyes. "As governor, I was all about *common sense leadership*. I think the country could use some of that right—"

Barrish makes a choking sound and clutches her chest. For a moment she seems suspended, a look of shock in her eyes. Then she collapses to the floor.

Erica freezes for an instant. The room is silent. *What's happening?*

Then she's on the floor beside Kay. She puts her hands over the other woman's heart and pushes down again and again, then she tilts Barrish's head back, chin up, pinches her nostrils, clamps her mouth over Kay's and forces one breath, two breaths, three breaths—*life!*—into her lungs. There's no response. Now Audra Ruiz is on the other side of Barrish's body doing the chest compressions as Erica continues the rescue breaths, and now Kay's husband is there, too, one of Kay's hands in his own, saying, "Stay with us, my love, stay with us!" There's controlled panic in the room as Lesli calls 911 and Greg yells, "Cut away!" into his headset.

EMTs arrive in less than five minutes and take over. They insert a breathing tube into Barrish's windpipe and attach defibrillator electrodes above and below her heart and then deliver a jolt of electricity; her upper body jerks but her heart doesn't start beating. The seconds tick by. They jolt her again. Still nothing. The seconds turn to minutes. They load her onto a stretcher—Bert Winters by her side, still holding her hand—and carry her away to the hospital.

Silent shock settles over the room. To go in a seeming instant from all of that energy and life force to . . . nothing. It's over. Kay Barrish is gone.

Erica's mind is blank, like a whiteboard, a flat line, then disassociation, as if she's hurtling away from this scene, away, away into another world, a better world. Her legs feel weak and she grabs the back of a chair. She feels an arm around her shoulders.

"Are you okay?" Greg asks.

Then she remembers: she's a reporter, and the most powerful woman in America has just died in her arms. She has a job to do. "The hospital, Greg, I have to get to the hospital and file a report!"

"No, Erica, an anchor from our local affiliate is already on the way there."

"Greg, no, I want to go, I *have* to go!" She moves toward the front door, frantic.

Greg grips her by the shoulders and looks into her eyes. "Erica, you're in shock. You're in no condition to report on anything."

She looks at him and somehow he gets through. And she knows he's right.

As she died, Kay Barrish looked into Erica's eyes—with eyes that were filled with disbelief and terror. Erica knows she will never forget that look And she wants to cry—for Kay, for herself, for the country, she wants to just weep and weep.

But Erica doesn't cry. No. Uh-uh. Growing up, tears only earned her more scorn from her folks—"Crybaby, crybaby!" Instead she takes the deepest breath of her life, holds it a moment, and then slowly exhales. The room comes into focus around her. People are crying, walking around in a daze, on their phones. Outside she can hear the arrival of news trucks and police cars.

"There's a lot of press outside," Greg says. "Do you feel up to making a brief statement? If not, I can do it."

"I'll do it," Erica says, suddenly thankful for the task and the purpose it brings.

Five minutes later she stands at the bottom of the driveway in front of a battalion of reporters and microphones, lights and cameras, a growing crowd of stunned onlookers—there are helicopters whirling overhead, their spotlights sweeping over the scene. Questions are shouted at Erica and she ignores them, saying in a steady voice: "At 8:04 tonight, while I was interviewing her, former governor Kay Barrish suffered what appeared to be cardiac arrest. Her chief of staff, Audra Ruiz, and I attempted CPR but were

113

unable to revive her. At 8:09 emergency personnel from St. John's Hospital arrived and took over the efforts. Governor Barrish remained unresponsive. At approximately twenty past eight her body was taken to the hospital. That's all I have to say." Erica turns from the cameras. And then, without thinking, she turns back and begins to speak again, this time slowly, in a more intimate tone. "I only spent two days with Kay Barrish, but that was more than enough time for me to know that she was a remarkable woman, a smart and kind woman who cared deeply about our country, about *all* of us. I've lost a friend. What our nation has lost is incalculable."

Greg takes her arm and gently leads her to a waiting car. She gets in. The driver, an older black man, turns and gives her a sad smile, his eyes red-rimmed. "Are you comfortable?" he asks.

Erica nods. As the car moves slowly down the street and the mayhem recedes, she leans back and rests her head against the soft leather. A sudden wave of exhaustion, deeper than bone, overtakes her, and she closes her eyes. She just wants to sleep, to sleep forever.

Chapter 21

Erica wakes up adrift in a vast bed—a sea of pillows and duvets and sheets so smooth they must be silk. She arrived at the hotel last night to find she'd been moved to a suite. She gets up, slips into a plush robe, and walks into the enormous living room. There's a bouquet the size of Delaware on the coffee table—the card reads: *With sympathy and admiration—Nylan.* Beside the flowers are a tray of tiny chocolates, a basket of fruit, a bottle of Dom Pérignon—everywhere she looks there are creamy fabrics, plush furniture, plump pillows, thick carpets. And the California sun shining in the window makes it all sparkle and shine and glow.

Erica takes in the bounty and has one thought: coffee. She picks up the phone, dials room service and orders it—then suddenly she's ravenous and adds an omelet, bacon, fruit salad, oatmeal, juice, pastries and muffins and marmalade.

She sits on a sofa that looks like it's never been sat on before. It's a little past eight o'clock; she slept for nine hours, the most sleep she's had in years. She feels so rested—and that feels like the greatest luxury of all. There's so much to think about, to sort out, to make sense of. But she pushes it all away, wanting to hold on to the sweet, soft nothingness for a minute more.

The hotel phone rings.

"This is Erica."

"Hi, Mom."

"*Jenny* . . ."

"I saw you on TV a hundred times. You're famous."

"Am I?"

"I'm sorry the lady died."

"I am too, sweetheart."

"You tried to save her."

"I just did what anybody would have."

"I'm proud of you."

Erica feels her throat tighten. "Well, I'm proud of *you*."

"I have to go to school now."

"I love you, baby girl."

"I have *repeatedly* asked you not to call me baby."

"I'll try my best, sweet thing."

"I'm not a candy bar either, Mom."

"Yes, you are. You're *my* candy bar, whether you like it or not."

Jenny laughs and her laughter is like water, cleansing, life giving, and Erica feels her blood flow and her mind sharpen.

"Bye, Mom, I miss you."

The food arrives and Erica pours herself a cup of coffee and reaches for the remote. She clicks on GNN, then FOX, then CNN, then MSNBC, then ABC and CBS, then the local news and sees . . . herself. The coverage is wall to wall. Beloved Kay Barrish—movie star, governor, philanthropist, perhaps future president—died on live television, and Erica Sparks's brave, instinctive attempt to save her is riveting footage.

She clicks off the TV—watching the clip is disturbing and shocking and sad and . . . thrilling. At the start of the interview, before Kay's collapse, Erica is both a commanding and charming presence, holding her own with one of the most formidable women in the country. Their rapport is obvious. And then the heart attack and Erica's response. And now, less than twenty-four hours later, she's a household name.

It's a terrible way to achieve her dream. But the undeniable fact is she *has* achieved it. She knows the old adage to beware of answered prayers. She must consider her next steps carefully. *Very* carefully. In fact, she feels like she's already in a minefield with her information about the hacking of the Staten Island ferry—navigating it is going to take some delicate and cunning footwork.

Erica looks over at the bounteous room service cart and thinks, *But right now, it's time to indulge.*

Chapter 22

Just as Erica is polishing off a morning glory muffin—good thing it's not frosted or she'd swear it was a cupcake—there's a knock on her door.

"Erica, it's Greg."

She lets him in. He looks like he hasn't slept, his jaw is stubbly, his clothes wrinkled, his eyes sunken. Does he look a little haunted? She reaches up and touches his cheek. Erica realizes how *comfortable* she feels around him. Their history may be short but it's dense, and he has proved his friendship and loyalty again and again.

"Have you been up all night? How about a cup of coffee?" she asks.

"I think my blood must be three-quarters caffeine right now. How are you?"

"Dazed."

"Not surprising."

"Was it a heart attack?"

"They're almost certain, but they've scheduled an autopsy. You were incredible last night."

"If only it hadn't been under such terrible circumstances."

Greg nods, and there's a moment of silence between them. Punch-drunk, frazzled, fried—he has never looked more attractive to Erica. She has a sudden urge to kiss him. Instead she says, "I should get out of this robe."

She goes into the bedroom and slips into jeans and a T-shirt. She gives herself a quick check in the mirror. She stretches her arms over her head, arches her back. Her body feels so relaxed—in a way it hasn't in a long time. She looks over at that huge welcoming bed and imagines . . . making it, hospital corners and all!

Tempting as the bed may be, today, the first day of her new life, is not the time to take that kind of emotional and professional risk. She grabs a dark blazer, puts it on, and walks into the living room. She has an agenda, an important agenda. Greg is sitting in a chair, working on his blood-coffee level, a thoughtful expression on his face.

"Erica, I'd like to talk seriously for a moment."

She sits on the sofa across from him. "Go ahead."

"Kay Barrish's death was sad and traumatic, but it happened. And because it happened, your life is about to change dramatically. Do you think you're ready for it?"

"I do. It's what I want."

"That's what I hoped you would say. There's really no limit to how high you can go. Our ratings last night were among the best in cable history. GNN's whole profile has changed. We're now firmly on the map. Nylan is over the moon, and when I spoke to him this morning, he said it's time to think about giving you your own show."

Erica feels a surge of triumphant euphoria—which she disguises by reaching for her coffee cup and taking a sip. "I don't want to rush into anything. We've all seen what happens when someone is given a show before they're ready. It's not pretty."

Greg nods. "More immediately, I've been fielding calls all morning from shows that want you on—everyone from *Good Morning America* to *E! News* to *60 Minutes* to Stephen Colbert."

"I'm going to be very selective. As I've said, I'm in this for the long haul. I don't want to be known as a one-trick pony—the blonde who tried to save Barrish. I also don't want to spread myself too thin, and I don't want to wear out my welcome before I've arrived. I'll do *60 Minutes*. Nix the others."

Greg nods. "It carries the most weight."

Erica feels it, the subtle shift in power—the network needs her as much as she needs them. It's a nice feeling. She hopes Kay Barrish would be proud of her. And maybe now Nylan will back off.

"Now, Greg, there's something serious I want to discuss with you."

"Shoot."

"A source I trust explicitly has contacted me regarding the Staten Island ferry crash."

Greg leans forward, elbows on knees.

"This source was able to get into the ferry's computer system. The system was hacked. The crash was an act of terrorism."

"Whoa." Greg stands up, paces. "Erica, do you know what you're saying? The NTSB said it was a computer malfunction, an accident. Who is this source?"

"I can't reveal that, Greg."

"Is it Mark Benton?"

"I said I'm not saying. But they know their stuff. Well."

"Do they know who's responsible?"

"They're working on that."

"When did the source contact you?"

"Night before last."

"You should have told me immediately."

"We were consumed with Barrish."

"Have you told anyone else?"

"Just you."

Greg rubs the back of his neck, exhales. "You know this is a *major* story?"

Erica nods.

"We have to handle it *very* carefully. This is information that was obtained illegally."

"We're dealing with *terrorists* here," Erica says. "People who want to kill us and maim us, destabilize our society, destroy the United States of America. No, this wasn't on the scale of 9/11, but it was a warning shot about the power of cyberterrorism. I don't care *how* my source got this information, we have it and we have a responsibility to act on it. Which probably means sharing it with the National Security Agency."

Greg goes still for a second. Then he nods, almost to himself. "You're right, of course. We're dealing with evil here, and we have to do everything we can to find them. We have a responsibility to the nation."

"To the world. Cyberterrorism makes borders obsolete."

Greg runs his fingers through his hair. "We have to think through contacting the NSA. The Feds can be very ham-handed. They'll demand the name of your source and immediately want to take over. Which may well short-circuit the source's work on finding the location and identity of the terrorists."

"Good point."

"How much time does your source need?"

"I haven't gotten a timetable. They're working around the clock."

"Let's give them forty-eight hours before we go to the NSA." He stops pacing and gives her a sympathetic smile. "Talk about out of the frying pan."

"I grew up with Maine winters. I can handle the heat."

Chapter 23

Erica and Greg are in the car heading to LAX for their flight back to New York. They've only been on the freeway for a couple of minutes when the driver exits.

"Aren't we going to LAX?" Erica asks.

Greg smiles. "We have a little surprise for you."

Within minutes they've pulled into Santa Monica Airport, past the terminal, onto the tarmac, and then up to a large private jet with *Universe* written on its nose. A steward stands at the foot of the air-stairs. "Nylan sent this for you," Greg says.

Wow. How many times has Erica suffered through the indignities of teeming airports, glacial security checks, jammed flights filled with screaming babies, and seatmates with questionable personal hygiene habits. And now this—drive up and you're on board.

Erica and Greg get out.

"Welcome. The *Universe* is yours," the steward says before retrieving their bags from the back of the SUV.

Erica walks up the steps and into the cabin. And there sits Nylan Hastings. Surrounded by two men and one woman.

"There she is!" Nylan says, standing, and they all break into applause.

Erica has never been fond of surprises, and she turns to Greg. "Did you know about this?"

"I swear I had no idea."

"You were breathtaking last night," Nylan says, smiling at her in a proprietary way.

"I was just doing my job."

"I'd like you to meet Margaret Dempsey, GNN's lead counsel; George Wilkins, our chief financial officer; and Fred Wilmot, our chief visionary officer."

In contrast to Nylan, who is his usual study in faux casual, the others are all dressed in dark suits and perfectly groomed, with erect posture and too-bright smiles—the Stepford execs.

A second steward appears with six flutes of champagne. Erica accepts one.

"To our future together," Nylan toasts.

Erica pretends to take a sip—the dry, fruity effervescence tickles her nostrils, and she feels a split second of seductive nostalgia. Then she puts the flute down.

The captain appears. "Welcome to the *Universe*. I'm Captain Sutter. Our estimated flying time to New York this afternoon is five hours and eleven minutes. We've been cleared for takeoff, so I'd ask you to please sit down and fasten your seat belts."

He returns to the cockpit and the plane begins

to taxi. Erica sits in one of the impossibly comfortable leather seats—which are arranged in a circle around a large coffee table—and gets her first good look around. The plane is decorated like the lobby of a hip luxury hotel, all clean lines and soothing hues punctuated with bold pops of color and arresting art, including a Jeff Koons dog sculpture, which sits between the seating area and the dining table. Past that, Erica gets a peek into the kitchen, where a female chef is hard at work.

"There are two bedroom suites in the back if you'd like to take a nice, hot shower," Nylan says as the stewards bring out hot towels and take drink orders.

Erica notices that no one, except Greg, who asks for a beer, orders alcohol. Nylan runs a sober ship. And a tight one. All three of his deputies have that same laser focus, that intensity that Nylan tries—with limited success—to disguise.

Takeoff goes as smoothly as whipped butter on warm bread. As they glide through the ether, Nylan plays host, keeping the focus squarely on Erica. New ratings numbers have come in—the Barrish interview is the fifth highest-rated program in cable news history. But it goes way beyond that—hits on YouTube have passed a hundred million worldwide, GNN's website has experienced a fifteenfold jump in visitors, Erica is approaching half a million Twitter followers, and all of GNN's programming has experienced a surge in viewership.

"Erica, overnight you have become the global face of GNN," Nylan announces. "I want to give you your own daytime show."

Erica skips a breath. "Thank you, I'm honored. I'll do my very best."

Her own show! Erica can almost feel her head expanding. *Cool it, kid! The day before yesterday you were just one more hardworking reporter. What goes up can come down—and just as quickly.* Shooting stars burn out. We live in a fickle culture that has collective ADD, is always looking for the next hot thing, and loves to turn on its celebrities. Can online haters and tabloid and TMZ headlines be far behind? Keep things in perspective.

What Erica is most excited about is her new power. Power to uncover the truth, to report on important stories, to help drive a national, even global, dialogue on the future of our dangerously divided nation and our imperiled, war-riven planet. And, on a personal level, the power to take charge of her destiny, to make some kind of uneasy peace with her past, both her miserable childhood and the terrible mistakes she's made as an adult. The power to give Jenny the life she deserves. She wants her daughter living with her in New York, going to one of the city's best private schools, having advantages that she could only dream of in St. Albans, Maine. Advantages that, Erica will stress, come with responsibility. Most of all, she wants Jenny to be happy. She suffers from bouts of moodiness and her grades are erratic. The divorce was hard on her; she was exposed to some real ugliness. Erica wants to make amends. She wants to be a wonderful mother.

Somewhere over the Midwest one of the stewards announces, "Dinner is served."

As they move to the table, Erica gets a text message. She takes out her phone—it's from Mark and reads: **Getting closer.** "It's from my daughter," Erica says, before answering: **See you tomorrow.** And then she flashes to the black glasses placed so carefully in front of her computer screen. She puts her phone on the table facedown and glances at the implacable faces of Nylan's aides—they're all looking at her with identical inscrutable expressions. Let them look. Erica has a lot more power at GNN than she did yesterday. She just has to learn how to handle it.

Once everyone is seated, the chef comes out from the kitchen; she's dark-haired, slender, and polished.

"This is Rebecca Atkins," Nylan says. "Rebecca's London restaurant Beside the Point receive two Michelin stars this year. I've hired her just for this flight."

Atkins smiles becomingly and says in a crisp British accent, "We will be starting this evening

127

with artichoke bisque infused with lemon-apricot oil and topped with sheep-milk sour cream and Scottish caviar. After a sedum and baby beet green salad, our main course is pumpkin-seed-and-truffle-crusted tuna served with a grilled-grape-and-baby-pea ragout."

Listening to this lavish litany—which the others are absorbing with studied nonchalance—Erica has a sudden flash of insecurity: she doesn't belong in a private jet with a private chef, eating food like this. And there are so many utensils, what if she uses the wrong one? Everyone is smiling at her, but what are they thinking? Can they tell she grew up on canned stew and Little Debbie snacks? Erica pushes the thoughts away—something she's trained her mind to do since those first excruciating days at Yale. She exhales and picks up the fat soup spoon, thankful that it's the obvious choice. Greg, who is sitting next to her, gives her a wry don't-worry-about-it smile, almost as if he knows what she's thinking.

She tries the soup; it sets off a series of sequential taste explosions in her mouth—rich, deep artichoke cut with a whisper of citrus tang and fruity sweetness, giving way to creamy sour-cream comfort and finally the intense burst of the salty fish eggs. She can hardly believe that there are people who eat—and live—like this every day. And they're welcoming her into their world.

At one point Erica looks over at Nylan and

catches him watching her intently. She's quiet during the rest of the meal, marveling at the revelatory flavors and listening to the others talk about their plans for the network. She notices that Nylan speaks the least. He listens like a hawk, his eyes flashing with that restless intelligence, but he seems to be conserving his energy. This flight, after all, is celebratory; there are no battles being fought—he saves his firepower for when he needs it. Erica suspects there's a lesson to be learned there.

Dessert is a raspberry, cashew, meringue napoleon—rich and light and fruity all at once. It's cleared, coffee orders are taken, and then, suddenly, a beautiful little box made of polished teak appears in front of Erica.

"What's this?"

"Open it," Nylan says.

She lifts off the lid and looks inside. There sits a crystal orb the size of a baseball. She gently lifts it out. It's a globe, etched with a map of the world. The GNN logo is inscribed over the North Pole. Suspended inside the globe is a mint silver dollar.

"It's exquisite," Erica says. Everyone else at the table nods in agreement.

"It's Lalique. Nylan only gives out one or two a year," Fred Wilmot says.

Erica holds it up and examines it. She can make out the date on the silver dollar: 1978.

"That coin was struck the year Nylan Hastings was born," Wilmot solemnly states.

There's a render-unto-Nylan moment of silence at the table. The hushed devotion is a little too much for Erica. Her enjoyment and pride at the gift gives way to a feeling that's less pleasant. The globe is just so self-reverential and solipsistic. It's creepy. She and Greg exchange a glance—does he feel the same way?

The plane hits a sudden wall of turbulence. Without thinking, Erica's hand goes to Greg's thigh under the table. Then his hand is on top of hers. He gives her hand a gentle squeeze. She should pull away. Shouldn't she? She looks at the globe. She's queen of the world at thirty thousand feet.

She leaves her hand on Greg's thigh. And as for the turbulence? Bring it on.

Chapter 24

Erica sits in her new office, which has a seating area, a view of Central Park, and a large closet. It's two days after her return from Los Angeles. She paid a quick visit to Mark Benton yesterday, and he reported that the cyberterrorists are highly skilled—he's finding it close to impossible to track their whereabouts. He also reiterated the possibility that the terrorists have detected *him*. And the danger that holds for both of them. They agree that they shouldn't be seen together in the office anymore. From now on they'll arrange outside meetings that appear serendipitous.

Erica is preparing for the first development meeting on her show, which has a tentative timeline to go live in two months. There's so much to do: big things like hiring a director, writers, and other staff; designing the set; coming up with a basic format and recurring segments; and a thousand details large and small, like the show's music and lining up go-to experts on a host of issues. Erica is determined to avoid ideology—is there anything more annoying and less elucidating than two ideologues from opposite sides of the spectrum yelling over each other? She wants to keep the focus on the facts, and she wants to mix in some aspirational, inspirational, and even spiritual segments. And some pop culture to provide pure entertainment—and a ratings boost.

Greg strides into her office. "ISIL has just claimed credit for the Staten Island ferry crash."

Erica stands up. "So it *is* terrorism. And ISIL no less. Do they have that kind of capability?"

"Apparently. They've been recruiting globally —young people with tech skills. They're threatening another cyberstrike against the US. The president is going to speak in fifteen minutes. We need you on-air in ninety seconds."

"I thought the ferry crash was Claire Wilcox's story now."

"*Was* is the operative word in that sentence." Erica races down the hall toward the studio.

Chapter 25

Erica looks into the camera and begins: "We have breaking news: The Middle East caliphate ISIL has claimed credit for the crash of the Staten Island ferry on the morning of April 13. The crash claimed five lives and injured eighty people, two dozen of them critically. Ten remain hospitalized. ISIL claims that it hacked into the ferry's computer system and froze its steering mechanism. If true, this is the first major act of cyberterrorism committed on American soil. President Garner will be speaking to the nation ten minutes from now."

GNN runs the footage of the crash and Erica interviews, by remote feed, one of the nation's leading experts on cyberterrorism. Then they go to the White House feed. President Garner is grave, strong, and succinct: this evil act will be punished. He tells the nation that the Department of Homeland Security's cyberterrorism division is working to determine the location of ISIL's technology infrastructure. When it does, appropriate action will be taken.

After the president's remarks, Erica is on-air for the next six hours, anchoring GNN's coverage of the unfolding story. This is the first time she's been on for this long, anchoring a story this big. Her adrenaline reaches a high level and plateaus—she's on her game, cruising along. Greg is right with her the whole time. Once the initial story is reported and the footage of the crash shown, it becomes a challenge to fill the airtime. Greg rounds up senators from both parties in Washington, the mayor of New York City, GNN's chief Middle East correspondent in Damascus, a survivor of the crash, a cybersecurity expert who explains how cyberterrorism works, and a general with expertise in the field.

Erica knows from her years of experience in Boston that it's a gamble to pull people in at the last minute, especially those with limited media experience. Some folks freeze, others are staggeringly inarticulate, others stray off topic. That's where the art and craft of her job comes in—Erica's goal is to get people to give relevant, timely, insightful answers. In some ways she loves the tough guests the best—they force her to up her game. She has to size them up in seconds, try to connect, and then draw them out in the right direction. She has the opposite problem with several of the network's regular political commentators, whom she finds to be self-important, with little original insight, imagination, or wit.

The main challenge with these gasbags is getting them to shut up.

One of Erica's most important interviews is with Allen Menkin, a former NSA official who now works for a private intelligence contractor.

"Mr. Menkin, how do we know ISIL's claim of crashing the ferry is the truth and not just an opportunistic ploy? After all, it makes them a hero to Muslim extremists around the world, generates fear here in the United States, and no doubt helps with recruiting."

"That's a crucial question," Menkin answers. "My sources inside the intelligence community assure me the government has third-party confirmation that the hacking originated from a location in ISIL-controlled territory in Syria. Without such information I highly doubt the president would have addressed the nation."

Erica finally turns over the reins at eight p.m. —to Claire Wilcox, no less. The two share a split-screen handoff in which Claire, after thanking Erica for the good work, says, "You look *exhausted,* my friend. Get some rest." Erica takes the high road, advising viewers to stay tuned for "Claire Wilcox's hard-hitting reporting and always intriguing insights." Claire looks momentarily shocked by her rival's magnanimity. Poor Claire, she's had a rough week. There's no Lalique crystal globe sitting on her desk.

Erica decompresses in her office, kicking off

her flats and massaging her feet, checking her e-mails, and sipping a cup of green tea. Greg appears in her doorway. She motions him in. He closes the door behind him.

"If the hacking came from ISIL in Syria, I guess it makes your source a moot point," he says.

"Which is something of a relief."

"It's out of our hands."

"You did an amazing job today, Greg. You just kept those guests coming. Although I do think it's time to send Senator Ferguson out to pasture. He's an angry old man who hasn't had an original thought since Reagan was in the White House."

"He's a media whore—turn on a camera and there he is. They thrive in the native climate down there in DC."

"Swamp creatures."

The two share an easy laugh. The laugh feels so good—release from the intensity of the day. They're silent for a moment, both realizing how strong and instinctive their bond has become. Their relationship has passed through another crucible. They worked together seamlessly for hours—in a pressure-cooker environment—anticipating each other's needs, confident in each other's ability. She's never had a work experience that went quite so smoothly.

"How about I walk you home?" Greg asks.

"Sounds good to me."

Chapter 26

It's a cloudy, humid New York night as Erica and Greg walk up toward Fifty-Seventh Street—rain seems imminent. She remembers the last time Greg walked her home. It was just a month ago, but it feels like a lifetime—and she feels like she was a different person then. Green. Untested. At the bottom of the pyramid. Now she's at the top and the dynamic between Greg and her has flipped. Which he seems to have no problem dealing with. One thing she's loved about him from day one is his lack of overweening male ego—so many men she's worked with feel the need to always be right and in control. And to make sure the women around them know it. Greg is the very opposite—he seems close to gender-blind.

"I love you!" a woman screams, rushing up to Erica.

Erica recoils, stepping backward. She does a quick scan: middle-aged, clean, looks sane.

"You were so amazing with Kay Barrish—I cry every time I watch it. And today, with the terrorism story, you *care,* you really care."

"Thank you," Erica manages.

"I can't believe I just met you. My husband

isn't going to believe this. *I love you!*" The woman retreats, pulling out her phone.

Erica has never experienced anything like that. Sure, she's been recognized, but this wasn't recognition, it was adulation. How can that woman *love* her, when she doesn't even know her? Talk about power. It's strange, and she feels a combination of exhilarated and wary. She's entered a brave new world, one in which privacy and boundaries are erased.

"Welcome to Xanadu," Greg says with a smile.

Erica slips her arm through his—she can feel his lean muscle. Then it starts to rain, just a few steady drops at first and then a clap of thunder and a downpour. Greg whips off his jacket and holds it over her as they duck, laughing, into a nearby doorway. They huddle, their bodies pressed together, as all around them the city scurries for cover. Erica's hair is dripping and Greg's shirt is soaked.

"I guess there are times in life when all you want is an umbrella," he says.

There's another thunderclap and the wind picks up. Erica blinks to clear the rain from her eyes.

"Greg?"

"Yes?"

"I'm going to kiss you now."

And she does.

Chapter 27

Erica floats into her apartment on the trail of the kiss. She feels light and electric and alive, so alive. In the bedroom she takes off her clothes and slips into a robe. She walks into the bathroom, grabs a towel, and dries her hair. She looks at herself in the mirror and smiles—*It's happening, Erica, it's really happening.*

Her phone rings. Who could that be? Greg wishing her good night?

"Erica, it's Mark." He sounds agitated.

"I guess our work is done."

"Not exactly. I never take authority at its word, so when the ISIL news broke today, I kept working."

"And?"

"I've uncovered something. Something important."

It takes Erica a moment to switch gears, to accept the news. The kiss fades to a distant memory as she slots into work mode. "What is it?"

"Erica, as we discussed, the deeper I get into this, the more chance there is that the terrorists will sniff me out. Which puts me in serious danger. And by extension, you. We have to be more careful. I'm calling you from a prepaid phone. Buy one yourself. We'll use them for all future communications. Meet me at six tomorrow morning at the Starbucks at Fifty-Second and Eighth."

"I'll be there."

"And, Erica, don't tell anyone about this call. *Anyone.*"

Erica hangs up, reaches into her bag for her playing cards, sits on the couch, and deals a hand of solitaire on the coffee table. What could Mark have uncovered? And why is he suddenly so worried about their safety? Just when she thought that the ferry story was out of her hands, she's suddenly back in the mix. Neck deep.

She tosses down the cards and stands up, looks out the window—the rain is over, the streets are crowded again, but now the city looks hard-edged, unrelenting, overwhelming. Who knows who is out there, and what their motives are? She draws the curtains as a wave of fear sweeps over her. She begins to pace with one thought in her mind: a drink.

Chapter 28

Erica arrives at Starbucks at five forty-five. In a nod to her new reality, she's wearing a baseball cap and sunglasses. They work—she gets some second glances, but with her blonde hair hidden and her unmade-up face obscured, people can't quite place her. She orders the latest frappa-whatever and sits on a stool at the back. Even at this hour the place is jammed with early risers, a mix of groggy construction workers and bushy-tailed young A-types determined to get to the office an hour before everyone else. Since she got about an hour's sleep, she feels more kinship with the groggy crowd—but as she sips the coffee and inhales the city's energy, her adrenaline starts to kick in.

Of course she didn't have a drink last night—but she did have a moment where she just wanted *out*. A low-level fear has lodged itself at the corners of her consciousness. This ferry story feels radioactive, carrying risks not only to her work but to her life. Is she in real danger? She pushes the thought out of her mind. She wants to use her time developing her own show, building a platform for the long career. But walking away from the story is out of the question. So she spent a restless night fighting for sleep as various scenarios—none of them pretty—galloped through her head.

But now she's up, alert and ready for whatever news Mark brings. She's certainly impressed with him—he's smart, fearless, thoughtful, and amazing at what he does. One of the good guys. And at GNN, she needs every good guy she can find.

It's six and he hasn't shown up. She watches the baristas—they turn fulfilling coffee orders into a ballet. Then her mind flits back to the kiss with Greg, her hand on his cheek, the light stubble, the taste of his tongue, his arm around her waist, their bodies pressed together in the doorway, the city disappearing around them. She wants another kiss . . . and then another.

Now it's 6:22 and there's still no sign of Mark. She fingers the prepaid cell phone she bought at the twenty-four-hour Duane Reade on Fifty-Seventh Street. Should she call Mark's? She does. It rings and rings, no answer, no voice mail. She hangs up. What could Mark's news be? He said it was important. A thought that has festered at the edge of her mind—half formed and willfully ignored—pushes its way to the fore.

It was an incredible coincidence that she happened to be reporting from Battery Park when the ferry crashed. Fine. Coincidences happen. But then for her to be interviewing Kay Barrish at the moment she had a heart attack.

Does lightning strike the same person twice? Can fate be that random?

It's 6:34. Where is Mark?

Suddenly the coffee shop seems chaotic—it's so noisy a gun could go off and you wouldn't hear it. And everyone is so impatient, so intense; there's a woman with greasy hair carrying six bulging plastic bags, mumbling to herself. A wave of paranoia floods Erica. She looks around her. Why is that man staring at her? And so intently. Then he smiles—the excited smile of a fan. Erica manages to smile back, but now other people are looking at her. She feels exposed, vulnerable. She's famous now; she has to be careful. People want a piece of her. There are a lot of crazies out there.

It's 6:42. No Mark. She grabs her bag and flees.

Chapter 29

Erica feels somewhat better in her office, grounded by the work at hand, with Greg just down the hall. She fights the urge to go down to the third floor and see if Mark is there. He was adamant about no contact at the office. Erica opens the file on her show—there's a development meeting at nine—and starts to write down ideas. When her mind is engaged, everything else falls away, her synapses click, her motor hums.

She jots down thoughts on the set—she envisions a news desk, which will be her home base, and then a comfortable seating area for the more human-interest and lighthearted segments. She also wants to get out of the studio regularly, doing segments and interviews that take her around the region, the nation, even the globe.

There's a knock on her open door, and Greg steps into the office. Erica wants to get up and run into his arms. Instead they exchange a conspiratorial smile. They agreed that displays of affection are off-limits at work. Which only makes it more exciting. Their secret.

"Good morning, Sparks."

"Ditto, Underwood."

"There's breaking news. Our sources at the Pentagon tell us the president has unleashed an airstrike on ISIL's suspected technology center outside Alleppo, Syria."

"He's not wasting any time. Does this mean our development meeting is canceled?"

"No, just delayed. I want to put you on the air to discuss this development. As for your show, Nylan called me this morning. He wants it on the air ASAP. He's going to build you your own studio, green room, dressing room, hair and makeup station, the works. He wants to start running teaser promos in two weeks."

Erica stands up. "All very exciting. But let me go get presentable."

"You look exceptionally presentable to me."

"*Shhh*—loose lips."

"You had to mention lips."

Erica sits down in the makeup chair, and Andi gets to work on her hair. A somber Rosario asks, "Did you hear about Mark Benton?"

"The IT guy?"

"Yes. He was mugged this morning on the way to work."

Erica's heart starts to race. "Oh no. That's terrible news. Is he all right?"

"He got beaten up pretty bad. He's in Beth Israel Hospital in a coma." Rosario picks up the spray gun. "Are you all right, Erica?"

"Me? Oh yes, I'm just sorry to hear this news."

"Do you know him?"

"We've met a couple of times. He seemed very nice."

"And a real genius with computers," Andi says. "My laptop crashed once and all my files got erased. I was in a crazy panic, I went down to IT, he fixed it for me in ten minutes."

"I hope he's going to be okay," Erica says.

The women work their magic. But by the time Rosario is done, she has to blot and repowder Erica's sweat-dappled hairline.

Chapter 30

It's seven p.m. and Erica is in her office, done for the day. Willpower got her through it—she put blinders on and forged forward. She's been on the air six times to update the ISIL bombing story. The Pentagon released photos of the suspected ISIL technology nerve center before and after the American air strikes. It is obliterated. But Erica is quickly learning to question every claim.

When she was a local reporter up in New England, these big national and international stories were out of her purview. No longer. She feels a very real responsibility to her viewers—and to the nation and even to the world—to be skeptical. Like Ronald Reagan said: trust but verify. Sometimes government agencies make mistakes. And sometimes they willfully lie, usually to cover up those mistakes. Or for rank political reasons. Now she has the power to uncover the truth, a power the average citizen can only imagine, and she isn't going to be hesitant about using it. And so in every appearance today she stressed the word *suspected* when describing the ISIL technology center. And she reiterated the fact that while ISIL has claimed responsibility for hacking the Staten Island ferry's navigational system, no *proof* has been offered or discovered.

The development meeting on her show went well. Erica, Greg, Lesli, and several other associate producers were present. They went over writers' résumés, decided on a 60/40 ratio of hard news to human interest and celebrity stories, and hired a designer, a brilliant young Italian woman who will be responsible not only for the set, but for the logo and all graphics—Erica wants a unified look, fresh and distinctive. The word *brand,* like *teamwork,* is so overused that it's almost lost its meaning, but the fact is that's what she's creating. It's a crowded marketplace and she wants to stand out.

Of course without meaningful reporting it will all be for naught—and delivering that is up to her. Then there's the fact—which in her less modest moments she admits to herself—that she's demonstrated star power. She wants to put it all together in one seamless package: tough, honest reporting, informative and entertaining stories, a great crisp look, and at the center of it all—Erica Sparks.

Erica straightens her desk. She's eager to get down to Beth Israel to visit Mark. Just as she's about to stand up, Greg appears in her doorway.

"It was a good meeting," he says.

"What do you think of *The Erica Sparks Effect* as a name for the show?"

"I like it. It's got energy and it promises results." Greg puts his hands in his pockets, frowns. "Did you hear about Mark Benton down in IT?"

"I did, yes. Very upsetting."

"Did you know him?"

"I've met him a couple of times, I asked his opinion on the cause of the ferry crash. He was helpful." Erica has an urge to open up to Greg, to tell him everything that Mark has discovered and about their scheduled meeting at Starbucks. Then she hears Mark's voice: *Don't tell anyone at GNN. Anyone.*

"He's one of the best. Hopefully he'll be okay," Greg says. He gestures toward a chair. Erica nods. Greg sits, leans forward, lowers his voice. "You seem a little preoccupied. How are things going with Jenny?"

Erica feels a moment of relief—he may have picked up on her being distracted, but he guessed the wrong cause. "Things are okay. The divorce was difficult for her. She has some anger towards me."

"Divorce does that."

"This is an important time in her life. I think it was the right decision not to bring her to New York with me, I'm just so busy, but I do doubt myself." Erica feels that tug of guilt for neglecting to mention that bringing Jenny to New York was never an option. Thankfully the details of why it wasn't are buried in those sealed court records. "I want her to know that I'm here for her, even if we're not living together."

"I can't wait to meet her."

Erica's face lights up with a huge smile. "Oh, she's wonderful, Greg, curious and funny and sweet—when she's not being awful to her mom." They laugh. "But she's growing up. She's not a little girl anymore. In fact, her birthday's coming up in two weeks and her addled mother has no idea what to get her."

"She's turning . . . ?"

"Nine. I'd like to take the day off and go up to Massachusetts and see her. Is that going to be possible?"

"Of course. You're still officially a field reporter. I'll find someone to cover for you. Of course if the ISIL story takes some dramatic turn . . ."

"Kids don't really understand dramatic turns. It would mean a lot to Jenny if I showed up. And to me."

Greg is quiet for a moment, then he rubs his palms together in a gesture she has come to recognize—his wheels are turning. "Say listen, just off the top of my head—why not bring Jenny down here? We can have a small party for her in the studio."

"I'm not sure that's a good idea. She's a little shy with new people. It might be too much attention."

"We could make it very low-key. She'll get to

see where Mom works, what she does, how admired and popular she is."

Erica considers Greg's idea. After the toxicity of the divorce, she would love for Jenny to see her in action. She even admits to some vanity—she's successful, something of a hot ticket, and she'd like Jenny to know that. And Jenny might get a kick out of a behind-the-scenes look at television news. Other people bring their kids to work all the time.

"You know what, I think I like the idea. I'll ask Lesli if she could arrange the party."

Greg sits back, runs his hand through his hair. "Any chance of dinner?"

Erica looks down at her desk, shuffles a few papers. "There's nothing I'd like more. But I really want to spend the evening organizing my notes on the meeting."

"All work and no play makes . . . *The Erica Sparks Effect* the most exciting show in cable news."

"Here's hoping."

When Greg leaves, she quickly grabs her things and heads down to the elevators. She waits impatiently, her foot tapping. The car comes and she gets on, presses 1. The doors close and the elevator descends for several floors, then lurches, then shudders, then stops. Panic rises in a wave through her body, then the lights go out and she's plunged into blackness. She's trapped. Her throat closes. She wills herself to breathe. She freezes and listens—there's no sound, no commotion, no raised voices, nothing she'd expect to hear if it was a full-building blackout or if there'd been an explosion or an attack. It's just her. Alone in the dark. What if the elevator drops suddenly, all the way to the basement? She'll die on impact. She feels her way along the wall to the control panel and gropes for the emergency button, which sticks out from the panel. She presses it. No alarm sounds. Nothing. Just blackness and silence, as silent as death.

Erica can't control her panic, sweat breaks out all over her body, she screams, "Help!" She gropes her way to the closed doors and, using all her strength, tries to pry them open. They don't give. *"Help me!"* Her voice just seems to be swallowed up by the dark. And then, suddenly, the elevator lurches and groans. The lights flicker on, and it begins to descend. Erica sighs in a great gush of relief, her panic ebbs.

When the doors open at the lobby, a suited security agent and an elevator maintenance man are standing there. Erica steps off, dazed and shaken.

"Are you all right?" the maintenance man asks.

"I think so, yes."

The security agent says nothing, just stands there with a grim expression on his face.

The maintenance man puts an Out of Service

pedestal sign in front of the open elevator door, then steps into the cab and turns off the power.

"Why did it happen?" Erica asks.

"We're going to look into it. Could be mechanical. Or it could be a glitch in the software. These cars are all computerized."

"Could it have been intentional?"

The maintenance man looks incredulous. "I guess so. But what kind of sicko would want to put someone through that?"

What kind of sicko?

Erica heads out into the welcome air. As she steps to the curb to hail a cab, she looks back at the GNN building and thinks, *That is not a safe place.*

Chapter 31

Beth Israel Hospital is on First Avenue and Seventeenth Street. Erica jumps out of the cab, heads into the main entrance, walks up to the front desk, and gets Mark's room number.

She hesitates before stepping on the elevator. As the car rises, she says the Serenity Prayer several times. It centers her, gives her strength and faith. Which she badly needs right now. She feels as if she's moving into uncharted territory. When she dreamed of her career, she never imagined she would find herself caught up in a story this big, with national security implications, where people's lives are at stake. Where she herself may be in danger.

In some core way Erica feels like she's been in danger her whole life—when a little girl's parents use her as an emotional and physical punching bag, a foil for their sad, sick lives, can she ever really feel safe? She thought fame and success and money would protect her, buffer her from pain and fear. Now that hope seems naive. She takes a deep breath, trying to calm the telltale beat of her troubled heart.

Erica walks down the wide hallway. She doesn't like hospitals—all the plastic, all the sickness, all the depressingly cheery colors, all the downcast people coming out of the rooms after visits, all the patients shuffling down the hallways with walkers. She smiles at a passing nurse. Nurses, on the other hand, she loves—they're on the front line, in the trenches every day, doing the dirty work—the ones she's known tend to be caring, no-nonsense, and a little eccentric. They're real people doing real work that really matters. Heroes.

Erica reaches Mark's private room. The door is open but she can't see him because the curtain is drawn. She can see a middle-aged couple sitting at the foot of his bed, watching him with deep concern.

She knocks gently on the door. "May I come in?"

The woman nods. Erica walks past the curtain and gets her first look at Mark, and her stomach turns over. His head is wrapped in bandages and his face looks like one big bruise, red and yellow and purple and green, grotesquely swollen, blood caked at the corners of his open mouth, several teeth gone, one eye shut tight, stitches along his temple and cheek. There are tubes everywhere, drips and catheters and bags.

Erica and the couple exchange sad, stricken looks. "Are you Mark's parents?"

The man nods. "Chuck Benton. This is my wife, Marie."

"I'm Erica Sparks, a colleague of Mark's."

"Mark mentioned you. He likes you," Marie says. "Thank you for coming."

The Bentons look like they're still in shock. There are two suitcases beside them.

"I'm so sorry this happened," Erica says. "How long have you been here?"

"A couple of hours. We flew in from Cleveland."

"Do you have a hotel?"

"We got a reservation at the Holiday Inn on Houston."

That sounds depressing. Erica goes out to the nursing station and approaches a young male nurse who is writing on a clipboard.

"Can you recommend a nice nearby hotel?"

He looks up and smiles. "Everyone loves The Inn at Irving Place. It's about three blocks west, small and very homey. A lot of patients' families stay there. It's not cheap though."

Erica takes out her phone and calls the hotel. She manages to book the Bentons a room, requests fresh flowers, and tells the hotel to put it on her credit card. Then she calls the Holiday Inn and cancels the reservation there. She walks back into Mark's room and tells the Bentons. Marie Benton's eyes tear up with gratitude. Chuck Benton protests but Erica fibs and assures him GNN is paying, is happy to pay.

A doctor walks into the room. Clearly the Bentons have met him earlier. The doctor recognizes Erica and stands a little taller. "Mitch Kaminer. Nice to meet you."

The Bentons and Erica watch as the doctor scans the chart hanging at the end of Mark's bed.

"How is he doing?" Erica asks.

"No change. Which is good news at this point."

"Can you tell me a little bit about his injuries?"

"With his family's permission I can."

Chuck Benton nods.

"Mark suffered a serious beating with blunt force trauma to the skull. There was swelling on the brain, and we removed a portion of his skull to alleviate the pressure. He also has a broken left arm, a broken right orbital bone, numerous cuts, and severe bruising. Right now his prognosis is uncertain." The doctor hesitates and then says without much conviction, "But I've seen people recover from worse injuries."

Poor dear Mark. Erica reaches out and squeezes his hand. "Keep fighting, my friend, keep fighting! You've got a lot of windsurfing left to do."

The doctor leaves and Erica sits beside Mark's parents, numb, until she loses track of time and all she hears is the hum and gurgle of the machines that are keeping him alive.

A black man of around forty enters the room—he's wiry, kinetic, handsome, with a closed, wary face and eyes that have seen too much.

"Detective George Samuels," he says without a smile.

Introductions are made. Samuels walks over beside the bed and looks at Mark. He doesn't flinch.

"Can you tell us where and when Mark was mugged?" Erica asks.

"It happened on Charles Street in the West Village, a half block from his apartment, at approximately five thirty this morning. No witnesses have come forward. But this wasn't a mugging. Muggers steal the wallet, the laptop, the cell phone, and then get the hell out of there. This guy—or guys—stuck around to administer . . . this. Which is assault with a deadly weapon, probably attempted murder."

"But why my Mark? He never hurt anyone," Marie Benton says. Then she starts crying.

Erica feels guilt rise up like a wave inside her. This happened because of her. She's the one that pulled Mark into this story. It's her fault he's lying in this hospital bed fighting for his life. What if he dies?

"When we see this kind of overkill, it usually means that someone wants to send a message," Detective Samuels says.

As Erica feels her short hairs stand up, she thinks, *Message received.*

Chapter 32

It's a solid wall of stainless steel, his kitchen. Kitchens are so messy otherwise. Food is so messy, a necessary inconvenience. Like sleep. Not that Nylan sleeps much. A couple of hours a night is all he's ever needed, and he can function at warp speed with none at all. Sleep is boring. It has no momentum, no juice.

It's a little before three in the morning, Nylan's favorite time of day. He loves the feeling of being disassociated from the everyday rhythms that the masses live by. Poor things. What meaningless little lives they lead. He's at the stainless-steel kitchen wall, which is at one end of his sixty-foot living room on the seventieth floor of One57. The room has floor-to-ceiling windows—he's floating above the whole tapestry of glittering, glowing New York. The view bores him too. He touches a panel on the wall and an espresso maker appears; he presses a button and it hisses to life.

She's even more intriguing and alluring than he'd expected. And so cunning and curious in her own stunted way. And so heartrendingly sincere. Even idealistic. Idealism is so touching. And so weak. Weakness enrages him.

But she's so beautiful. Her face, her body, the proportions, the curves and swells. She's a genetic masterpiece. And she's *his*.

But how did she spring from such barren soil? From a trailer in Maine? From crude, stupid stock. Nylan has always felt people like that should be culled. Sterilized at least. They weaken the gene pool. But then, by some miracle, they bring an Erica Sparks into the world. He should send them a tower of gifts from Harry & David as a thank-you present. He laughs out loud at the thought.

Of course she's made terrible mistakes. You can't throw a guttersnipe into Yale without some growing pains. Like everyone else, she has a breaking point. And she broke. And she'll break again. He smiles at the prospect.

Nylan doesn't break. He never has. And his life

hasn't been easy; his childhood was traumatic too. Poor Nylan. His mother died when he was nine. Plowed her car into a tree. It changed everything, didn't it? After all, he grew up so deeply privileged. How many boys have a house with thirty rooms to explore? That grand two-story staircase, the paneled library imported from an English castle with cherubs carved into the woodwork, the living room that seemed to stretch on forever, the nooks and crannies and hidden attics full of secret dreams and secret desires. His private kingdom. Until *she* arrived. He was eleven years old. His father sat him down and explained how lonely he'd been since Nylan's mother died, how the house needed a woman to run it, how he needed a wife by his side, how he was sure Nylan was going to fall in love with Gwen just as he had.

Well, he didn't. He didn't fall in love with Gwen. He fell in hate with her. With her edicts and oozing smiles and swept-back hair, she treated him like he was an afterthought, an interloper in his own house. Ordering the maids not to clean his room. Telling him to stay upstairs when she threw one of her fancy parties. Stealing his father, who stopped taking him to the country club for golf and a club sandwich and a sneaked sip of his Scotch. Forgetting his birthday. *She forgot his birthday!* And then when he told her, she acted all innocent and contrite, but he could tell that she was lying and that she forgot it on purpose. That was the last straw.

And so he pushed her. Pushed her down that grand staircase that she loved so much—waiting until all the guests had arrived before appearing at the top, to oohs and aahs and laughter and a hundred tipsy, admiring "Gwen!"s tossed up her way. But there was no one in the vast entry hall that night and Father was away on business and he waited in the linen closet—one of four—with the door cracked, waited until he saw her leave her bedroom and walk down the long hallway on her way down to the bar for her nightcap of some girly-Gweny liqueur made from some stupid delicate flower that only grows in the Alps, and just as she set foot on the top step, he stepped out of the closet as quiet as a ghost—*Rush! Rush! Rush up behind her and PUSH! PUSH HARD! SHOVE HER, SHOVE HER DOWN THE STEPS!* And she tumbled, too shocked to even cry out, and fell over herself again and again and again, her head cracking, then cracking again.

And then she lay limp at the bottom. Like a little doll with its limbs akimbo and blood oozing from its ears. And he slipped back to his bedroom and spent the whole night shivering in triumph.

His father was never the same. Served him right.

Ah, youth.

Nylan takes his perfect little cup of espresso and heads down a long hallway, past his bedroom and library, deep into the bowels of the apartment, far from the glittering view, far from the world.

His safe room is dark, with several large club chairs facing a bank of screens. Nylan settles into one of the chairs. He takes a sip of his espresso, carefully places it on a small table, picks up a remote. The footage of Erica reporting from Battery Park comes on one screen. He watches as she makes her perfect intro and then all hell breaks loose as the ferry crashes. The tape is on a loop and it starts again. He clicks the remote and Erica's interview with Kay Barrish comes on a second screen. She's so composed, so charming, and then Barrish clutches her chest and falls to the floor, and Erica falls after her, gallantly performing CPR. That tape is also on a loop and starts again. He clicks again and Erica stepping into the elevator comes on a third screen. And then the elevator stops and a look of panic comes over Erica's face, and then the elevator goes dark and she screams in the dark, "Help! Help me!" This footage is on a loop too. He clicks again and a fourth screen fills with Erica in her office, undressing. She slips out of a dull dress and now she's standing there in nothing but her bra and panties, just her bra and panties covering her curves and swells, and she doesn't know she's being watched, that his eyes follow her everywhere, and her undressing plays on an endless loop . . .

And now the room, the world, is filled with Erica, and Nylan's eyes move from screen to screen, his pulse quickening, his arousal growing—Erica charming, Erica undressing, Erica screaming, Erica undressing, Erica screaming . . . *Scream, Erica, scream . . .*

And he thrusts, lurches forward, and his elbow knocks over the espresso.

And he slumps back in the chair. Oh, Nylan, you've made a mess.

Silly boy.

Chapter 33

It's six a.m. the following morning. Erica is walking to work, her armor—baseball cap and sunglasses—in place. Her phone rings. It's Greg.

"Good morning."

"I've got a bombshell, Erica. The LA County's medical examiner just announced a press conference for seven their time. Kay Barrish's autopsy revealed that she didn't die of a heart attack. She was poisoned. Cyanide."

Erica stops cold on the street, the morning rush surging around her. How could this be possible? "You mean she was *murdered?*"

"It certainly looks that way."

"How? When?"

"It must have been right before your interview."

Erica's wheels start racing, she replays the minutes before the interview in her mind. "In the food, it must have been in the food. But lots of people ate the food. Wait—there were those individual tamale pies."

"I want you on-air ASAP."

"Of course. Poor Kay. There was the caterer and that boy, that Mexican intern. But why would *they* murder Kay Barrish? I saw the boy hand her the tamale pie, right from the oven."

"So did I. I'm sure the LA police are going to send a detective east to question us."

"Greg, the coincidences here are unnerving me. The ferry crashes when I'm there, and now this. Do I attract disaster?"

"It's disturbing, I understand. But the terrorists were planning that crash for a long time. And Kay Barrish had political enemies. There are a lot of people who didn't want to see her in the White House. They saw an opportunity and took it. It has nothing to do with you."

Greg is right. Isn't he? "I'll see you in a few," she manages.

Erica hangs up and stands there. She's gained so much from tragedy. It almost feels as if she's made a pact with the devil. Then she sees Kay's face as she died, the terror in her eyes. She hears the screams from the ferry. And then Mark's battered face. Evil. Evil did that. There's evil in the world. Everywhere. *But you knew that, you grew up with it.*

Grow up. Grow up.

Erica feels light-headed, her throat tightens, she's going to faint, she's going to fall, fall on the sidewalk and crack her head open. She looks around wildly—there's a church, a small redbrick church squeezed between two apartment houses. A sign reads: Church for All Nations. Erica ducks inside. The sanctuary is modest, with plain walls and wood trim. There are a couple of solitary worshipers in the pews, and it's so quiet, hushed, the only sound is the gentle *whoosh* of the broom the elderly custodian is pushing down the aisle.

Erica slips into a back pew. The sanctuary smells clean and slightly woodsy with the comforting acrid tang of half-burned candles. And that gentle, rhythmic *whoosh* of the broom. She's in a safe place, where good people aren't mugged and poisoned, where kindness lights the way. She closes her eyes and feels that goodness within herself, her best self, and she knows that as long as she holds on to that she'll be okay.

Slowly her breathing returns to normal, her head clears. Has she gained from some terrible coincidences? Yes, she has. But that only strengthens her resolve to pay back her good fortune, to make a difference. Is she in danger? Quite possibly. But danger demands courage. She has to find that courage.

All her life Erica has felt like she was running on quicksand, with nothing to save her but her own speed and strength and determination, and no one to pull her up should she start to sink. When she finally found faith—through acts of kindness both simple and profound by teachers and strangers and Archie Hallowell and Moira O'Donnell and fellow addicts she met in rehab—she found herself on firmer footing for the first time in her life. Her faith is her bridge over the quicksand.

The custodian comes up the aisle with his broom—its soft *whoosh* is the most soothing sound Erica has ever heard, and she smiles at him and he smiles back, and in that moment she finds the grace to go on.

Chapter 34

As Erica leaves the church and rushes to work, her phone rings.

"This is Erica."

"Nylan Hastings here."

Erica stops, holds the phone close to her ear, and covers her other ear with her fingers. "Nylan."

"I want you to come to the White House Correspondents' Dinner with me," he says. The dinner is the most glittering journalistic event of the year, drawing the biggest names in media and a flock of Hollywood stars. "Jimmy Fallon is the MC, Meryl, Brad, and Denzel are all confirmed."

Erica feels slightly disoriented for a moment. Sure the dinner is a big deal, but what about Kay Barrish's murder? And does he consider this a date of some kind? Because that's out of the question. "Um, of course, Nylan, I'd love to come."

"Spectacular. I can get Harry Winston to loan you some diamonds."

"Nylan, you've heard about Kay Barrish?"

"Terrible."

"And sad and horrifying and disturbing."

"I want you to fly out there today. You own this story. Our ratings are going to go through the roof."

"Lesli told me you've worked with that caterer, Lisa Golden, before?"

"*I* don't work with caterers, Erica. I have people who handle that. Listen, I'll arrange a few appointments with designers. Do you have any favorites? Jason Wu, Tom Ford, YSL? You just let me know. Even I'm putting on a suit. We'll make a beautiful couple."

"Nylan, I'm going to represent the network," she says firmly.

165

"Touchy-touchy," Nylan says. Then he laughs.

Erica is creeped out—and shocked. He doesn't really care about journalism, about truth—they're just a means to an end. And that end is ratings and parties—and *power*. And what about Kay Barrish herself, the woman, and the hopes she held for the nation?

"Best for last: George Clooney is at our table."

Erica hangs up and picks up her pace. To even mention designer clothes and movie stars in the same breath as the murder of Barrish. The man has ice water in his veins.

Still, she must admit, the Correspondents' Dinner is a big deal. All her idols will be there: Diane Sawyer, Katie Couric, Barbara Walters. But swathed in diamonds? Not her style. She has been told, however, that sapphires do wonders for her eyes.

Chapter 35

Moira is renting a small Spanish-style house in Los Feliz. She greets Erica at the door and the two friends share a hug. It's just after noon. Erica's flight out of New York landed forty minutes ago and she had her driver take her right to Moira's. A visit with her old friend, no matter how short, always centers her.

"I just got back from the station ten minutes ago, but I managed to whip up some amazing Vietnamese takeout."

"Superwoman."

"Look who's talking."

"My pod is picking me up here in half an hour. Lesli, my field producer, flew out with me."

"We're just two busy career gals."

Their friendship is just so easy—no matter how long it's been since they last saw each other, they immediately pick up where they left off. They walk into the charming house with its terra-cotta tile floors, arched doorways, and decorative tiles.

"LA agrees with you," Erica says. Moira—tall, with beautiful café-au-lait skin and improbable amber-green eyes—looks terrific, toned and glowing. Her father is Irish-American and her mom is black, and they met at work—two Boston cops.

"I've become one of those annoying yoga freaks."

"Namaste, baby."

Erica follows Moira into the kitchen, where her friend spoons the Vietnamese food into dishes and carries them out to the dining room.

"So bring me up to the minute on the Barrish story," Moira says.

"The caterer has been cleared. Arturo Yanez, her apprentice, had only been working with her for a couple of weeks, but she swears by his character. Well and good, *but* . . . she took her dog out for a walk and left Arturo alone in her kitchen for twenty minutes. A trace of cyanide powder was found on the kitchen backsplash in the exact spot where he made the tamale pies. Then he disappears the same night. The math ain't tough."

"So finding Yanez is the next step."

"Yes. I'm not optimistic about the prospects. Alive, at least."

"This whole town, the whole state really, is in shock. That woman was loved."

"I'm obsessed with solving this, Moy."

"Don't get *too* obsessed, Erica," Moira says, a cautionary note in her voice.

"Thanks. I'm feeling pretty solid these days."

"You know where I live."

"What about you? Work life? Love life?"

"Work is great. I'm no Erica Sparks, but we've known that for a while. As for a man—affirmative. We're having fun but it's too soon to tell. And you?"

"I've been seeing a little of Greg Underwood."

"Eri-*ca,* mixing business and pleasure is a recipe for combustible."

"I'm taking it *very* slow."

"Listen, you've gotten very famous very fast. Mostly good. Mostly fabulous. Entirely deserved. *But* . . . people are going to want a piece of you now. I'm serious about this. Fame buffers you from reality. I see it in this town all the time. I want you to take *everything* slow."

There's a knock on Moira's front door.

"My pod has arrived. Duty calls."

Moira reaches across the table and squeezes Erica's hand. "You have me on speed dial."

"I love you, Moira."

"Oh shut up and get to work."

Chapter 36

"This is Erica Sparks reporting live from outside the apartment building in East Los Angeles that was home to Arturo Yanez. Yanez is the seventeen-year-old high school student who is suspected of serving Kay Barrish the cyanide-laced food that killed her last Saturday. Yanez did not return here after leaving Governor Barrish's house that night. His current whereabouts are unknown. Yanez, who is an undocumented immigrant from Juarez, Mexico, shared a one-bedroom apartment with three cousins and two unrelated persons." The camera pulls back. "Standing next to me is one of his cousins, Felipe Munoz. What can you tell us about your cousin?"

"Arturo was worry for long time. Very worry."

"What was he so worried about?"

"His mother. In Juarez. She's sick."

"Sick?"

"Cancer. In her stomach."

"Has he been back to visit her?"

"No, Arturo is afraid to go. If he goes, he maybe not get back into States. He wants to stay here. Work in a restaurant. He's a good cook. He feeds all of us."

"Did he have any unusual visitors? Any meetings? Did you notice any change in his behavior recently?"

"He's happy to be with Recipe for Success. But he worries. So much worry for his mother."

Lesli, Erica's producer, is standing behind the camera. Her phone vibrates. She steps out of earshot and answers it.

"Have you spoken to Yanez's mother?"

"I call her. But she is very sick. Too sick to talk."

Lesli, still on the phone, listening intently, motions Erica to wrap it up, *fast*.

"Thank you for your time, Mr. Munoz. And now we'll go back to GNN headquarters in New York."

The camera and lights are turned off. Lesli rushes up to Erica. "I just got word from the LAPD. A hiker came across a dead body out in the desert near Joshua Tree. Hispanic teenager. Description sounds like a match for Yanez."

"Let's head out there." Erica helps her pod load the van. As soon as they're on the road, she turns to Lesli and says, "Book us a flight to Juarez."

Chapter 37

The California desert is an alien landscape to Erica. They leave teeming Los Angeles behind and head southeast, driving through a barren pass lined with hundreds of slowly spinning windmills—they look futuristic, surreal. As the city recedes and they get further into the desert, there are giant rock formations, cactuses, and spiny-leafed Joshua trees.

They reach an unmarked track and turn onto it. They drive deeper into the desert and within minutes civilization seems like a distant dream. As far as the eye can see, it's sand and sun, sun and sand, broken only by the huge rocks looming up from the desert floor—all of it shimmering and wavy in the heat. It's stunning, but so bleak and forbidding. Erica wonders how anything—or anyone—could survive out here.

And then, in the distance ahead of them, looking at first like a mirage, are the red lights of police cars and an ambulance. As they get closer, they see police tape forming a rough circle, and inside the circle a lifeless body lies on the ground.

They park and Erica gets out of the van. The air is like a furnace, a searing, dry heat she has never felt before. A masculine Asian woman in a dark pantsuit with a detective badge on her belt seems to be in charge. Erica walks up to her.

"The first vulture is here," the woman cracks. She has short black hair and a tough face with a turned-down mouth and darting dark eyes.

"Happy birthday to you too," Erica says. "I've got a job to do."

"As long as you don't interfere with mine."

"How about we cooperate?"

"I've had investigations compromised by sloppy reporting."

"Thanks for the benefit of the doubt. I'm going to do whatever I can to find the people behind Barrish's murder. You want to stand in my way or help me?"

The woman narrows her eyes and looks at Erica, softens a little, kicks at the sand. "Detective Sergeant Betsy Takahashi, California State Police. And I know who you are."

Erica looks over at the body—it's sprawled facedown, with a single gaping bullet hole in the back of the head. "Where do things stand?"

Takahashi points to a somber Hispanic man who is speaking to another detective. "That's Martin Alvarez, the head of Recipe for Success. He just identified the deceased as Arturo Yanez."

"How long has the body been here?"

"Approximately seventy-two hours. He was killed elsewhere and dumped here."

"Any leads?"

"Not so far. We'll be removing the body shortly and taking it to the lab for a complete forensic analysis. Dead bodies have a way of giving up information."

"What are you thinking?"

"That this was a contract killing. Someone persuaded Yanez to poison Barrish. The persuasion probably came in the form of hundred-dollar bills. But once he had done his job, he had to go."

"But would Yanez kill Kay Barrish, or anyone for that matter? He seemed like such a nice kid. I thought he was doing well."

"Doing well? He was an unpaid intern at Recipe for Success. He was an illegal, living on the edge, picking up day work, trying to survive. Desperate people do desperate things." Takahashi blows out air and kicks at the sand again. "This is a tough one. I met Kay Barrish a couple of times, I saw her in action. She treated everybody from a senator to a cleaning woman with the same respect."

Erica nods. Finding Barrish's killer transcends her journalistic instincts. It reaches right into her heart and soul. Erica believes deeply in democracy and, like Barrish, is profoundly troubled by ideologues who cast compromise as a bad thing. Compromise builds unity, and unity is strength. A house divided will not stand. We're all in this together. Barrish was America's best hope—and she died in Erica's arms.

"Can I get a statement from you?" she asks Takahashi.

"Keep it short. I've got work to do."

Erica's pod only takes a couple of minutes to get ready. Lesli calls New York and Erica goes live. Takahashi sticks to the facts and so does she. The sun is starting to set and Erica—a small speck in the vast, unforgiving landscape—closes by stressing that the discovery of the body raises more questions than it answers.

Chapter 38

Lesli booked them a flight from Palm Springs to El Paso. As the plane begins its descent, Erica looks out the window at the glittering nighttime sprawl of El Paso and Juarez, Mexico—separated only by the shimmering black ribbon of the Rio Grande. The plane lands and they head to an airport hotel, where Erica falls into a deep sleep.

Lesli has arranged for a van and a Spanish-speaking driver to take them across into Mexico, and they set out early the next morning. The little bit of El Paso Erica sees looks poor and scruffy, but nothing prepares her for Juarez. As soon as they cross the border, any semblance of order disappears. The traffic is dizzying—cars, bicycles, and scooters dart in and out, cut each other off, fill the air with honks and curses. Shops seem to be exploding out of their storefronts, the sidewalks are filled with multicolor displays of everything from fruits to dresses to toys to electronics, music blares from tinny speakers. There are shaved-ice carts, tortilla stands, and stray dogs by the dozen.

They drive through town and soon they're in a vast slum that stretches as far as the eye can see. Thousands and thousands of shack-like houses jammed together, their walls leaning in ominous indecision, windowless, waterless. Wires carrying pirated electricity, barefoot children, smoke from ten thousand cookstoves mixing with the dust and sand to haze the air and—coupled with the filth—assault the nostrils.

Children run alongside the van with their hands out, shouting for money. Adults stare warily as they pass. The driver turns down a narrow street, so tight it feels as if the van could knock against one of the houses and set off a domino reaction that would level half the slum. Then he stops. "This is it."

Erica and the driver get out. The house they are in front of looks just a little bit nicer than its neighbors. The outside is freshly painted, there's a flowerpot beside the door, the curtains in the window look new. Erica knocks on the door, and an older teenage girl opens it. She looks smart and hard. The driver asks her name and she says,

"Dolores." Then he begins to explain in Spanish who they are and why they're there.

She cuts him off. "I speak English." Then she turns to Erica. "And I know who you are. Arturo is my brother."

"Do you know . . . ?"

"That he's dead? Yes, of course I know. It's been all over television, all over the neighborhood. Thanks to *you*. What do you want? Why did you come here?"

Erica motions to the driver and he returns to the van. "I'm very sorry," she says.

"No, you're not. People like you play games with people like us. You get famous, you get rich. We die."

"I want to find out who killed your brother."

"I told him not to go to the States. I told him! *Idiota! Estupido idiota! Estupido! Estupido Arturo!*" Dolores clenches her fists and for a moment Erica is afraid the girl will hit her—but then her shoulders slump and her mouth opens and tears pour from her eyes. *"Arturo, mi Arturo, mi hermano Arturo . . ."*

In that moment Erica hates her job, hates the voyeurism, the intrusion onto private sorrow. *Is Detective Takahashi right, are we all vultures?* She wants to put her arms around this girl, wants to bring her solace, wants to bring her brother back. But she can't bring him back. And she didn't kill Barrish or Yanez. In fact, she's trying to find out who did. She takes a deep breath. She has a job to do.

Dolores slowly pulls herself together—clearly this isn't her young life's first sorrow. She reaches into her jeans and takes out a tissue, blots her eyes and blows her nose. "Do you want to know why my brother is dead?" she asks in a remarkably matter-of-fact voice.

Erica nods. Dolores leads her into the house. It's just two small rooms, with a curtain over the doorway that leads to the back room. The front room has a rudimentary kitchen, several day-beds, and a flat-screen TV.

Dolores pulls back the curtain. A woman who is probably forty-five but looks ninety is on the bed, skeletal, unconscious, near death. "This is our mother. Cancer is eating her alive. It is over. But a month ago she was still getting up, still eating. We had hope. Stupid us. There is a doctor who says he can cure cancer, but he wants twenty thousand dollars. Arturo sent ten thousand and said the other half would be coming soon. The doctor took the ten thousand and gave Mama some stupid blood treatment. But Arturo was so proud. He thought he bought Mama life." She laughs bitterly. "But he bought himself death."

"Did he say where he got the money?"

"He told me he won it gambling, but Arturo could never lie to me." Dolores walks over to the bed and strokes her mother's forehead.

"So that's all he said, he gave no hint of who paid him?"

Dolores shakes her head.

"We'll find out who is behind all this. I *promise*."

Dolores sits on the side of the bed, takes her mother's hand and kisses it, holds it to her cheek. "No matter what you do, it won't bring Mama back. Or Arturo."

Erica heads out to the van and her flight back to New York. As she sits in her window seat looking down at the endless brown expanse of southern Texas, she feels frustrated but determined—the trip to Juarez didn't bring her any closer to knowing who hired Yanez, but she'll get there, yes she will.

Chapter 39

The first thing Erica does the next morning is call Dirk.

"Hi, Erica," he says, antipathy dripping off the two words. He would never come out and admit it, but he's jealous of her success. Erica knows she has to tread lightly.

"I wanted to talk to you about Jenny's birthday."

"We're taking her on a whale watch tour. That's what she wants."

"Our daughter, the marine biologist." No response. "That sounds wonderful. Do you think she would enjoy coming down to New York and seeing where I work?"

Dirk sighs. "It would be difficult logistically. I'm not just going to put her on a train by herself."

"Of course not. I'll send a car and driver to come up and get her."

" 'Send a car and driver'? Honestly, Erica, success is ruining you."

Former husbands can be such a-holes.

"I guess I flourished in failure." As soon as the words are out of her mouth, she knows they're a mistake.

"I can live without your sarcasm. And I don't think it's in Jenny's best interests to go down there. She's finally settling down in school. Linda is a steadying influence. Being exposed to all that New York razzle-dazzle could easily throw her off."

"Linda is a steadying influence." Which means one thing: Erica is an unsteadying influence. Here comes that mocking voice in her head: *bad mother, bad mother, bad mother.* Yes, she *has* been a bad mother, but that's in the past. Today is today.

"It's just one day, Dirk, and the party is going to be small and low-key."

He sighs again, but this one sounds like

surrender. Then there's a long pause before, "Erica, I can't provide for Jenny the way you can. She'll come home and see me as a disappointment."

Erica appreciates his honesty. Dirk is a high school history teacher. He's basically a well-meaning guy. When they first met, Erica was attracted to his passion for history and his idealism about teaching. These days he's in mid-burnout and he takes out his frustrations on Erica.

"On the other hand, Dirk, she may spend one day here and say, 'No thanks to that stress fest.' "

Dirk chuckles. It's a nice sound. Erica flashes back on a weekend camping trip they took in Vermont's Green Mountains early in their courtship. Erica had never been camping but wanted to be a good sport. The first day out—after a dinner of slimy, lukewarm ramen noodles—they spent an unromantic night shivering on lumpy ground in a flimsy tent surrounded by animal noises that to Erica sounded like hungry bears licking their chops. She learned a valuable life lesson that night: man invented houses for a good reason. In the morning Erica pleaded with Dirk to head back to civilization. He chuckled—that sweet, indulgent chuckle of his—and packed up the tent.

"Erica, are you on the beam with the drinking?" he asks, suddenly deadly serious.

She wants to say, *Do you really think I could*

function at this level and *drink?* But she holds her tongue. It's a legitimate question. "I am, yes."

"All right then. Jenny can come. But just for the day."

Erica hangs up. So Jenny is coming down to see her next Monday. A birthday visit. How wonderful! Erica takes out her cards and deals a hand of solitaire, trying to convince herself that the visit doesn't fill her with anxiety and dread.

Chapter 40

Erica ducks into Beth Israel Hospital. It's a week since Mark was mugged, and she's arranged to meet Dr. Kaminer in Mark's room to discuss his progress. She's wearing jeans, flats, and a cashmere pullover, and is hiding behind sunglasses and a scarf.

She walks into Mark's room. Chuck and Marie Benton are sitting at the foot of the bed, looking as if they haven't moved in the week since he was attacked.

"How's my friend doing?" Erica asks.

Marie gives her a wan smile. Erica can see why: Mark's facial swelling has gone down but he still looks badly bruised, his right eye is still swollen shut, he's still hooked up to the tubes and machines. He's still in a coma. Erica goes over to the bed and strokes his arm. "Hi, Mark, it's Erica. You look better, buddy. You're doing great. We're all here for you, all rooting for you. Hang in there and keep fighting." She gently touches his cheek, wills him to get better.

"You're a good friend," Chuck says.

Erica can't tell them about the guilt that is burning up her insides. About the aborted meeting at Starbucks. About the fact that Mark may have uncovered something about the cause of the ferry crash that has national security implications. Instead she asks, "How are you two holding up?"

"The hotel is lovely, but we're moving into a short-term rental tomorrow," Marie says. "We're going to be coming back and forth from Ohio, and we wanted our own place, with a kitchen."

Dr. Kaminer walks in. Marie Benton instinctively stands up and moves beside her son.

"How's it looking?" Erica asks.

"I'm getting cautiously optimistic," Kaminer says. "It's hard to tell from looking at Mark, but we're seeing progress every day. His vitals are strong. The swelling in his brain is down to the point where we hope to reattach the piece of skull we removed in the next two to three days. Now we just have to hope he comes out of this coma."

"And if he does?" Erica asks.

"It's going to be a tough journey back. We're

looking at months of intensive rehab. Will there be permanent brain damage? Hard to say. I've seen remarkable recoveries from brain trauma."

Chuck Benton joins his wife beside Mark and takes his hand. "Do you hear that, Mark? It's time for you to come out of this stupid coma. You better listen to your dad or there'll be hell to pay." Then he leans down and kisses Mark's forehead, leaving his lips there for a moment as if he's willing strength and life into his son.

Chuck straightens up. Mark's left eye blinks three or four times. Then it stays open—and he turns his head toward his father.

Chapter 41

The emerging facts about Kay Barrish's murder keep it the country's top story, and Erica is on the air so often—repeating what is essentially the same information about Barrish and Yanez—that she begins to feel like a mechanical doll. She's learning a new craft: how to make news interesting the tenth time she's reporting it. The keys are to not let her energy flag (or her boredom show), to switch up the opening so she introduces the story from a slightly different angle each time, and to continuously search for some new piece of information that adds interest (if not import) to the story.

It's midafternoon and Erica is in her office. She's become increasingly guarded and uneasy at GNN. She's also taken a step back with Greg. She's been consumed with the Kay Barrish story and with concern for Mark and burning curiosity about what he uncovered before his beating. There's just no room on her plate. Greg understands, he's also crazy busy. They're both being pros, although sometimes when their eyes meet, Erica feels an urge to rush into his arms.

Hoping to scare up something fresh on the Barrish story, Erica calls Detective Betsy Takahashi out in LA.

"We've pinpointed the time and place Yanez disappeared," Takahashi tells her. "It was the night of the murder. He helped Golden, the caterer, load up. The scene at Barrish's house was pretty chaotic, so they didn't get out of there until after ten p.m. They drove to Golden's house in West Hollywood and unloaded. Then she drove him to the bus stop on Santa Monica Boulevard, where he was going to pick up the Number 4 bus home to East LA. She remembers the time as approximately eleven fifteen. We've located two witnesses who were at the bus stop. A car drove up, the passenger window went down, a Hispanic man inside was wearing a hat that obscured his face. He called Yanez over, they exchanged some words, and Yanez got in the backseat. That's the last time he was seen alive."

184

"Any information on the car?"

"Newish, black, and midsize is all we can get out of the witnesses. They're both restaurant workers who were heading home after a long shift. They were half asleep."

"Can I go with this story?"

"Get it out there."

Erica hangs up and heads down to the studio to report the breaking news on Yanez's disappearance and Kay Barrish's murder.

Chapter 42

It's Monday, Jenny's birthday, and Erica is standing on Sixth Avenue outside the Time and Life Building, waiting for her arrival. She's going to show Jenny around the network and then there will be a small party in one of the studios. Lesli is in charge of the preparations. To lessen the chances that Jenny will feel self-conscious, Erica has invited Andi's ten-year-old son, Lesli and her wife's three kids, and Rosario's five-year-old granddaughter. Not wanting to fulfill Dirk's prophecy that the visit will spoil Jenny, Erica has asked for no presents. She'll give Jenny the birthday iPod in her office.

A car pulls up to the curb, the back door opens, and Jenny climbs out. Erica's first thought: *She's grown up so much.* Erica feels a stab of sadness at what she's missing. But Jenny is here now—they have this day together. She rushes to her.

"Jenny!"

Erica sweeps Jenny up in her arms, squeezes her tight, kisses her, swings her with joy. Passersby stop and watch.

"This is embarrassing, Mom," Jenny says.

Erica freezes and then puts her down. She's messed up already. "I'm sorry, honey, I guess I got carried away."

"I guess you did." Jenny looks up at Erica with an exasperated, indulgent expression, as if she's the parent and Erica is the child. "But that's okay, Mom, you can't help it."

"You're right. I can't help loving you very, very much."

Jenny is wearing a navy-blue dress and matching flats, her brunette hair hangs down her back, and she's carrying a backpack. Erica suddenly feels at a loss, awkward and vulnerable around her daughter. She smoothes Jenny's hair. "You look very pretty."

A well-dressed woman approaches. "I hope I'm not interrupting, but I just wanted to say I'm a big fan."

"Thank you," Erica says, wanting to kiss the woman for her perfect timing.

"As far as I'm concerned, you're the best thing on cable news these days."

"I agree," Jenny says, taking Erica's hand.

Erica beams like a lighthouse and leads her daughter inside.

She takes Jenny to Greg's office first. He stands up, a big smile on his face. "I think I know who you are."

"Nice to meet you," Jenny says quietly, then she looks down. Erica finds her shyness so touching.

"I'm delighted that you're with us today. Your mom is always telling us how wonderful you are and how proud she is of you."

"Don't all moms have to say that?"

Erica has an urge to lean down, take Jenny by the shoulders, and say, *No, honey, no, they don't. Some moms belittle their kids, let them go to school with filthy hair and filthy clothes, never cook them meals or help with homework. In fact, some moms hate their children.*

She doesn't say it, of course, but someday she wants her daughter to know her history, to understand how hard she's worked to make some kind of peace with her childhood, to build a career and a life for herself. And for Jenny. For the two of them. *Together.* Soon. It has to happen soon or her daughter will slip away from her forever.

"Maybe all moms have to say it, but your mom *means* it," Greg says.

Jenny can't disguise her wonder at Erica's office, with its views up to Central Park. She walks around examining everything, asking questions about the files on Erica's desk, watching the huge TV that—its screen split in four—shows all the major cable news networks at once.

"Are you going to be on TV today?"

"No, Greg gave me the day off so I could spend it with you."

"What if there's breaking news?"

"Then I may have to step in. But only if it's about the Kay Barrish story."

Jenny is thoughtful, nods her head. "That's a big story. I hope they find out who paid Yanez to kill her."

"I hope they do too."

"There has to be justice," Jenny says.

Erica feels like her heart could burst right out of her chest. "Yes, honey, there does."

Jenny walks over and opens the closet door. Nancy Huffman has filled it with suits and dresses for Erica. "Wow, Mom, are these all yours?"

"I guess you could say they are. The wardrobe woman picked them out for me."

"She did a good job."

"You can tell her that yourself. She'll be at your party."

"I like this one," Jenny says, taking down an above-the-knee white dress with a stripe of bold black abstract pattern running on a diagonal across the front.

"That's pretty cool," Erica agrees.

"Try it on."

Erica slips out of her workaday grayish-blue dress and into the black-and-white one. "What do you think?"

"You look like a star, Mom."

In that moment Erica realizes she not only loves her daughter, she *likes* her. Any kid who cares about justice *and* fashion is a kid she wants to know.

"Now that I'm properly attired, shall we head down to the party?"

"Do we have to?"

"I know you don't like parties, honey, but it's going to be small. Some of the people I work with are eager to meet you. We won't stay long, then we'll walk up to Central Park, just the two of us. How does that sound?"

"Nice."

Erica and Jenny walk into the studio where the party is being held. Erica stops short. *What the—?* There are at least forty people milling around—including Claire Wilcox—streamers and happy birthday signs, a three-tiered cake, a food table manned by a caterer, and a disc jockey spinning some annoying pop tune at earache volume. Nylan is standing at the edge of the festivities, watching with a patriarchal smile. The other girls at the party are much more urban-outfitted than Jenny—wearing leggings

189

and sparkly sneakers and bright tops. Jenny looks like a suburban girl whose grandmother picked out her dress. She shrinks into herself.

In spite of all the forced gaiety, the party feels tense—people are a little too convivial, as if they're extras in a party scene in a bad movie. Suddenly the music stops, the singing of "Happy Birthday" starts, a confetti gun goes off, and nine candles are lit on the cake. The off-key cacophony feels like it's triggering the mother of all migraines. Erica sucks air and fights to control her anger.

The singing ends and Claire takes center stage, shushing the crowd. She's beaming like a spotlight. "On behalf of everyone at GNN, I want to welcome Jenny to our family. Today is a big day. You're turning nine. Which is a wonderful age, because you're still little, but you're getting big! So I got you a big present . . ."

An assistant appears carrying a six-foot-tall stuffed giraffe that she presents to a mortified Jenny as everyone laughs.

". . . And a little one." Claire hands Jenny a small blue box from Tiffany's. The crowd coos. Claire looks right at Erica and says, "I know this was a no-gifts party, but honestly, what's a birthday without a present or two? Am I right?"

The party shouts agreement.

Nice work, Claire, making the whole party about you. The music restarts. Then Erica sees a cameraman taping it all. That's when she goes white-hot.

"I'll be right back, honey," Erica says. She walks over to Lesli, struggling to control her voice. "What's going on here? I asked you for a small party."

Lesli looks at her—her eyes hold apology. "Nylan insisted on this, Erica."

"Did he ask for it to be taped?"

"He did. He wants to use the footage in promos for your show."

Erica crosses to Nylan. "I want the filming to stop."

"Calm down, Erica. This footage is gold for your image."

"Jenny is my daughter, not a prop in my career. The taping should have been cleared with me, and I want it to stop."

Nylan says nothing, does nothing. Erica can feel herself start to sweat. This is the last thing she needs today, Jenny's day. Still Nylan says nothing, does nothing. But his eyes hold something . . . What is it? . . . Is that desire? . . . Is he getting off on watching her twist in the wind? Unreal.

Erica strides over to the cameraman. "Please stop filming."

He looks over to Nylan for guidance.

"If you don't stop filming right now, I'm going to rip the camera out of your hands."

He turns off the camera.

Nylan comes over. "You have a lot of passion, Erica. Which makes us kindred spirits." He gives her a half smile. "I'd like to see you in my office tomorrow morning at ten."

"What about?"

"You'll find out soon enough."

Jenny comes over. Nylan drapes his arms around her neck and says, "Hi there, pretty girl."

Erica shudders with revulsion and rage. She removes his arms and pulls Jenny close to her.

"Aren't you going to introduce us?" he asks.

"Jenny, this is Nylan Hastings, the founder of GNN."

"How do you do?"

"I do well. Thanks to your beautiful mom."

"Oh look, there's Nancy," Erica says.

"See you in the morning," Nylan says, walking out of the party.

Erica wills her game face on—this is Jenny's party and she's going to do what it takes to salvage it. "Jenny, this is Nancy, the lady who picks out all those nice outfits for me."

"I chose that one," Jenny says.

"It looks terrific on your mom," Nancy says.

"I *love* it," Erica says. "It makes me feel like a New York sophisticate. There's no label. Who's the designer?"

"I guess I'm busted," Nancy says.

"Wait a minute—you designed this?"

"Without you it was just fabric on a hanger."

Who needs Jason Wu when you have Nancy Huffman? "We have to talk."

Over Nancy's shoulder, Erica spots Greg arriving. He comes over.

"I thought this was going to be a small party," he says.

"You and me both."

Greg chats with Jenny. He's so easy with her, has no problem drawing her out. She laughs at something he says.

"What's in the little blue box?" he asks. Jenny opens it—it's a necklace with a silver *J* pendant. "Do you like it?"

"I don't wear jewelry," Jenny says.

Greg gives Erica a this-is-a-great-kid smile. Erica starts to relax. It's not the party she wanted, but so be it. She and Jenny sit and share a piece of cake. Claire comes over and kneels in front of them with a syrupy smile on her face.

"What a lot of excitement!" she says. "Have you named the giraffe yet?"

"No," Jenny answers. "I'm kind of too old for stuffed animals. I'm going to donate it to Toys for Tots."

Claire is momentarily taken aback but recovers in a flash and slaps on her empathy face. "Ooooh, that's *so* sweet of you." Then she turns to Erica. "How's Mom holding up?"

"Mom is great. Actually, we're just on our

way up to Central Park. Would you be a doll and deal with this?" Before Claire has time to answer, Erica hands her their paper plate with the half-eaten piece of cake on it. Then she takes Jenny's hand and they slip out of the party.

Chapter 43

"I googled the park, Mom," Jenny says as they head through the Sixth Avenue entrance. "It opened in 1857. Before that it was open country. There were even some farms with cows. It has four lakes and two streams, and guess who lives here? Possums, raccoons, and skunks."

"Now skunks are nocturnal, aren't they, honey?"

It's a lovely May afternoon, mild and blue-skied, and the park is filled with people of all ages and colors and persuasions strolling, running, biking, boarding, clutches of friends young and laughing, elderly on benches chatting, pigeon feeders and iPaders, artists and executives, the driven and the drifting, New York in all its glorious humanity—Erica simply can't get enough. And being here with Jenny takes it all to another level, to a place that feels close to . . . happiness.

They walk past the park's southernmost lake and head north toward the carousel.

"That party wasn't much fun, was it?" Erica says.

"It was okay."

"You're a good sport."

Jenny shrugs. "Greg is nice. Is he your special friend?"

"Well, maybe. Yes, kind of. I hope so. Do you like him?"

"He's interesting. And *cute*." Jenny smiles at her mom, and for a second they're girlfriends talking about cute boys.

But they're not girlfriends, they're mother and daughter, and Erica wants to have a meaningful talk with Jenny, find out how she's feeling, what's going on inside her. At the same time, she dreads it.

She screws her courage to the sticking place and strokes Jenny's head. "Can we talk about something serious, honey?"

Jenny nods.

"I know I hurt you when I was drinking. I'm sorry for that."

"Why did you drink so much, Mom?"

"Well, I was probably working too hard. Putting a lot of pressure on myself. Your father and I weren't getting along. And I'm one of those people who can't stop drinking when they start."

"An alcoholic?"

"Yes."

"You did hurt me. I hated you."

The words sting—but their honesty soothes. "I don't blame you. I hope you can try to forgive me."

"You hurt Daddy too."

"I'm sure I did. When two people are married and it doesn't work out, there's a lot of pain. It takes time to get some perspective. I think your dad and I are on a more even keel these days. One thing that will always bond us is our love for you."

"I'm glad I'm not a grown-up."

Erica laughs. "You know, you will be one of these days."

"Not too soon, I hope."

"What do you think of New York City?"

"It's big and there are *a lot* of people."

"I find it exciting."

"People look at you. You're famous."

"Do you like that?"

Jenny nods. "Do *you* like it?"

Erica looks around. People do recognize her—but she's not a movie star like Reese Witherspoon or Anne Hathaway; she's a newscaster associated with a national tragedy, so the response she gets is more muted and respectful. But it brings a sense of power nonetheless. "Yes, I do, honey. It's a strange feeling, but I hope I've earned it. I work hard. Look, there's the carousel."

Jenny's face lights up at the sight of the venerable old amusement ride with its brightly painted horses and calliope music. They sit on a bench and watch it go round and round, filled with excited children laughing and shrieking with joy. Erica feels a moment of envy. But it gives way to solace—with all the chaos and evil in the world, children still know how to laugh and play.

"How are things at school, honey?"

"I got an A in science."

"Did you? I'm so proud of you. I don't think I ever got above a C in science."

"Why don't you want me to live with you, Mom?"

This is the question Erica dreads most. "Oh, but I do, baby girl, I do more than anything. It's just that, well . . ." She takes a deep breath and dives in, dives into the lies. *No, they're not lies, they're fibs, temporary fibs, just until . . . until . . . ?* "I didn't want you to have to switch schools in the middle of the year. And I sometimes have to fly out of town on a moment's notice, so you'd be left alone—we'd have to find you a nanny. And my hours are so unpredictable, you'd be eating way too much cold pizza and microwave dinners."

"My friend Bridget's mother does it all alone. She's busy too."

Erica is at a loss as to how to answer. "Do you *want* to live with me?"

Jenny folds her arms and looks down. "I don't know. I don't trust you."

Erica takes Jenny's chin in her hand and gently raises her head. "Will you give me a chance to earn your trust?"

Jenny considers this. Then she nods. Erica wants to wrap her arms around her but resists. "I promise you that *as soon* as I can make it happen, we'll be living together." She runs her fingers through Jenny's hair. "May I see what's in your backpack?"

"It's private."

"Okay."

"But you can look."

Jenny hands her mom the backpack. Erica takes out the new iPod, crazy bands, a dog-eared Judy Blume book that she recognizes as her own old copy, a brush, and then . . . Mikey, the small stuffed monkey that Erica gave Jenny on her second birthday. The little fella looks threadbare but well loved.

"Mikey," Erica says simply. Jenny reaches over and strokes his head. They sit quietly for a little bit as the excited city swirls around them. Then Erica puts everything back in the pack, hands it to Jenny, stands up, takes her hand, and gestures toward the carousel. She'd ask Jenny if she wants to take a ride, but the lump in her throat would make it difficult to speak.

They ride around, Jenny happily bouncing on her horse. Just as they get off the carousel, Erica's phone rings—it's Detective Takahashi from LA.

"I have some news on the Barrish murder. We've found the probable car that picked up Yanez at the bus stop. It's a Lexus rental stolen from a beach parking lot in Santa Monica. It was abandoned on the street in Covina. It's being taken to the lab for analysis. There's copious blood in the trunk, including splatters consistent with a single gunshot wound. A jacket matching the one Yanez was wearing was also found in the trunk."

Erica puts her phone back in her purse.

"Who was that, Mommy?"

"A detective in Los Angeles. There's a new development in the Barrish murder."

"Breaking news?"

"Yes."

"Well, come on then, we have to get you to the studio!" Jenny grabs Erica's hand and starts to run.

Chapter 44

Erica is in her office the next morning. After getting back from Central Park yesterday, she put Jenny in the car that took her home and then spent six straight hours on the air, trying to squeeze maximum news value out of the discovery of the car in which Arturo Yanez was probably killed. The network ran footage of the car itself being loaded onto a flatbed truck in Covina for transport to the forensics lab, of the Santa Monica parking lot where it was stolen, of the bus stop in West Hollywood where Yanez was last seen alive. The big question, of course: Who stole the car? Finding that out would be a big break.

Erica feels it was a good day for her and Jenny, an important day between them. Yes, she choked on that crucial question of why they aren't living together, but she'll deal with that when . . . when she can.

Almost time for her meeting with Nylan. She's never been to his office. Which everyone tells her is a blessing—if you're called in, it's probably not to receive good news. She's hoping this visit is an exception. She drops in on Rosario and Andi before heading up there. She worked hard last night, there's an awful lot on her plate, and she's feeling a little ragged around the edges.

As she heads down the hall toward the elevators, her prepaid phone rings.

"It's Chuck Benton."

"Hi, Chuck, how's Mark doing?"

"He's doing pretty well. His skull was put back together."

"That's great news."

"And he spoke. One word. Barely audible. But I leaned down and he repeated it right into my ear."

"What's the word?"

"Erica."

Erica stops in her tracks, scans the hallway, lowers her voice. "I've got a meeting I can't skip, but I'll be down ASAP."

In the elevator heading up to Nylan's office, Erica marshals herself. There is no one more important to her career, to her future, than Nylan Hastings. No matter how creepy he may be, he's responsible for all the good things that are happening in her life. A million possible scenarios are careening around in her. Then she shuts down her internal guessing game. *Just be yourself. It's working so far.*

She gets off the elevator and comes face-to-face with a middle-aged woman sitting behind a vast, intimidating counter. A man in a dark suit with an earpiece in his right ear stands nearby and scrutinizes Erica. Everything feels hushed and tightly controlled up here; there's a crackle in the air, like static electricity. One spark and it could all blow up.

Erica smiles at the gatekeeper. "I'm here for my appointment with Nylan."

The woman finally smiles, although it's just with her mouth. She picks up her phone. "Erica Sparks is here."

Nylan appears almost instantly and leads her down a wide hallway hung with posters of the network's anchors and their shows. *The Erica Sparks Effect* will fit right in.

Nylan's office is bigger than most New York one-bedroom apartments, but furnished minimally, with a couple of elegant sofas and chairs and a large glass desk with nothing on it but a softball-sized plastic globe of the world. This man is organized to the point of obsession. There's a Rothko on one wall, a Pollock on another, and a Calder mobile hanging in a corner. The views up to Central Park are staggering. Fred Wilmot, GNN's chief visionary officer, is standing in one corner, impeccable in a dark suit and silk tie. His face is a mask, implacable. Nylan is in sneakers, a loose black T-shirt, and jeans—even dressed like an overage skateboarder, there's no mistaking that this is *his* office.

"Erica, you remember Fred Wilmot."

"Of course. How nice to see you."

"And you," Wilmot says with a tight smile.

Nylan gestures for Erica to sit. She chooses one of the couches.

"Do you know what geolocated news is, Erica?" Nylan asks. There's no innuendo, no loaded looks. He's being completely professional and it's a relief. Hopefully he got the message.

"Basically customized news?"

"Yes, delivered wherever you are on the planet. You live in Seattle, you're hiking on Mount Kilimanjaro and there's a gas explosion a block from your house? You're instantly informed in a targeted news blast sent to your smartphone."

202

He strolls around the room, lithe and coiled. "That's the kind of scope this network is going to have. We are in the process of *redefining* what news is. We are going to reach into every corner of this planet to connect and unite humanity—and write a bold, new history for mankind."

He spins around and looks at Erica. She hopes she looks appropriately enthralled.

"Cybertargeting will allow us to respond to crises within minutes. We used it in partnership with Doctors Without Borders to track and contain a recent outbreak of Ebola in Senegal. We partnered with the World Wildlife Fund to crack a poaching ring that was killing elephants in Thailand. This network is going to *transcend* news as we know it—we are going to be nothing less than the planet's central nervous system."

Wilmot picks up the globe on Nylan's desk and hands it to him. Nylan tosses it in the air a few times—he's got the whole world in his hands. From where she's sitting, Erica can make out the continents. Nylan faces a blank wall, taps South America, and a projection pops up on the wall:

Brazil
Connected: 140 million, 70 percent of
  population
Currently online: 82 million

He taps Asia and the projection changes to:

203

Pakistan
Connected: 108 million, 62 percent of
  population
Currently online: 53 million

He taps Greece, Chile, and South Africa in
rapid succession, and the same set of statistics
comes up.

It's a dazzling display and Erica is awed.
"Nylan, that's *amazing*."

"This is just the big picture. We can instantly
mine this data and know *exactly* where these
people are, what site they're on, and who they're
communicating with. We can reach *all* of them
simultaneously. Or we can reach one specific
person out of billions." Nylan's voice rises, and
for a moment his casual aspect falls away. "We
are building one world, one future, *one universe!*"

Erica half expects laser beams to shoot out of
his eyes. The man is possessed. Brilliant? Yes. A
visionary? Obviously. But also messianic. Which
is disquieting. But Erica knows that there's a
fine line between genius and madness. And parts
of Nylan's vision are thrilling—look at the work
he described with Doctors Without Borders and
the World Wildlife Fund. The potential for good
is enormous. So is the potential for not-good—
for control, for invasion of privacy, for manipula-
tion, monopoly, forced conformity, autocracy.

Wilmot presses on a blank wall, and it springs

open to reveal a refrigerator. He reaches in, grabs a bottle of green juice, and hands it to Nylan, who sits at his desk and gazes out toward Central Park with a faraway look in his eyes.

Fred Wilmot takes over, all business. "Our cyber division built all this. They are the best in the world, bar none. Our capabilities even surpass those of the Pentagon. Of course, that's only part of the picture. We're in the process of monetizing our abilities. Right now the network is running at a loss, but we're exceeding projections. Thanks in large part to you, Erica. Your ratings speak for themselves, but we've also convened a series of focus groups to gauge opinions and feelings toward you. The public loves you, but more importantly they *trust* you. Every great enterprise needs a public face. We want you to be that face. Your own show is in development. We want to move it to prime time and make it two hours long. We are prepared to offer you a three-year contract at three million dollars a year. We will also pay you a two-million-dollar housing allowance. And provide you with a car and driver. We'll send the contract to your lawyer."

Erica tries to take it all in. Part of her finds it disturbing that they ran focus groups on her without her knowledge. Another part of her wants to leap up and scream, "I'm rich!" But she contains herself and says calmly, "I look forward to getting the contract."

Nylan turns toward her and smiles, the proud smile of a small boy who has just won a prize at the county fair. The man is an enigma wrapped in a riddle wrapped in seven billion dollars.

"George Wilkins, our CFO, will negotiate any fine points," Wilmot says, signaling the meeting is over.

Erica stands. "I better get to work."

"There is one thing, Erica," Nylan says. "I appreciate your journalistic instincts, and the investigative reporting you've done on the Barrish case. But you're more valuable to us on-air, behind a desk, than you are down in the weeds of Juarez or anyplace else. We need you pulling stories together, making sense of disparate information, putting field reports in context. In a word: anchoring."

"Nylan, I'm more than a news reader. I'm a *journalist*."

"I realize and respect that." He looks at her, his eyelids lowered to half-mast in an almost seductive gesture. Uh-oh. "But your value is dependent on your stature. Having you report from the slums of Juarez is not consistent with being the global face of GNN. We have field reporters to do that." He smiles, and this smile feels like ice. "Are we on the same page?"

Erica hesitates. The last thing she wants is to be stuck behind a desk for the next three years. She needs to be out there, covering stories on the ground, searching for the truth. But there's no way she's going to walk away from the financial independence and the level of power she's being offered. She'll be able to get custody of Jenny, buy them a beautiful apartment, put Jenny in private school, give her every advantage of a privileged Manhattan childhood. Erica has to pick her battles carefully. She's willing to acquiesce on this one. For now. "Yes, we're on the same page."

As she rides down in the elevator, Erica tries to digest what just happened. She feels like she both got the biggest break of her career *and* was cut off at the knees. Nylan basically told her to stop her investigation—and there was an implied *or else*. What would that *or else* be? Erica feels her throat tighten. Billionaires really do make their own rules. Erica pulls out her phone to call Moira. Then she remembers she's being watched.

Chapter 45

As Erica cabs down to Beth Israel, she takes out her prepaid and makes the call to Moira.

"Hey, Moira, I was just offered a prime-time show and a three-year contract at three million per."

Moira hollers so loud that Erica moves the

phone away from her ear. "Baby, I am *so* proud of you."

"Hey, thanks, and I mean it when I say it wouldn't have happened without you. You reached down and picked me up when I needed it most. You're the best friend I've ever had."

"Can you lend me a hundred K?"

"At 15 percent."

"This calls for a celebration."

"Let's hold off until the ink is dry. Listen, can you do me a big favor?"

"Name it."

"Can you see what you can find out about Fred Wilmot? He's our chief visionary officer."

"Sure. Why the interest?"

"There's something cold and . . . *scary* about him. What do you make of Yanez's death?"

"It feels like gang work to me. The stolen rental car MO is popular with Hispanic gangs out here, and they've used the desert as a dumping ground before."

"Why would a gang want to kill him?"

"Follow the money."

"So you think they were paid?"

"Absolutely. Whoever engineered Barrish's murder is smart. *Very* smart. I'm sure they put at least four or five layers between themselves and the crime. Yanez was the first layer, whoever killed him is the second layer. This is going to be a tough onion to peel."

"There's no way I'm letting go."

"Erica, you don't sound like a woman who has just scored a life-changing triumph."

"Moira, Hastings and Wilmot want me to stay behind the desk, stop field reporting. I feel like they want to muzzle me, use me almost as a figurehead. They ran focus groups on me without telling me. And there's something very . . . *bizarre* about Nylan Hastings. The network has this secretive cyber department. He seems power crazed."

"Why would they want to muzzle a reporter as talented as you?"

The question hangs there.

"Talk soon," Erica says as the cab pulls up to the hospital. As she rides up in the elevator, she thinks, *Until my show debuts I'm still a field reporter—it may be time for another trip out to LA.*

Chapter 46

Erica walks into Mark's room at Beth Israel to find him asleep. He looks better—the bandage around his skull is smaller, his bruising is less livid, and he has come out of his coma. Erica gently touches his hand. His eyes slowly open. It takes him a few beats to register where he is.

Then he focuses on Erica and a small smile forms. He looks beautiful in that moment.

"Hey, buddy," Erica says.

Mark opens his mouth and struggles to speak. He finally chokes out a barely audible "H-hi there."

"You look so much better, my friend." That sweet smile again. "How are you feeling?" He thinks about it for a moment and then nods. "Dr. Kaminer tells me you're going to be moving to rehab in a couple of days. That's *great* news. He said your progress is slow and steady, which is the best kind."

Mark looks as if he has suddenly remembered something. His brow furrows, he seems to grow agitated. He opens his mouth and struggles to speak, but he can't form the words.

"Mark, what is it?"

He's working so hard to talk, and the inability is frustrating him. He looks like he might start crying.

"Take it easy, take it easy, my friend." With his eyes he implores Erica to come closer. She leans down. "What is it? Do you want to tell me something about the ferry crash?"

His eyes open wide and he nods his head. Again he opens his mouth but can't find speech. Then finally he manages a few slurred words that sound like "nice till." He repeats it, only this time it sounds like "nasal." What sense does that make?

Mark shuts his eyes, takes a deep breath, marshals his strength, and slowly, unmistakably articulates, "Not ISIL."

"Not ISIL? The ferry crash wasn't the work of ISIL?"

Mark nods. Then he sighs, exhausted from saying the two words, closes his eyes, and falls back on the pillow.

On the sidewalk outside the hospital Erica calls Detective George Samuels.

"What can I do for you?" he asks.

"Have you made any progress on the attack on Mark Benton?"

"We have a person of interest. The surveillance camera at the Sheridan Square subway station recorded a man entering the station at 5:41 that morning, which is consistent with the time of the attack. He was wearing a cap that obscured his face, but he was definitely furtive and in a hurry, and he was carrying a computer case that matches Benton's."

"How do we find him?"

"We're in the process of enlarging and enhancing the camera footage. When we can see his face more clearly, we'll have an artist draw a full rendering and then we can start publicizing it and looking for a match in our databases."

"Keep me posted."

"I have a question for you. Do you know why anyone would want to attack Benton?"

"He was helping me investigate the Staten Island ferry crash. He was tracing the source of the hackers who froze the ferry's computers."

"The ferry investigation was over when he was attacked. ISIL claimed responsibility and we took out their capability."

"They *claimed* responsibility. It hasn't been *proven*. Mark told me today that ISIL didn't do it."

"What, does he have magic powers?"

"No, but he understands hacking."

"So does my ten-year-old son."

"Mark Benton not only understands it, he can *do* it. There's a big difference. Look, I'm handing you the motive and you're giving me a hard time."

"Ms. Sparks, I'm paid to be skeptical."

"So am I. So let's work together. Mark called me the night before he was attacked—he'd found something out and he didn't want to tell me on the phone. He asked me to meet him at Starbucks the next morning. He didn't show up. Put it together. And call me Erica."

There's a pause. "It's certainly the strongest theory we've got. This was definitely not a random attack. So it was carried out, or at least ordered, by whoever *did* sabotage the ferry. Does Benton have any theories on who that might be?"

"He has more information. But speech is very difficult for him. He's getting a little stronger every day. Listen, is there any chance we could get a police guard stationed outside his room?"

"As of now, this is just a mugging. There's no way the department is going to pay for a guard. I'll go see him tomorrow."

"Let me know if you learn anything. And please light a fire under the folks who are enhancing the subway footage."

Erica hangs up and steps off the curb to hail a cab. The traffic is fierce but flowing, there are surges of people on the sidewalks, in the crosswalks, there is music and honking and yelling, the smell of asphalt and exhaust and tacos from a nearby food truck—the city feels like one great wave racing toward the future, and she's riding the wave—riding it toward the truth.

Chapter 47

Erica returns to her office to find a bouquet of red roses on her desk. The card reads: *You just keep blooming—Your GNN family.*

Erica fingers one of the roses and leans down to smell it—suddenly a huge water bug crawls out from the petals and onto her hand. "Yuck!" She shakes it to the floor, where it scuttles away. Then another bug appears on the flowers, and then a third—it's crawling with them. Erica grabs the vase and runs down to the ladies' room, where she dumps the whole thing in the toilet. The blood-red roses are surrounded by a swarm of flailing water bugs. Erica flushes the toilet and watches the petals and bugs swirl round and round and then get sucked down into the pipes. Nothing remains but the bare, thorny stems. She shudders.

As Erica walks back down the hall, fighting to slow her heart rate, she thinks, *Someone wants me off balance and on edge. Makes me easier to control.* Then she feels anger rising like a tonic in her veins. *You're not going to stop me.*

Back in her office, Erica calls down to building maintenance and reports the rose stems, casually, joking. "It was an only-in-New-York moment."

Then she gets a call from Greg. "Any chance of dinner tonight?"

"That would be nice."

"My place? At seven?"

Erica has a moment of wondering whether she's ready to be alone with Greg in his apartment. She trusts him—but she's not sure that she trusts herself. It's been a long time since she's been with a man and Greg is so kind and she craves being held, touched, shutting off her overactive mind and imagination and letting go.

Oh, Erica, grow up. You sound like some love-struck coed who's taken one too many poetry classes. You and Greg are both adults. You can handle a simple dinner.

"Your place at seven sounds perfect." Erica hangs up and immediately wonders what she should wear.

Paul Elliot, the network's lead producer of promos and teasers, knocks on her open door, carrying a laptop. "I've got a rough cut of the first promo for *The Erica Sparks Effect*."

Elliot plays the thirty-second spot. It opens with the footage of Kay Barrish collapsing and Erica giving her CPR, cuts to the ferry crash, and then goes to a series of quick cuts of Erica reporting various other stories. As pulsing music plays underneath, the breathless male announcer says: "The *New York Times* calls her 'the most exciting new face in network news.' The *Washington Post* says, 'Sparks is setting new standards of excellence.' And Huffington Post raves that 'Sparks leaps off the screen with a rare combination of charm and smarts.' Don't miss *The Erica Sparks Effect*, debuting on June 15 on GNN."

Erica puts her imaginary helmet on—the one that keeps her head from swelling. "Nice work, Paul."

"I got a call from Nylan this morning—he put a rush on it. It's going to start airing tonight. He also wants a camera to trail you at the White House Correspondents' Dinner—he wants footage of you with the movie stars."

Paul leaves, and Erica calls Nancy Huffman.

215

"Do you have a couple of minutes you could spare?"

Erica steps into her large walk-in closet and checks out the clothes. They're arranged by piece and by color—rows of dresses, separates, shelves of sweaters and pullovers, racks of shoes, a dresser filled with scarves and hose and topped by an array of purses and accessories, a jewelry box filled with bracelets, necklaces, and her clip-on earrings. There's also a red-leather ottoman. It may not be *Real Housewives* ostentatious, but it's all pretty drool-worthy. Looking at it, Erica feels some guilt—she knows how many girls and women in the world would be thrilled with a tiny fraction of her bounty.

Nancy appears, looking divine in the world's crispest white shirt worn over loden-green leggings and black sandal heels. How does she make it look so effortless?

"Fashion panic. What should I wear to a sorta-maybe but not-too romantic dinner?"

"Erica, you'd look great in a potato sack. Cinched with the right belt, of course."

"You pick the belt and I'll find the sack."

"Is this restaurant or home?"

"Home."

"His or yours?"

"His."

"Okay, you're on his turf, so you want to up the armor quotient just a tad. I'd recommend slacks . . ." She walks into the closet and pulls a pair of fitted black slacks that have just a hint of shimmer. "Silk blouse . . ." She pulls a Caribbean-blue blouse. "Last pedi?"

"Three days ago."

"Good." She pulls a pair of metallic-silver sandals. Then she opens the jewelry box and chooses a pair of simple sterling circle earrings with a single blue topaz in the center. She holds the ensemble up for Erica—everything just *works*. And Erica's confidence about the evening soars.

"Will you marry me?" Erica says.

"Let me check with my husband."

"One more thing, Nancy. I'd like you to design a dress for me to wear to the White House Correspondents' Dinner."

Nancy stops cold for a moment. "Seriously?"

Erica nods.

"I'd be delighted and honored. Are you going with Greg?"

"Nylan."

"Oh." Nancy's eyebrows go up, something shifts in her face.

Erica steps into the closet and gestures for Nancy to join her. She lowers her voice, "What is it?"

Nancy also lowers her voice. "Nothing."

"Nancy, I saw that look."

"Discretion is the better part of holding on to my job."

"You have my word nothing you say will leave this room."

Nancy moves around a few pieces, generally fusses with the clothes in a make-work way, and asks with feigned nonchalance, "Have you seen the women Nylan dates?"

"I know they're young and beautiful."

Nancy pulls a dress and hands it to Erica. "Hold this up." Erica does and Nancy steps back in scrutiny. "Some of them are in our business. And others rent by the hour." Nancy shakes her head at the dress, takes it from Erica, and tosses it onto the ottoman. "I think we can winnow that one." She pulls a pair of shoes with clear Lucite high heels. "Tack-y. These shoes are positively"—she looks Erica in the eye—*"predatory."* She tosses them on top of the dress and pulls a teal cardigan. "I actually bought this for Sue Williams."

"Sue Williams?"

Nancy holds the cardigan up in front of Erica, saying breezily, "She was the top-rated anchor at the Phoenix CBS affiliate. One of Nylan's first hires before GNN went on the air. Then they went to Davos together. Sue never came back to the network . . . Some men don't take rejection well. All wrong for your skin tone," she announces, tossing the sweater on the reject pile.

"All wrong."

"A woman in your position has to be so careful about what she wears," Nancy says.

"I don't want to end up on the 'What Was She Thinking?' list."

Chapter 48

Greg lives in a graceful prewar building on the corner of Eighty-Second and Riverside Drive. Erica is curious to see what his apartment is like, how it's furnished, what it says about him. When she enters the ornate lobby, the doorman smiles in recognition and says, "Mr. Underwood is in 1014."

Greg answers the door wearing cargo pants, a black pullover, and beat-up sneakers. His green eyes light up in a welcoming smile and Erica feels this *pull* toward him.

"Welcome to my thank-you-Nylan-Hastings abode."

He ushers her into the foyer, and she hands him a dozen irises.

"Twenty-first-century gender roles are pretty confusing, but if they include men getting flowers, I'm all for it. Let me grab a vase."

Greg disappears into the galley kitchen and Erica walks into the living room. The room has great bones—a box ceiling and a fireplace flanked by built-in bookshelves—and is filled with comfortable furniture, framed prints, and photos. Windows face a small balcony and the river below.

"I picked up some awesome Italian grapefruit soda. Can I interest you in a glass?" Greg calls from the kitchen.

"Sure. And did you just use the word *awesome?*"

"Tragic, huh?" he says, walking in and handing Erica the drink.

"This is delicious."

He picks a tray up off a side table. "Tuna tartare?"

She takes one. "Wow, a lot of horseradish."

"You like?"

"Delicious. Please tell me you didn't make this."

"I love to cook."

He loves to cook.

They sit on sofas on either side of the coffee table.

"So, you had an exciting day," Greg says. "You're getting the coveted nine p.m. slot. And I heard some numbers. Welcome to the one percent."

"I'll believe it when I spend it." Erica puts down her drink. "Greg, Nylan wants me behind a desk pretty much all the time. That's not where I want to be."

"I know it isn't. My advice: Let's get your show

up and running. If the ratings are as good as we hope they're going to be, you can . . . well, *demand* may be too strong a word . . . but you can *suggest* that you cover certain stories personally, out in the field. I'll back you up. At that point it will be very difficult for Nylan to say no."

What would she do without Greg's savvy? "You're right, of course. I think I was anticipating problems. Not a great attitude." She wants to discuss some of her qualms about Nylan himself—his grandiosity, his cold eyes, his suggestive looks, his rabid fervor, the nagging fear he generates in her, the sick little stunt with the flowers—but wonders if it would be indiscreet. After all, Nylan signs Greg's checks. She focuses on what matters most to her. "I want to stay front and center on the Barrish murder, even if that means spending more time in LA."

"Have there been any new developments?"

"I'm waiting for the results of the forensics on the car. I think this was clearly a murder for hire. And the people doing the hiring have to be pretty far up the food chain."

"Meaning?"

"Yanez was obviously the last link. A pawn who sold his life for 10K. There are layers between him and whoever ordered the murder. It could be a terrorist organization with sophisticated operations in this country. Or a political rival who is *really* ruthless. Or a foreign leader.

I wouldn't put it past Putin. I suppose it could be some homegrown American crazy like Timothy McVeigh or Cliven Bundy, but those guys are pretty basic at the end of the day. They have the motive—hatred of the government—but not the smarts or the means to pull off something like this."

Greg is looking at her but he's only half listening. Erica knows that look. She's been getting it—and ignoring it—pretty much since she hit puberty. When he sees her note it, he rubs his hands together to cover his raw desire. "You do know that the crime may never get solved."

"Not from want of trying," Erica says.

"Dinner will be ready in about fifteen minutes. I made chicken Provençal."

"Sounds yummy."

There's a loaded pause, and that look comes back into his eyes. "Would you like to see the view?"

"Yes, I would . . ."

They go out to the balcony. It's a beautiful spring night with a silver moon cresting the endless sky—and down below, the river glows like phosphorescence and the city glitters like a billion jewels. And Erica is above it all and, yes, her dreams are coming true. Is she dreaming now?

Greg stands behind her, wraps his arms around her, and kisses the back of her neck, and his lips are warm and soft and rough and tender and insistent. His hands run down her arms and waist and hips, and he gently turns her body and his eyes are pools of kindness and promise, and then they kiss and her chest is rising and falling with each breath, rising and falling into his arms, his lips, and she runs her hand down his cheek and she wants him, she wants this . . . and there's nothing but their kisses and the night . . .

He takes her hand to lead her inside and she whispers, "Greg, I'm . . . I'm not ready . . . not yet."

And he looks at her and smiles away his disappointment. He tenderly brushes her hair off her forehead, then leans down and kisses her one more time. "Speaking of ready, it's time to eat."

"I'm so hungry," Erica says, although food is the furthest thing from her mind.

Chapter 49

Erica is somewhere in deepest Queens, sweating and straining, huffing and puffing—and it feels so good.

"Run the pattern one more time," Grandmaster Nam Soo Kyong tells the class, which obediently runs through the Tae Kwon Do series of stretches, kicks, and lunges yet again.

The dojang is crowded; about half the practitioners are Asian, the rest are the usual New York mosaic of colors, shapes, and ages. Erica found the place online, where it earned rave reviews. Then she dressed down, stuck a cap on her head, and took the subway out to Flushing. She walked down from the elevated station to find a thriving neighborhood of fruit-and-vegetable stands selling exotic produce she'd never seen before, restaurants, clothing stores, fish markets spilling onto the sidewalks thick with shoppers. Every sign is in Korean, incomprehensible chatter fills Erica's ears, the air is aromatic with exotic spices, car exhaust, and fresh fish—immigrants bring such entrepreneurial energy to this city, to this country, she thinks. These are people hungry for the American dream, and she hates the way they've been demonized by xenophobic ideologues.

Nobody in the dojang seems to recognize Erica, which is both disappointing and liberating. After the warm-up, the class breaks into partners and the sparring starts. Erica finds herself facing off against a teenage Korean girl—who is fierce. She and the girl exchange head-height kicks and blocks, jumping and spinning—the whole body focused on the foot, concentration fierce. And then, between kicks, total relaxation, which conserves and marshals the energy. All of it performed with breath control—exhale on the kick.

Tae Kwon Do was developed in Korea in the 1940s, a hybrid of Japanese karate, Chinese martial arts, and ancient Korean self-defense and combat exercises. It goes beyond the actions and moves—stressing courtesy, integrity, perseverance, self-discipline, and invincibility.

Erica took her first class when she was a freshman at Yale. She had two motives. One was to make sure that her father was the last man who ever hit her. The other was that Yale's urban campus was foreign territory to a girl who'd grown up in all-white rural Maine. The uncomfortable truth was that it took her some months to get comfortable with all the diversity. Once she did, she fell in love with the melting pot. And with Tae Kwon Do.

Erica came to think of her classes in New Haven as lessons in adulthood. Early on, she was tempted to go home and test what she'd learned on her father. But that rage for revenge faded as her practice strengthened. Why sink to her parents' level?

The fact is Erica has never been back home since that late-August day when she left for Yale. Her mother drove her to the bus station. When they arrived, there was a moment of silence. They sat there, the engine running, daughter off to forge a life out of the trauma and chaos of her childhood, mother back to the leaky prefab, her pot pipe, and her black-market painkillers. Sitting in the rickety Chevy, there was so much to say. And nothing to say. Her mother lit a Kool. Erica got out of the car, got her one suitcase out of the backseat, and turned toward the tiny bus depot.

"Erica," her mother called.

Erica turned back. Her mother was leaning across the front seat toward the open passenger window.

"Listen, you're off to that fancy school now. No one in this family has ever had that kind of chance. Then again, no one's ever had your brains."

Erica was buoyed—her mother was going to send her off with words of encouragement.

"But just remember, you can change a lot of things in your life, but you can't ever, *ever* change where you come from. And deep down, you'll never be better than any of us." She snickered, took a drag of her cigarette, and drove off.

With each Tae Kwon Do move, Erica feels herself growing more centered and engaged in the moment. She tries to stare down the fear that has been festering inside her since she found those glasses in front of her computer, that ratcheted up after the elevator jerked to a sudden, terrifying stop, that was further fueled by the water bugs crawling out of the red roses. But no matter how deeply she breathes or how graceful her moves, she can't shake the sense that she's in danger.

The class ends. Erica thanks her sparring

partner and the grandmaster. She is so glad she came. Not only because her practice feels tuned up and sharpened, but because she renewed her connection to a discipline that has been important to her, that helped her survive at Yale. And that may help her survive in the days ahead.

As she walks out into the New York evening, she turns on her cell phone and sees there's been a call from Moira. She calls her back on her prepaid.

"Hey, Erica, we just heard from a source in the LAPD that there's been a break in the Barrish case. No word on what it is."

"Thanks for the heads-up. I'll call Detective Takahashi."

"And, Erica, I did some serious digging on Fred Wilmot."

"Find anything interesting?"

"I'd call it disturbing. Wilmot and Nylan Hastings have been best friends since grade school. They grew up together in Winnetka, a rich suburb of Chicago. Hastings went off to Stanford, Wilmot to Brown. He was the first person Hastings brought on board when he founded Universe. When he was at Brown, Wilmot was accused of selling cocaine to his classmates. It was never proved and the school handled it internally."

"Not exactly the best character reference, but we all make mistakes at that age."

"It's the mistake he made when he was ten that disturbs me. With his best friend Nylan watching, he doused a neighbor's golden retriever with lighter fluid and set it on fire."

Erica stops dead on the sidewalk. "Oh no."

"Then they stood there and watched it burn."

"I feel sick, Moy."

"Erica, you're working for men who have ambitions beyond our imagining. Cold, ruthless, predatory men, men who light dogs on fire. Be careful."

Should she tell Moira about the glasses, the elevator, the water bugs? She doesn't want to alarm her friend even more. And she doesn't want to jeopardize her career by leaping to any unproven conclusions. Those glasses were probably a cheap stunt by Claire Wilcox. She has no proof the elevator incident was intentional. The water bugs were pretty juvenile in the end. Erica has an awful lot at stake—her future with Jenny, her show, her power, her salary. She can't let overblown fears derail her. She's got an investigation to pursue.

"Thanks, Moy, I will be careful. Now let me look into this development in the Barrish case. You may see me soon."

"Every cloud."

Erica hangs up and calls Takahashi.

"Erica, you must have some good sources."

"Starting with you."

"The DNA results are back on the blood that was found in the trunk of the stolen Lexus. Arturo Yanez is a match. No big surprise there. But we also found some prints and got a match. They belong to one Miguel Fuentes. Six priors including attempted murder. Member of the Nortenos, one of the most notorious gangs in East LA."

"So Yanez's murder was a paid gang hit."

"Yes. "

"Do you have a location on Fuentes?"

"We have a last known, but we've already been there and he's long gone. He's probably trying to get out of the country. The airlines, bus companies, and border crossings have his name, picture, and description."

"I'll be in the studio in about forty-five minutes. Can I get you on for an interview?"

"Call me ten minutes before you're ready to go live."

"Are you at LAPD headquarters?"

"Yes."

"I'll get a crew down there ASAP. And listen, would I be in your way if I came out there?" This question is strictly a courtesy—the press can go where it wants—but Erica is developing a relationship with Takahashi and wants to be deferential. It could pay off later.

"A *good* reporter is always welcome."

Erica hangs up and calls Greg. He'll deal with

getting an LA crew to police headquarters. "I may want to fly out there to cover this."

There's a pause. "I understand why you want to, Erica, but it has to be cleared with Nylan. And as you know, he wants you *elevated,* not out in the field where you're just one of many reporters."

"Kay Barrish died in my arms. This is *my* story."

"Agreed. But we have to be very strategic. Figure out the best way to present it to Nylan. Let's talk when you get here. Now let me get that LA crew in place for your Takahashi interview."

Erica hangs up. Even Greg seems to be backing up Nylan. Even Greg. And that elevator, shuddering and then stopping . . . she was all alone in the dark. Trapped. Is it a trap? Erica steps into a nearby doorway and hugs herself. The fear that she's been fighting—that she's not safe at GNN, that she's being watched and controlled and manipulated by Nylan and his money and power and sickness, that she's in danger, not safe, not safe—springs to full leering life.

Several passersby look at her, curious. Do they recognize her, the blonde woman huddled in a doorway? An elderly Korean man approaches her. He smiles, a kind smile. "Do you need directions?"

"No, no . . . I'm fine. I was just, um, talking on the phone. I'm going to the subway now, that's all, thank you."

As Erica crosses the street, she tries to rid her mind of the image of that poor golden retriever burning to death on a suburban street.

Chapter 50

Erica spends the rest of the afternoon and evening reporting on the break in the Yanez murder. She interviews Takahashi and broadcasts Fuentes's mug shot. During a break she confers with Greg about the best way to approach Nylan about her heading back to LA, and they hatch a plan. On her next break she calls him.

"Nylan, I want to do an hour-long piece on the Barrish murder, frame it as a commentary on American culture and our national loss, with a focus on California. I've got a request in with the governor for an interview—his press aide was very receptive. I've lined up the state's most respected historian and a UCLA expert on collective trauma. I've got interview requests out with Streisand, Schwarzenegger, and Spielberg. Their people all responded positively to the idea. I think this could be a fascinating and important piece." She recalls the words of Archie Hallowell: *Sometimes you have to lie your way to the truth.*

There's a pause. "I like it. But keep the focus on the sociology and the collective trauma, not on the investigation. High-minded. Milk the celebrities for all they're worth. Soft focus. See if you can wring a few tears out of Streisand. How soon can you get started?"

"I thought I'd fly out to LA tomorrow."

"Can you pull the piece together by the end of the week?"

"Yes."

"Don't forget we have a date in DC on Sunday night. The Correspondents' Dinner."

"I can't wait," Erica says, a shiver of revulsion racing up her spine.

Chapter 51

On the flight to LA, Erica sits in her first-class seat, laptop open, perusing the websites of New York's best girls' schools: Chapin, Spence, Brearley. She thinks Jenny would do better without boys around, one less distraction. She also feels strongly that Jenny needs continuity and stability in her life; she'd like to find a school that's a good match for the long term, a place Jenny can put down some roots and flourish all the way until college.

There's something intimidating about the schools, with their history and traditions, their impressive alumnae, their websites bursting with positivity, good works, and academic promise. Many of her snootier Yale classmates went to these schools or others just like them. And now—she thinks with no small satisfaction—she'll be sending her daughter to one. If, of course, she's able to gain custody. Big *if.* Big and potentially ugly *if.* But Erica has been in touch with Morris Ernst, one of the country's best child-custody lawyers. He told her that with her profile, he believes she can gain custody—that they can reason with Dirk, make it clear to him that with her resources, Erica can provide Jenny with so many advantages that Dirk, with his teacher's salary, simply can't.

Erica clicks off the Spence site and onto Stribling real estate. It's time for a little guilty pleasure—she looks at several apartments on the Upper West Side, which is close to work and schools and bracketed by two beautiful parks. The prices are staggering—a million dollars buys you a nice one-bedroom. She'd love to be in a prewar co-op and lingers over the photos of a two-bedroom on West Eighty-First facing the Museum of Natural History—it has a large living room, lovely views of the museum and the small park that surrounds it, a fireplace, wide hallways, a sense of solidity and space.

She imagines Jenny coming home from school, rushing down the hallway to fill Mom in on her day. The two of them in front of the fireplace on winter Sundays, Jenny doing homework and Erica working her way through the Sunday *Times*. Tucking Jenny in at night, the twinkling park lights out the window. Both of them in a safe place. A safe place. The apartment is 1.75 million. She can hardly believe she can afford it. But she can.

She's on an early flight—it lands in LA at nine thirty a.m.—and as the flight attendant brings her a small tray of exquisite breakfast pastries, Erica feels ready for what lies ahead. There's a lot on her shoulders, but maybe that's a good thing—there's no room left for that fiery demon that likes to perch there and hiss in her ear . . . *"You can't ever, ever change where you come from. And deep down, you'll never be better than any of us."*

Erica picks up her rental car and drives to Moira's house in Los Feliz. She finds the fake rock tucked under the cactus in the side yard, slides it open and takes out the key, and lets herself into the house. There's a note on the dining room table that reads *Mi casa es su casa* and a bouquet of fresh flowers in her bedroom.

Erica unpacks, washes off all traces of makeup, changes into sweat pants, running shoes, and a shapeless top. She tucks all her hair up under an unflattering canvas hat and puts on a pair of clunky sunglasses.

Driving southeast from Los Feliz through

Silverlake and Echo Park and into downtown LA is like moving through the layered strata of ancient rock. The large houses and perfect landscaping give way first to modest bungalows, and then to neglected apartment houses and rundown commercial buildings, and finally to teeming Skid Row—down-and-out in LA—thousands of people who are some combination of poor, addicted, struggling, defeated, crazy, or lost. It's a great sea of humanity and they're all drowning—in the shadows of the gleaming towers of the city's revitalized downtown business district.

This is the neighborhood of Miguel Fuentes's last known address. Erica drives slowly, searching the faces. She's looking for Fuentes, of course, but she's also fascinated by this raw underbelly of Los Angeles, in part because she sees her own parents, her own childhood reflected here in an urban mirror. The sidewalks are lined with tents, mattresses, shopping carts, cardboard boxes, clothing, sleeping dogs, and nodding people. She sees a little girl, no more than five, sitting on a garbage bag full of clothing. She's eating cookies out of a huge package; she and her clothes are filthy, but the little girl looks happy, savoring each bite of her lucky find. Then a man walks by and snatches the package out of her hands, and the girl starts to wail and wail. Nobody comes to comfort her.

Erica finds the address where Fuentes lived. It's on the far edge of Skid Row; the streets are marginally less chaotic and filthy here. The building itself is a two-story 1950s motel-style apartment house with outdoor walkways, way past whatever prime it may have had. There are low-lifes loitering around, and a sense of malevolence pervades the air. Erica parks in front and heads toward the stairs. Fuentes was in apartment twenty-one.

"Save your time, the cops have been crawling all over the place." Erica turns to see a skinny old woman sitting in a lawn chair, greedily sucking down an unfiltered cigarette, swimming in a muumuu, her lips painted a florid red. "That kid took a powder weeks ago."

"Do you know where he went?"

"I'd say 'to hell'—but he was already there." She laughs at her witticism, showing perfect movie-star dentures.

"Did he live here alone?"

"That place was a revolving door. I'd say never less than five or six of them were living there at any time."

"Do you think they were fellow gang members?"

"No, they were the string section of the LA Philharmonic." She laughs again. "I was assistant prop master on *Father Knows Best*. I'm Old Hollywood. What do you think of them apples?"

"Are they all out of the apartment?"

"Yeah. The landlord is renovating the unit. Granite, stainless steel, spa tub." She laughs again. "I *am* having it fumigated."

"You own the building?"

"Bought it fifty years ago. I'm a smart cookie, got into real estate. I like renting to gang members. They pay in cash. Or drugs, if I'm in the mood." She cackles again, then narrows her eyes. "Are you looking for drugs?"

"I'm looking for Miguel Fuentes. Can you help me out? Anything that sticks in your mind? Anyone who might help me find Miguel?"

The woman makes an exaggerated *I'm thinking* expression. "The air conditioner in unit sixteen is on the fritz. I'd tell them they're on their own but there's a baby in there. Poor little tidbit in this heat."

Erica came prepared. She pulls a wad of cash out of her pocket, peels off a hundred.

"I said *air conditioner,* not fan," the woman says.

Erica hands her another hundred.

"He had a sister. She stayed about a week, was right over the border. Pretty girl, classy as hell. Smart. Always carrying books. I think she was a schoolteacher back in Mexico. They were fighting all the time—she was screaming at him to get back in school. She got outta here fast. Like I said, she was smart."

"Do you remember her name?"

"Samantha."

"How long ago was this?"

"It's been awhile, four months, maybe six. Time bleeds at my age."

"Did you tell the police?"

"They didn't ask."

When she gets back to Moira's, Erica 411.coms *Samantha Fuentes*. There are seven listed in LA, but the site only lists landlines, and what kid has one of those nowadays? Then she does a Google search, and LinkedIn pulls a Samantha Fuentes who is a twenty-five-year-old tutor in West Los Angeles specializing in Spanish, English, reading, and writing. There's a phone number and Erica calls.

"This is Samantha Fuentes."

"Hi, Samantha, this is Erica Sparks, reporter from GNN."

There's a chill on the line and then, "Yes?"

"I wanted to talk to you about your brother. I was hoping we could meet for coffee."

"I have nothing to say about my brother. If he had anything to do with that murder, I hope he's sent away for many years."

"You can help make that happen."

"How?" she asks warily.

"A public plea to him to surrender would be one way. How about that cup of coffee?"

There's a pause and then, "I would like to help. Okay."

"Would this afternoon work for you?"

"Yes. I'm out in Pacific Palisades. Meet me at the Coffee Bean and Tea Leaf in an hour."

"See you then."

Erica heads out to Pacific Palisades and finds that the California Dream is alive and well—the cushioned enclave is so sparkly, lush, and lovely that you could almost forget that things like deceit, murder, and evil exist.

Erica has changed out of the sweatpants—one of the least flattering garments ever invented—and gone with a cap instead of the canvas hat, but otherwise is covered up enough not to draw many glances of recognition. Of course, in a celebrity-thick neighborhood like this, she's small potatoes.

She walks into the coffee shop, and a young woman with a lovely, open face waves her over to a table.

"Samantha."

"Erica."

"I guess we're both psychic."

Samantha has a beautiful smile and an easy-going, endearing manner that almost disguises her wariness.

"Can I get you something?" Erica asks.

"I've got my green tea."

Erica gets a double espresso and joins Samantha. "Thanks so much for agreeing to meet me."

"I'm an admirer."

"This all must be very hard on you."

"It is. But I'm not surprised. My brother has been in trouble before. Even as a kid. But nothing like this. I was a big fan of Kay Barrish. She did a lot for my people."

"Do you have any idea where your brother might be?"

"I don't. I would guess that he's back in Mazatlan, but that's only a guess."

"Have you spoken to any family members down there?"

"I have and they haven't seen any sign of him. The Los Angeles police sent down a detective to talk to my parents."

"He may not have been able to get out of the country."

"I'm sad for him, but I have no sympathy. He chose his path. When I first arrived here, I lived with him for several weeks. His life was filled with anger and ugliness. And he did not want to change."

"Would you be willing to speak on camera?"

"I thought about that, and I would not. You know, Erica, I have ambition. I have come here to make a beautiful life. I have found a good job. I am the live-in tutor for the family of Mort Zimmer."

"The television producer?"

"Yes. He and his wife are kind, generous people who want to help me. I am living in a nice apartment over their garage. I am enrolled in UCLA extension working towards my master's degree in education. If I become identified with my brother, it could hurt me. Do you understand?"

"I do, of course, and the admiration is mutual. But if it could help us find justice for Kay Barrish?"

"My brother has never listened to me. He's not going to start now. And I don't think I should give you an interview. Kay Barrish is a popular woman, people love her. I don't want to be connected to her murder."

Erica sips her espresso. "Fair enough."

"What I can do is call you if I hear anything. My family will tell me if he shows up down there."

"I would appreciate that. Do you think there's any chance he'll contact you?"

Samantha laughs ruefully. "I doubt that. We haven't spoken since I moved out of his apartment. And he doesn't know where I live."

"Stay in touch."

On the drive back to Los Feliz, Erica replays her meeting with Samantha. Everything the young woman said made perfect sense. Even the lies.

Chapter 52

When Erica gets back to Moira's, she calls Greg in New York and asks him to have a local LA crew on standby in the morning. Moira comes home and makes them dinner of tuna steak, green beans, and wild rice. As they eat, Erica brings Moira up to date on her investigation. Her friend offers her usual level-headed advice and reluctantly approves of Erica's plan for the next day, urging extreme caution—the gangs of LA consider murder a participatory sport.

Erica gets up at five, does her Tae Kwon Do, dresses down, and heads out to Pacific Palisades. She found the Zimmers' address online and she drives past it—the house is large, Spanish style, with a circular parking area in front. Erica parks around the corner where she is almost hidden but has a clear sight line to the house.

She sits and waits. After about ten minutes the front door opens and a boy and girl, around ten and twelve, come out, followed by Samantha. The kids have their backpacks and Samantha is carrying an insulated bag. They all get in a Lexus SUV and head out of the driveway. Erica pulls down her visor, turns the corner, and follows at a distance.

The SUV makes its way down Temescal Canyon Road to Route 1 and then turns south. Worried Samantha will see her in the rearview mirror, Erica lets a car get between them. The Lexus gets on the Santa Monica Freeway and heads east for about a mile, getting off at Exit 18. Erica follows for several blocks and then stops as the Lexus pulls up in front of the Crossroads School. The kids pile out and wave good-bye.

Erica follows as Samantha drives back to Route 1 and heads north. But she doesn't turn onto Temescal Canyon Road she keeps going for about a half mile before turning right onto Topanga Canyon Boulevard.

Driving up the canyon road is like entering another world, with tawny brown hills home to scrub oak, tall grasses, and bamboo—there are few houses, and the urban energy of Los Angeles seems to vaporize in the sweet-smelling air. Erica stays three cars behind Samantha as they drive the winding road deeper and deeper into the still canyon. The houses they pass are mostly older, fanciful, whimsical; many look benignly neglected. They pass a small village with a post office, some shops, a restaurant, a nursery. The people, young and old, mostly look like hippies, rich and otherwise; there is a lot of flowing hair and flowing clothes.

Just on the other side of the village, Samantha turns left onto Greenleaf Canyon Road and heads up into the hills. Civilization falls away, it feels like wilderness up here, the houses are scattered far and wide. No one would hear you scream. The road branches and Samantha bears left. Up ahead—set back from the road in a small field—there's a collapsing stable, its last horses long gone. Samantha slows. Erica quickly veers off the road, onto a dirt track where she's able to drive the car behind a copse of trees. She gets out and runs to the edge of the road in time to see Samantha get out of the Lexus, look around, reach into the car and grab the insulated bag, put it down behind a tree, and get back in the SUV. Erica falls to the ground in high grass and watches as the Lexus drives past her back down the hill.

She lies there, watching. After a minute, Miguel Fuentes pokes his head out of the stable and looks around. Confident that the coast is clear, he rushes across the field, grabs the insulated bag, and darts back to the stable.

Erica stands up, takes out her phone, and calls Greg. "Send the crew up to Greenleaf Canyon Road in Topanga. As fast as possible. And be ready to go live as soon as they get here."

Erica wants to give her crew a head start, so she waits ten minutes before calling Betsy Takahashi and giving her the location of the fugitive.

Chapter 53

"This is Erica Sparks reporting live from Topanga Canyon in Los Angeles, where there has been a big break in the Kay Barrish murder case. Twenty-seven-year-old Miguel Fuentes—whose fingerprints were found in the car in which Arturo Yanez was murdered—has just been arrested by the Los Angeles police. Yanez was the caterer's assistant who allegedly poisoned Barrish. Fuentes was discovered hiding out in a crumbling stable in an isolated section of Topanga Canyon. They're leading Fuentes into a police car now."

The camera pans to a scowling, handcuffed Fuentes being led from the stable, across the field, and then into a squad car.

"Fuentes is a known member of the notorious East Los Angeles gang called Nortenos. He has six prior arrests, including one for attempted murder, for which he served three years at San Quentin. The unanswered question is, what was the gang's motive for murdering Yanez? To help me answer it, I have Los Angeles police detective Betsy Takahashi." The camera pans back, and Takahashi is in the frame. "Thank you for your time, Detective. Can you shed any light on why Fuentes would murder Yanez?"

"This has all the hallmarks of a gang murder—the execution-style shooting in the back of the head, a stolen car used to commit the crime, dumping of the body out in the desert. The witnesses who saw Yanez get into the stolen car at the bus stop on Santa Monica Boulevard the night of Barrish's death report seeing at least two men in the car. So Fuentes didn't act alone. And Yanez got into the car voluntarily, which indicates he knew the men."

"Are you suggesting that the same people who murdered Yanez may have hired him to kill Barrish?"

"I am, yes."

"But why would an LA street gang want to murder Kay Barrish? For one thing, she was beloved in the Hispanic community."

"These gangs are known to commit murder for hire."

"And hopefully Fuentes will be able to supply you with the name of whoever hired him."

"Exactly."

"Will the district attorney be offering him a plea deal?"

"You'd have to ask the district attorney that question."

"Are you confident today's arrest will lead to the solving of this case?"

"The only time I'm confident that a case is solved is when the perpetrator is behind bars."

"Thank you for your time. This is Erica Sparks reporting live from Topanga Canyon. Now back to GNN headquarters in New York."

The camera is turned off. Detective Takahashi asks, "So, are you going to tell me who led you to Fuentes?"

Erica remembers her meeting with Samantha Fuentes, the young woman's warm smile and honest ambition. "I'm not going to reveal my source," she says simply.

Takahashi's eyes narrow. "Whoever it is could be material to the investigation."

"If at any point I think that might be the case, I'll reconsider."

Almost simultaneously, news vans from the other networks race up the canyon road and arrive on the scene and crews pour out, hurrying to get shots of Fuentes in the police car before it leaves. They've all been badly scooped by GNN. Erica smiles to herself—*Sorry, guys, but that's the news biz.*

Chapter 54

Erica and Nylan are in the back of the limousine on their way to the Correspondents' Dinner. There's a tense silence between them, has been since he picked her up at her hotel. Erica feels uncomfortable being this close to him; she crosses and uncrosses her legs.

"I'm sure you understand, Nylan, that once I got the tip on Miguel Fuentes's location, I had to put the special report on Barrish's murder on the back burner."

"I didn't like seeing you out there in the weeds of Topanga looking like some second-rate field reporter."

"Second-rate field reporters don't get tips on the biggest murder case of the decade. And I understand our ratings spiked significantly."

Nylan turns away from her, looks out at the rainy night, casually brushes at his pants leg. "I'm not sure there ever *was* a special report in the works."

Should Erica compound her lie? "Do the ends justify the means?"

"Are you asking rhetorically?" He turns to her. "If so, you and I agree on one of life's great moral questions." He crosses his leg so that his foot is inches from her dress, almost as if he wants to kick her or wipe his sole off on the exquisite red fabric.

Erica wants to move away from him but wills herself to remain steady. "Sometimes a small sin in pursuit of a great goal is justified."

"Only a small sin?" He reaches out and touches her shoulder. Erica flinches. "A hair out of place."

"Yes. Only a small sin," Erica says, turning and looking him in the eyes.

Erica's words hang in the air between them as the limousine pulls up in front of the sweeping curve of the Washington Hilton. Ropes hold back the gawkers and celebrity hounds. Nylan and Erica step out of the car and into the blinding light of a thousand flashbulbs. A production assistant leads them to a small staging area where they stand and pose for more pictures. Erica has to admit Nylan looks handsome, dapper and almost grown-up in a perfectly tailored black suit. He puts an arm around her waist—she takes a step away from him. Anger flashes across his face. Too bad.

They make their way up the red carpet toward the hotel entrance when another production assistant steers them over to Giuliana Rancic and Kelly Osborne, who are covering the red carpet live on E!

"Welcome to GNN's superstar newscaster Erica Sparks and her date, Nylan Hastings, the founder of the network. OMG, Erica, that dress!" Giuliana gushes.

"I'm *obsessed*," Kelly says. "Who are you wearing?"

"It's by a New York designer named Nancy Huffman. She has a small atelier in the East Village."

When Nancy first showed Erica the simple

red, strapless gown, she wasn't sure about it. Then she tried it on, looked in the mirror, and was ecstatic—the drape, the color, the simplicity—it's a dream. And tonight, with her hair and makeup exquisitely done and the simple ruby necklace by Bulgari and matching red-paste clip-ons from Etsy, she feels more beautiful than she ever has in her life. Was she really a complete unknown just six weeks ago?

Erica and Nylan enter the hotel lobby and are walking toward the ballroom when Meryl Streep approaches. It's a surreal moment for Erica to see the actress—whom she adores—just a few feet away. "I'm a fan," Meryl says. "I think you've shown true grace under pressure."

"I'd say thank you but I'm speechless."

She shares a laugh with Meryl Streep—*with Meryl Streep*—and then she and Nylan enter the ballroom and make their way toward their table. Erica sees Katie Couric, who waves; and Bill O'Reilly, who calls, "Keep up the no spin, Sparks!"; and Megyn Kelly, who gives her a thumbs-up; and Kathie Lee Gifford, who blows her a kiss. There's also Kerry Washington and Julia Roberts and Sofia Vergara and Denzel Washington and, yes, George Clooney. *At their table!* President Garner and First Lady Ginny Garner are at the dais, along with senators, cabinet members, and media executives.

The energy in the room is crackling, dazzling,

dizzying, everyone is groomed and glistening and golden, strangers are smiling at Erica as if she belongs. And she does belong. Doesn't she? No matter where she came from. No matter how many mistakes she's made in the past. This is now, the present racing into the future, a future filled with infinite promise.

Erica is too keyed up to eat. Nylan works the table like he owns it, which he probably does. Jimmy Fallon is hilarious skewering Washington politics. There's a lot of tablehopping, huddled conversations, drinking and laughing. Erica excuses herself to go to the ladies' room.

When she's checking her makeup, Lois Wittmer appears. Wittmer is the great female pioneer in television news—the first woman to have her own show, to anchor the evening news, to develop and exploit the celebrity interview. She occupies a unique place in the fiery pantheon of feminism. Although now, in her late seventies, she's rarely seen on the small screen.

"This is embarrassing, but you're kind of my idol," Erica says.

"I never, *ever* get tired of hearing that," Wittmer says with a lopsided smile—she's clearly enjoyed a glass of wine or four. "I hear you're getting your own show."

"Will you be a guest?"

"Sure I will."

"Score!"

They laugh and then Wittmer grows serious—in that slightly exaggerated way people do when they're tipsy. She reaches out and gives Erica's hand a squeeze. "I think you have a lot of talent, Erica Sparks. *A lot* of talent. But lemme tell ya, this is a fickle business. Don't take a stinkin' thing for granted. Not one stinkin' thing. And remember—the SOBs who run the business will drop you on a dime if your ratings go south, or when you grow wrinkles, or just when they feel like it. On. A. Dime. Speaking of SOBs, that guy you work for, Nylon Haystacks or whatever the hell his name is."

"Nylan Hastings."

"Bingo! That guy gives me the creeps big-time. Isn't it great how you guys are always one step ahead of the news? Like with that ferry crash—you just *happened* to be there. Then Kay Barrish, bless her heart, buys the farm in the middle of your interview. Awful coincidinky, if you ask me."

Erica isn't sure what to make of this outburst. Is it the bitter ranting of a has-been? Or wisdom out of the mouth of a drunk? Before she can figure out how to respond, Jennifer Lawrence walks into the ladies' room. She gives Erica a warm smile.

Erica tries to dismiss Wittmer's admonition. Nylan may not be perfect, he may be cold-blooded and more than a little sleazy, but he's led

Erica into a career, a world, a life beyond her imaginings. *Don't bite the hand that feeds you.* Or she may end up sour and cynical, like her fallen idol, who has just wobbled out of the ladies' room muttering to herself.

As she makes her way back to her table, Erica's prepaid rings.

"George Samuels here. We've got a tentative match on the suspect seen entering the subway the morning Mark Benton was assaulted. His name is Anton Volodin. He's twenty-four, a low-level member of the Russian Mafia."

"The Russian Mafia?"

"Yes, they've been establishing a toehold in this country for the past decade. They're mostly involved with drugs, prostitution, and extortion. And they're ruthless."

"Why would they be after Mark?"

"If and when we find Volodin, that will be our first question. And, Erica, Mark is moving to rehab tomorrow. His speech is a lot better. He keeps asking to see you."

"I'll be down as soon as I get back to New York."

As Erica wends her way past tables ringing, singing with laughter, champagne, jewels, and insider whispers, it all grows muffled and falls away—as she realizes what she really cares about.

Chapter 55

Erica cabs down to the Rusk Rehabilitation Center on East Thirty-Eighth Street—it's a nondescript, could-be-anywhere building, but she knows it's one of the best rehabs in the world. She gets Mark's room number and heads up to the fifth floor. The elevator doors open and she sees him making his way down the hallway on a walker with an aide by his side. The bandage on his head is much smaller, revealing his shaved skull. Erica is touched by his determination as he methodically places one foot in front of the other. Then he looks up and sees her—a beautiful smile breaks across his face, and Erica feels an intense wave of affection for her brave friend.

"Look at you," Erica says, going to him. Without thinking, she cups his face in her hands and kisses him on the forehead. "You're up and about."

Mark struggles to speak and when he does, it's slowly, but his voice is stronger, his enunciation clearer. "G-g-goo-*d* . . . mor-*ning* . . . E-e-*ri*-ca."

Erica feels her throat tighten but she fights off the sentiment—it's not what anyone needs right now. "You sound *so* much better. Not quite ready for voice-over work, but getting there."

They make their way to his private room, where the aide helps him into bed. He sighs with relief.

The aide leaves, and Erica and Mark are alone. He indicates the rolling bedside tray, and she maneuvers it in front of him. There's an iPad on the tray. Mark slowly but steadily pecks out the letters: I need my home computer.

"Do you want me to get it for you?" Erica asks, and Mark nods. "Is it in your apartment?"

Mark nods again. Then he types: 704 Greenwich St, #7

"I'll need your keys."

Marks nods to his bedside table. Erica opens the top drawer and takes out his keys.

"N-n-*now,*" Mark says, then he types: Laptop on table

"Back in a flash."

Erica cabs downtown to Mark's building in the West Village. It's a converted stable—four-story, brownstone and brick, with two enormous doorways in front. She climbs two flights to Mark's place. It's one large room. A windsurfing board hangs on one wall like a sculpture. There's a bed with a cool steel headboard at one end of the room, and a modern kitchen with a rustic farm table at the other. The place is minimal, masculine, and cool, hardly the nerd pad Erica was half expecting. As she picks up the computer and slips it into its case, she takes another look around and wonders about Mark's love life. He's a catch.

She cabs back up to the hospital. When she walks into Mark's room and he sees the computer, his eyes light up. He indicates his tray, and Erica takes out the computer and opens it up. Mark turns it on, and as the screen comes to life, he comes to life, sitting up in bed, leaning forward—alert and engaged at a whole new level. For the first time since his assault, Erica allows herself to think, *He's going to be okay.*

"Mark, what was it you were going to tell me at Starbucks?"

His face grows serious. He moves his attention from the laptop to the tablet and types: The ferry hack originated in the United States.

"Are you *sure?*"

He nods emphatically.

"Do you know *where* in the US?"

He types: Determining that is much trickier. There are so many servers and overlapping networks. It's going to take some serious dig-ging. But I'm working on it.

He smiles, and at that moment he looks like a happy kid with his favorite toy, and Erica again feels that swelling of emotion toward him. She puts a hand on his shoulder and gives him an encouraging squeeze. He takes her hand in his and holds it to his cheek for a moment, in a gesture whose innocence takes her breath away.

"You've made amazing strides, my friend, and you're just going to keep getting better. And I am going to be here for you every step of the way, for as long as it takes."

As Erica is leaving Rusk Rehab, she runs into Detective Samuels on his way in.

"How's he doing?" the detective asks.

"His progress is pretty remarkable. I found out what he was going to tell me the morning he was assaulted: the Staten Island ferry was hacked from within the United States."

Samuels rubs his chin. "If that's true, it's a game changer. Can he prove it?"

"Yes. Hacking leaves a trail. It's a matter of having the skills to follow that trail. He's working on determining the exact location."

"That information would break this thing wide open."

"Any leads on Volodin?"

"He's connected with Bratstvo D'yavola, a Russian Mafia crew out of Brighton Beach in Brooklyn, led by one Leonid Gorev. We've staked out their clubhouse but Volodin hasn't been seen. I wouldn't be surprised if he turns up dead. At this point he's worth more as a corpse."

"Where are they in Brighton Beach?"

"They operate out of a caviar shop on Brighton Beach Avenue. But don't be getting any ideas, Erica."

"Ideas?"

"Do you know what Bratstvo D'yavola means?"

Erica shakes her head.

"The Devil's Brotherhood."

As Erica steps off the curb to hail a cab uptown, she thinks, *I really should educate myself about caviar*.

Chapter 56

"Is this desk a little too big?" Erica asks, sitting behind a desk the size of a conference table. "I'm afraid it's going to cut me off from viewers. Remember, our format is less talking-headsy than most news shows. We're going to have more medium shots, and I'm going to be moving between the desk and the seating area. And occasionally out into the audience. Otherwise, I love it."

Erica is test-driving the set of *The Erica Sparks Effect*, which premieres in three short weeks. The show's director, Ali Cheung; its designer, Natalie Ferro; and Greg are with her. The studio is a state-of-the-art space with seating for a small audience, a first for a newscast.

"The desk gives you authority," Ali says. She's serious, low-key, one of the best in the business.

"I want authority, not autocracy." Erica has

had conversations with Ali and Greg about the sort of culture she wants backstage—one that's gener-ous, respectful of everyone no matter what their rank, its high standards leavened with humor and caring. If someone is doing a good job, they'll receive absolute support. No backbiting, no drama, no divas.

Erica understands that at the end of the day, she's the captain of this ship. It's up to her to model the behaviors and work ethic and consider-ation she expects everyone to deliver. It's about bringing her best self to work every day—and inspiring everyone else to do the same. If she can accomplish that, the show will soar.

"I want the show to be a dialogue with viewers, not a lecture. I really want us to be fresh—a little bit of Ellen, a little bit of Oprah, and a lot of hard-driving investigative reporting. The desk feels like armor."

"Out with the desk!" Ferro, chic and cool in all black, says in her Italian accent. "I'll have a smaller one in this afternoon."

Erica gets up, walks over to the seating area, and sits in one of the two love seats facing each other over a coffee table. The tones are soothing beiges and creams with pops of color on the pillows and accessories. Erica wants a balance of comfortable and stimulating, and Natalie has delivered.

Suddenly music pours out of the speakers and

fills the studio. It's the latest iteration of the show's theme music. Everyone stops and listens—it's bright and melodic with a pulsing underbeat that gradually grows stronger, holding a promise of important things to come.

"This is fantastic!" Erica says. A wave of elation sweeps over her—she's dreamed of having her own show for a decade and now it's all coming together. She leaps up and does an impromptu little jig. Everyone in the studio laughs, the good energy flows—and Erica feels like she's at home.

As she's walking down the hall to her office, Nancy Huffman appears.

"Erica, I've been *swamped* with orders since the Correspondents' Dinner. I've had to hire three dressmakers to keep up."

"You may have to quit your day job."

"Stranger things have happened." She grasps Erica's hand. *"Thank you."*

Erica heads down to her office and opens the door. Then she screams.

Chapter 57

There's a rat on her desk, a large rat, a large dead rat—*no, it twitched*—and blood is oozing from its mouth and nose and eyes, and Erica watches in horror as the rat struggles to crawl across her desk, leaving a trail of smeared blood in its wake. Her stomach turns over, she's going to heave, and then Nancy is there and then Greg, and they turn her away and close the office door and lead Erica to a chair in the hallway and sit her down. She opens her mouth and a thin stream of watery vomit pours out.

Greg is on the phone, and now a top man from the building's maintenance department appears and he takes one look at the rat and says it's eaten anticoagulant poisoning but that the building has never seen a rat above the second floor and in any event there's no current problem and no poison has been laid out in at least three months. And then a low-level maintenance guy appears and puts the rat in a bag and cleans off Erica's desk. And Nancy hands Erica a warm, damp towel and she wipes herself off.

"Do you want to take the rest of the day off?" Greg asks.

And even though all Erica can feel is fear, she

answers, "No." And she stands up and walks into her office. Nancy and Greg follow. She sits behind her desk, takes shallow breaths that slowly deepen. Nylan's behind this. Nylan and Wilmot. They have a thing for dead animals. And dead people?

If they think this is going to stop her investigation, they're wrong. Dead rat wrong.

"I've got work to do," Erica says simply to Greg and Nancy.

"Erica . . . ," Greg begins.

"I said I have work to do."

Chapter 58

The next day Erica hires a car service to take her out to Brighton Beach. They drive along the Hudson to Lower Manhattan, through the Battery Tunnel to Brooklyn, onto the BQE and under the Verrazano Narrows Bridge. They pass Coney Island, honky-tonk and romantic with its boardwalk and amusement rides, crowned by the Cyclone, the iconic wooden roller coaster. The change in scenery is good for Erica, even though she knows she will never get the image of that dying rat crawling across her desk out of her mind.

They reach Brighton Beach Boulevard, which

runs under the elevated subway. Bursting with vitality, the streets are filled with Russians of all ages—some are well-dressed, others look working class and even poor—and lined with Russian shops, bakeries, restaurants, and over-the-top nightclubs. Erica scans the shops looking for A Taste of St. Petersburg, and when she sees it, she asks the driver to stop and wait for her.

The store is immaculate and filled with a dazzling array of gourmet delicacies—its center-piece is an enormous refrigerated case filled with a lavish display of loose and tinned caviar set on mounds of ice. A solidly built young man stands proudly behind the case. Unfortunately there are no customers for him to wait on, which doesn't seem to bother him in the least. Clearly, selling caviar isn't the store's real purpose; it was set up to wash illicit cash—and it's a great-looking laundry.

A pretty, very Slavic-looking young sales-woman approaches Erica with a polished smile. "Welcome to A Taste of St. Petersburg."

Erica has dressed down in jeans, a blouse, flats, and no makeup, but the woman looks as if she's trying to place her.

"Can I help you find anything?"

"I'm looking for Leonid Gorev."

"I do not know if he is available. May I tell him who is here to see him?"

"Erica Sparks."

The woman disappears into the back of the store. "How's business?" Erica asks the young man behind the caviar counter.

"Oh, very good!" he says, smiling and gesturing around the deserted store as if it was filled with shoppers.

"Have you worked here long?"

"Two months!"

"How long have you been in this country?"

"Two months!"

"So you came over here to work in the store?"

"To work for Mr. Gorev."

"Oh. Do you know Anton Volodin?"

A dark cloud sweeps across the young man's face, and he opens the back of the caviar case and starts to rearrange jars and tins.

"Erica Sparks, what a pleasure and an honor!" booms a bulky middle-aged man in an expensive suit—sporting a Rolex and a gold ring a rapper would envy—as he crosses to her. "I am Leonid Gorev. And you are far more beautiful in person than on the television set. You are here for some caviar! How wonderful! Maybe you will do a TV show story on our caviar! Come, come with me! Gregor, bring us back the finest selection."

He takes Erica's arm and leads her through the store, down a hall, and into a large, opulent office. The place looks like it was put together by a decorator with an unlimited budget and multiple personality disorder—it's a dizzying mishmash of plush fabrics, leather sofas, sleek midcentury pieces, and gold-plated rococo—on second glance, maybe it's not plated. In spite of a desk Louis Quatorze would think was ostentatious, it feels like a party room, and Erica can imagine all-night revels filled with drinking contests, raucous Russian laughter, and sentimental tears, a blizzard of cocaine and passels of expensive hookers.

"Please sit, Erica Sparks. Make yourself at home. We will start with vodka. You can't have caviar without vodka! I have the finest vodka in the world! Vodka of the czars!"

"I'm allergic."

"Oh, I'm sorry, would you like . . . *something else?*" he asks with a mischievous twinkle before pouring himself a shot of vodka and knocking it back.

"I'm fine, thanks."

Gregor appears with a large silver tray, which he sets down on the coffee table. It holds iced mounds of shimmering black and red caviar, little triangles of toast, and a silver bowl of butter. Then he bows and leaves.

"Do you know how to eat caviar the Russian way?"

"I don't."

"We don't use any nonsense like hard-boiled eggs or chopped onions! Take a piece of toast, spread with butter, top with caviar—and eat!

Enjoy! Live!" Each exclamation is punctuated with a shot of vodka.

Erica follows his directions with the black caviar. The deeply salty, fishy taste is a little off-putting at first bite—and more so at second. She politely tries the red and then says, "Delicious."

"Perhaps you will put our caviar on the television set, Erica Sparks!"

"I'm here for a reason."

"Everyone is everywhere for a reason."

"I'm looking for Anton Volodin."

Gorev's head jerks slightly, then he walks over and helps himself to a heaping serving of caviar. "Very nice young man. I miss him. He worked for one of my other businesses."

"What business would that be?"

"Automobile repair and salvage. There are so many automobiles in America. They are all over the streets."

"You say you miss him. Where did he go?"

"Anton went back to Russia."

"He's wanted for questioning in a brutal assault on a colleague of mine, Mark Benton."

Something flashes in Gorev's eyes—something that makes Vladimir Putin look like Johnny Appleseed. "Anton? Assault? No. Never. He's a sweet Russian boy."

"The police have video footage of him leaving the scene of the assault with Benton's computer case." Slight exaggeration—the footage shows him at the subway station just after the assault—but they're not playing footsie here. "Are you sure he's back in Russia?"

"Of course I am sure."

"When did he leave the country?"

"Oh, I don't know. I am a busy man. Maybe two weeks ago. I have many employees. I don't keep track. You ask a lot of questions, Erica Sparks."

"I'm a journalist."

"What is it you say in America? . . . Curiosity killed the cat."

"Satisfaction brought her back."

Gorev breaks into a satisfied smile, and Erica has the feeling she's just stepped into a cat-trap. He goes to his desk and presses an intercom. "Peter!"

Within moments a sweaty, obsequious middle-aged man in a too-tight suit appears. He looks vaguely terrified.

"I want to speak to Anton Volodin."

"Of course, Leonid, of course."

Peter sits down at the ornate desk, presses a button, and a large TV screen rises out of a console. Then he takes a laptop out of a desk drawer, does some typing, and Skype appears on the screen. Ringing. The ringing is answered—a sexy, heavily made-up woman with some serious mileage on her, wearing a negligee and sitting on a sofa, appears on-screen. She and Peter

267

exchange words in Russian. She turns her head and calls out. Anton Volodin appears, disheveled and shirtless, and plops down beside the woman, putting an arm around her shoulders. He's twenty years younger than she is, and his smile at the camera is louche and lascivious.

Gorev walks behind Peter, puts his hands down on the desk, and leans into the frame. "Hello, Anton."

"Leonid! Hello."

"There is a beautiful woman here who I want you to meet. Her name is Erica Sparks."

"Hello, Erica Sparks, beautiful woman," Anton says, laughing, all sleazy male ego.

The pervasive decadence of the whole scene is starting to turn Erica's stomach. This man almost killed Mark Benton, Leonid Gorev was almost certainly an accomplice, and yet here they are smug and laughing, surrounded by mounds of caviar, opulence, and indulgence.

"Erica Sparks has a crazy idea that you beat up a man," Gorev says.

They laugh again. "That is silly, Erica Sparks. I am a pussycat." He licks the woman's neck, and she arches her back and moans.

Erica stands up, says, "I've seen enough," and walks out of the room, trailed by their laughter.

As the car makes its way back to Manhattan, Erica calls Rusk Rehab.

"Mark Benton's room. This is Chuck Benton."

"Hi, Chuck, it's Erica. How's my friend doing today?"

"Obsessed. I can't get him off of his computer."

"That's a good thing, no?"

"That's a very good thing. Marie and I feel like we're getting our son back."

"Can I talk to him a minute?"

"Sure thing."

"Hi, E-*ri*-ca."

"I was wondering if you could hack into someone's Skype account."

"N-not easy . . . but d-d-doable."

"His name is Leonid Gorev. G-o-r-e-v. I need the last number he called, about ten minutes ago. It should be a number in Moscow and it should belong to one Anton Volodin. Also, any information you could find on Volodin would be helpful."

"I'm o-on it."

Erica hangs up. As her car makes its way up West Street, she looks out at the mighty Hudson and hears echoes of the Russians' taunting laughter. It reminds her of something, something she can't quite place. She feels like she just came face-to-face with venality, mendacity—the human spirit at its ugliest and most depraved. And that's when she realizes what the mocking laughter reminds her of—the sounds she heard on the other side of the flimsy plasterboard for the first seventeen years of her life.

Chapter 59

Erica called the real estate agent Greg recommended and now she's walking through a bright, spacious bedroom in the West Eighty-First Street apartment she admired online. She imagines where Jenny's bed would go—and her bookcase and dresser and desk with a bulletin board above it filled with pictures of boy bands and animals and ideas. Then she inspects the walk-in closet and imagines it filled with Jenny's dresses and shoes and sweaters. She walks to the window and looks down at the Museum of Natural History, surrounded by its gracious park in the full blush of spring. Jenny has always loved science, and she'd be able to walk across the street and be immersed and inspired.

Erica walks down the wide hallway to the living room—the place is even lovelier in person than it was in the pictures, filled with south light, large and welcoming rooms, high ceilings, floors of honey-colored oak, French doors into the dining room, and a beautiful carved mantel over the fireplace. Erica walks through the kitchen—it's done in black and white and looks more than adequate for someone who believes that takeout food is one of mankind's great evolutionary leaps. There's a doorman downstairs. The building is impeccably maintained and exudes a sense of security and stability, which is so important for Jenny—and for her mother. Erica imagines them at home here together, sharing a wonderful life—a secure and stable life. Life *can* be secure and stable. Can't it? Even in a world where someone puts a dying rat on your desk.

Erica feels a growing sense of doubt about her position at GNN—clearly Nylan is trying to stop her investigations, to frighten her, undermine her confidence, play sick head games on her. She wants to buy an apartment fast; once it's in her name, he'll have a tough time getting it back. Her housing allowance will pay for it, and no matter what happens she'll walk away with a juicy piece of Manhattan real estate. Two can play this game of wits, Mr. Hastings, no matter how high the stakes.

Madge Miller, in her sixties, glasses around her neck, simple blue dress, looking more like a librarian than a real estate agent, gestures Erica to the back of the kitchen, where there's a service entrance and a set of folding doors. "Ta-da!" she says, opening the doors to reveal a washer and dryer.

"Sold!" Erica says, and Madge smiles indulgently. "No, seriously, sold. I'd like to make a full-price, all-cash offer."

Madge is nonplussed. "Don't go anywhere,"

she says, taking out her cell phone and walking into the living room.

Erica opens the service entrance, the apartment's back door. There's a small landing with an elevator, two large trash barrels, and doors leading to two other apartments. The landing is painted battleship gray, dark and claustrophobic. It looks grimy and smells faintly of trash. Erica gets a creepy feeling at the back of her neck. Someone could sneak onto that service elevator, ride up here, break into the apartment. Kidnap Jenny. Harm Jenny. Harm Erica. She quickly shuts and bolts the door. She'll add another lock.

"The apartment is yours," Madge says, coming into the kitchen. "Let's head over to the office and get started on the paperwork."

As they walk through the foyer toward the front door, Erica turns and takes a look back at the empty apartment. Instead of the safe, secure place she saw just fifteen minutes earlier, the quiet, echoing rooms and slanting afternoon sun seem to hold menace and danger—the pristine setting for some terrible crime.

Erica leaves Madge's Upper East Side office after formalizing her offer with a check for $175,000, 10 percent of the purchase price. She feels a combination of trepidation and triumph. As she walks downtown toward GNN, her prepaid rings—it's Detective Takahashi.

"Listen, Erica, there've been some developments with Miguel Fuentes. The DA has offered him a deal if he'll talk. We won't charge him with first-degree murder, meaning there'll be no chance he'd get the death penalty or life in prison."

"Has his lawyer responded?"

"We're waiting. But we're optimistic he'll take it. The case against him is strong. DNA doesn't lie. Either way, we've scheduled an interrogation. It's a tool to force an answer. If he accepts the deal, he'll talk freely. If he doesn't, he'll sit there with his lawyer and we'll try and scare the hell out of both of them with our evidence."

"When's the interrogation?"

"It's at one p.m. our time today."

"Is there any chance you can patch me in so I can watch?"

There's a pause and then, "I guess you didn't get where you are by being a shrinking violet."

"Barrish died in my arms, Detective."

"Yeah. I'll do it. "

"Much appreciated."

"But it's just for you. None of it can be broadcast without the DA's and the LAPD's consent."

"Agreed."

"I'll call you fifteen minutes before to confirm."

Back in her office Erica sits making notes for her meeting with Morris Ernst, the lawyer who will be handling her petition for custody of Jenny.

She's told him she wants to play softball—her great concern is that the negotiations may traumatize Jenny, and that's not acceptable. She also leaves a message for Detective George Samuels, asking him to call her.

Greg appears in her doorway. "Are you okay?"

"I think so."

His face darkens, and for a moment he looks like he wants to say something but then decides not to. He switches gears. "Do you have a minute? I want to go over a list of possible guests for your first show."

"No time like the present."

He comes in and sits across from her. "I lied," he confesses with a disarming smile.

"Shame on you."

"Well, I do have a list. At the top of it is 'Spend more time with Erica.'"

"Funny—there are days when I wish I could spend *less* time with Erica."

"She's a busy gal," Greg says.

"All work and no play—"

"—makes Erica a lonely girl?"

She looks into his eyes and sees a touching insecurity. Men, for all their bluster in the public square, are filled with private doubts and vulnerability. If only more of them could admit it. Erica nods.

"How about we be lonely together?" Greg says.

"I want that, Greg. But I'm up to here with

show prep, I'm buying an apartment, seeing a lawyer about reworking my custody arrangement with my ex, and dealing with rats—dead *and* alive."

"You have to breathe. We could go on a nice, innocent date—see a Broadway show, go down to Chinatown for dinner, explore Williamsburg." He leans forward, elbows on knees, looks so sincere and hopeful and adorable.

"I'm afraid a nice, innocent date is the last thing I have time for."

Greg frowns in frustration.

Erica gets up, walks to the office door, and closes it. "A nice, romantic date, on the other hand, could maybe be arranged."

Chapter 60

The camera feed from the LAPD interrogation room is a little grainy. A glum and handcuffed Miguel Fuentes and his lawyer sit on one side of a conference table, Betsy Takahashi and an assistant DA sit across from them. Erica is in her office with the door shut, riveted to her computer screen.

"Miguel, we're glad that you've decided to accept our plea deal," the DA says. "What we would like you to do is walk us through everything that you know about the murders of Kay Barrish and Arturo Yanez."

"I don't know anything about the murder of Kay Barrish."

"You know that Arturo Yanez was paid to murder her?"

Fuentes nods.

"So you *do* know something about Barrish's murder. The more open and honest you can be with us, the easier this will be for all of us. Did you make the original contact with Yanez?"

"No."

"Do you know who did?"

Fuentes hesitates before saying glumly, "Ricky Martinez." Sweat breaks out on his brow. He may have just signed his death warrant.

"Is Martinez a member of Nortenos?"

"Yes. He is above me."

"Have you done jobs with him before?"

"Yes."

The DA turns to Takahashi. "Get a warrant and an APB out on Martinez."

Takahashi leaves the room, and everyone waits silently until she returns about ninety seconds later.

The DA continues. "Was Martinez in the car with you when you picked up Yanez at the bus stop on Santa Monica Boulevard?"

"Yes. I was driving."

"How did Martinez find Yanez?"

"They are both from Juarez. From the same street. Ricky knew that Arturo's mother was sick and that he needed money bad."

"After you picked Yanez up, did you drive straight out to the desert?"

"Yes."

"Where did you kill him?"

"I did not kill him!"

"So Martinez fired the shot?"

"Yes."

"Where?"

"In the desert."

"And what did he do with the gun?"

"He buried it in the desert."

"At the spot where you dumped his body?"

Fuentes slumps forward, a look of self-pitying regret on his face. "Yes."

"So you drove into the desert, Martinez opened the trunk, shot Yanez, and buried the gun?"

Fuentes puts his head in his hands, looks like he might throw up.

"Answer the question."

"Yes."

"And then you drove back to Covina and abandoned the car?"

"Yes."

"Who stole the car from the beach parking lot?"

"I did."

"All right, Miguel. Thank you for your cooperation. Now I want to ask you a very important question. And I want you to think before you answer. Will you do that?" the DA asks.

Miguel nods.

"Do you know who contacted Ricky Martinez to find Yanez in the first place?"

Erica leans forward, studies Fuentes's face.

"I don't know . . ." Fuentes says, and it's obvious he's lying.

"Think hard, Miguel."

"I don't know," he says in exasperation, looking like he might start to cry.

His lawyer leans in and whispers in his ear. Fuentes takes a deep breath. "All I know is a man came from the East, from New York, he met with Ricky, he knows Ricky. That is *all* I know."

The DA waits. Lets him sweat. The seconds tick by.

Finally: "They will kill me, even in prison they will kill me. They are the hardest of all." Now Fuentes looks afraid, very afraid.

"Who are?" the DA asks. Again no answer. The DA waits. And waits. Finally he says, "We can arrange for protection for you in prison. Put you in a segregated unit. But you have to tell us everything you know."

More waiting. More sweating. More seconds ticking by. "He has money. Lots of money. He gives everyone money. He gets what he wants."

"Who is he?!" the DA barks.

"I never met him! His name is Leonard Gorf or something! I don't know! All I know is—he is fat and rich and Russian and he lives in New York!"

For a moment Erica feels like the world has stopped. Then she feels a jolt of pure adrenaline rock her body. One more layer of the onion has been peeled back—and there is Leonid Gorev. The Devil's Brotherhood.

On-screen, the Los Angeles interrogation ends. Erica immediately calls Detective George Samuels. "Can we find out if a Leonid Gorev flew out to Los Angeles anytime in the month before May second, the day Barrish was killed?"

"We can try."

"Can you meet me tomorrow? I want to go over an idea I have."

"I hope it's a good one."

"How about at Mark's room at Rusk Rehab? We can check on his progress. And see if he's made any headway in locating the source of the ferry hacking."

Erica hangs up. Her thoughts are racing. *"They will kill me, even in prison they will kill me."* They killed Kay Barrish and Arturo Yanez. They almost killed Mark. And they may kill Fuentes. Would they think twice about killing Erica Sparks? Erica hugs herself and thinks of Jenny.

Chapter 61

Erica is at her desk on her fourth game of solitaire. And the cards aren't helping. Her mind is racing like a runaway train. Gorev and the Russian Mafia were involved in the attack on Mark, which means they were involved in the Staten Island ferry crash. Were they also behind Kay Barrish's murder? Were both the ferry and the murder acts of terrorism carried out by the Russian government, ordered and directed from the Kremlin? Or was Gorev hired by someone in this country to carry them out? If so, who? It's deeply disturbing to think that some person or organization or cabal in the United States would want—let alone have the means—to inflict this kind of trauma on the country. What would their motive be? Destabilizing our democracy? These are evil acts. Whoever engineered them is a psychopath. Just like that dog-torturer Fred Wilmot and his accomplice Nylan Hastings.

Fred Wilmot and Nylan Hastings. Erica stops mid-deal and the cards fall from her hands into an unruly pile on her desk. What was it Lois Wittmer said to her in the ladies' room at the White House Correspondents' Dinner?

"Isn't it great how you guys are always one

step ahead of the news? Awful coincidinky, if you ask me."

Claustrophobia grips Erica's neck like a noose. She quickly tosses out the absurd conjecture: that somehow Fred Wilmot and Nylan Hastings were involved in these crimes. They have too much to lose. But then again, the ferry crash caused ratings to soar, and Barrish's murder put GNN—and Erica—on the map. Erica feels her body flush with a wave of prickly heat. She has to move, to get out of this room, away from these thoughts.

She heads into the hall and toward the ladies' room. Suddenly the hallway—with its bland gray carpet and off-white walls—feels like a tunnel, a tunnel that leads to someplace dark and dangerous. And she can't turn back; there's no way out but forward.

There's no way out but forward.

Erica ducks into the ladies' room, heads over to the sink, grips its sides, and looks at herself in the mirror—*stay calm, stay calm.* She turns on the cold water and holds the insides of her wrists under it. The cold is soothing, her breathing slows down, her fevered imagination slowly cools.

She had a paranoid attack. Just like she did when her mom and dad left her alone for three days when she was five years old, and the only food in the house was a half-eaten bag of

Cheetos, and the heat was turned off because they hadn't paid the propane bill, and it was November in Maine, and Erica huddled under her skimpy covers sure that *they wanted her to die*—but it turned out they had just driven to the casino in Montreal on an amphetamine-fueled whim and won six hundred dollars, and they came back with a package of filet mignon, three bottles of champagne, and a gram of coke and had an all-night party to which Erica wasn't invited.

Of course Wilmot and Hastings had nothing to do with these crimes. Wilmot may have committed a heinous act as a ten-year-old, and Hastings may be a megalomaniac, but that doesn't mean they're capable of evil on this scale.

There's no way out but forward.

Journalism is about putting one foot in front of the other in an inexorable march toward the truth. There's no place for ridiculous imaginings, wild conjectures, off-the-wall theories. Facts are the only valid measures. Whoever committed these crimes put layers of cover between themselves and the actual perpetrators. In the Barrish murder they've uncovered Yanez, then Fuentes and Martinez, and now an unidentified Russian who may well be Leonid Gorev. She has to keep following that trail—it will lead her to the source.

"Awful coincidinky, if you ask me."

Chapter 62

Back in her office, Erica forces her mind to move on. It's not as if she doesn't have other pressing responsibilities. Like the guest list for her first show. Erica leaps at the task like it's a life preserver.

The show is generating lots of anticipatory buzz, and agents and press reps of politicians, entertainers, and athletes have all been making known their clients' availability. Erica wants to go big, wants to do something that's never been done before. But she doesn't want to strain to be original, or come off as desperate or cheesy or exploitative. She wants substance *and* she wants big names. She reminds herself that her audience is going to be predominantly women. She picks up her cards and deals a game.

She loses the game. Which is when an idea strikes.

Michelle Obama, Laura Bush, and Hillary Clinton together, talking about their heroes—the women who have most inspired and influenced their lives. Completely nonpartisan. The opposite, in fact. Unifying. Inspirational. Fascinating. Fun. And amazing, even historic, television.

Erica races down the hall toward Greg's office thinking, *I am going to make this happen.*

Chapter 63

Erica walks into Mark's room at Rusk Rehab to find him sitting at a table that has been turned into a makeshift desk. He sees her and breaks into a big smile. His computer is open in front of him, his iPad and several yellow legal pads beside it, and there's a printer on the floor.

"You're not wasting any time," Erica says, crossing to him. She puts her hands on his shoulders and gives the top of his head a kiss—scratchy stubble is coming in. He reaches up and squeezes her hand. How comfortable they are with each other, almost like they're brother and sister. His progress is amazing and she feels close to overwhelmed with some combination of affection, admiration, gratitude, and relief. This guy is a fighter, solid, and she feels like she's made a friend for life.

"I brought you a cronut," Erica says, handing him the bag.

"Are you t-try-ing to kill me?"

"Apparently you don't need me for that."

Mark takes the cronut out of the bag—it's slathered with neon-pink, allegedly raspberry frosting. He takes a bite.

"T-this is totally d-d-dis*gusting!*" he says, taking another gleeful chomp.

"I think that's the idea."

Detective Samuels walks in. "Is that a cronut?"

Mark nods and says, "Erica b-brought it."

"In that case, you're both under arrest for crimes against your waistline."

"Mark's been busy," Erica says.

Mark presses a button and the printer comes to life, spewing out several pages. He hands them to Erica—they contain Leonid Gorev's Skype account and password, Anton Volodin's phone number, his address in Moscow, his birth record, and his military service in the Russian navy.

"You found all this on the Internet?" Erica asks.

"You j-just have to know where to look," Mark says.

"Any luck determining the location of the ferry hackers?" Samuels asks.

"It's d-difficult. The hackers are v-very sophisticated."

"Is it hopeless?" Erica asks.

"No! I'm making p-progress. I'm p-p-pretty sure they are within a hundred miles of New York City."

"So are twenty million other people," Samuels says.

"O ye of little f-faith," Mark says.

"It's a job requirement."

"You wear it well," Erica says.

"Don't mean to be rude, but I w-w-want to get back to work."

"Here's your hat. What's your hurry?" Samuels says.

As soon as they're in the hallway, Erica asks, "Did you find Leonid Gorev on any passenger list?"

"No. He may have flown under an alias. When it comes to passports and other identifying documents, these people are expert forgers."

"Still, it's a setback."

The two of them head across First Avenue to a coffee shop and sit in a booth. After they order, she brings him up to date on the Barrish case. "So I've got these two separate investigations— the ferry crash and Barrish's murder. I see them as parallel tracks and it seems to me the tracks are converging—on Leonid Gorev."

"Who is just a point man for someone higher up the food chain," Samuels says. "Barrish's murder was a real-body blow to our country, and the ferry crash was a very effective act of terrorism. Could it be the Kremlin? I wouldn't put anything past Putin."

"We have to get Gorev to talk," Erica says. "The best way to do that would be a full confession from Volodin that he attacked Mark and that he was paid by Gorev to do it. We can then take that confession to Gorev and force him to spill."

"Unfortunately Volodin is in Moscow."

Erica holds up the printout from Mark. "But we have this. Does the NYPD have any contacts in the Moscow police?"

"We do."

"Do you have any Russian-speaking detectives on the force here?"

"Affirmative again. With the Russian Mafia expanding its reach in the city, they're in great demand."

"Would you consider sending one over to Moscow?" Erica asks. Samuels gives her a skeptical look.

Erica leans across the table and details her plan. Samuels considers it for a moment. Then he says, "Don't breathe a word of this to anybody. If Gorev knows we're getting close to him, he'll be on a flight out of the country before we can tie our shoes." He stands up and buttons his jacket. "And meet me at police headquarters in forty-eight hours."

Erica pushes away the cup of metallic-tasting coffee as the waitress comes over, plops down beside her and—without asking—takes a selfie of the two of them.

Chapter 64

It's the next morning and Erica is in her office, once again quelling her fears by throwing herself into her work. She's one phone call away from securing the Dream Team for her first show. She's already spoken to Michelle Obama and Hillary Clinton. They were both warm and friendly and agreed to appear. But without Laura Bush it won't be complete. Erica hates hyper-partisanship—she considers herself a militant moderate and wants the show to foster a sense of unity and shared purpose among viewers, no matter where they sit on the political spectrum. For that to happen she needs the final link.

The office phone rings.

"This is Erica Sparks."

"I have Laura Bush on the line," a woman's voice says.

"Erica, this is Laura." Her voice is welcoming.

"First of all, Mrs. Bush, I can't thank—"

"Please . . . *Laura*."

"As you can imagine, Laura, I'm a little nervous," Erica says.

"So am I."

They share a laugh. Why are famous women so much easier to deal with than famous men?

"I know my producer has outlined my vision for the segment with you, but let me elaborate. It's called 'Three First Ladies—Nine Extraordinary Women.' We'll open the show with the four of us discussing what it means to be First Lady, and especially the causes you espoused while you were in the White House. I know how passionate you are about literacy. And as someone who grew up in a house without books, I can't tell you how moved I was by your efforts."

"There's really nothing I enjoy more than curling up with a good book. And I must say that I was moved by your actions with Kay Barrish. She was a friend of mine," Laura says.

"It's a loss that continues to reverberate, isn't it?"

"I miss her," Laura says simply.

"After we talk, I want to introduce short segments on three women of your choosing—women who have inspired and enriched you in some way. Michelle and Hillary will do the same, and then we'll look for common threads."

"It sounds worthwhile—and great fun. I accept."

"You have just made my year."

"I'm always delighted to see my fellow First Ladies and compare war stories. Tell me, have Michelle and Hillary signed on?"

"They have, yes."

"Oh, so you reeled in the big fish first?" Laura says, tongue firmly in cheek.

They laugh. "Not at all. They just took the bait first."

"I'm not buying that—hook, line, *or* sinker."

Erica hangs up with a smile on her face. She can't believe she exchanged corny banter with a former First Lady. That she spoke to *three* First Ladies in one day. That they're all going to be on *her* show. She's about to call Greg and tell him the news when her prepaid rings. She walks into the closet before answering.

"Erica, it's George Samuels. We have a problem. Our contact in the Moscow police wants ten grand for 'operating expenses.'"

"Wow."

"I should have seen this coming."

"Can the NYPD pay it?"

"We have a no-bribe policy, which has a little give in it, but this case is too sketchy right now for anyone to sign off on a payment this size."

"So without the 10K, we're at a dead end."

"I'm afraid so."

"Let me work on this."

Erica hangs up. When you need water, you go to the deepest well. She goes back to her desk and calls Nylan—thank God he can't see that her hands are shaking.

"Erica," he says in a flat voice.

Erica ignores his antipathy and says brightly, "I just had the nicest chat with Laura Bush. She's in. As are Hillary and Michelle."

"This is the kind of thing you should be focused on."

"Your faith in me has made it all possible," Erica says, laying it on thick.

"I hope that faith continues," Nylan says.

"I do have one other issue. I'm working on a story about price fixing by the major drug companies. Millions of Americans are forced to sacrifice their financial security to pay for drugs they need to stay alive. This is major. I have a source who swears he can deliver incriminating documents. But he wants to be paid for his services."

There's a pause, and Erica can almost hear Nylan switching gears. His voice stays casual, but the undertone goes from honey to ice. "Erica, I want you charming First Ladies, not chasing half-baked conspiracy theories."

"This isn't—"

"I want to leverage your star power, not squander it. There's nothing sexy about price fixing."

Erica feels frustration boiling in her veins. This man is acting like he owns her. *Like he owns her.* Time to cut her losses. And she can hardly claim the moral high ground.

"All right, Nylan. I'll move on." *I sure will move on.*

"That's my star talking."

Erica hangs up, walks back into the closet, and

calls Samuels. "I've got the money," she tells him. "How do you want it?"

Samuels gives her the transfer codes for the Moscow bank account. Then she heads out to her bank.

Chapter 65

NYPD headquarters is tucked between City Hall and the Brooklyn Bridge, at the southern edge of New York's vast Chinatown. Nearby are two imposing courthouses—one federal, one state— and other magnificent municipal buildings. Erica is awed by the grandeur.

Police Plaza, on the other hand, is a hulking, brutalist box dating to the early 1970s when Americans were rioting in the streets and public architecture crouched into a defensive posture. Erica wonders what they would build today if given the chance—surely something with more grace and fidelity to its stately neighbors.

Erica passes through security, where she is greeted with smiles of recognition, and heads up to the eighth floor. The windowless conference room is nondescript, with just a table and chairs. Samuels is alone in the room, sitting in front of a large-screen laptop with Gorev's Skype account open on the screen. He's talking on a landline, is serious and keyed-up.

"Hang on, Ed," he says into the phone, putting it down on the table before turning to Erica. "We're just about ready to go."

Erica nods, her pulse quickens, her breathing grows shallow—if this doesn't work, her investigation will hit a dead end.

"It's one a.m. in Moscow, the lights are out in Volodin's apartment," Samuels says. "We want to wake him up, get him when he's groggy and vulnerable."

"And probably half drunk," Erica says. She sits down next to Samuels close enough to see the screen but not so close as to be in the computer's camera eye.

Samuels picks up the landline and asks, "You ready? . . . Great. Hang tight." Samuels dials on Skype. The phone rings. And rings. And then it's answered—a bleary-eyed, underwear-clad Volodin appears on-screen.

"Leonid, it's the middle of the night," he croaks, not yet focused.

"I hate to interrupt your beauty sleep, Volodin, but this isn't Leonid. It's Detective Samuels of the New York Police Department." Samuels holds up his badge as he barks "Go!" into the landline. Suddenly there's violent knocking on the door of Volodin's apartment and shouted commands in Russian.

Volodin's head spins from the computer to the door and back. "We've positively identified you as Mark Benton's assailant!" Samuels shouts as the knocking and yelling from outside the apartment grows louder. And then there's a crash as the door is kicked in. Volodin tries to scramble over the back of the sofa as two men—one a Moscow plainclothes cop who looks like he's about six foot six of pure muscle, the other Detective Joe Ortiz of the NYPD—grab him and slap on handcuffs. "You're under arrest for the attempted murder of Mark Benton," Samuels says.

"You're coming back to New York with me," Ortiz says.

"That's right, Anton, we got the extradition papers all ready to file. Right, Serge?"

"Yes!" the Russian cop hisses.

"You're going to be standing trial for assault with a deadly weapon and attempted murder. Those punches left some evidence behind— your skin cells and DNA. We've also got positive identification from a witness. You're toast. Say good-bye to Moscow because you won't see it again in this lifetime."

Volodin's swagger is a distant memory—he looks completely dazed, lost, desperately trying to gather himself and make sense of what's happening.

"You look pretty pathetic, Anton," Samuels continues. "You're a two-bit thug, a worthless worm. I wish we could just off you and get it over with, save everybody a lot of time and money. You sicken me."

Volodin's jaw drops open and he looks down.

"Look at me, you creep!"

Ortiz and the Russian cop each grab an arm and yank Volodin up. He raises his eyes.

"You're a spineless worm. A cheap thug for hire. I'm after bigger fish than you. You tell me what I want right now and I'll try and cut you a deal."

"Can I stay in Russia?" Volodin asks.

"I'm asking the questions. Who hired you to beat up Mark Benton?"

"If I talk, you will get me a deal?"

"Depends on what you say. I'll tell you this though—you *don't* talk and you're looking at twenty in prison. There are no women in prison, Anton, no vodka, no cars, no nothing. Just a cellmate who might take a liking to your young Russian ass."

There's a pause, and then Volodin spits at the camera. Serge slams his fist into Volodin's face— blood spurts from his cheek.

"There's more where that came from. Now who hired you to assault Mark Benton?" Samuels demands.

Something hard sets in Volodin's face as self-preservation takes over. He shakes free of Ortiz and Serge and looks right into the camera. "Leonid Gorev."

"How much did he pay you?"

"Fifteen thousand dollars."

"And you worked for him at the time?"

"I stole cars for him."

"So on the morning of May second at approximately five thirty, you waited across the street from Mark Benton's apartment at 704 Greenwich Street. When you saw him come out of the building, you followed him onto Charles Street and attacked him."

"Yes."

"Aside from your fists, what did you use?"

"Pliers from the car garage."

"Did you think you had killed him?"

"I was paid to kill him."

"Do you know why?"

"Because he was too curious about what happened to the ferryboat."

Erica leans in.

"Why did Gorev care about the ferryboat?"

"He didn't," Volodin snorts in derision.

Erica and Samuels exchange a glance—they're getting close.

"So somebody paid Gorev to hire you?"

"Smart American policeman. Give him a gold star."

"Who paid Gorev?"

"You think he would tell me? I'm just a stupid worm thug."

"Once again—who paid Gorev?"

"Take off the handcuffs."

296

"Take them off," Samuels says, and the cops do it. Volodin shakes out his hands, wipes at the blood on his face.

"Some woman."

"What was her name?"

"I don't know her name."

"What did she look like?"

"I only heard her on the phone with Leonid. After they talk about the money, she tries to sell him an apartment house."

"Sell him *an apartment house?*" Samuels asks.

"He said she sounds like a leprechaun. Then he says leprechauns eat babies." Volodin laughs.

"So he was contacted by a real estate agent with an Irish accent to have Benton beat up?"

Volodin makes a mock-clueless expression. "Stupid worm don't know."

Samuels mutes his voice. "So, Erica, we've got his confession and he's nailed Gorev. Is there anything else?"

Erica looks at Volodin on the screen, his sleazebag bravado back in place, and she thinks of Mark in his room at Rusk Rehab. She wishes she could kick right through the screen and knock that smirk off his face. "Is this enough to get him extradited?" she asks.

"We're sure going to try."

"I can't think of anything else."

Samuels unmutes. "All right, Volodin, we're done with you."

"I told you what you want. Can I stay in Russia?"

Samuels turns to Erica and smiles before turning back to the screen. "Sure you can, buddy, sure you can."

They hang up. Erica's first thought is how skillful Samuels is. He got everything they needed out of Volodin—and more.

Back at GNN, Erica calls Madge Miller, her agent on the Eighty-First Street property, and asks if she can drop into her office this afternoon. Madge readily agrees, telling her that the contracts have been signed and they can set a closing date when she arrives. And while they're at it, Erica thinks, help her find a leprechaun with an apartment building to sell.

Erica hangs up. She feels like she's getting close with her investigation. Yes, there have been fits and starts, but by keeping her eye on the prize—the truth—she's been able to make steady progress. But it has come at a price. She's afraid. Her imagination keeps leading her into some dark places.

Erica takes out her cards and deals a hand. Her office phone rings and she starts. *Blocked* comes up on the caller ID.

"This is Erica."

"Hi, sweetie, it's your mommy."

Chapter 66

Erica can't remember the last time she spoke to her mother, but it's been at least six or seven years. It might as well have been yesterday—she feels that familiar mix of rage, vulnerability, and hurt bubble up inside her, the toxic alchemy that defined her childhood. Sitting in her fancy office with its view of Central Park, she feels at a loss, hollow at her very core, as if the ground has been pulled out from under her. She can handle thugs and First Ladies, murder and sabotage, fame and men, but she's not sure she can handle "mommy." She struggles to maintain her emotional footing.

"Hi, Susan," she says flatly.

"Oh, honey, it feels so good to hear your voice, my little sweetie girl."

Yeah, the little sweetie girl you ignored, belittled, and abused.

Erica lets the pause, the tension between them, just hang there. She's not throwing out a lifeline to this woman.

Finally her mother says, "Well, honey, aren't you going to ask how your old mama is doing?" Her voice sounds raspy and ragged after decades of cigarettes and pot.

Erica says nothing.

"I turned fifty this year. AARP sent me something in the mail. They want me to join!" she says, laughing. The laughing sets off a coughing fit, which sets off a hacking fit. Charming.

AARP, huh? I'm not sure you can retire from welfare.

"I fell and broke my arm, honey. I'm all laid up. And my car died. I miss your daddy. I'm awful lonesome, sweetie."

Erica's father took off for points unknown when she was still at Yale. At the time she held out faint hope that having that pig out of the house would lead to Susan pulling herself together a little bit. But no, it just added one more notch to her self-pity belt.

Erica reaches for her deck of cards. Susan hasn't asked her one question about how she's doing, about her life, her success, Jenny. Erica doesn't have time for this. She knows where this call is heading and she decides to take a shortcut.

"How much do you want, Susan?"

"What did you say, pumpkin?"

"I asked you how much money you wanted."

"Oh, Erica, sweetie, I don't want any money. I just wanted to talk to you, to get back in touch with my little girl. There isn't a day goes by that I don't miss you. I was looking at the sweetest picture of you and me the other day, on the swing set back behind Kennedy Elementary. Rcmember that day, honey? I came to pick you up from school like I always did, like I mostly did, and that nice man said hello to me. He was a cafeteria food salesman, he was at Kennedy to talk to the principal. Do you remember, honey? Handsome and well-dressed and he was flirting with your mommy and I grabbed your hand and pulled you over to the swing set and we each got in a swing and had a contest to see who could swing higher and the man was laughing and I swung higher than you but then I let you win 'cause that's what mommies do, and he took our picture and then when he came back to Kennedy, it was on a day when I didn't pick you up and he gave you the picture and you brought it home. I always wondered, honey, what would've happened if I *had* picked you up from school that day. That man was sweet on me, I was just a little twenty-three-year-old thing, cute as a button. Remember how cute I was, honey? I bet he lived in a *nice* house. All carpets and cozy with a big screen and ice cream. We could have lived there, pumpkin. I know he wanted to marry me, we had *chemistry*. But I didn't pick you up that day. You asked me not to. Sometimes I think you were *ashamed* of me."

You got that right—I was ashamed of you. And I still am.

And now Erica feels something worse than anger coming on—sadness. A terrible, cosmic sadness about her mother's terrible, sad life. Susan grew up poor, her parents were illiterate, she dropped out of school at thirteen, never visited a doctor or a dentist, had an abortion at fifteen, the year before she met Erica's father and got pregnant again. She never had a chance in this world. Poor Susan. Poor, sad Susan. Erica feels herself falling into a black chasm, an abyss of grief and longing and pity for her mother.

No! It's not an abyss, it's a trap, a trap set by Susan, to play on those very emotions. Yes, she had it rough, but so do millions of other people—people like Erica herself, thank you very much—and they don't turn into monsters who abuse their children, they don't retreat into a netherworld of pot and pills. Erica feels herself pulling back from the black chasm, into the here and now, into the life she has built for herself, through hard work and tenacity and respect for herself and others. When she fell—and she fell far—she picked herself up, patched herself together, and got back in the game. She doesn't owe this woman—this Susan, her mother—anything.

"I've got a very busy day ahead of me," Erica says.

"So do I. Thank God I got a taxi voucher to take me to Hannaford, otherwise I would starve to death right here in this lousy dump."

"I'll send you a check for a thousand dollars," Erica says, wanting to be over and out.

"Oh, honey, I told you I don't want your money. If you send me a check, I'll just rip it up into tiny pieces," Susan says, her voice growing quivery as the tears start to flow. "I just want us to be friends again, like we were that day on the swing. I know I wasn't the greatest mommy, I wasn't an Oprah mommy, I even know I was a bad mommy some-times, but I was dealing with that sonofabitch father of yours, I just always loved you, you were my little tidbit, my little Necco wafer, and I'm so proud of you, baby girl, of everything you've done, oh, baby girl . . ." Now she's drowning in her tears, sniffling, bawling.

In spite of everything, the tears get to Erica. She can't help it, can't stop it, it's her *mother*— the woman who gave her life, brought her into the world, and Erica does have some early memories of her mother smiling at her, holding her up and nuzzling her, talking silly talk, squeezing and hugging her. Loving her. Does her mother love her? She wants so much for her mother to love her. And not to cry. *Please don't cry, Mommy.*

And now Erica's throat is tight and her eyes are wet and she can't let her mother know she's crying, but she can't stop and they're crying together and she wants to forgive . . . to forgive this poor, sad woman her sins as she wants to be forgiven for *her* sins. It's the only way forward . . . to a healed heart. And they cry and they let themselves cry and it feels cleansing.

"Oh, baby . . . my sweetie baby . . ." Susan sobs.

The crying tapers off and there's a strange silence between them—to Erica it feels as if the plates have shifted, they're in uncharted territory . . . Is a fresh start really possible? It will take baby steps at first . . . baby steps . . . baby and mommy steps . . .

"Can I call you again, sweetie?" Susan asks.

Erica takes several deep breaths. "Yes, yes you can."

"Maybe we can be . . . friends," Susan says.

"Maybe we can."

"Can I ask you one question, pumpkin sweet?"

"Of course, ask me anything."

"Like I said, my car died, and living up here you just *need* a car, you need one, otherwise you go crazy, people freeze to death up here, they freeze and starve to death, you remember how cold it is, sweetie, and my friend Wilbur—yes, Mommy has a special friend—has found a Honda Accord with only 58,000 miles on it and it's only six thou, and if you could loan me the money, I'll pay you back on a regular payment schedule 'cause I'm going to go down and apply for a job at Walmart. Could you do that for your old mommy?"

A door—a thick metal overhead door, the kind bullets bounce off of—slides shut in Erica's heart and mind and soul. What was that old song? "Won't Get Fooled Again"? Yeah right, fat chance.

You are a fool, Erica. Only a fool would go back to a dry well again and again hoping that by some miracle she would find it full of water.

Erica sits up in her chair, throws back her shoulders. This is over, o-v-e-r, *over*. "I'll send you a check today."

Susan starts to gush with gratitude and promises, but Erica is deaf to them. She hangs up and feels a dark hole where—just ten minutes earlier—her heart had been.

Chapter 67

Erica is in Madge Miller's office at Sotheby's Real Estate on East Sixty-First Street. The office is perfectly organized and decorated in soothing beiges. Madge herself—in her understated gray dress and pearls, glasses on a chain around her neck and hair in a bun—seems like a throwback to a more genteel New York. This is exactly the kind of calm, ordered place that Erica needs to be in right now. The call from her mother left her rattled; demons she thought she'd conquered flared back to life, screeching, teeth bared, red eyes glowing.

Madge looks at Erica—there's concern in her

eyes. "How about a cup of tea? We have some lovely herbals."

"That actually sounds nice," Erica says. She never drinks herbal tea.

Madge presses her intercom. "Rufus, could I get a cup of chamomile-lavender for Ms. Sparks? . . . So, we're all ready to close. I must say, Erica, I think you've made a very good decision. It's a lovely apartment."

Rufus—young, wearing an expensive suit—brings in Erica's tea. She holds it up and inhales the gentle fragrance, takes a sip—it's soothing. Madge is soothing. Why can't Madge be her mother—this lovely, understated, understanding woman.

"Does June fifteenth work for you? That's in two weeks and gives us time to make sure all the t's are crossed."

Erica takes another sip of tea—the office is soothing too, immaculate and ordered and sane, and her chair is so comfortable.

"Erica?" Madge gently prompts.

Erica is pulled out of her reverie. "Oh, I'm sorry. It's been an . . . *intense* day."

Madge chuckles in sympathy. "We all have those."

"The fifteenth works."

"It's very exciting."

"I can hardly believe it," Erica says. She pictures her mother, back from Hannaford, unloading her beer and frozen pizza and Little Debbie snacks in her kitchen with its grimy corners and cheap cabinets and long-busted dishwasher. Erica doesn't feel a lick of guilt about her new apartment, not a drop, not a crumb, not a scintilla. Why would she? How could she? She sits up straight, puts the teacup on a table.

"Listen, Madge, I wonder if you could help me with something?"

"I'd be delighted to try."

"I'm trying to track down a real estate agent who has an apartment building for sale."

"Erica, there are over twenty thousand real estate agents in this city. It's true that the majority of us don't deal in apartment houses, but you're still talking about a large number. Do you have any other information?"

"She's a woman. And she has a strong Irish accent."

"The Irish accent helps. Most brokers from abroad try to lose their accents. Except the British—high-end buyers love a British accent. Irish? Not so much. So if this woman has retained her brogue, it may be because she considers it an asset. Which means she may have a largely Irish customer base. Which means she may operate in one of the city's remaining Irish enclaves."

"Which are?"

"There's Marine Park and Gerritsen Beach in Brooklyn, Broad Channel and Sunnyside in

Queens, Woodlawn in the northern Bronx. Many of these old neighborhoods still have mom-and-pop real estate agencies. Hold on, let me do a quick search." Madge starts typing. "I'll just get the zip codes for those neighborhoods . . . Here we go . . . Now let's do a zip code search for real estate agencies . . . Okay." Pages start to flow out of her printer. She hands them to Erica. "Here you go."

Erica looks down at the list of about two dozen agencies. "Madge, if you ever want to switch careers, let me know. My show is hiring researchers."

Madge smiles in bemusement. "I'm not sure you could meet my quote."

"I'm sure we couldn't. I can't thank you enough."

"My pleasure. And your request was easy. I've had clients ask me to babysit."

"Don't give me any ideas."

Back at her office, Erica starts working her way down the list. When she tells them she's interested in investing in a small apartment building, most tell her they have none listed. And the two agents that do have buildings also have New York accents. It's drudgework and she's beginning to wonder if maybe she's barking up the wrong list. She reaches the last neighbor-hood, Woodlawn in the Bronx. She calls Celtic Home Realty.

"Welcome to Celtic Home, your home away from the homeland," says a woman with a lilting Irish accent that she's milking for all it's worth.

Erica sits up straight, suddenly alert and focused. "Hi, my name is Erica Sparks."

"Now why does that name ring a bell?"

"You may have seen me on television."

"I'm not a big one for television, but never mind that. I'm Fiona Connor. How can I help you today?"

"I'm thinking of investing in some real estate. I know how strong the rental market is, and I'm considering a small apartment house."

"Well, you've come to the right place. I've got a nice little apartment building, eight units, been in the same family for forty-two years, maintained with great Irish pride. Would you like to schedule an appointment?"

"I would, yes. Does tomorrow morning work for you?"

After the call, Erica feels restless and out of sorts. She gets up and paces, goes to the window—down below rush hour is starting and thousands of workers are pouring out of office buildings and joining the throngs on the already crowded streets in a great surging wave of humanity. The sight only exacerbates her loneliness. She feels like there's a piece missing from her essential self, that no matter what she does or how far she travels, something is *off,* that her family's sickness and depravity and self-sabotage is hardwired into her DNA.

And then there's her fear, which has grown constant—sitting still has become difficult, getting to sleep has become a nightly battle. In the long, dark hours she falls prey to terrifying thoughts, horrible scenarios—many involving Jenny being harmed. She feels a sudden, overwhelming urge to see her daughter. She picks up her phone.

Dirk answers. "Hello, Erica."

"Hi, Dirk. How are you?"

"Pretty well. Linda and I are engaged." Is there an edge of gloating in his voice?

"Oh. Well, that's . . . that's wonderful."

"Yes, yes it is. Jenny will have a complete family. Which she needs at this point in her life."

The dig hurts but Erica ignores it. "May I speak to her?"

"Hmm . . . yes. Okay."

"I'd like to come up and see her."

"Aren't you swamped? I saw a promo for your new show."

"I am busy, but I'd like to see my daughter. I could fly up, just for an afternoon."

"It took her a week to get back in the groove after her trip to New York. As I predicted, your glamorous life unsettled her. It seemed to exacerbate her insecurities."

What a lousy thing for him to say. When they

first got together, Erica confided in Dirk, told him about her childhood, about Susan, about her own insecurities and fears about motherhood. She had no role model and hoped the combination of her maternal instincts, common sense, and abiding love would guide her. She wants to be a good mother more than anything in the world, to break the chain of negligence and abuse that| goes back for generations in her family. All her other success will be meaningless if she fails at that. For him to throw that in her face is a low blow. She wants to lash out at him, to defend herself, to say that Jenny seemed excited and enriched by her New York experience. But she knows that— at least for now—Dirk holds the cards.

"Well, if I come up to Massachusetts, that shouldn't be a problem. Jenny and I could go out to lunch, go to a museum, maybe do a little shopping."

"If you take her shopping and buy her a lot of fancy things, she'll start comparing it to what I'm able to buy her."

"Does that mean that I'm never allowed to spend money on my daughter?"

He has no answer to that question.

"Listen, Dirk, you know I'm in recovery. I haven't had a drink in over two years. I've apologized to you for my past behaviors. You told me you accepted my apologies, but I'm not so sure."

Erica can sense him softening.

"I know you've worked hard, Erica."

"Jenny is *our* child. Our marriage may not have worked out, but it produced a wonderful young woman we can both be proud of."

"Yes, yes it did. Hold on, I'll get Jenny. And, yes, you can come up and see her."

"Thank you, Dirk." Erica waits, and in a moment Jenny comes to the phone.

"Hi, Mom."

"It's so great to hear your voice. I've missed you. How's school?"

"It's good. I had a lot of fun in New York."

"Did you?"

"Yes. Dad doesn't like me to talk about it, but I did. I think he's jealous."

Erica allows herself a small gloating smile. "Well, dads can be like that sometimes. But he loves you very much."

"I like to watch you on TV in my bedroom. I like Linda okay, but she's not my real mother."

In that moment Erica learns something new: tears can just start to flow. Without warning, without fanfare and sobs and sniffles, they just flow, like water from a spring.

"I'd like to come up and see you, hang out for a day," she manages.

"Cool."

They chat about this and that, easy banter, mom-and-daughter stuff, for a few more minutes.

When Erica hangs up, she feels a tentative confidence. She's not an iota like her own mother. She *is* breaking the chain, the sad, sordid legacy. She's giving Jenny confidence and support and guidance. She's a real mother. She's not a fraud. She's an imperfect woman doing the best she knows how.

Erica's prepaid rings. It's Mark. She goes into the closet.

"Hey there, Mark."

"Erica, I'm g-getting close. The f-ferry was h-hacked from somewhere in Man-hattan."

Erica's short hairs stand up. "Do you think you'll be able to pinpoint the exact location?"

"Yes."

Erica hangs up and starts to pace. The ferry crash has fallen off the news, but when they can identify the terrorists, Erica will be sitting on a story every bit as big as Barrish's murder. And it will be her exclusive. But the closer she gets to the truth, the more of a threat she becomes to the perpetrators. Erica feels a sudden chill. She goes back to the closet and slips into a cardigan, hugs herself—but the chill remains. Then she closes her office door and leans against it, slowly sinking to the floor.

Chapter 68

The boat is rocking, rocking slightly in the wake of a cruise ship that lumbered past filled with three thousand peons off to spend a drunken week trying to forget their crummy, meaningless lives. Nylan chuckles. People are so pathetic. He picks up the bottle of Roederer Cristal—off the teak table, handmade in Antwerp, that sits on the deck of the yacht *Universe*, handmade in the Lürssen shipyard in Bremen—and pours himself another glass. The boat, which cost $143 million to build, is only a toy. An amusement, a divertissement, a plush little ha-ha. Fun, yes, but he's after much bigger game. And he has it in his sights. He doesn't wear jewelry, but if he did, they'd all be on their knees waiting to kiss the ring and grant him three wishes—unless he wanted six: presidents, prime ministers, movie stars, popes, titans of the brave new world. *Kiss the ring. Kiss my ass. Kiss of death.*

Nylan looks out at the glittering Hudson, up at the glittering Manhattan skyline. All hail! GNN has roared into the black, defying expectations. Just two years ago he founded the network from scratch and now it's in the stratosphere, the highest-rated cable news network. He's on the cover of *Fortune* and too many other magazines and websites to count, he's being begged to join consortiums developing ski resorts in the Andes and building artificial islands in the Red Sea, he's preparing a TED Talk, publishers are clamoring for a book, Donald Trump—that bloated, orange-faced freak—wants to be his BFF. He could go on. And on—he's surfing the crest of the biggest swell in history. But he won't go on. Because tonight is about humility. Nylan looks up to the glowing night sky, to the planets and stars, and knows he's just a speck, just a wink of a blink in the ceaseless tide of eternity. How could he be anything *but* humble?

And here come Fred Wilmot and Dave Mullen walking down the dock! This night is about *them*. He loves them. No, he does. Really. They're his true friends. His soul mates. His partners. His puppets.

The two men walk across the ramp and make their way up to the aft deck. Nylan hands them each a glass of Roederer.

"To an epic night," he toasts. They clink and sip and smile, the anticipation among them palpable, pulsing, tumescent.

"How about a little amuse-bouche to start the festivities?" Dave Mullen asks in his deeply hip drawl. In spite of his laid-back manner, he looks drawn, anxious around the edges. He takes out a small silver box, presses a button on the side, and the lid pops open—it's filled with sparkly white powder.

"That looks delicious," Nylan says. Dave hands him a silver straw and he dips down and *snorts* and a sweet shot of ecstasy shoots through him.

But something's wrong; Fred is looking so serious. "Frederick—why the long face?" Nylan asks.

"We have a little problem. It's blonde and very inquisitive."

"She's a temporary irritation, not a problem," Nylan scoffs.

"A new poll came out today. She's now the second-most-admired woman in America after the First Lady."

"So what? She's just about outlived her usefulness at this point."

Outlived her usefulness. Nylan loves that phrase. It has so many implications, it promises so much. Death. Death is such a beautiful thing. The finality. The removal. The power.

"That's just the thing, Nylan, I'm not sure she *has* outlived her usefulness. Her effect on ratings and social media is instantaneous. Commercial time on her show is presold for four months at 600K for thirty seconds. The money is gushing in. It's what sent us into the black. But it feels like a house of cards—if we lose her, it could all come tumbling down. We *need* her."

Nylan hates the idea of *needing* anybody. All

316

Nylan has ever needed is Nylan. Fred can be such a wuss sometimes. But Nylan is no fool, he's not about to shoot the messenger. "So she's as inquisi-tive as ever?"

"I've detected an unknown presence," Mullen says. Then he takes a snort and then two more. His eyes are darting around. "I don't like unknown presences. They mess with my head."

Nylan starts to pace. He can feel anger rising in his veins. And a begrudging respect for the white-trash blonde. He underestimated her. But, seriously, who does she think she's playing with? She has *no* idea.

"I have the goods on her," Nylan says.

"I know you do, Nylan, but if we destroy her reputation, where does that leave us?"

Nylan pays Wilmot *a lot* of money to ask these tough questions. But that doesn't mean he likes to hear them. And he can't believe that boozy little trailer-trash blonde has backed him into this corner. It's time to turn on the cunning tap and let it flow.

Think.

He *does* need her. For now. Until he can replace her. With another star. He has to make that happen. Soon. *Very* soon. That's really all he needs. Once he has another girl—and he'll find one—Erica Sparks will suffer a tragic and unfortunate death. There are so many creative ways to kill a person. Maybe a drive-by shooting as she walks to work—a single bullet to the brain. Fired by some pathetic soon-to-die lackey.

Think of the publicity her death will bring. The network will go into collective mourning, broadcast her funeral live, set up a foundation in her name that provides journalism scholarships. And then, tears still flowing, the next GNN superstar will be introduced on a wave of sympathy and goodwill.

Nylan takes another snort. What a beautiful plan, stunning in its simplicity.

But it has to happen soon. Mullen is jittery. And Mullen never gets jittery. It's time to send Erica Sparks out in a blaze of glory. One last story that transcends even Kay Barrish's death. That cements her place in history. But what? What? Nylan's wheels start racing faster, faster, *faster.*

He takes another snort, Dave and Fred follow. "Hey, cheer up, baby boys, Daddy's got this one. Everything is under control. Now let's have some fun!" Nylan goes over to a console on the wall and presses a button. Bruno Mars comes on the speakers and Nylan does a little dance. It's a tingly New York night—

And here come the girls. Down on the dock, three of them, long-legged, young and beautiful with long hair and short skirts and smooth skin and perfect bodies. One black, one Asian, one blonde—just what Nylan ordered. And Nylan owns them. He *owns* them. And he loves owning them. Fred arranged it, he's good at things like that. Fred has contacts, contacts that reach right down, right down into the sweet underbelly of pleasure and pain and pull out . . . beautiful girls like these.

And now they're boarding and now they're in the main cabin and now they're snorting and sipping and now Nylan takes the blonde's hand and leads her down, down into his suite and locks the door behind them and takes her beautiful, perfect face in his hands.

"I'm so happy to see you . . . ," he purrs. He leans in and kisses her oh-so-gently on her lovely lips. ". . . Erica." And then he hauls back and slaps her hard, really hard, and tears fill her eyes and a little trail of blood trickles down from the corner of her mouth. She's a good girl. And the suite is soundproofed. No one will hear her screams.

Chapter 69

Erica dresses way down, with her unflattering floppy hat and large sunglasses in place, and walks across town to Lexington Avenue, where she ducks into the subway and catches the 4 train to its northern terminus in the Bronx—Wood-lawn. As with Flushing and its Koreans, and

Brighton Beach and its Russians, she finds herself in an insular ethnic enclave. The main shopping street, Katonah Avenue, is lined with pubs—Mulligan's, Behan's, Coachman's Inn— that offer "rashers and Guinness." A grocery store window displays pickled beetroot and "bread flown in from Dublin." There are shamrocks everywhere, and a large mural painted on the side of a building features fiddlers and football players. Above the stores are small apartment buildings, and the side streets are lined with a mix of single-family houses and more small apartment houses. The faces Erica passes are, with rare exceptions, white and on the ruddy side.

Celtic Home Realty is a small, nondescript storefront. Erica walks in and a little bell rings. There are two desks, several filing cabinets, and a small seating area. A large map of Ireland is on one wall and a map of Woodlawn on another. A woman of around fifty—short, chunky, sour-faced, her hair dyed a garish red and styled into a series of tight undulating waves—is on the phone exchanging unpleasantries. When she sees Erica, she quickly ends the call and stands.

"You must be Erica Sparks."

"And you're Fiona Connor."

They shake hands. Fiona has a handshake like a prizefighter, and under her smile Erica sees a set jaw and shrewd little eyes.

"I did a little poking around, and now I know

who you are," Fiona says, folding her arms over her chest. She's dropped the thick-as-marmalade brogue.

"I hope you won't hold it against me."

"Hardly. We Irish love the green—and it sounds like you've got plenty." She laughs mirthlessly. "So, have a seat and tell me what you're looking for."

"I'm suddenly making a fair amount of money, and my financial adviser says I should consider investing in real estate. He advised a stable neighborhood and something multiunit."

"Well, you've come to the right place. Wood-lawn is as solid as you can get. Very few properties come up for public sale. We prefer to do things by word of mouth—it helps to preserve the . . . *character* of the neighborhood. Other-wise we'd be overrun."

A young man walks into the office from the street. He's skinny and jittery—his whole body seems to be quivering. Gray skin, greasy hair, desperate sunken eyes: Erica doesn't need a blood test to spot a junkie. Fiona's mouth turns down in annoyance.

"Hey, Ma."

"Can't you see I'm with a customer?" She turns and gives Erica an oily smile. "This is my boy, Desmond."

Desmond's darting eyes look over at Erica. "Hey there," he says. "Listen, Ma, some creep sideswiped my side mirror. I need two hundred bucks for the repair." His eyes are glassy with need.

Fiona shakes her head, and her tight little mouth gets tighter still. Clearly she's been through this scene a hundred times before. If Erica wasn't there, who knows how she would react. But she wants Desmond to disappear, so she opens her purse, withdraws two bank-fresh hundreds, and hands them to him.

"Hey, thanks, Ma, I'll pay you back as soon as I get my paycheck. I swear it, I will."

"I think a job comes before a paycheck."

"You're the best, Ma." He lurches toward her and kisses her cheek. Then he turns and rushes out of the office.

Fiona looks after him in anger and disgust, then turns all business. "The building is eight units, the rent roll is 12K a month, the price is $750,000. Good return on investment, especially if you're paying cash money. Would you like to go take a look at the property?"

They leave the office and set out along Katonah Avenue. Fiona has a peculiar heavy step, slightly bowlegged, almost a tromp. She nods to several people they pass, but Erica notices that the returned greetings are far from effusive. In fact, some people seem to shrink from her. They reach a handsome four-story redbrick building. Fiona unlocks the front door—the small lobby is freshly painted.

"All the apartments are identical one-bedrooms, two apartments a floor, no elevator. Good for the legs. There's one vacant unit. Follow me."

They climb to the second floor. The unit is also freshly painted, light and spacious, with a galley kitchen and original black-and-white tile bath.

"This place would easily rent for eighteen hundred a month. I'll find you a *nice* tenant. Whenever you have a vacancy, you come to me. I fill it."

Erica looks at her, incredulous. Fiona shrugs. "That's how we do business around here. Like I said, we have to protect the character of the neighborhood."

"Funny, Leonid Gorev didn't mention anything about you finding the tenants."

Fiona's head jerks—she quickly catches herself, but now there's a feral look in her eyes. "Leonid Gorev? Never heard the name before in my life."

"That's funny, he referred me to you. He said that the two of you do business together."

Fiona purses her mouth, turns and runs her fingertip along a windowsill and then turns it over, checking for dirt. "I do business with a lot of people."

"Do you?"

Fiona sucks on her teeth with exaggerated nonchalance. "I'm from Belfast. I left because of the Troubles. I don't like trouble."

"Who does?"

"Some people make trouble for themselves."

"That's true. They put themselves in the middle of things. And then they get squeezed from both sides. Just as an example, someone could have . . . oh, I don't know . . . Leonid Gorev on one side. And on the other side . . ."

"You interested in the building or not?"

"I need a little more information."

"You're the curious type, aren't you?"

Erica looks at Fiona's hard-set, shrewd little face. She's not going to get anything more out of her today. "Let me think about it. Thanks for your time." She crosses to the front door. "I'll show myself out."

Chapter 70

For the rest of the day, Erica fights her frustration. She feels like she's so close, but with a murder investigation *close* doesn't cut it. She has another lousy night, tossing in bed, edgy and fearful, filled with dark thoughts, and in the morning she feels aggravated, thwarted, fidgety, out of sorts—as if a way forward is tantalizingly close, in front of her but just out of her grasp. She sits up in bed and replays her time with Fiona. Her mind keeps going back to Desmond. If she could get to him at the right time—aka when he needs a fix—she might be able to buy a little information pretty cheap. Or maybe Samuels could apply a little pressure on him—after all, heroin possession is a felony.

Erica skips her morning Tae Kwon Do. She just can't focus, and she can't eat either—she's too keyed up. An appetite seems like some distant luxury. She flips on the local news. The anchor reports on a large hurricane forming in the south Atlantic and heading northwest toward Florida, and then says, "Now let's go to reporter Gabriella Garcia in the Woodlawn neighborhood of the Bronx, where a well-known local business-woman was killed in a tragic hit-and-run accident last night."

The screen cuts to Garcia: "I'm standing on the corner of Katonah Avenue and East 237th Street where, at just after eleven o'clock last night, Fiona Connor was walking her Rottweiler when a car ran a red light and struck her. The vehicle did not stop. Connor, fifty-seven, was pronounced dead at the scene. The lone eyewitness, an eighty-two-year-old male, is reported to be in shock and unable to recall any details about the accident."

Accident? I don't think so.

Erica switches off the set. She fights to contain the fear that floods over her. Another dead body. Another hit. Another killing. But under the fear, she senses an opening. Her hands shake slightly as she calls Fiona's office.

A woman's voice answers, "Celtic Home."

"This is Erica Sparks, I was a client of Fiona's. I'm so sorry about her death."

"It sucks. This is her niece, Maureen Scarpetti. Yeah, I married an Italian. Almost got kicked out of the family. Oh, there's another call coming in. It's crazy around here."

"Can you tell me where the funeral will be? I'd like to pay my respects."

"She's being waked tomorrow, starting at two at her house, 421 East 232nd Street."

For the rest of the day and the next morning, Erica keeps her blinders on, head down, goes through the motions. She shows up at the office, tries to get some work done on her show, but she can't focus. Finally it's time to head up to Woodlawn—she calls Uber. She wants to arrive early at the wake so she can clock who comes and goes—she doubts the person she's looking for will show up, but there's no substitute for eyes and ears on the ground.

Fiona's house is redbrick, looks like it was built in the 1930s, with a wide front porch. Erica gets out of the car. It's a few minutes after two and already the place is jammed, people spilling out onto the porch, most of them with drinks in their hands. There's lots of loud laughter, the kind you hear when people who've known each other forever are dragging up the greatest hits from the glory days. Erica is dressed casually, wearing just a touch of makeup, but as she heads up the walk, she notices stares of recognition. Someone on the porch calls her name, but she pretends not to hear and goes into the house.

To the right of the foyer is the dining room, the immense table covered with scores of mismatched casseroles and dishes. There's a bar set up in one corner—it's a popular spot. To the left is the parlor—with Fiona's open coffin at the far end. Except for the ghoulish, somewhat surreal fact that there's a heavily made up, perfectly coiffed corpse in the room, the wake feels like a drunken bash. Erica makes her way through the crush toward the coffin, hearing snippets of conversa-tion:

"Ding-dong, the witch is dead."

"What she put up with . . . that boy."

"Is Diaz here yet? He's going to miss her, for sure."

"I hear she has millions stashed away in the Caymans."

"Eddie Spellman never comes back to the old neighborhood."

"I hope Saint Peter takes bribes."

Erica wonders who Diaz is and why he's going to miss Fiona. She reaches the coffin. The embalmers have done their best, but she still looks many miles from "at peace." Desmond is standing next to the coffin, swimming in a cheap suit, greeting mourners. His eyes are lidded—the man is definitely high—but he seems pretty broken up.

"I'm sorry about your mother," Erica says.

"The world won't see the likes of her again." He starts to cry—and it starts to feel like a performance.

Erica feels intrusive but can't let that stop her. "Listen, Desmond, do you think we could talk at some point?"

He nods his head. "The funeral's tomorrow. I'm flying to Vegas two days after that. It was Mom's favorite place."

"How long will you be out there?"

"Week or two. I'm staying at the Bellagio." He can't contain a tiny smirk—someone just came into some money.

There's a murmur in the room, and Erica turns. A middle-aged Hispanic man, an aide on either side of him, is making his way through the throng. He's working the room, shaking hands, touching arms, leaning in to listen.

"Who's that?" Erica asks a woman standing next to her.

"That's Assemblyman Ruben Diaz. Fiona was involved in local politics. She knew how to deliver votes. Among other things."

Diaz reaches the coffin and looks down at Fiona's dead body with exaggerated sympathy.

Then he turns and hugs Desmond. "I'm so sorry for your loss."

"Thanks, Ruben. It's rough."

"You need anything. Ever. You call me."

"Thanks, man."

Then Diaz notices Erica. "Wait a second . . . It's Erica Sparks!" He beams and holds out his hand. "What a pleasure to meet you." Diaz is nice looking, expansive, charming, with cunning eyes. "Did you know Fiona?"

"She showed me a building."

"Erica Sparks wants to buy a building in my district? I'm honored."

"We were also in preliminary discussions on another matter," Erica says.

"Oh?" Diaz's voice grows wary. "And what might that be?"

Erica senses she's hit a nerve. "I'm not sure this is the right place to talk."

"Agreed. Why don't you call my office and we can set something up." He nods to one of his aides, who pulls out a card and hands it to Erica.

"Actually, do you think we could talk outside? The matter is pressing."

Diaz's eyes narrow. He looks around the room as if he's searching for an escape hatch. He rubs his jaw. "Yeah, sure, of course. I'll be right out. We can talk in my car."

Erica puts his card in her purse and then gets Desmond's cell number. As she makes her way out of the party, she's cajoled into several sloppy selfies. The whole scene starts to give her a bad case of claustrophobia—the screaming voices, slurred speech, exaggerated emotions—boy, is she thankful she's sober.

Down at the curb Diaz is standing in front of a long black car, talking intently on his cell. As Erica approaches, he hangs up and gives her another big smile. Then he opens the car door and gestures her in with a little bow.

The inside of the car is a hushed world of buttery black leather. Sweat has broken out on Diaz's hairline.

"So, Erica, you're the last person I'd expect to see in Woodlawn, at Fiona Connor's wake. She seems like pretty small fish." He laughs nervously, his suave showing some cracks.

"Some small fish swim with sharks. I understand you and she had a mutually beneficial relationship."

Diaz takes out a handkerchief and mops his brow. "Fiona was very committed to her community."

"To maintaining its *character,* you mean?"

"You might put it that way." Diaz looks at his watch, looks out the window, looks at Erica, beseeching. "Look, we rubbed each other's backs, okay?"

"I'm listening."

Diaz takes a deep breath, slumps a little in

resignation. "A halfway house wanted to come into the neighborhood. Fiona didn't want them. I was able to get the zoning . . . adjusted. Quickly. Without a lot of people noticing."

"That's your scratch. What was hers?"

Diaz leans forward, elbows on knees, palms clasped, eyes closed, silent. He stays that way for a long moment, and when he speaks, it's in the steady voice of truth. "I love my wife. More than anything in the world. But we've been married for twenty-five years. There's a lot of temptation out there. I'm human. Fiona owns apartments . . . quiet apartments on quiet streets."

Erica sighs to herself. Midnight zoning changes and enabling extramarital affairs are a million miles from where she wants to be.

"Look, I talked to my lawyer," Diaz says. "What I did was stupid, but it's not a felony. And what Fiona did wasn't even illegal. But it's humiliating. For my wife and kids. You understand. I don't want it plastered on the front page of the *Post*."

Erica likes Diaz, he seems like a sincere guy. She just has to make sure.

"Did you know Fiona was involved in Kay Barrish's murder?"

Diaz jerks upright and looks at Erica, his mouth open. She nods. A big smile of relief spreads across Diaz's face.

Chapter 71

Erica is in a lousy mood on the long ride back to Midtown. The trip was a bust. As the car makes its way down the West Side highway, she looks out at the Hudson and thinks. Whoever Fiona was working with on Barrish's murder wouldn't go anywhere near that wake. She replays the scene in her head, searching for anything she may have missed.

"What she put up with . . . that boy."

"I hear she has millions stashed away in the Caymans."

"Eddie Spellman never comes back to the old neighborhood."

Eddie Spellman? Can't hurt to google him. When she gets back to her office, that's the first thing she does. A bunch of Edward Spellmans come up—she quickly winnows them by adding *Woodlawn* to the search. There's only one match, but it piques her interest. Apparently this Ed Spellman is a well-known figure around New York—a consultant with wide-ranging contacts. *New York* magazine ran an article on him several years ago titled "The Insider's Insider."

Erica clicks on the link and reads:

When a senator wants to know if his wife is cheating, he turns to Ed Spellman. When an Upper East Side heiress wants to make sure the Italian count she's dating didn't buy his title on the Internet, she turns to Spellman. When a male movie star wants to hush up a coke-fueled weekend of S&M at the Gansevoort that landed him in the ER, he turns to Spellman. With connections from Buckingham Palace to the White House, from the Catholic Church to the Mafia, from the Clintons to the Kochs, from the art world to the netherworld, Ed Spellman is the man who can get things done without leaving finger-prints—and who knows how to keep a secret.

Erica races through the article—which mentions Spellman's working-class Woodlawn childhood—and then stops dead when she reads:

Spellman got his start when he founded a consultancy with business executive Fred Wilmot, who is currently Nylan Hastings's second-in-command at Universe Entertainment.

Erica gets up and closes her office door. She goes back to her desk and sits there. She pieces it together—the trail from the lowly caterer's assistant to the LA gangs to the Russian Mafia to Fiona Connor to Spellman and then . . .

"Isn't it great how you guys are always one step ahead of the news? Like with that ferry crash—you just happened to be there. Then Kay Barrish, bless her heart, buys the farm in the middle of your interview. Awful coincidinky, if you ask me."

But it's not "you guys" who are always there. It's her. Erica. Is she being manipulated? Is she part of their web? Their plan? She remembers frantically blowing her breath into Kay Barrish's lungs, holding her as she died, the fear in her eyes.

And what followed? Her fame, her contract, her show, her apartment, the prospect of getting Jenny back.

Think it through, Erica.

She's getting ahead of herself. She has no *proof* that Nylan or Wilmot was involved. Journalism—and justice—demand the truth. Yes, the trail leads in their direction, but she has to keep investigating until she has proof. The closer she gets, the greater the danger, but she can't stop now, she can't.

There's a knock on her door. She clicks away from the Spellman article. "Come in."

Greg enters. "Are you okay, Erica? You look spooked."

"Oh, I'm fine. Just feeling a little swamped."

"I know that feeling. Listen, are we still on for tomorrow night?"

"Tomorrow night?"

Greg walks over to her desk and sits opposite her. He lowers his voice. "Are you sure you're okay?"

"I'm hanging in."

"Dinner at your place? Don't you remember, you invited me last week? After we'd . . . well, made out like a couple of teenagers."

Erica does remember their make-out session— it was giddy and . . . passionate. "Oh yes, of course, dinner. I've been so busy, I forget what day it is."

"Does tomorrow still work for you?"

Maybe she should tell Greg what she's learned. They could become allies in nailing down the final piece of the investigation, no matter where it might lead. Yes, she'll do that. She'll tell him tomorrow before dinner, slowly, with no detail left out. He'll be able to help her make the right decisions.

"Yes, it works fine. I have been known to make a halfway decent omelet."

"Sounds perfect." He reaches across the table and gently strokes her hand. His hand feels so warm—the warmth spreads through her body. But another feeling flares up, for the first time with Greg—wariness. She can trust him. Can't she?

"I better get cracking. I'm doing a promotional interview for the show in twenty minutes."

Erica sits in the makeup chair, and as Rosario works on her face, she goes over the key points she wants to get across in her interview. She puts the troubling information about Ed Spellman—and all its implications—out of her mind for the moment. As the makeup goes on, so does her game face.

"Nylan Hastings was in the chair today," Rosario says.

"Oh, why?"

"He was doing an interview on the business show."

"How was he?"

"He was okay at first and then he got a text that upset him. He became agitated and angry."

"I wonder what it could have been."

"I read it over his shoulder," Rosario says. "I read everyone's texts. How else can I gossip?"

"Well, what did it say?"

"It said 'she knows'—Erica, please try not to flinch when I'm spraying your face."

"Just 'she knows'?"

"Yes. Maybe Nylan's girlfriend found out he's been sleeping with Claire Wilcox."

"Yes, yes, that must be it," Erica says, looking at herself in the mirror—can anyone else see the terror in her eyes?

Chapter 72

Erica gets almost no sleep and when she finally does doze off around five a.m., she wakes up suddenly an hour later in a cold sweat. Out the window the gray dawn is oppressive, unforgiving. There have been many times in her life when she's felt alone and vulnerable, but never anything like this.

Her mind keeps circling back to that text: **She knows.**

If she knows, she goes.

Erica gets dressed and heads up to the Whole Foods at Columbus Circle to shop for her dinner with Greg. It's tough to concentrate, and the store is jammed with people, too many people, they're all around her, writhing and streaming, she can barely move, a cart bumps against her, people whisper and point. Why are they looking at her? Claustrophobia grips her throat. She needs to get out of here. In a near panic she grabs what she needs and rushes to the express checkout.

After dropping off the groceries at home, Erica heads down to GNN. Today is blocked off for work on her show, including a couple of rehearsals. In her office she has a hard time sitting still, can't even get through a hand of solitaire. Then Claire appears in the doorway. She seems subdued, as if she's turned her wattage down a few notches.

"May I come in?"

"Sure."

Claire is even dressed down, in a dark pantsuit. "Listen, Erica, I know I've been horrible. And I'm sorry. Sometimes my ambition gets the best of me. I also know we're probably never going to be besties, but I'd like to try and clear the air. So we can all move forward." She smiles, and it actually looks sincere—or at least in the ballpark. "Any chance we could get a cup of coffee and chat?"

Erica is wary—sharks don't suddenly turn into minnows. But it's in her own best interests to get along with Claire, especially if she's sleeping with Nylan. "Yes, coffee would be nice."

"Great. What time works for you?"

"How about four?"

"The Four Seasons?"

"Why not."

Rehearsal is called, and Erica knuckles down and does her best to focus. But the mood on the set is subdued, there are no smiles or quips. When her eyes meet Greg's, his light up with anticipation. She gets through the day and heads off to her meeting with Claire.

Chapter 73

Erica is awed by the lobby of the Four Seasons—it looks like the set for one of those glamorous 1930s movies—soaring, exquisitely lit, Art Deco details. She sees Claire sitting on a cozy sofa and crosses to her. Claire stands up—she's changed into a little silver dress and looks sensational, if a little overdone—and they air kiss, which feels so phony. Heads are turning; they've both been recognized.

"Isn't it fun being famous?" Claire says with giddy girl-talk intimacy.

"It has its perks."

A waiter comes over and they order coffee.

Claire grows serious. "I'm going to cut to the chase, Erica. What I really wanted to tell you is that I have tremendous respect for you. As a journalist. I know how high your standards are and I think your example is good for all of us at the network."

"Thank you."

"The truth is, I've been a little jealous of you. You arrived and I felt overshadowed. Nylan suddenly seemed to turn all his attention to you."

"You've held your own."

The coffee arrives and they both take sips.

Claire puts her cup down and says, "It's been tough at times, to watch your star soar. You've forced me to up my game. I appreciate that."

"We all have a stake in GNN's success," Erica says.

"Exactly. I hope we can move forward in that spirit."

"So do I."

Claire raises her coffee cup and clinks it against Erica's. "Cheers then." She puts down her cup, runs her fingers through her hair, gives her head a shake, sits up a little taller, and lowers her voice. "I don't know if you've heard, but Nylan and I are seeing each other."

"I might have heard a rumor."

"He's the most intriguing man I've ever met. His intellect, his ideas never fail to astonish me. He's just so passionate . . . in *all* areas, by the way." Claire smiles with satisfaction.

Erica is unsure how to respond to this over-share, and for a moment she wonders if she should warn Claire about Nylan's predilections—she wouldn't want her to end up in the emergency room—but it's their business. "He's certainly passionate about the network."

"I believe he's a great man, Erica. And that we're seeing—not just seeing, are actually *a part of*—history in the making."

Someone drank the Kool-Aid.

"I hope I can use my show to move the arc toward justice," Erica says.

Claire reaches out and grasps Erica's hand. "That's another reason I have so much respect for you. You *care*." She fiddles with an earring, her expression darkens, becomes regretful. "I feel very protective of Nylan. Of what he's working to build at GNN. That's why I felt compelled to do some digging. I discovered something that I felt I should share with you. It's upset Nylan. I think he views it as a threat to the network's future."

Erica feels a wave of foreboding. "Is it something to do with me?"

"I'm afraid it is, yes." Claire gives Erica a look of pitying sympathy. Then she takes a deep breath and exhales with a sigh. "I got hold of the court records of your divorce."

Erica feels all the blood drain from her head, she's afraid she'll faint—she grabs a sofa arm to steady herself.

"Are you all right, Erica?"

Erica sits stock-still—and then a welcome wave of anger sweeps over her. "No, no, I'm *not* all right. Those records were sealed. What you did is illegal and immoral and . . . wrong, just wrong." She'd like to slap that pitying look right off Claire's face.

"Oh, Erica, can anything really be kept hidden in this day and age? Besides, this isn't about you, or me, it's about protecting the man I'm falling in love with. Imagine if one of your *enemies* had gotten hold of it. They could torpedo your whole show." She takes a sip of coffee. "I wouldn't worry about it *too* much. Of course Nylan is upset, I've never seen him so angry. But I'm sure he'll calm down. I just wanted to give you fair warning. . . . You look a little flushed, sweet-heart."

"Do I? Let me use the ladies' room."

As Erica crosses the lobby, she wills herself to walk tall when what she really wants to do is lie down on the plush carpet and curl into a fetal position. She sees the bar across the lobby and takes three steps toward it. No! Not with Claire here, the Queen Bee of the Mean Girls . . . *"You look a little flushed, sweetheart."* The woman has the ethics of a gutter rat.

A dying gutter rat oozing blood as it crawls across her desk.

Erica makes it to the ladies' room. She looks at herself in the mirror—her eyes look hollow and haunted. The past has crawled out of its hole like a snake and is wrapping itself around her neck. She won't give in, she can't give in—she silently says the Serenity Prayer but finds no serenity. She wets a paper towel with cold water and holds it to her temples, takes measured breaths. She has to get out of here, she has to think, and she has to deal with Greg, who'll be arriving at her apartment in about ninety minutes.

Erica crosses the lobby to Claire, willing herself to stay composed. Claire is checking messages on her iPhone and looks up innocently.

"I've got to run," Erica says.

"I'm so glad we did this," Claire says with a warm smile. "Sisterhood is powerful."

"I don't have a sister."

Chapter 74

As Erica makes her way down Fifty-Seventh Street, people are staring at her and she hates her fame—it's intrusive, assaultive, a trap. Has she stepped into a trap? Her secret-in-a-box has just sprung open and a leering clown has popped out—she's shocked, scared, humiliated. And angry—at herself. She paid a heavy price for her transgressions, but the records were sealed and she felt that the slate had been wiped clean. She believes in redemption, and every step she took in getting to GNN brought her closer to it. How could she have been so naive as to think the records would never come to light? Or be dragged into the light by someone like Claire Wilcox. Imagine if the tabloids and gossip sites get ahold of it?

She passes a liquor store. She needs a bottle of

wine. For Greg, of course. She ducks inside. It's a lovely liquor store with wood accents and soft jazz playing, filled with bottles of expensive vodka and gin and exotic whiskies and fine wines from all over the world. Erica feels herself relax; she walks down an aisle, reaches the vodkas, and stops in front of the display of Belvedere. She loves the image on the frosted bottle—a palace reached through mysterious, beckoning branches. *Belvedere.* Her friend. She runs her fingers down a bottle. She was famous for her Belvedere and tonic. First pour thevodka into the chilled glass —two fingers' worth—then squeeze in a whole lime, yes, a whole lime, and then add the tonic—those lovely effervescent bubbles—and finally two lime wedges. It was an elixir more than a cocktail, stimulating, invigorating, it heightened all of her senses, made her so witty and care-free—*la-di-da!*

"May I help you?" a young male clerk asks.

"Oh . . . I'm looking for a nice bottle of wine to go with a mushroom omelet."

"I would suggest a white, perhaps a Sauvignon Blanc. What's your price range?"

"Price range?" Erica remembers she's rich, she's rich and famous, she's a star. "No budget. I want the best. It's for a dear friend. I don't drink. I mean it's not some sort of *rule* or *edict*. I just don't. Not that I *can't* or *won't*. I just don't. Today. Tonight."

The clerk's brow furrows. "We have a really superior Sauvignon Blanc for eighty-five dollars."

"I'll take a bottle." As the clerk goes to retrieve the wine, Erica calls after him, "Make it two."

Chapter 75

Greg will be here any minute.

After getting the wine, Erica picked up flowers. A beautiful bunch of white and blue hydrangeas. Then she grabbed a dozen red tulips—so simple and elegant—and then a stunning mixed bouquet. She spent two hundred dollars, good for her. But now—as she moves the three vases from one table to another—she worries that the flowers are too much, that they come off as a desperate attempt to impress. She grabs the tulips and rushes into the bathroom and puts them on the counter. No, too fancy for a bathroom. She goes into her bedroom and puts them on her dresser. That's better. Isn't it? Should she light a scented candle in here? Candlelight is romantic, but is it cutesy, presumptuous, jumping the gun? Is romance even still a possibility?

And what about music? She grabs her iPhone and goes to Spotify—something for the soundtrack of the evening. Nothing too hip or jangly.

Classical? No, too fusty. What about Michael Bublé or Celine Dion? Too Vegas-y?

Erica is desperately trying to ignore the elephant in her head: how to deal with Claire's news about her court records. Does she tell Greg? What will he think of her when he finds out? Does he know already? And what about her plan to bring him in on her investigations?

Erica stands still and sucks air, closes her eyes and wills herself to calm down. Tony Bennett! He's timeless. She puts on Bennett and moves the hydrangeas to the side table in the entryway. She goes to the galley kitchen. The small red potatoes are already roasting in the oven. Are they done? If they are, will they dry out? She pours olive oil into a frying pan and starts to sauté the mushrooms. She should have done this earlier. She doesn't want Greg to arrive and find her sautéing mushrooms. But what *should* she be doing when he arrives? Not watching TV, not just sitting around.

Before she has time to decide, the intercom sounds.

"Greg Underwood is here," comes the doorman's voice.

"Send him up."

Erica checks herself in the entryway mirror, smoothes out her little black dress. Is it too short? Is it wrong for what might turn into a very serious evening? The doorbell rings.

Greg stands there looking exhausted and

stubbly, his black mop even more unruly than usual. Clearly he's come straight from work. They look at each other for a moment—there's no kiss, no touching—and Erica can't read his look. It leaves her more unsettled. She has to take things one step at a time, not get ahead of herself, not get desperate. *Don't get desperate.*

"Welcome," she says.

Greg hands her a bouquet of lilies.

"They're beautiful. Thank you." The place is starting to look like a mortuary.

They walk into the living room. "This is nice," he says politely.

"It's fine for now." Does Greg seem oddly subdued—or is that her imagination? "How about a glass of wine?"

"I could use one."

Erica goes into the kitchen, sticks the flowers in a vase, and opens a bottle of the eighty-five-dollar wine. She holds the bottle under her nose and inhales the dry, fruity bouquet. She'd love a glass, just one . . . but that's out of the question . . . with Greg here. She pours him a glass and brings it to him—he's sitting on one of two facing sofas. He takes a sip. "This is fantastic wine." He definitely seems serious, almost preoccupied.

Erica sits on the opposite sofa. "So I thought the rehearsal went well," she says, brushing at a nonexistent spot on the sofa.

"Yes, it did. We're moving in the right direction."

"Things seem to be coming together," Erica says, feeling inane.

Greg looks so uncomfortable, even morose. He takes a long swallow of wine and looks like a man steeling himself for an unpleasant task. "Erica, there's something I need to talk to you about. I'm afraid it's serious."

"Is it my court records?"

"You know?"

"Claire told me."

"Nylan gave them to me to read," Greg says.

"Who else knows?"

"Just Nylan, Claire, and Fred Wilmot."

"And you, of course."

"Nylan felt I need to know because it could impact our show. I reassured him that you were sober now and there was no chance of another incident."

No chance?

"Did he accept that?"

"He wishes you had told him."

"What Claire did is despicable."

"I'm not convinced she actually unearthed them. I think Nylan may have fed them to her."

"Why would he do that?"

"To exert his power and control. Knock you down a peg. But, listen, how the records were obtained is secondary at this point. We have to deal with what's in them."

Erica stands up abruptly and starts to pace. "What's in them is that I drove drunk with my Jenny in the car." Just saying the words makes her nauseated. Erica hates self-pity, but for a moment it washes over her.

It all happened that fateful day she was fired from WBZ. Dirk had moved out of their lovely house—the house Erica's salary paid for—and taken Jenny with him, to some crummy rental, basically kidnapped her, really. Yes she started drinking early, yes she drank all day, yes she got angry, yes she went to Dirk's crummy rental to confront him and found Jenny with a babysitter, yes she snuck Jenny out of the house and into her car—but she put her in the backseat and fastened her seat belt—yes they drove to some crummy motel on Route 9 and Jenny was crying and Erica left her alone in the room and went to go get some ice cream—*oh all right, she went to find a liquor store*—and yes she slammed into a pickup truck.

But she paid a terrible price—losing custody of Jenny. And then, after the records were sealed, she pretended they didn't exist, would never come to light. So now another price must be paid. Erica faces the bitter irony that she, who is so committed to finding the truth, may be undone by her own sin of omission.

Erica is still pacing, feels like she could jump out of her skin. How is she ever going to get through the rest of this night? "I made a big mistake," she says.

"We all make mistakes, Erica."

The smell of something burning wafts into the room.

"Oh no, the mushrooms!" Erica cries, racing into the kitchen. She's glad to be away from Greg for a moment, from his sympathy and scrutiny, from the awful truth of her transgression, her self-inflicted wound. She turns off the burner, but the mushrooms are cinders. She opens the oven, the potatoes are dark and shriveled. Dinner is ruined. Just like her career, and maybe her life—she'll never get custody of Jenny if this becomes public. It's all crumbling. She's lost in a labyrinth with no idea which way to turn, which path to take—she needs to turn off her racing mind. She picks up the bottle of wine, opens the refrigerator door, and steps behind it. Hidden, she raises the bottle and takes a gulp.

Greg appears in the kitchen archway. "How's it going in here?"

Erica furtively shelves the wine and closes the refrigerator. "How do you feel about Thai take-out?"

"A woman after my own heart." Greg goes to Erica and places his hands on her shoulders. She flinches. "This is rough for you, I know, but we can get through it."

Why is he being so nice? Why isn't he angry

and disappointed? Like she is. Erica pulls take-out menus from a drawer, grateful that she has something to occupy her hands.

"Pad Thai?"

Greg nods, she calls and orders.

They return to the living room and sit on opposite couches. "I think we have to look at it from Nylan's perspective," Greg says. "He has a lot invested in you—financially, yes, but beyond that you're the global face of GNN. There's a lot riding on you. He has compelling reasons to keep it between the four of us."

Between the four of us? So is Greg one of them now—Nylan, Wilmot, Claire and . . . Greg? One of a group of people she can't trust. Who have the power to destroy her. Has she misjudged him? Is his ultimate allegiance to Nylan and his own career?

The thought chills Erica to the bone and beyond. She can't look Greg in the eye, he'll see her suspicion—or is it paranoia? She stands up, she needs to move, she walks over to the mixed bouquet and fusses with it.

Greg is sitting forward on the couch with his elbows on his knees, his palms clasped together—sympathetic, analytical, practical. But is it a front, a performance? He has all the answers at his fingertips, as if they were rehearsed.

"But what about Claire? Isn't she gunning for me?" Erica asks.

"Yes, but she just fired her best shot. And the real prize she's after is Nylan."

"So snaring him is even more important to her than ruining me?"

"Let's hope."

Greg gives her a meaningful look, and another thought occurs to Erica.

Is Greg the messenger? Sent to reiterate that they have the goods on her?

"I think the best thing to do is nothing," he says. "Let Nylan make the next move. Don't let him know that you know."

Of course he knows that I know. Isn't that the whole point, Greg? Friend, mentor, ally, fascinating man, attractive man . . . man I was going to hold in my arms tonight.

But she can't be sure. Her imagination feels like a runaway train. He's never been anything but honest and supportive. Erica feels dizzy with confusion.

Mercifully the doorbell rings. She goes and collects the food. "Stay put, I'll plate it," she says as she heads into the kitchen. She opens the fridge and steals another gulp of the wine. Then another. The edges of her anxiety soften. Is she crazy in questioning Greg's motives? She plates the food and brings it into the living room.

"Could I get another glass of wine?" Greg asks.

"Oh, of course, I forgot all about it." Erica goes back into the kitchen. She takes another gulp.

Will Greg notice that the bottle is emptier than it should be? She turns on the cold water and holds the bottle under the tap for a second. Then she returns to the living room and hands him the bottle. Will the wine taste watered down? He pours himself a glass and takes a sip. Does he frown slightly?

Erica sits. She has no appetite, pushes the food around on her plate. Greg digs in with gusto, like a hungry teenager. Oh please let him be the man she thought he was.

"Greg?"

He looks up.

"How does what's in the court documents make you feel about me?"

He puts down his plate. "Erica, I went through a divorce and I know how painful it is. I behaved in ways that I'm not proud of." He gets up, crosses the room, and sits beside her on the couch. He takes her hand in his. "We all carry our demons, don't we? They're never going to go away—we just have to fight them to a draw." He strokes her hand. "As to how this news makes me feel—it makes me care about you even more."

His words are a momentary balm, and having him this close, smelling his pine soap, feeling his hands enfolding hers is sweet torture. She wants to believe he's on her side . . . she wants it so badly . . . she works so hard, feels so alone, has taken on so much, it's all on her shoulders, she feels like she's walking a tightrope, a tightrope over a black abyss . . .

"Erica, you went from zero to a hundred in the time it took you to try to save Kay Barrish's life."

"Too much too soon."

"You're strong, Erica. I have faith in you." Greg pulls her to him, puts his arms around her, and cradles her to his chest. "You've had a rough day, you need to rest, just rest, beautiful girl. I've got you, I'm holding you . . ."

His voice is soothing, hypnotic, he strokes her hair. Erica snuggles up on the sofa, closes her eyes, and leans into his touch, feeling his warmth, his body, his gently beating heart . . . Is she in a safe place? . . . Is she? . . . Can she let go? . . . *Let go . . . let go . . .*

Erica wakes with a start, disoriented. Where is she? She's lost in a strange place. She bolts up, out of Greg's arms, looks at him, and for a brief sad second imagines they're somewhere in the country, in a house with a garden and a fireplace —then the mirage evaporates and her terrifying reality is back. "How long was I asleep?"

He brushes her hair from her forehead. "About a half hour. I should probably head home. I've got some loose ends to wrap up tonight, and we have a big day tomorrow."

Erica nods and walks him to the door. He leans in to kiss her but she turns away and then rests her head on his chest for a moment.

"Good night," he says.

"Good night."

He opens the door and then turns. "Oh, there's one thing I forgot to mention. I think I blocked it out."

Erica looks at him quizzically.

"Nylan wants to see you in his office at nine tomorrow morning."

Erica closes the door after him, turns the dead bolt, and then leans against the door, feeling like she's tumbled off the tightrope and is falling, falling . . .

Chapter 76

After polishing off the first bottle of wine and most of the second, Erica crashes into a deep sleep. When she wakes up, her head feels like it's stuffed with cotton candy and her mouth tastes like sandpaper. Her brain starts spinning—what's Nylan's next step? What's hers? And Greg? She *thinks* she trusts him. Does she trust herself? Outside, the city is enveloped in a drizzly fog. She wraps herself in the covers and wishes she could stay in bed all day. Or forever.

Erica stumbles into the shower, turns on the cold water, steps in. As the frigid water runs over her scalp and body, she forces herself to face the truth about last night. She slipped. And she loved every wine-softened second of it—would love to spend today, tomorrow, and all the days after in that tender haze. But she knows that wine would turn into vodka and vodka would turn into hiding and lies and slurred speech and work screw-ups and on and on . . . and now she's shivering, trembling, her whole body is shaking. She steps out of the shower and dries herself, running the towel roughly over her skin. But even when she's dry, the shaking won't stop.

Erica walks down to GNN. After her meeting with Nylan at nine, there's a technical rehearsal for her show at eleven—the first with full lights, music, makeup, and wardrobe. In her office she looks over her notes on the show, but the letters blur, she can't focus, she's too restless. She gets up, walks into the closet, and tries to pick an outfit to wear for the rehearsal. There are so many choices, it's overwhelming—she'll ask Nancy for some help. She goes to her desk and calls her extension.

A woman's voice she doesn't recognize answers, "Wardrobe."

"Oh, this is Erica Sparks, I'm looking for Nancy."

There's a pause and then, "Nancy Huffman doesn't work here anymore."

"*What?* What happened?"

"That's all I'm at liberty to say."

Erica sits there in shock, then she calls Nancy's cell. Voice mail picks up. "This is Nancy Huffman. I'm not available right now, but please leave a message." Hearing her voice is . . . eerie. "Nancy, it's Erica. I just heard. Call me, please."

Erica calls Greg. "Do you know what happened with Nancy Huffman?"

"She was fired yesterday, escorted out of the building."

"Why?"

"Theft. They claim she was billing for more than her garments cost."

"That's ridiculous. And why didn't you tell me last night?"

"I found out this morning. Aren't you due at Nylan's in a few minutes?"

Erica hangs up. The news about Nancy is disturbing but she has no time right now, no time . . . She checks herself in her office mirror. Does the fear show on her face? She can't let it show, she can't let him know. *He knows. She knows.* She stands up straight, the trembling has stopped, hasn't it? She throws back her shoulders and heads to the elevators.

Chapter 77

Erica gets off the elevator and is facing the mirthless receptionist and the suited security guard.

"Mr. Hastings is expecting you."

Erica heads down the hall and walks into Nylan's office. Fred Wilmot is standing there, alone, holding a manila folder.

"Erica," he says without a smile.

"Hello, Fred. Where's Nylan?"

"He's not in the room at the moment, is he?"

"I'm here to see him."

"The morals clause in your contract specifically states that there is nothing in your past that could adversely affect your public image. By failing to disclose your aberrant and criminal actions, you've given us due cause to terminate you. The public will forgive a lot of behaviors. Kidnapping your daughter and then driving drunk with her in the car isn't one of them."

"I did not kidnap her."

Wilmot opens the folder and reads: ". . . *Unauthorized removal of Jenny Sparks from her father's house in Dedham, Massachusetts.* I'd call that kidnapping. You then drove your daughter to the Monticello Motor Inn in Framingham where you rented a room and immediately abandoned her alone in the room while you went out in search of a liquor store. On Route 9 you rear-ended a Toyota Tacoma truck and suffered cuts, contusions, and sprains. Your blood alcohol level at the time of the accident was .31 percent, almost four times the legal limit."

The cold hard words, the cold hard truth, make Erica queasy. A bead of sweat rolls down from her left armpit.

"Do you have anything to say for yourself?" Wilmot demands.

Erica wills herself to stay composed. She doesn't want to give him any satisfaction. Yes, she made a terrible mistake, but *she* didn't commit acts of terrorism and murder. "We all have to answer for our behaviors, Fred. Sooner or later. Was there something you wanted to tell me?"

Nylan strides into the room, casual as day. "There she is, our superstar." He gives Erica a big smile and sits at his desk. "Please have a seat."

Erica remains standing.

"I am over-the-moon excited about your show. *Three* First Ladies. Every other network is pulling their hair out. How did you do it?"

"Dumb luck."

"Dumb like a fox." There's tense silence, he runs his hand over his glass desktop, grows serious. "You know that we've become privy to your court records."

A bead of sweat rolls down from Erica's right armpit. The sun is pouring in the room, it's too warm, almost stifling. "Yes."

"Well, I don't give a damn about your past. You paid a price for your actions and you had every reason to believe you could move on. That's what I want to do. Move on. We expect your opening show to set ratings records. You inspire us all, and I want us to be a team for many years to come." The good cop is on a roll. "I want to demonstrate my faith and commitment by paying you a five-million bonus on the first anniversary of your show. All taxes paid."

What? Erica is thrown off balance. It's a bribe, but a seductive one. Her salary is paid monthly, and taxes take a fat bite. A year from now she'd be a rich woman. *Secure. Safe.* She flashes to her high school days, the exhausting hours working at Burger King, trying to find a quiet corner to work on her homework during her breaks, leaving with the stench of cheap beef and rancid oil clinging to her clothes.

"There is one thing I'd like in return," Nylan says.

Here it comes. "What's that?" Erica asks as sweat breaks out on her brow.

Nylan leans back and smiles, ignoring her question, switching gears. "GNN is building our bench, creating the next generation of stars. I'm about to hire a brilliant young reporter named Laura Gordon, who anchors the evening news at our Tucson affiliate."

Wilmot takes an 8x10 photograph out of his folder and hands it to Nylan, who holds it up for Erica to see.

"Isn't she pretty? And so bright—and only twenty-four. She's *very* popular, our ratings have spiked down there. She reminds me of you, although she's very confident."

Did Nylan turn the heat on? The office is starting to feel like an oven.

He hands the photo back to Wilmot. "Listen, Erica, with so much riding on your shoulders, I need you to pull back *completely* on any investigative work and concentrate on the show."

Erica decides to force his hand—but can she keep her voice steady? "What specific investigation are you referring to?"

Nylan leans toward her, lowers his voice. "The whole country was traumatized by Kay Barrish's death. Since it happened on my network, I feel a sense of responsibility. I know you do too, and that, in fact, you're conducting an informal investigation. I think it's time to leave it to professionals. I've hired the best private detective in the world." Nylan stands up, crosses to the front of his desk, and leans against it, just a few feet from Erica. "I've given him carte blanche to take any actions he feels may be necessary to find Barrish's killer or killers."

Wilmot walks out of the room and returns moments later with a well-groomed man of around fifty, his thinning hair slicked back, his muscular frame encased in an expensive suit.

"Erica, I'd like you to meet Ed Spellman."

Chapter 78

Erica can't stop her sharp inhale but otherwise hopes her poker face holds. The fox is in the chicken coop. And she's the chicken.

Ed Spellman crosses to her and extends his hand. They shake. He smells citrusy and rich, his nails are coated with clear matte polish, his hair looks like it was cut with a diamond blade.

"What a pleasure," Spellman says.

"Likewise," Erica manages. The room feels like a sauna. Prickly heat races over her body.

Spellman steps back, next to Wilmot and Nylan. Erica looks at the three men—the three rich, powerful white men—standing over her. Even David didn't face a hydra-headed Goliath.

"Erica, I considered Kay Barrish a friend. Her death was a terrible loss." Spellman's voice is edged with emotion. "We are going to make sure whoever is responsible pays the price."

"Do you have any idea who that might be?" Erica asks.

"At this point we believe the murder was engineered by the Kremlin. Barrish had said some very harsh things about Vladimir Putin. He did *not* want her in the White House. We've been able to identify one of the middlemen in the plot. He's a capo in the Russian Mafia."

"What's his name?"

"Leonid Gorev. Unfortunately he's disappeared. He probably sensed that we were closing in on him and returned to Russia. Without Gorev, I'm afraid the trail has gone cold. Temporarily, of course."

"Of course," Erica says. *It's called hitting a brick wall you built.*

"I'm a bulldog, Erica, and I'm not letting go until justice is served."

"Keep me posted."

"I'll let you know the minute we learn anything new." He takes out his card and hands it to her. "Call me anytime night or day. I'm at your service," Spellman says with a smile that stops at his upper lip. "Let me get back to work." He nods to Nylan and Wilmot and leaves.

"I hope this addresses your concerns," Nylan says.

"As for your court records," Wilmot adds, "I can guarantee you they will never see the light of day."

Nylan and Wilmot are staring at her, smiling, expectant.

Think. Think fast. You're cornered. You need room. You need time.

"It does address my concerns. Spellman seems highly competent." She sits up in the chair and slaps the arms. "So! I am officially dedicating all my time and energy to *The Erica Sparks Effect*. Let's make great television together!"

Erica stands up and thrusts out her hand. Nylan ignores it, opens his arms, and hugs her. She shudders but covers it up with a halfhearted hug back.

Nylan nods at Wilmot, who opens a cabinet to reveal a large television. He clicks a remote, and footage from Jenny's birthday party fills the screen. There's Claire: "On behalf of everyone at GNN, I want to welcome Jenny to our family." Wilmot pauses the footage—Jenny's sweet, tentative face fills the screen.

Erica's stomach turns over.

"What a wonderful future the GNN family has together," Nylan says.

Erica knows a thing or two about families—but she forces out a bright "Indeed."

Chapter 79

Erica heads down the hallway to rehearsal—she's rattled and enraged. Does Nylan really think she would sell her soul for five million dollars? And bringing up Laura Gordon—*"She reminds me of you, although she's very confident."* And that little trick with the Jenny footage was despicable, sick. Her daughter is her life. They touched the third rail, and Erica is going to bring them down or die trying. But how? Both Samuels and Takahashi have told her there isn't enough evidence to bring charges.

Right now she has to keep her head down and think. And she has to get through this rehearsal.

In her dressing room Erica changes into a color-block dress Nancy picked out, and then Rosario and Andi do her makeup and hair. Both of the women are subdued, tentative, even fearful.

"I heard Nancy was escorted out yesterday," Erica says.

Rosario lowers her voice. "Like a criminal."

"But why?" Erica asks.

Rosario looks down.

"Is it because she was friends with me?"

Rosario's somber silence is her answer.

Rosario and Andi leave and Erica is alone. She

looks at herself in the mirror. Who's the real Erica behind the pretty makeup and perfect hair? The battered little girl who huddled in her room night after night, afraid to venture to the bathroom for fear it would trigger one of her mother's fits? Or the teenager who studied until her eyes burned and became the first ever graduate of her high school to make it to the Ivy League? Or the mother desperate to do right by her daughter, to make amends, to protect her and nurture her? Or a woman trapped in a situation that has spun out of control and threatens her life?

There's a knock. "Erica, it's Greg."

"Come in."

"How did it go with Nylan?"

Erica has an urge to pour out her fear and anger and vulnerability, but some instinct pulls her back. Is he one of *them?* "We reached an agreement."

"About?"

"I'm trying to stay focused here, Greg."

A look of hurt flashes across his face, but he recovers quickly and says, "I've got an ear anytime you want to bend it."

The floor manager comes in and tells Erica they're ready for her. She takes her place behind her desk. The crew—lighting, camera, sound—all run checks, and Erica responds to their requests to stand, look at cameras one, two, or three, move to the seating area. She struggles to stay engaged, but she feels disassociated from the scene, as if she's watching her own stunt double go through the motions.

Soon they're ready to run a mock show. Interns have been recruited to stand in for guests. Ali Cheung calls for quiet on the set and then, "5, 4, 3, 2, 1. Go!"

Erica looks into camera one and reads from the teleprompter, "Welcome to *The Erica Sparks Effect*—where the truth rules. I'm Erica Sparks, and today's top story is . . ."

She struggles through the copy, sweating profusely, feeling as if she could slip into gibberish at any second. "The National Weather Service has upgraded Tropical Storm Carl to a Category 3 hurricane. As it barrels toward South Florida, the storm continues to gain strength. If this continues, the weather service is predicting it could be as devastating as Katrina or Sandy."

She interviews an intern standing in for the head of the National Weather Service. Then she goes to the first commercial break.

Erica stands up and takes a step away from her desk—she feels a slight rush of air behind her, followed by screams and a thundering, floor-shaking crash. She instinctively drops to the ground and covers her head. She looks over—a heavy strip light fell off an overhead beam and landed right where she was sitting three seconds ago, smashing her desk in half. If she had been sitting there, it would have crushed her skull like a ripe melon.

Everyone freezes for a moment, then Greg rushes over to her, kneels beside her, puts a hand on her shoulder. "Are you all right?"

Erica lies there on the floor; she can feel herself going into shock, the blood is draining from her limbs, racing to her heart, she feels icy-cold and struggles for breath, she opens her mouth but can't find her voice. Now the crew has encircled her and they're all staring. Why won't they leave her alone? *Leave me alone!*

"Are you all right?" Greg repeats, and she manages to nod. Greg turns to the crew. "All right, everyone, this was a terrible accident, but thank God no one was hurt. I'm canceling the rest of the rehearsal. I want every light up there triple-checked."

The crew slowly disperses and Greg helps Erica to her feet. She takes an unsteady step, then another. "I'm okay," she says, hoping the words don't sound as hollow as they feel.

Chapter 80

Erica wants out of the building; it's not a safe place. She'll head home and try to gather herself, to figure out what to do next. As she walks out into the plaza, she notices a young man on a bike standing nearby; he has a short beard and is wearing a helmet and dark glasses, obscuring his face. When he sees Erica, he mouths something—he's talking on an earphone. As she turns north up Sixth Avenue, he gets on the bike, moves into the bike lane, and heads north too. Erica slows down, he slows down. Erica speeds up, he speeds up. She starts to shake, fighting to control her fear, she stops, pretends to look for something in her bag—her hands are trembling—then she quickly looks over: he's pedaling slowly, watching her, making no pretense. Even though she's in public, on a busy avenue, Erica feels cornered, her throat tightens, adrenaline surges through her—it's fight or flight.

Oh look, there's that nice liquor store, its window filled with beckoning bottles—there's a bottle of Belvedere! Lovely Belvedere! Her friend. *Flight.* It's all too much for her, her crazy, scary life, a snowball that's turned into an avalanche—but she's minutes away from relief, comfort, oblivion. She heads toward the liquor store. And then a young girl steps off the curb without looking, is heading right into the crosstown traffic. "Mollie!" her mother screams, racing to catch her, grabbing her hand at the last second, swooping her up in her arms, holding on to her for dear life, loving her, holding her, protecting her from the world and its dangers. That's what mothers do.

Erica turns away from the liquor store and heads back uptown. She turns west on Fifty-Seventh Street, and the man on the bike does the same. She picks up her pace and reaches her building. Up in her apartment, she crosses to the window and looks down. There he is on the sidewalk across the street, looking up at her.

Erica paces. The falling light was no accident. But if Nylan had wanted to kill her, the light would have dropped three seconds earlier. It was a scare tactic. Just like showing that footage of Jenny. *Jenny.* They wouldn't harm her daughter, would they?

Wake up, Erica, of course they would. They'd kill her without blinking.

Erica races to her computer and frantically researches private security firms in the Boston area—she finds one, Sentinel, that's been around for over a hundred years. She calls and speaks to the president. Then she finds the nearest car rental agency—it's a Dollar down on Fifty-Second Street—and calls. "This is Erica Sparks.

I need a car, any car, as soon as possible. I'm at 457 West Fifty-Seventh Street. I need you to drive the car into the parking garage. I'll meet you down there. How soon can you be here?"

"Twenty minutes."

Erica washes off her makeup and changes into jeans, a blouse, and running shoes. She goes to the bedroom window—the man is still down there, still watching her. Around him the crowds stream by, going about their business as if this were just another day, an ordinary day. She goes into the living room and turns on the lights and the tele-vision. Then she puts on sunglasses and a base-ball cap and heads down to the garage.

They gave her a silver Accord, which is good, nondescript. She pulls the baseball cap low on her forehead and drives out of the garage. Across the street the man with the bike is texting, then he looks back up at her windows.

Erica gets on the West Side Highway and heads north to the Cross Bronx Expressway and then gets on 95 North toward New Haven. She tries to stay at a reasonable speed, but it's not easy, she's leaning forward over the wheel, willing the miles to disappear. Every time she turns on the radio, she hears another update on Hurricane Carl—wind speeds are still increasing and it's expected to make landfall within thirty-six hours. At New Haven she gets on 91 North to Hartford. Her phone rings.

It's Nylan. Should she answer it? You can't run from your enemy.

"Nylan."

"Erica." There's a pause, and it's thick with the unspoken, thick enough to suffocate her. "I just wanted to tell you how sorry I am about that falling light."

"Accidents happen."

"They do, don't they."

"They do."

"Listen, this hurricane is shaping up as a *major* story. I'd like you to go down and cover it."

"I thought you wanted me in the studio."

"I don't want any more wild goose chases. But with a hurricane of this magnitude, our viewers will expect our biggest star on the ground. This could end up bigger than any of us imagine."

Is this a setup? But she has to maintain her front, she has to stay a pro—and maybe the storm will buy her a little time. "Of course I'll go."

"Good girl. And Erica?"

"Yes?"

"Say hi to Jenny for me."

Chapter 81

Erica is heading east on the Mass Pike. She calls Dirk.

"It's Erica. I'm in Massachusetts. We need to talk."

"What about?"

"I'd rather tell you in person. Can I stop in? Is Jenny home?"

"Erica, what the hell is this about? You can't see Jenny on this short of notice. And what do *we* need to talk about?"

"Something important."

There's a sigh, and then, "When will you be here?"

"In about a half hour. Is Linda there?"

"She is."

"Can you come out and meet me in my car first?"

"If this is some kind of game—"

"It's not a game, Dirk. I'm in a silver Accord."

Erica arrives in Dedham and drives through the quiet suburban streets—who knows what terrible things go on inside these tidy houses? She reaches Dirk's modest rental. She has an urge to rush into the house and take Jenny in her arms, but she waits. Dirk comes out, walks to the car, and gets in, frowning. He's put on some weight and lost a little more hair. Was she really married to this man—this stranger sitting a foot away from her—just two years ago? It feels like a hundred lifetimes.

"What's all this about?" he asks.

"Dirk, I'm caught up in something serious, maybe dangerous. It will be over soon—one way or another. In the meantime, I've hired a security company to watch Jenny."

"Are you telling me you've put my daughter in danger? *Again?*"

Erica thinks she might throw up. Because his words are true. She *has* put Jenny in danger. She never should have started her investigation. She's a fool, thinking she can save the world. How about saving your own daughter first, Erica? You mess up everything you touch—

"You can't ever, ever change where you come from. And deep down, you'll never be better than any of us."

Erica slumps against the steering wheel, fighting exhaustion, fighting fear, fighting herself. "Yes, I have. I have put her in danger. And I'm very, very sorry that I have. But the only way out of this is forward. The detective will watch over Jenny, mostly from his car, here and at school. You won't even notice him. And you and Linda should keep a close eye on her, too, a very close eye."

Dirk looks down at his hands, his mouth tight. "I can't believe you brought this on us."

Erica explodes. "Well, I did. Okay, *I did*. I'm a horrible, terrible mother, I've made nothing but mistakes, I've scarred Jenny forever! Is that what you want to hear? *Is it? Is it? Is it!*" Erica feels the hot tears welling up behind her eyes—she uses every ounce of her energy to will them down. And then her stomach hollows out, and she says in a quiet voice, "I'm just trying my best, Dirk. I'm just trying my very best."

The car is quiet for a long moment and then Dirk says, "We'll keep a close eye on Jenny."

"Thank you. I'd like to see her now."

They get out of the car and head into the house. It's neat and clean and Erica feels a terrible stab of envy and longing. Linda comes out from the kitchen, wiping her hands on her apron. She's a handsome woman, fit and freckled, and Erica wants to hate her, but she can't, she can only feel a begrudging gratitude—and a sense of urgency.

"Thank you for everything you do for Jenny," Erica says. "She may be in danger. Dirk will fill you in."

Linda's face darkens.

Dirk calls upstairs, "Jenny, there's someone here to see you."

"Who is it, Daddy?" Jenny appears at the top of the stairs, looking heartbreakingly beautiful.

"Mommy!" She flies down the stairs, and Erica sweeps her up and twirls her around, and they're both laughing—or is Erica crying?—and she never wants to let her go.

"What are you doing here, Mom?"

Erica kneels so they're eye to eye. "I came to see you."

"I'm doing my homework."

"I'm sorry to interrupt."

"You're more important than homework."

Erica brushes Jenny's hair off her face. "Am I?"

"Of course. You're my mother."

"Why don't we take a little walk?"

"Just around the block," Dirk says. "Dinner is almost ready."

As Erica and Jenny head down the front walk, Erica scans in both directions, looking for anything unusual, strange cars, strange people. There's a gray sedan parked up the street, on the other side, with a man sitting in the driver's seat; he has an open newspaper in his hands but he's looking over the top of it, to Jenny's house. "Wait here one second, sweetheart." Erica crosses to the car and says, "You are?"

"Kevin Nealy. From Sentinel." He opens his wallet and shows Erica his license.

"I'm counting on you to protect my daughter." Erica crosses back to Jenny.

"Who is that man, Mom?"

"He's a nice man. He's looking out for you. I want you to be very careful for the next couple of weeks. Don't let any stranger get near you."

"Why?"

"Because your mother says so. Will you *promise* me?"

Jenny nods, and Erica takes her hand and they start to walk. Erica wants to remember every detail—the feel of Jenny's hand in her own, the sound of her voice as she talks about friends and school, the evening sky—but she has a hard time focusing, she can't stop looking around, checking every car that drives by, every person they see.

"Are you okay, Mom? You seem so nervous."

"I'm fine, honey. Remember your promise."

"Are you going to Florida to cover the hurricane?"

"Yes, I am, tomorrow morning."

"No wonder you're nervous."

They're back in front of Dirk's house. Erica kneels down and puts her hands on Jenny's shoulders. Her throat tightens as she says, "Jenny, I want you to know that I love you, I love you more than anything in the world. Will you always remember that, always and forever?" Jenny nods, and Erica brushes her hair from her face, cups her chin, kisses her cheek, inhales her sweet smell. "Now go have dinner and then finish that homework."

Erica watches as her beautiful baby girl walks up to the front door. When she gets there, she turns and says, "Be careful, Mommy."

Erica waves, then blinks—a tiny insect must have flown into her eye. Why else would tears be flowing?

Chapter 82

Night falls and Erica pushes eighty as she heads back to the city. When she reaches New Haven, she calls Desmond Connor on her prepaid.

"Hey there, Erica." Then he calls out, "Hey, people, Erica Sparks is calling me! This calls for another round. On me." There are cheers.

"Listen, Desmond, could I stop by and talk to you? In about an hour. It's about your mother. Her death."

"Hey, well, whatever, sure. I'm at Mulligan's."

Erica hangs up just as the radio reports that the National Weather Service has upgraded Carl to a Category 5 hurricane.

Using her GPS, Erica makes it to Woodlawn and drives slowly down Katonah Avenue, scanning the streets. She parks and ducks into Mulligan's. It's a classic Irish pub—lots of dark wood and loquacious drunks. Desmond is sitting at the bar holding forth. His eyes are at half-lid and his head has a gentle nod—it's clear he's mixing his medicines.

"Desmond," Erica says. "Can we talk at a table?"

"Yeah, sure, why not? Hey, you look all keyed up. You want a little something to chill with?"

"Thanks for the thought." They move to a corner table. "Do you know Ed Spellman?"

"Everyone in Woodlawn knows Eddie Spellman. Mr. High and Mighty."

"Did he do business with your mother?"

Desmond nods. "Oh yeah, those two got into some shady tricks, man. I mean I'm not exactly Mr. Clean, but I never did the kinda sick stuff they did."

"Like what?"

"Like *offing* people."

"Seriously?"

"You wave enough money in my mother's face, she woulda offed *me*."

"I don't think your mother was the victim of a hit-and-run. I think she was murdered."

"Whoa. That's some heavy thinking."

"I think Ed Spellman had your mother killed. They were involved in a very serious crime. He wanted her out of the picture. I need you to talk to a detective."

"I'm allergic to law enforcement. No can do."

"Desmond, I'm talking about the people who murdered your mother."

He smiles to himself. "When you find them, let me know where to send the thank-you note."

Erica walks out of the bar and looks around—is that someone running, running away, someone dressed in black, several blocks down? It's hard to tell at night and then the figure is swallowed up by the dark. She has to get out of here, off this dark street, she has to escape.

As she drives downtown, she keeps checking the rearview—wondering if she's being followed. And then she wonders if she'll ever be able to escape.

Chapter 83

It's close to midnight when Erica gets home, and as soon as she walks in the door, she turns on the television—it's wall-to-wall coverage of Carl. A Doppler radar image of the hurricane fills the screen—the storm is vast and projected to make landfall within twenty-four hours. The governor has ordered an evacuation of all oceanfront residences in Broward, Palm Beach, and Dade Counties. There are massive traffic jams as people flee north, out of the storm's path. Erica switches off the television and looks out the window. A different guy on a bicycle is across the street, looking up at her windows. She goes into her bedroom and starts packing. Her prepaid rings.

"Erica, things are breaking open," Mark says. "I'm inside the computer that hacked into the ferry's navigational system. It belongs to Dave Mullen."

Erica feels light-headed, sits on the bed, stunned into silence for a moment. "Are you positive?"

"Yes. But I haven't cracked the master password. When I do, the computer will think I'm him and I can search its history, e-mail, files, and current activity."

Erica feels a fourth wind coming on and can barely control her rising excitement. "We'll be in the brain of the beast?"

"Yes. And most important we'll be able to find out who ordered the hacking."

"Listen, I'm heading down to Miami to cover Carl. Stay in close touch."

"There's a lot of activity on this computer. I think they're working on some new scheme."

"That's a terrifying thought." Erica hangs up and immediately calls Detective Samuels. She brings him up to date and then says, "You *have* to station a twenty-four-hour guard outside Mark's room."

"You think his life is in danger?"

"I think *all* our lives are in danger."

Chapter 84

It's just after nine a.m., and Erica, Greg, Derek, and Manny are in a small jet approaching Miami International Airport. All commercial flights have been canceled, and Erica asked Greg to charter a plane—there's no way she was going to fly on one of Nylan's jets.

They're gripping the arms of their seats as the plane is buffeted, tossed around by winds that seem to be increasing by the second.

"You okay?" Greg asks.

Erica nods, although she's far from okay. She was on the phone with Mark off and on all night, getting updates and offering him moral support. He's so close to hacking his way into the very heart of Nylan's secret world.

They hit a wind shear and the plane is knocked upward, they all gasp as their laptops and phones go flying. Erica grips Greg's hand—a charge passes between their bodies. Her feelings for him are so strong they scare her; she's afraid to give into them, afraid they might cloud her judgment.

But she's getting ahead of herself. In spite of everything, she has to keep pushing forward, functioning. She's covering a storm that threatens the lives of millions of people and animals, untold trillions of dollars in property damage, and devastation to the fragile South Florida ecosystem.

The pilot's voice comes on the speaker. "Hang on, folks, we're coming in."

The plane approaches the runway on a diagonal, its tail blown off center, then comes a series of jerks and bumps before the wheels touch down with a thud, followed by a bone-rattling shudder.

Erica walks down the flight steps into the humid, turbulent Florida air. The airport is eerily deserted—there are no takeoffs or landings, no support vehicles buzzing around. A broadcast van—provided by GNN's local affiliate—is waiting for them across the tarmac. An associate producer hands them the keys. Greg gets behind the wheel, Erica sits up front next to him.

They head for their hotel, the Biltmore in Coral Gables, a few miles south of the airport. The roads are a hazard course, with trash cans and debris tossing around like tumbleweeds and palms groaning in the gusts. The few people they see are racing to hammer plywood over windows. One woman is running down the street, leash in hand, frantically calling for her dog.

Suddenly the Biltmore looms up from its low-slung residential neighborhood. It's a pink Spanish-style palace that was built in the 1920s.

They park and duck inside. Like the airport,

the lobby is almost deserted, and what staff there is seems spooked.

The network has set up a command center in one of the hotel's mezzanine function rooms. Erica and her crew check in and are handed long rubber coats and hats and knee-high boots.

"I'm going to head up to my room and change," Erica tells Greg.

"I want to file a report from Miami Beach. We'll leave as soon as you come back down."

Erica goes up to her room and changes into jeans and a sweatshirt, then puts on her storm gear and checks herself in the mirror—makeup and a brush are futile; within seconds of being out there, she's going to look like a dripping doll.

Erica, Greg, Manny, and Derek set off for Miami Beach. The sky is dark and low and ominous, glowing slightly in the reflected lights of the megalopolis. They get on Route 1 north— it's crowded with fleeing cars, their occupants anxious, exhausted; there's a sense of barely controlled panic, in backseats mothers cradle children, frightened faces peer eastward, toward the Atlantic and the destruction it holds.

They reach the MacArthur Causeway to Miami Beach. Around them the sea is heaving—as they reach the low end of the causeway, sea-water sprays up and splashes their windshield, momentarily reducing visibility to nil.

Erica texts Mark: **Any progress?** He texts back: **Hang tight.**

"If this gets much worse, we're going to turn back," Greg says.

They enter Miami Beach and head across Fifth Street and reach the iconic stretch of Ocean Drive that's lined with Art Deco hotels. Greg parks the van and they pile out. Across the street is Lummus Park and then the ocean—the cresting, crashing surf rising higher and higher. The façades of the hotels are swarming with workmen battening down the doors and windows and hauling outdoor furniture and plants inside. The wind is howling and now the heavy rain starts, blown horizontal, stinging Erica's cheeks and eyes.

"Let's shoot you in the park with the hotels behind you!" Greg yells.

Manny and Derek swing into action, and within minutes the camera and sound are ready. Greg is on his headphones to New York. "Go!" he screams.

"This is Erica Sparks reporting live from Miami Beach, where Hurricane Carl has turned the region into something resembling a war zone. The storm's frontal system has just begun to lash the coast. The National Weather Service is reporting that wind speeds inside the hurricane have reached two hundred miles an hour, the highest ever recorded. That blunt force is expected to make landfall tonight. Millions of Floridians have taken to the roads and are fleeing north and west." A beach chair sails by in front of Erica, narrowly missing her. "As you can see, it's dangerous to be outside in these conditions. The Federal Emergency Management Authority is advising those who are unable to evacuate to seek shelter in an interior, windowless room. Tonight's storm surge may swamp the entire island of Miami Beach and inundate the Florida coastline as far north as Daytona Beach. The hurricane's size, scope, and ferocity are unprecedented."

A wind gust almost knocks Erica over. Greg gives her the signal to wrap it up. "This is Erica Sparks reporting live from Miami Beach in South Florida, which is under siege from Hurricane Carl. Stay tuned to GNN for the latest developments."

Erica, Greg, and the crew—all soaked to the skin—race to the van and head back to Coral Gables. Route 1 is virtually traffic-free heading south, and they reach the hotel in twenty minutes.

Everyone in the command center is gathered around the console—a grave President Garner is speaking to the nation. "To coordinate the federal response, I'm sending Vice President Dalton down to South Florida. She will be accompanied by Marshall Wolman, the head of FEMA; as well as the secretaries of Health and Human Services, Defense, and Housing and Urban Development. FEMA has established a hurricane command center at Homestead Air Force Base, ten miles south of Miami."

Erica looks around for Greg. There he is, in a corner of the room, on the phone. He hangs up and pulls Erica aside. "I just got off the phone with Dalton's chief of staff. Air Force Two is scheduled to land at three thirty this afternoon. The vice president has granted you five minutes of time after her arrival."

"How did you make that happen?"

"They wanted to give one interview, and Nylan pulled some strings."

"Nylan pulled some strings."

"Will the interview be at Homestead?"

"No, Nylan convinced them to do it at the airport. It's a great visual."

"Isn't getting the vice president to command central more important than a television visual?"

"It's just five minutes, Erica."

In the news business "just five minutes" never is. But she can't deny it will be a powerful visual to cover the landing of Air Force Two and then have an almost immediate interview with Dalton. Still, Erica feels a sharp stab of foreboding.

She pushes aside her doubts. Her interview with the vice president will be televised globally, so she has to be at her best.

"We've got a couple of hours. Why don't you go lie down?" Greg says, as if he's reading her mind.

As she heads upstairs, her phone rings. It's Moira.

"I saw your report from Miami Beach. Good job," she says.

"We're close to nailing Nylan, Moira, and he knows it."

"Are you safe? Is there anything I can do?"

"If anything happens to me, contact Mark Benton. And be a friend to Jenny, help her remember her mom."

"Oh, Erica."

"Please, Moira."

"Don't be a dead hero. Listen, Greg called me. He told me you slipped."

"It was just one night, Moy."

"One night leads to a thousand. I'm concerned. And so is Greg."

"Do you think it's changed his feelings toward me?" Erica asks.

"Yes. It's strengthened them. Isn't it obvious? Erica, he's in love with you."

Erica stops in the corridor and leans against the wall. She *can* trust him. He called Moira. He *does* care. It's what she's been hoping for, dreaming of, but it seems overwhelming now, here, in the middle of a hurricane, on the cusp of nailing Nylan, with her life in danger; she's so overloaded, running on fumes, and now this. *Oh, Greg.*

Erica retreats to her room. Outside, the wind

is a muffled howl. She throws off her rain gear and collapses on the bed, praying for rest if not sleep. She tries deep breathing but her heart is pounding too fast. She gets up and runs a hot bath and gets in. The water feels creepy against her skin. She gets out and dries herself.

Her prepaid rings.

"Erica, it's Mark. I got deeper into Mullen's computer."

"And?"

"I got into some encrypted e-mails. Mullen hacked the ferry on orders from Nylan."

"No . . ."

"There's more, and it's very worrisome. A new project has been started in the last twenty-four hours. It's being thrown together in a hurry, the initial security has been easier to breach."

"Do you have any idea what it is?"

"I'm getting close, but Mullen has just set up a series of last-minute firewalls. He's on to me."

Erica has no doubt Nylan will order Mark killed if he knows he's inside Mullen's computer. "I'm going to call George Samuels. Hang tight."

Erica picks up the hotel phone and calls Samuels's cell. "George, it's Erica Sparks. Call me back on a landline at this number, it's urgent." She paces the room—she's already put Mark's life in danger once. The hotel phone rings.

"What's up, Erica?"

"Mark is deeper inside Mullen's computer and

he's discovered a new project. We need to put a second cop outside his room. And I think we should alert the FBI. Do you have a contact there?"

"Yes. I'll call him right now."

"Stay in touch."

Erica gets suited up in her rain gear and heads down to the network's nerve center. In the elevator her phone rings. It's Nylan.

Chapter 85

His safe room doesn't feel safe. He should have had stainless steel walls put in. They could get in, his enemies. They're everywhere. Nylan snorts another line of coke. That's better. It was just a paranoia burst. It's over. Another snort. He's safe. He's in control. Things are fine. They're *fine!* If only he didn't have to deal with sycophants, these weak, pathetic wannabes.

The room is littered with pizza boxes that hold congealing slices, soda cans, beer bottles; there are cigarettes and overflowing ashtrays and an empty gin bottle and half-smoked joints, and it's all so messy and disgusting.

Spellman's over in the corner on the phone, frantic, frantic fool. Everything's fine. Except for Spellman's mess. He better pull it out of the bag. He better. He *has* to.

Nylan crosses to him. "Is he there? Is he ready? Is it happening?"

"I'm trying to find out!"

Nylan can smell himself, he's disgusting too, the sweat has congealed on his body like the cheap oil on the pizza. His T-shirt is dark with sweat, so dark it looks like blood.

Mullen is over in another corner on his laptop, freaking out. Another loser. The Great Hacker got hacked himself. That's when it all started to unravel. *It's not unraveling.* Snort! There. Better.

"He's in! He got into my encrypted files! *Ahhhh!*" Mullen leaps up, paces around, takes another toot. Man, has he lost his cool. He's lost in Loserville. He stinks too, he smells like old, wet boot leather, rank.

"I thought you were the best in the world, Mullen. You told me you were the best in the world, and *that joker Benton in IT got into your encrypted files!*"

Mullen's eyes bulge out, he looks like a freak, a strung-out freak. Pathetic.

Nylan goes over to the table and huffs up a line. He's fine. He'll get everything under control. He's done it before, he can do it again. It's all going to go down just as he planned. Just waiting for confirmation from Spellman. Then he has to make sure Erica is there. It'll be the most spectacular news story ever. In history. As big as Lincoln's assassination, as big as Dealey Plaza.

He makes the news; he creates history. There's never been anyone like him.

There's that stupid dog, Wilmot, slumped, crumpled on the floor in the corner holding a bottle of whiskey, his body shaking. Is he sobbing? That's sickening. Boy, true colors, huh, Fred, fold in the clutch, pathetic, blubbering slob.

NEVER GIVE UP. NEVER, EVER GIVE UP.

"It's a go! He's in place!" Spellman screams.

Nylan feels a surge of triumph. He calls Erica.

"Nylan," she says.

"How's the weather?"

"Terrifying."

"Funny, you don't sound scared."

"It takes a lot to scare me. You know that, Nylan."

"Just make sure you get to the airport. This is going to be the biggest story of your career."

"I'm heading that way."

"Don't mess this up, Erica. There's too much at stake. Don't forget who made you a star. Where would you be without me? You'd be covering a Kiwanis Club picnic for some tenth-rate station in Buttcrack, New Hampshire. That's where you'd be. Nowhere! *I made you a star!*"

"You sound a little stressed, Nylan. Is everything okay?"

"We're not talking about me, we're talking about you. I'm fine. I'm in control. I'm always in control. Don't forget it, Erica. And get to that airport."

He hangs up. He looks around the room at his loser lackeys. And the mess, the disgusting mess. He sucks up a line. He'll get his cleaners in, everything will be spotless. Sparkling. Good as new. Like nothing ever happened. Beautiful. Perfect.

King of the Universe.

He picks up a filthy dish towel from the floor and mops the sweat off his face.

Chapter 86

The atmosphere in the nerve center is crackling—reporters, producers, technicians are all huddled around television screens, live feeds, and the large control board. Greg is glued to the airport feed. Everyone is in that place beyond exhaustion, running on sheer adrenaline. This is the civilian equivalent of war, and Erica feels a wave of respect for Greg's courage, for his years as a war photographer. Studying the screen, he looks so vital, so engaged.

"Isn't it obvious? Erica, he's in love with you."

Greg sees Erica, and they instinctively move to a quiet alcove. They stand close to each other, lower their voices to near whispers.

"Are you holding up okay?" he asks. Erica nods. "The vice president's plane is due to land in less than forty minutes. We have to head up to the airport."

"I'm ready . . . and, Greg?"

"Yes?"

"Thank you for calling Moira." She reaches up and touches his cheek. For a moment there's no storm raging outside, no anxious colleagues across the room, just the two of them, alone in a hotel in Miami. And then they kiss and a wave of desire sweeps over Erica's body, her skin, her soul.

They reluctantly part. Greg says, "Tonight."

Tonight? Erica wonders. And then she understands. Not even a hurricane can keep them apart. "Yes," Erica whispers. "Yes."

Then her prepaid rings and the world is back.

"I just got into Nylan's current project," Mark says, his voice taut. "He has an operative at the Miami Airport Industrial Park, just west of the airport. He's going to fire a shoulder-launched missile and bring down the vice president's plane."

An icy vise clamps Erica's spine. Nylan is going to shoot Air Force Two out of the sky. It will traumatize and destabilize the nation. Which is exactly what he wants. She remembers his desperation to get her to the airport for another Erica Sparks exclusive. Now it all makes sense.

"Mark, we have to do something. Is Samuels there?"

There's a quick pause and then the detective comes on. "I'm here. The FBI knows. I'm about to call the Secret Service."

"I'm only fifteen minutes away from the industrial park. We're going to head up there," Erica says.

"That's a dangerous move."

"I've got to try and stop this." She hangs up.

"What is it?" Greg asks.

Time to come clean. "I've been working with Mark Benton since the ferry crash to uncover the hacker. He's inside Dave Mullen's computer right now—Nylan plans to blow Air Force Two out of the sky. He has a mercenary with a shoulder rocket at an industrial park next to the airport."

Greg goes white. Erica can see his mind racing behind his eyes.

"He could be wrong."

"Greg, he's *in*. He's in the brain of the beast. In real time. This is happening."

Greg takes a step back, as if he's absorbing a blow. "Has he contacted the FBI? The Secret Service?"

"Yes."

"Well then, it's in their hands."

"We're a lot closer. We have to try and stop this."

Greg rubs his forehead, looks down, a man at a loss.

"Greg, why are you hesitating? What is wrong with you? What is going on?"

"Oh, Erica . . ."

"Oh, Erica *what?*" she demands. Then she has a moment of terrible clarity. When she speaks, it's softly. "You knew, didn't you? You knew all along what Nylan and Wilmot have been doing."

"No! I did *not* know. I suspected. I had no proof."

"So you kept your mouth shut."

Greg can't look her in the eye. Erica feels like the ground has gone soft beneath her feet. A cosmic hurt sweeps over her, a terrible betrayal. *Oh, Greg, how could you?*

"No. I *didn't* keep my mouth shut. I went to Nylan and told him my suspicions. His reaction was blanket denial, and then he got ugly. He made some threats. I backed off because I thought I was protecting you."

"Protecting *me?* What the hell does that mean? How were you protecting me?"

"Nylan said—" Greg begins.

Suddenly there's a terrible crash as an uprooted palm tree slams into one of the room's tall windows, smashing it, spraying glass across the floor. Rain lashes in.

"I don't have time for this right now. I've got to

get up to that industrial park," Erica says. "Are you with me?"

"Of course I'm with you. I want to always be with you."

They race down to the lobby, where Manny and Derek are waiting.

"Listen, we're not going to the airport. We're heading into a very dangerous situation. Worse than the hurricane. Are you up for it?" Erica asks.

The men jump to their feet. Manny asks, "What's up?" as they all rush out and pile into the van, which is rocking ominously.

"I'll explain on the way," Erica says.

Greg takes the wheel, Erica is shotgun, Manny and Derek in the back. Erica punches Miami Airport Industrial Park into the GPS.

They take off, heading up Route 959. Greg dodges lawn chairs and grills, and debris that flies through the air and skitters across the road. He fights to stay in control as the wind pushes the van back and forth. Erica looks at him, his focus is fierce, he's sweating, and she wants to grab him and demand the truth. *Protect her? From what? From him?*

They pass under the Dolphin Expressway and turn west on Perimeter Road. The van is rocking like a toy, the roar of the wind is deafening, a big chunk of roof flies by. The abandoned airport is right in front of them—and then Air Force Two appears like a ghost ship through the clouds.

Erica imagines the vice president on board, surrounded by cabinet members and aides, not suspecting that these may be the final moments of their lives.

They turn right on Milam Dairy Road, which turns into NW Seventy-Second Avenue. They reach the industrial park and turn into the parking lot. There's no sign of the shooter. Could Mark be wrong? Could Dave Mullen have purposely sent them to the wrong address? Greg speeds around a long, low building—and there, up ahead, in an empty expanse of parking lot, they see the assassin, a rocket launcher on his shoulder, aimed and ready. Greg drives straight toward him. The shooter turns and sees the van. He pulls out a pistol but Greg doesn't waver; the assassin raises the gun and shoots. The left front tire blows out, the van lurches violently. The next bullet pierces the windshield. Greg is hit, thrown back in his seat, losing control of the van, which careens on three tires. Erica grabs the wheel.

"Run him down," Greg cries, his teeth clenched in pain. As Erica struggles to get control of the vehicle, Greg also grabs the wheel, and the two of them aim the van at the shooter, who gets off another shot before the van bears down on him. He jumps out of its path but they manage to graze him, knocking the rocket launcher from his hands, sending him to the ground.

Greg floors the brakes. Blood is seeping from the hole in his poncho. The van careens wildly before stopping about twenty feet past the assassin. Erica leaps out. The shooter is rattled and dazed, but he's young and strong. He stands and picks up the launcher and aims it at Air Force Two, which is moments from touchdown.

Erica races toward him, and he swings the rocket launcher at her—it smacks into her right shoulder and she's knocked to the asphalt. Searing pain shoots through her right side. He aims the pistol at her head and Erica looks down its barrel and thinks she's about to die. *Jenny.* Then she rolls lightning fast just as he pulls the trigger, and the bullet hits the asphalt. Erica leaps up and aims a kick to the killer's head with all her force —the force of her childhood, her hard work, her drinking, her daughter—and she connects with his jaw and his head flies back and he drops to the ground, knocked out. Bruised and gulping for air, she picks up the gun.

She turns to see Air Force Two touch down. The vice president is safe. But is Greg? She races back to the van. Derek and Manny have moved him to the back and laid him flat with a jacket under his head. They've taken off his poncho and Manny is holding a white cloth to the wound in Greg's chest. The fabric is soaked with blood, which oozes out between Manny's fingers.

Erica climbs into the back of the van and cradles Greg in her arms. His eyes are half closed; she can see the life ebbing out of him.

"Film me, Manny, I want this on record," Greg moans. Manny hesitates. "Film me! Use your phone."

Manny takes out his phone and shoots.

"Erica . . . I'm sorry . . ." Greg's breath is coming in short jerks. "Nylan was obsessed with you, he was going to make you a star. I thought the ferry crash was just coincidence. Then Barrish . . . it was too much. I was suspicious . . . but happy for you . . . and for me." He runs his hand down her cheek, then winces and clenches his teeth. "Then your court records . . . I realized he had them all along . . . I got angry and confronted him . . . told him what I suspected . . . he said if I told anyone, he would kill you." Blood trickles from the corners of his mouth. "That's what I meant when I said I was protecting you. I could have stopped this . . . but then I might have lost you . . ."

Erica brushes the dank hair from his forehead.

"I'm sorry, Erica . . . I . . . love you . . ."

"Please hang on, Greg, please don't give up." Erica's tears fall onto Greg's face and mix with his sweat and blood. The hurricane calms, the world disappears, it's just the two of them.

And then the world is back—an FBI helicopter touches down and a convoy of police cars, ambulances, and Secret Service vehicles—lights flashing and sirens blaring—roars into the industrial park.

Two EMTs rush over and load Greg onto a stretcher. Erica tails them as they carry him to their ambulance. "You're going to pull through, Greg. You're going to make it, hang on, please hang on . . ." she screams over the storm.

They load Greg into the ambulance, its doors close and it takes off, holding Erica's hopes.

A policewoman runs up to her. "Are you all right?"

Erica looks around at the mayhem, the flashing lights, the screeching sirens, the shattering storm. Then she says, "I'm still here."

Epilogue

Six Months Later

Erica is sitting in front of a roaring fire in her Central Park West apartment. Across from her, Barbara Walters is speaking to a camera, explaining why Erica was named the most fascinating person of the year. Jenny is watching the taping, along with Greg, Moira, Mark, Nancy, and Rosario—people Erica has come to think of as her "logical family." Looking at them, she feels a swell of affection and gratitude.

Walters recaps Erica's background and tumultuous year. She praises her for her interview with Oprah, in which she confessed to all her sins, including reliving that terrible night with Jenny. Erica smiles. It was a brilliant strategic move —suggested by Moira—that preempted any possible leaks of her court records, and actually deepened Erica's bond with her viewers.

Walters finishes the recap, the camera pulls back to a two-shot, and she turns to Erica and says, "Well, young lady, you must be exhausted."

"It's been an eventful year," Erica says.

"And look at your beautiful new apartment, with its lovely park views. This must feel like a refuge from the world."

"In my business, I'm not sure there is a refuge. When the world wants you, you can always be found. But it is nice to come home to."

After Nylan's arrest Erica pulled out of the deal to buy the place across from the Museum of Natural History—she couldn't live in an apartment that was bought with blood money. This apartment, just a few blocks south on Central Park West, was more expensive—but Erica can afford it. She hired a decorator, and the truth is she considers the apartment a little overdone. Some days she unlocks the door and feels like she's walking into a stranger's house.

"And you live with your daughter, Jenny, whom you've gained shared custody of."

"That's what has mattered most to me from the very beginning."

When it came to sharing custody of Jenny, Dirk proved himself to be a decent guy. Jenny told him she wanted to live with her mother and go to school in New York, and he was amenable. Then Linda got pregnant and that sealed the deal—in a couple of months Jenny will have a half brother. She's thriving at Brearley and loves exploring the city, but she still has bouts of moodiness. Has she completely forgiven Erica? Or maybe the real question is, has Erica forgiven herself?

"Your career, of course, is in high gear. After Hastings's arrest, GNN was bought by Amazon, and today *The Erica Sparks Effect* is the highest-rated news show on television. And you're one of the highest-paid newscasters in the business. Considering where you started in life, how does it all feel?"

Erica laughs charmingly. "To tell you the truth, it's a little hard to accept that it's happening to me."

What she doesn't mention is that there have been nights when she's bolted awake at four a.m. to the sound of her mother's mocking laughter. And then the middle-of-the-night terrors come marching in—the taunting in school, the stabbing pain of losing Jenny, the drunken nights, the drunken days.

"Nylan Hastings and his closest aides and accomplices—including Leonid Gorev, one of the leaders of the Russian Mafia in this country—are now in federal prison awaiting trial for terrorism, conspiracy, and murder. At what point did you begin to suspect Hastings was responsible for these crimes?"

"It was a gradual process, Barbara. And even after my suspicions were aroused, I had some denial. Evil on this scale is hard to grasp. Especially when it comes in a package as smart and successful as Nylan."

"Do you think he's accepted responsibility for his actions?"

"A psychopath has no conscience, no remorse, no empathy, and no sense of responsibility to anyone but himself. Look at his behavior since his arrest. He's acting as if he's the victim. It's chilling."

Even with Nylan in prison, when Erica thinks of him, she feels a tinge of fear—as if he could reach out from behind bars and have her murdered, or Jenny kidnapped.

"What do you think motivated him?"

"Power and grandiosity. Hastings had delusions that he could become the most powerful man in the world, using technology to manipulate events and engineer the news. He envisioned himself controlling the global flow of information and even social media. Human lives were nothing but pawns in his game. The thing you have to remember about Nylan Hastings is that he's not rational. He's playing by rules that he made up and that only he knows."

"Will you be a witness at his trial?"

"Absolutely. As you know, Nylan's chief fixer, Ed Spellman, has turned state witness. The evidence against Hastings is overwhelming and airtight. You'd almost expect to see an insanity defense . . . except he knew right from wrong."

"Erica, you took on Hastings and his entire cabal. Your own life was in danger. How were you able to hold up under such extraordinary pressure?"

"To be honest, Barbara, there were times when I *didn't* hold up. I had moments of fear, doubt, and retreat." She looks over to the sofa where Jenny is sitting—she looks half bored by the proceedings. Erica can't blame her—she's a little tired of talking about herself as well. "But I have a daughter. And I wanted her to be proud of me. And so I willed myself to keep moving forward."

"And now Jenny is attending Brearley, one of the nation's top private schools."

"Jenny knows that I struggled, and that most people struggle. She doesn't take her privilege for granted."

"And what's next for Erica Sparks?"

"I just want to be the best journalist I can be.

Which means uncovering the truth, no matter where it leads."

Barbara smiles coyly. "Aren't you leaving something—or maybe I should say *someone*—out?"

Erica looks over at Greg, who is fully recovered from a bullet that missed killing him by millimeters. They haven't gone public yet, but Erica knew this was coming. "Yes. I'm engaged to Greg Underwood."

Barbara can barely contain her satisfaction—even at the age of eighty-six, she loves a scoop. "When and where is the big day?"

"Oh, we haven't even begun to think about that. Maybe we'll go to City Hall on the spur of the moment."

Barbara wraps up the interview, and she and her crew pack up and leave. Everyone else stays for a dinner spread Erica orders in from a local burger joint. They fill their plates and sit around the fireplace enjoying the hearty food—and for a fleeting moment Erica feels safe and secure.

After everyone leaves, Erica and Jenny clean up together, side by side, a team. Erica doesn't have to ask Jenny to pitch in, she just does, and Erica swells with pride, both in Jenny and in herself. She's an okay mom, really she is.

Jenny washes up and gets into bed. Erica comes in, sits on the edge of her daughter's bed and tucks her in, brushes her hair from her forehead.

"I thought we could go ice skating in the park tomorrow. Does that sound like fun?"

Jenny nods. "And get hot chocolate?"

"And get hot chocolate."

"Know something, Mom?"

"What, honey?"

"You're not *that* fascinating."

Erica hugs Jenny and laughs. "You know what? I couldn't agree more."

Before going to bed, Erica walks around the apartment turning off lights. She stands in the darkened living room, illuminated only by the city lights pouring in the windows. The world is hushed, and for a moment Erica feels an emotion that is so foreign to her that she hardly recognizes it—contentment.

Her phone rings. She's tempted to ignore it, but as a journalist, she's always on call. The incoming number is blocked.

"May I speak with Erica Sparks?"

"This is she. And I've had a long day. Who is this?"

"I'm sorry to disturb you, Ms. Sparks. I'm calling from the White House. I have the president of the United States on the line."

Erica realizes that she now leads the kind of life where this isn't necessarily a prank call.

"May I put him through?" the staffer asks.

"You don't think I'm going to say no, do you?"

"Hello, Erica, this is President Garner. How did your taping with Barbara Walters go?"

"How did you know about that, Mr. President?"

"The intel is pretty decent around here. Which brings me to the point of this call. I'm sorry to disturb you at this hour, but your country needs you."

Erica looks out the window at the glittering lights of Central Park, sits on the sofa, slips off her shoes, and says, "I'm listening."

Discussion Questions

1. Global News Network (GNN) creates the news to drive ratings. What tools do the real cable news networks—FOX, CNN, and MSNBC—use to drive ratings?

2. Nylan Hastings uses fear as a management tool. Drawing on your own experience, do you think fear is an effective management tool? Was it effective for Nylan?

3. Erica Sparks is determined to rise to the top in the news business. Do you think she behaves ethically in her pursuit of this goal? For example, she lies about having secured an interview with the Duchess of Cambridge. Is this an understandable "fib" or unethical behavior?

4. Erica is sabotaged by Claire Wilcox, her rival at GNN. She turns the other cheek. Do you think this is the strongest response to Claire's underhanded behavior? Did you want her to confront Claire directly?

5. Erica grew up in poverty, with abusive parents. How did these circumstances shape

her personality? How do they continue to influence her behavior?

6. While a student at Yale, Erica grows dependent on alcohol as a tool to ease her social anxiety. In light of this, is her subsequent descent into full-blown alcoholism understandable?

7. After being fired from her local anchor job for on-air intoxication, Erica hits bottom and puts her daughter's life in danger. Is this forgivable?

8. Erica and Greg Underwood fall in love and by the end of the book they are engaged. Do you think they are a good match? What is your opinion of Greg?

9. Erica has a tortured relationship with her mother. Do you think she is right to cut off all contact?

10. Erica worries about her parenting skills. What do you think is the root of those insecurities? Do you think she is a good mother? If so, why? If not, why not?

11. When she becomes an enormous success, Erica is adamant about treating everyone

fairly and ethically, and with kindness. How do these values help her stay focused in the harsh glare of stardom?

12. Erica is obsessed with uncovering the truth. In pursuit of this goal, she puts her own life in danger. Do you think she is foolhardy or courageous? Or some combination of the two? Can you imagine putting your own life in danger in pursuit of a noble goal?

13. In the next book in this series, do you think Erica will succumb to her inner demons and start to drink again? Now that she is wealthy, secure in her work, and has custody of Jenny, do you think she will put her life in danger again? Do you think she and Greg will marry? If they do, do you think it will be a happy marriage?

Acknowledgments

Creating a new series means creating new characters, so thank you first to Erica Sparks. You are an amazing character, and I look forward to all of your adventures. Stay safe.

Thank you to all my friends at Fox, who continue to encourage and support my love of writing a good mystery. Thank you O'Reilly, from Wiehl. And Roger Ailes, for hiring a certain legal analyst and bringing me in to the world of cable news at the highest level. Thank you to Dianne Brandi and her mom Dolores.

A big shout out to my friend and bestselling thriller author, Steve Berry, who helped me think through the plotting every step of the way. It is an honor to be your friend.

Thank you to Stephen McCauley, who was an invaluable early reader. And to Michael Borum and Daniel Medwed, who provided wise advice and insight.

How to thank this publishing team? They are almost indescribable. They "got" the idea behind *The Newsmakers* right off the top. Imagine if the people reporting the news were actually the ones making it happen! Daisy Hutton, Amanda Bostic, LB Norton, Becky Monds, Jodi Hughes, Karli Jackson, Kristen Ingebretson, Elizabeth

Hudson, Kerri Potts, Kristen Golden, and Katie Bond.

Special thanks to Todd Shuster, my book agent and friend for many years. *The Newsmakers* would simply not have happened without your guidance.

And thank you to Jennifer Williams, my intern turned producer.

Thank you Sebastian, my collaborator and friend. I love your energy and spirit. Onward!

And always, thank you Mom and Dad. Thank you does not even begin to express how I feel.

All the mistakes are mine. All the credit is theirs. Thank you!

Lis

About the Author

Lis Wiehl is a *New York Times* bestselling author, Harvard Law School graduate, and former federal prosecutor. A popular legal analyst and commentator for the Fox News Channel, Wiehl appears weekly on *The O'Reilly Factor, Lou Dobbs Tonight, Imus in the Morning, Kelly's Court*, and more.

Center Point Large Print

600 Brooks Road / PO Box 1
Thorndike, ME 04986-0001 USA

(207) 568-3717

US & Canada:
1 800 929-9108
www.centerpointlargeprint.com